Also by Greg Greene

Newton's Law – Someone's Child

Alain LeDoux

NEWTON'S LAW

The Last IMMAM

BOOK TWO
OF
The Newton's Law Series

by
GREG GREENE

Our Hill Publishing
A division of
GGA

ISBN: **978-0-9810742-1-4**

For All my Children
And Eva

CHAPTER ONE

Tehran, Iran

Government ministers, no matter the type of government they belong to, are the same throughout the world. Here it was no different. They sat on both sides of a long table in rows with the president of the council at the head. Flowing away from him, their places denoting their power and prestige, were the heads of all the ministries. On the right hand side of the president in many countries you would expect to find the minister of defence, or perhaps the head of the internal police agency. In the Islamic Republic of Iran it was the head of the religious council. The long rows of seats now sat mostly empty, with the ministers of religion, science, defence, and internal security the only participants along with the president. Earlier, the room had rung with heated argument and rancour. Even in totalitarian regimes there was still strident discussion and an exchange of views. All those participating had, by experience, been able to judge the proper method of putting these views forward. This was a lesson which those who failed to practice were rarely given an opportunity to relearn. A difficult decision had to be made, and the time for discussion had been short.

The grand Mullah, Salim Al Rasheed, led off with the usual prayers and a reading from the Qur'an. His dark hooded eyes flooded with light as he began.
"The Prophet Mohammed, praise be to him, has given us the name of the twelfth Imman, the Mehdi, and the time of his rising is upon us."
"So it appears, Salim, but there is a difference between reality and the appearance of reality.. Can we truly be sure that this is the appointed time?"
"It is as I say it is."
"It may be so, but dare we risk that it is not? If we fail we will bring down the wrath of the world not only on ourselves, but on all of Islam, have we that right?"
"Not only the right, but the responsibility to do so," a new voice added.

The speaker was the President of Iran, a man small of stature but whose ambition encompassed all that he saw.
"The Grand Mullah is right; it is the time as has been prophesized, the time of the Mehdi. I would remind you that the purpose of this meeting is to begin the process of welcome. It is not the final act."

"Do you truly believe, Mr. President, that once we set our feet on such a path as this, that events can be stopped, decisions recalled?"

A former general in the Shah's army, Naquamm Benzir, leaned forward slightly. Folding his hands across his chest he took the president's gaze in his own and didn't blink.
"I take it you disagree?"
"I am a military man, as you well know, and as such I take a purely practical view. It is well known that any plan, military or otherwise, rarely survives contact with the enemy."
"This is not a plan made by mortals, but by Allah himself. It cannot fail."
"Any plan can fail, Mr. President, because the plan will be carried out not by Allah, but by men."
"By Allah's will, it will not fail."
"I only suggest caution," the general said, sweeping the table with his gaze. "Think well on this—think long and think hard—there is no path of return on this road."

The discussion continued for some time, long after the sun had receded from the sky and desert winds turned cold.
In the end, the president himself had cast the deciding vote and given the word.

Now that the time for discussion had passed, a hidden button was pressed and a small army of attendants, each wearing a white robe, descended upon the room from doors set cunningly into the walls. Wordlessly they cleared out the pile of plates, cups and saucers, serving dishes, and trays. Their last act before leaving was to set out a large tea service and place a cup before each remaining minister. Exiting as they came they saw little and heard nothing.

During the clean up, each member of the ruling group had a few moments to get up and stretch. There was none of the usual talking between them as there had been in almost all of their previous meetings. Each was alone with their thoughts. As they took their seats again, custom dictated they sip the fresh tea and consider for one last time the course of action upon which they had set their nation.

With a nod to the rest of the council, the Minister of Religion, who had been most strident in advancing the motion, brought out a small suitcase. He opened it in front of the president and entered a series of numbers onto a keypad. After a few seconds, a red light glowed on the panel above the keypad. There were no inscriptions or labels on the face of the unit. Everyone there knew its purpose already. The president spoke aloud three times "Allah Akhbar," God is Great, and pushed the red light down.

It was 5.27 AM on the morning of December 26, 2003.

The ancient City of Bam, located south and east of Tehran shook and crumbled.

El-Hahimin is to Iran what Lubyanka was, and some say still is, to Russia—a prison with doors that only lead in. Aram Mohammed Al Bazir had been a guard there since the days of the Shah. As a young man he had joined the army and risen to the rank of a junior officer. Then came the revolution. Unlike many around him, he had been judged to be redeemable by the new Mullahs who took over from the Shah's secret police. At first he, like many others, had willingly embraced the new regime that promised a return to the ways of Qur'an, the ways of his ancestors, the way to peace and a promise to be blessed in the presence of Allah. Each day he came to work, save Friday, the day of prayers, dressed in his long robe and Taqiyah, the white cap favoured in middle eastern countries.

The prison had become as familiar to him as his own home. He said nothing when men and women known to him and his father had passed through. Many former high ranking officials had taken up forced residence in the prison. As their corruption had been great, so the punishment would also be great. Some were on their way to camps, some to other prisons, and some on their way to the square in the middle of the prison where the walls were now patched with fresh mortar and reinforced by sandbags. Through the years he had kept his head down, going to all prayer meetings and attending the mosque within its walls. His son had gone to the new religious schools like other makes off his age. They were taken really, only to show up in the Basra marshes one day, and dead the next; a volunteer in Allah's Army, gone now to paradise. What does a 14 year old boy know of paradise? He wondered, but not out loud, never out loud.

The years had passed and he had both aged and risen in rank. First a squad of men, then a floor of the prison came under his command. A complete wing next, and finally, it was rumoured, the entire prison. He had left the business of torture, confinement, and execution long ago, and now his days were filled not with the screaming of the condemned, but the never ending insect like buzz of suppliers and bureaucrats and the demands of the current Mullah, whomever that may be. During the passage of time, his six foot frame had added weight, lost height, and was showing the ravages of time. His beard was turning grey, his eyes now required glasses, and perhaps thankfully, his hearing dulled. Every day he prayed five times, losing himself in the chants and prayers allowing them to push aside the concerns of his day to day life.

That was, until today.

Two things happened today that were to change not only the course of his life, but the course of world history. Like a tree branch that deflects an avalanche, small events sometimes had an influence far beyond their size even if he did not yet see it.

"Assalamu Alilkum Wa Rahmatulah Wa Barakatuh."
Aram looked up and responded to the traditional greeting from Sharmaq, the janitor.
"Thank you old friend."
"I will miss you, Aram."
"Really, are you going somewhere?"
"Not Im, you."
"And from where do you get this knowledge?"
Sharmaq smiled a toothless grin, "The walls have ears and they tell stories."
"I would not believe such rumours."
"I said they have stories, not rumours."
"Stories are just rumours told by many."
"That is true. Still I will miss you in any case." Sharmaq smiled again and the sounds of his footsteps echoed as he retreated down the long hallway.

The first to happen was the arrival of Mullah Shariz. He was in charge of all prisons in Iran, and he was known to be a hard liner, even by Iranian standards. Shariz had been born and raised in the mountains near the ancient city of Bam. As was the custom his formal education was interrupted at age ten when he was sent to a religious school. There he learned the Qur'an and Shariya, the Islamic civil code. There are as many interpretations to the Shariya code in Islam, as there are to the works of the Bible in christianity, or the Torah in judaism. As always, the interpretation in vogue being dependent upon who was on top of the heap at that moment in history. Shariz was now the one on top of the heap, and his interpretation was not subject to appeal of any kind, and it was harsh. It happened that on the day of his visit, one of the new guards, a boy really, just 17 years old, had brought a soccer ball to work. His home village had prevailed in a match against a powerful rival and in celebration the entire team had signed the ball and presented it to his father, who was the team's main sponsor. The excited teen had been showing the trophy to all who would pause long enough to look and listen to his tale of the heroic struggle. During the telling of this tale, Shariz happened upon the boy, and seeing the ball declared it to be an affront to Allah that anyone would celebrate such a thing as a soccer match in such a fashion. It might have ended there, but the boy, not realizing who he was talking to, protested that the match was sanctioned by the government, indeed some officials had even been in attendance. Shariz took this as a rebuke of his position and ordered the boy thrown into jail for "offending Islam" by worshiping a game instead of Allah. The despondent young man, alone and frightened, had taken his belt and hung himself.

The second thing that happened that day was as yet unknown to Shariz.

CHAPTER TWO

Office of the Secretary of State
Washington D.C.

Assistant Secretary of State Alexander Wells was not as tall as his voice. Those who had talked to him on the phone were invariably surprised that such a resonant baritone came from such a small body. Entering his office, they usually focused their eyes above his head, as if searching for someone else. At first he had been put off by this behaviour, but somewhere in his early twenties he had learned to live with it, and now it was like a game to him. He turned what would be, to some, a challenge of height to his own use. It actually gave him the advantage in negotiations, and put him in the driver's seat so to speak. His lithe body matched his height proportionally and he saw to it that any photos that went out were devoid of the usual reference points such as a desk, or lamp, which would allow others to accurately gauge his height. The camera angle was set from below, looking up, with objects in the far background. This little trick worked every time except of course when the new arrival was a Marine. Add to that, a female Marine whose stature was more diminutive than his own, and a beauty to boot, and the shoe was definitely on the other foot. Such was the case for him today when his new aide reported for the first time.

Marine Major Carol O'Conner was indeed a beauty, even more so in the crisp uniform of the day. A graduate of Harvard in less than the required four years to get her degree in political science, she was representative of the new era in the Corps. Today's battles often required more than a passing knowledge of the political considerations of the battlefield. The days of crushing your enemy and then helping him rebuild from the ashes, as set out in the Marshal plan, had proved far too expensive in terms of both financial and political capital for the 21st Century. The current line of thinking was not to "bomb the enemy back to the stone age," though that capability was certainly there. but to have the factions within them whose ideas matched yours, invite you in to provide assistance as required. This resulted in fewer casualties all around, less damage to the infrastructure that would need repair in the future, and, most importantly, more favourable press. Iraq had proved that newsmen would rather rush past a million folks risking their lives to vote freely for the first time in centuries in order to get a picture of yesterday's bomb crater. Somehow it was more ideologically fitting for the front page to show a water treatment plant that didn't work, than the dozen or so that did. Such is the news business.

Since the newly appointed Assistant Secretary of State gained his office more by virtue of delivering labour union votes, rather than his international political acumen, it had been decided that he should be afforded a little help in the running of his office. Further to that, the obvious fact that Major O'Conner was "every inch a dame" would show the administration's commitment to equality in the services, and her obvious photogenic qualities would keep the media happy. A win-win result all around. In addition, she was single, and so was he. Wells knew every job had its perks, and he fully intended to explore whichever ones that presented themselves.

Major O'Conner's area of expertise happened to be in Middle Eastern studies. And with the Palestinians and Israelis at last on the rocky and often detoured path to peace, the job there would require both the negotiation skills of Wells, and the political background of the good major. The future, if not looking bright, was at least a little less bleak for the department of state than it had been up 'til now.

Alexander Wells had spent the last two days being briefed by the top department heads on what to expect, what to say, how to address so and so and even how and what to eat at the official functions. Needless to say, the days of Krispy Kreme donuts and lukewarm coffee were in the past.

Odd thing was, his first meeting, according to the itinerary just handed him by Major O'Conner, was not in Haifa as scheduled, but the Iranian capital of Tehran.

CHAPTER THREE

43 Precinct NYPD

Detective Richard "the torch" Smith was halfway through the overnight reports and just starting his third cup of what passed for coffee when his concentration was interrupted by a head peeking around the now open door of his office.

"Hey, Richard, you gotta come see this, Kleinschmidt just brought in his first collar, and you'll never guess who it is." The head belonged to Richard's long time partner Sammy "the skunk" Nogales. Richard got his name when he was a young patrol officer, riding a Harley with a "suicide" shift and working traffic on the expressways. The Harley was one of the last of the breed requiring the driver to operate the shift with his hand off the handlebars by means of a lever down by his side. Doing that whilst driving along at almost any speed and still keeping the bike upright were beyond the abilities of many of the officers who attempted it. The traffic department had been trying for years to get rid of its complement of such machines and move up to the more modern and fashionable "Electra Glide" series, just like those the state trooper weenies used to escort the mayor. The problem was the traffic department, despite returning more in revenue from fines than the cost of operating the division, was lower on the priority list than other more favoured divisions.

One day Smith heard a call of a kidnapping in progress and being on a bike enabled him to get to the scene before any of the patrol cars. Thing was, he had to come up the alley. When he did, the kidnapper, still clutching his intended victim, a young girl, in one hand and a gun in the other, met him at the same time at the same spot. Richard reached for his gun with his left hand and in the excitement forgot to push in the clutch. The Harley stalled, and fell over onto the legs of the perp, who feeling the hot exhaust pipes burning his legs let loose of both the victim and the gun. Smith fell off on the other side, still clawing at his holster trying to get his gun out. Somehow as he left the contours of the Harley's air ride seat, he managed to kick the gas cap loose, or maybe he never really had it done up tight to begin with; mechanical devices being mostly beyond his area of expertise. In any event, the gas spilled from the tank, drenched the trapped suspect, and then ignited from contact with the hot pipes. The ensuing fire thus saving the taxpayers tens of thousands of dollars in court costs, at the expense of one Harley Davidson motorcycle.

Patrolman Richard Smith became Detective junior grade Richard "the torch" Smith and the traffic department gained a brand new Harley 1200 Electra Glide. Good results all around. The new detective was assigned to work with another rookie, Sammy Nogales, who unlike Richard had not had the good fortune to torch both an outdated motorcycle and a bad guy, whilst rescuing a very photogenic young lady. He had to earn his way with hard work and a sharp mind.

Unfortunately for him, Sammy was blessed with an all around bland selection of physical features.

This meant two things.

One, he was never going to get lucky with the ladies 'til closing time was well in sight, and, two, he was inevitably going to get picked for stakeout duty. He blended in so well folks never noticed him at all.

One such stakeout duty called for him to dress and act as a homeless person. He would frequent Central Park in search of a particularly persistent purse snatcher. The suspect in this case whizzed around the park on roller blades, leaving his would be pursuers and victims alike in the dust. The mounted patrol and their valiant steeds had been sent to find him, but horses stand out, even in Central Park, and when they appeared, the suspect wisely declined to snatch a purse.

Plan B was to have Sammy and some other similarly blended detectives roam the park and hopefully catch the suspect in the act. The thought was that while using roller blades may give him the edge in speed, it also confined him to the paved pathways, the speedy footwear being a liability on grass. On the appointed day, Sammy had adopted the disguise of a homeless man who entertained himself by feeding the squirrels, pigeons, and other park animals from a bag of bread crumbs. To get some visibility he had staked out a bench that sat on the edge of one of the main paths leading to the street. If anyone was wearing roller blades and looking to use that particular exit, they would have to go by him. As the stakeout dragged on for days he had seen many squirrels and birds, and also noticed the bush across the road was the home of another kind of park resident, a skunk. The creature had become accustomed to the noise and human content of the park and was no doubt enjoying life in what must it surely must have thought was the land of plenty. A veritable cornucopia of left over fries, burgers, chocolate bars, and other goodies magically appeared every day for its dining pleasure from the trash can set out by the path.

No hunting required.

In the natural course of things, the skunk became pregnant and sought out the bush for its den. There, supplied by the wealth of discarded food from the park she awaited the birth of her babies. The tiny cries announcing an increase in the skunk population reached Sammy's ears on the third day of the stakeout. At the same time he heard the cries of a newly purse-less lady screaming for help. Sammy had just enough time to drop his bag of crumbs and execute a perfect flying tackle at the figure speeding up the path wearing a black body suit and clutching a clashing red purse with its broken strap flailing in the wind. Said flying tackle was successful in knocking the wind out of both of them as they crashed into the bush. The resident of which was enjoying a peaceful snack of a half eaten hot dog. Expressing her indignation at this unwanted disturbance of her nursery, the skunk did what all skunks do in such circumstances, and so Sammy earned his name.

"So who did Kleinschmidt bring in," asked Richard, uncoiling his six foot five inch frame from the office chair and stretching. Like most men his age, he found it more and more difficult to hit the gym after work, and his increasing waist size attested to that fact. Sammy, on the other hand, was one of those people who could eat a cow and never gain an ounce. Some things in life just were not fair.
"Mickey the Mouth."
"You gotta be kidding."
"God's truth, he and his partner got him in interview room nine, as we speak."
"They start yet."
"Nope, I told them to wait 'til we got there."
"What's the collar for."
"Numbers."
"Oh man, this oughta be good."

The two detectives arrived to find the rookies, Kleinschmidt and D'Angelo, had placed Mickey in the interview room. He sat at a plain wooden table, in a chair that he had reversed so that the back of the chair faced the table and provided a resting place for his arms. Mickey was no stranger to the interview room. He knew that the front legs of the chairs were cut lower so the suspect would have to lean forward and become uncomfortable. The twinkle in his eye showed he was anything but.

Richard took a seat in the observation area, a small room with a single table and half a dozen chairs, separated from the interview room by a sheet of one way glass. Sammy rapped on the interview room door. When Kleinschmidt answered, Sammy told him that in his experience, the "good cop-bad cop" routine was a good bet.

"You sure about that Sammy, he looks kinda relaxed."

"Sure he does, that's why you gotta come at him hard, shake him up a little, bang your hand on the table—that sort of thing, and toss a chair around or something." Sammy spat out a bit of the cigar he was chewing on. "You're bigger than D'Angelo so you should be the bad guy. Didn't they teach you anything in the Academy?"

Kleinschmidt nodded and called D'Angelo over to the door to outline the plan.

When Sammy took a seat beside Smith, he nudged him in the ribs, "This is going to be great," he said with a smile. "A guy oughta have popcorn and beer for this show."

The observation room was filling up fast, the word having got around to the other detectives in the squad room. Detectives Kleinschmidt and D'Angelo, having finally agreed on who was playing what role, circled the table in the interview room like sharks on a school of tuna. D'Angelo pulled up a chair and taking a pack of cigarettes out of his suit jacket pocket, laid them on the table. Then he took the jacket off, rolled up his sleeves and loosened his tie. He turned to face Mickey.

"Mr. Knudson, do you know why you're here?"

"Sure," said Mickey, "everyone has to be some place." The crowd in the observation room grinned in anticipation.

"That's not what I mean, Mr. Knudson, I meant do you know the reason you're here?"

"Of course not, sonny," said Mickey, "that's the point of being here."

"Excuse me?"

"Well, think about it, if we know why we are here, then there would be no mystery to life, no drive to find out what's beyond the next bend in the road, the next mountain, across the uncharted vastness of the ancient oceans, even into space."

"No, you don't understand the question," D'Angelo began, shaking his head from side to side.

"Of course, I don't understand, none of us understand, it's only when we understand that we don't understand, that we begin to understand." D'Angelo stared, mouth beginning to open and a look of incomprehension spreading across his face.

"That's the key," Mickey continued, and cocked his head towards the mirror. Reaching into the pocket of his three day old shirt he took out a pack of chewing gum and popped a stick into his mouth. "You think they understand?" he said, nodding to the mirror. "They don't, but they don't want you to know they don't. 'Cause if you knew they didn't, then why would you think you did."

D'Angelo looked confused; this was definitely not going like the role playing exercises at the academy. He tried again. "No. Look, I mean, the reason we brought you in to, you know, talk to us about the numbers."

"Numbers?" Mickey said, "What numbers? You got a problem with numbers? I ain't no math teacher, you know. Hell, I almost flunked calculus in college, but I suppose I could tell you a thing or two about numbers. What base numbers did you have in mind?"

"Ummm what?" replied D'Angelo weakly

"You know what base, base ten the decimal system, base two the binary system, what base? Don't ya know about bases? What kind of education they give you anyway?"

"I meant the numbers slips you got caught carrying, the ones we found in your pocket."

"Numbers slips, what numbers slips? I don't know nothing bout no numbers slips."

"Those slips of papers we found with series of numbers on them!" D'Angelo replied. "The betting slips!"

"Betting slips? What betting slips? Why, they weren't nothin' but lottery numbers."

Kleinschmidt, sensing what his instructors called a 'Pivotal point', decided to step in and shake up the suspect. "Do you ever pick your feet?" He asked slamming his hand onto the table top. He had seen that in the movie "The French Connection" and thought it worked rather well.

"Hell, no," said Mickey. "They picked me!"

"What?" That part was not in the movie.

"My feet picked me, you know when you're a zygote," Mickey replied in his thick accent.

"Whose a Sci-goat?" retorted Kleinschmidt

"We were all zygotes," said Mickey, "when we were in the womb."

"What room, this room?"

"I think he means womb," interjected D'Angelo. "Like your mother's womb when she was pregnant."

"My mom's pregnant?!" Kleinschmidt asked incredulously - "She's 62, that can't be right!"

"No, when she was pregnant with you."

"Me, how can she be pregnant with me, I'm already born!" Kleinschmidt was beginning to lose his temper

"No, no. You don't understand," D'Angelo replied. "Before you were born."

"You saying I was a goat before I was born? Are you crazy you smart assed Wop?" Kleinschmidt spat.

"Listen! You brain dead Kraut, its Z-Y-G-O-T-E, one of the first stages of development when your mom's egg got fertilized by your dad, if it was your dad!"

"You calling my mom a whore?" screamed Kleinschmidt, reaching for his gun, which he had left by departmental ruling in a locked box outside the interview room.

"Christ, Kleinschmidt, you ain't got the brains God gave dust," D'Angelo spat in disgust.

Mickey rocked back and forth in his chair, turned to the one way glass mirror, and smiled. Life was good.

The observation room rang with laughter. Soon there were side bets on who would throw the first punch, D'Angelo or Kleinschmidt. Richard took a fiver on Kleinschmidt on the way out the door. This was fun to watch, but work was piling up. He returned to his office to find the inter-office mail wagon parked outside his door. Inwardly he groaned, Christ, more shit to sift through, just the thing to brighten up his day. The mail delivery was a daily occurrence, it brought questions, and he supplied the answers. More often than not, it brought more stupid questions than meaningful ones. Just yesterday he had to waste a whole hour explaining to his lieutenant, Jack "the rabbit" Horscheim, that no one really gave a rat's ass whether or not the yellow paint that marked the parking spots in the inadequate lot at the rear of the station was "environmentally friendly" or not. They didn't use but a can of the stuff in the entire time Richard had been a cop anyway. The god damn lines were so faint it would take a team of forensic investigators using an electron microscope a month to find the friggin' lines to begin with. Why the hell didn't he just ask the maintenance crew what the paint was anyway 'stead of taking up what little time he had. Smith later learned that the maintenance crew had told the lieutenant to "go pound friggin' sand," if he was that interested maybe he should "read the goddamn label hisself instead of bugging them."

Thus, it was that when Smith found a large red "confidential" envelope from said Lieutenant Horscheim on the top of the newly arrived pile he was tempted to stuff it straight into the shredder and claim he never saw it. Reluctantly he opened it with a sigh, and withdrew the neatly typed letter on the prescribed department letterhead. He read it twice, and then he checked the counter signed signatures of the various department heads that accompanied the rabbit's scrawled name.

Next he called in Sammy.

CHAPTER FOUR

Eastern Skies Inaugural Flight 196

 Modern airliners have been aptly described as "aluminum tubes with wings." On those wings usually sat an engine that provided the thrust required to move the tube through the air. The holy grail of jet engines was to convert as much of their power as possible into altitude and speed. With the WestCon Aerospace R1900 turbo fan engines on cruise, the new model 747 achieved a higher altitude and shorter transit time than its earlier cousins. This meant trans-Atlantic flights were able to be scheduled at more convenient times, and with the added fuel economy the higher altitude afforded, and could be offered at a cheaper rate. Consequently, the airlines were happy. That translated into happier flight crews. Happier flight crews meant happier passengers, and happier passengers meant more revenue for the airline. Everyone was happy with the new aircraft. Smiles all around—handshakes and parties--a regular love fest for all involved could breakout any minute.

 Well, not quite. If "smoking" Joe Zacardi had his way he would bulldoze the whole thing into a ball of aluminum, dump it into the nearest pit and go back to working on the previous models. Smoking Joe was the chief mechanic for Eastern Skies, and he knew from the moment he hit the factory floor at WestCon that these new engines were nothing but trouble. Just the thought of it caused him to spit out the half chewed Cuban cigar he had clenched in his mouth and unwrap another. He never lit the damn things, carrying matches and lit cigars around an engine maintenance shop was something only a damn fool would do. Smoking Joe was no fool. He had started out as a machinist literally at his daddy's knee, watching him work metal with a lathe and a file. By the time he was eight he could finish a block of aluminum to specs with basic hand tools alone. He had never even seen a computer controlled machine until he was in his thirties. In shop, while others made watering cans and ashtrays, he fabricated, from scratch, a working five cylinder model of a two stroke Gnome rotary engine. Just like the one hanging on the full scale spad in the hangar back on the farm.

 After apprenticing with Pratt & Whitney he got his ticket as an airframe and engine specialist and went to work with his dad. Quick to see that the real money was in jet engines, he started with Eastern Skies and steadily rose to the top position on the floor. When the move to the new model aircraft was decided on, it was his job to head to WestCon and learn everything there was to know about running the new turbofans. It didn't take long for him to see what his biggest headaches were going to be. The new engines were comparatively light on fuel consumption—that made them the darling of the marketing and accounting departments. They achieved this by using a new fan design that used larger and more efficient blades than their predecessors.

The downside of that was a larger rotating mass. A larger rotating mass meant more stress on the bearings. More stress meant a need for a higher oil flow.

In almost all aviation engines, oil is consumed as well as fuel, just not as much. Increased oil consumption would not present a problem with a new aircraft. The engineers would simply design in enough space for a larger oil tank. But in this case, for reasons of economy, and also because a design change would trigger a prohibitively large recertification cost, the new larger engine was to be shoehorned into the same old nacelles as the smaller ones. It was decided that an auxiliary tank would be fabricated and squeezed into the available space in the wing, and an oil feed line would connect that tank with the now smaller one in the nacelle.

Trouble with that was, as smoking Joe told anyone who would listen, any fool could see the auxiliary tank was flat and wide, with most of its area exposed to the cold air of the higher altitudes the plane was required to fly at. The damn thing made a better radiator than an oil tank. At those temperatures, the oil would congeal, making it hard to flow. The tank within the nacelle would benefit from the residual engine heat and thus not present such a problem. Now, in order to get the oil to flow correctly, they had to use newer, lighter weight oil and a pump and that meant two things. Lighter oil gets used faster, and more importantly, not every airport in the world carried it as a stock item. Just as icing on the cake, the oil tank within the nacelle carried factory markings, as required by law, for the regular oil weight, while the auxiliary tank was also marked, but for the lighter weight. The maintenance manual correctly listed the specific requirements, but that would only help if the ground crew happened to read it. Different procedures in different countries made sure no one could guarantee that would happen.

But in the end not enough of the people in a position of influence listened. It was much better to concentrate on the difference the new engines would make to the bottom line in an age of spiraling fuel costs. This was especially true when the engines consumed thousands more liters of fuel per hour than they did liters of oil. It was just a matter of time, thought smoking Joe, 'til the whole thing falls apart—as he ripped the wrapper off another Cuban—just a matter of time.

Alfred Newton sat in the window seat of row 23-B. Even with his large frame, he found to his surprise that it was very comfortable. With allowances for his close cropped hair taken into account, there was still adequate headroom when he stood up, and his legs didn't feel cramped. To his left was Elijah Longeyes, a Haida native from the Queen Charlotte Island on the west coast of Canada. Like Newton, he found the seating to his liking and a lot quieter than the twin engine Grumman Goose seaplane he was used to flying in.

Newton was from Victoria, on Vancouver Island out on the eest coast of Canada just above Seattle, Washington. A retired detective, he was now on his way to Spain for conference in forensic techniques used by small departments. Since his retirement, he had busied himself with a consultant's role. It was his way of keeping his hand in the game without becoming a major player. Elijah was a tribal elder, a Shaman, and a good friend. The two had been brought together by a series of deaths on the west coast. Elijah was coming along as an observer to the conference. He was not a police officer, the Haida had no such formal position in their culture. Instead they used a more effective way of dealing with those who strayed outside the tribal ways. A council of elders, chosen from the community, met and decided what course of action or restitution needed to be followed. Those outside the tribal community fell under the jurisdiction of the Royal Canadian Mounted Police. It was a system that worked well in their culture, better than the current justice system in the rest of the country. Newton had found Elijah a good friend and more astute than many of the officers he had served with.

The conference was held every two years, in different places throughout the world. Generally it followed the pattern of Europe, Asia, North America, and South America. The published reason was to discuss and disseminate information related to the advances in police work to each nation. Each meeting had a different theme, often reflecting the current troubles experienced in the host nation. Terrorism had been the last theme, and this time around, it was forensic investigation. There were of course, very well trained groups of highly motivated officers working in the most modern and well equipped laboratories in the world. But the resources of Scotland Yard, the FBI Crime Lab, The R.C.M.P. investigation divisions, and the

French Judicial Police were far beyond those of the bulk of the world's police services. This was especially true in emerging countries. It had been decided, therefore, to focus this year's discussion on the role of the small department with limited resources. Newton was one of a number of small department investigators invited to attend. Like him, most were newly retired. The reasoning behind that of course, was that they were free to talk much more openly about any cases they worked on, and, the lack of resources they had to overcome. A serving officer would not be able to be as candid as they might wish.

Published reason aside, the main goal of this, and most other like conferences, was to establish contacts amongst the new members, and nourish those of the old. Police work, as in all endeavours, required a certain level of what is now referred to as "networking." Apart from the electronic version, the Internet, which a surprising number of services had yet to gain access to, or make full use of, there has always existed the network of human contacts that are responsible for the communication of ideas and intelligence amongst like groups of people. More often than not, this "back door" intelligence consists of the experienced reasoning of a human being working with a limited set of facts and a lot of intuition. The "meet and greet" that Newton was scheduled to be at was at the top of his priority list.

Right now though, after five hours of flight and several cups of coffee, his priority was to put the new "passenger comfort station" to the test. Specifically he was at station number 2A, which was currently occupied, along with all the rest. Alfred waited patiently outside the door, feeling the vibration of the engines, and with his pilot's experience, appreciating the smooth and quiet flight. Sensing a presence behind him he turned to see a tall middle aged man with greying short hair leaning against the opposite wall. The man was seemingly at ease, but Newton noticed he stood on the balls of his feet, his hands free at his sides, sport jacket open, and tie loosened. His body language was relaxed, to a point, but not the relaxation one would expect after being on a plane for five hours. The man's eyes scanned the immediate surroundings, noting who was seated and who was not, then came to rest on Newton, and made eye contact. With a nod, he stuck out his hand.
"Richard Smith, NYPD."
"Alfred Newton, retired."
"Ever been on one these things before?"
"The plane or the conference?"
"Both, I guess," the New York detective replied with a chuckle. "First

time on both counts for me."

"Me too, but then, it's a new plane."

The door to the lavatory opened and a young boy came out, and with a quick look down the aisle scampered to his seat. He put on a pair of earphones and focused his attention on the combination TV screen/gaming station mounted on the back of the seat in front of him.

"Great idea - those things," Smith said, nodding towards the screens on the back of every seat. "Why weren't they around when we were young."

"As long as the kids have time to exercise their brains too," said Newton, stepping into the small metal bathroom. "That's one of the downsides of technology."

"So it is, me-boyo, so it is."

The door to the washroom on the other side of the aisle opened up and Smith went inside.

In the "front office" of the aircraft, as the younger set called the what is universally known as the "cockpit," the flight engineer was monitoring the myriad of instruments that kept him informed about the health of the various systems aboard the aircraft. The gauges and readouts that used to take up several square feet of space were nonexistent on this modern craft. Now, they were replaced by a bank of flat screen plasma monitors that cycled through the various readings. A row of electronic pushbuttons now took the place of the old mechanical ones of yesteryear. Using them, engineer Fred Westerkeep could summon up any reading he was interested in and have it shown as part of a cyclic scan, or continuously if needed. At this moment, the left hand screen displayed the usual readings one would expect. The remaining fuel on board, its rate of consumption, the temperature of the exhaust gasses from the engines, fuel and oil pressure, RPM, and other indicators of the internal workings of the massive rotating fans attached to the wings. On the right screen, he had selected the oil quantity, and the rate of flow from the auxiliary tanks mounted in the wings. So far, the new oil mixture was working just as the refinery had promised. No problems in sight or on the horizon.

Captain Scotty Jackson, a 31 year veteran of the airline, was watching his own bank of screens. A series of rectangular boxes appeared one behind the other on his and his copilot's monitor. In the middle of the nearest box was the outline of an airplane. All he had to do was keep the airplane centered in boxes as they marched towards him. Each box currently represented a distance flown of ten kilometers. He could set that distance down to ten meters if he wished, which he would do on landing. The electronics aboard the aircraft used information from the global positioning satellites orbiting the Earth to fix the aircraft's position down to the accuracy of one meter in any direction. Up, down, left, or right, it didn't matter; the airplane always knew where it was. Factoring in the mapping data supplied by another series of satellites, the boxes on the monitors represented airspace free of any obstructions. If you kept the plane in the centre of the box then the system guaranteed you would never fly into a hillside, mountaintop, or even another aircraft's airspace. This held true on the darkest night and no matter what the weather was doing. In the world of modern avionics, it was always a day with clear skies and unlimited visibility.

"Freddy, did you ever think you would be around to see something like this setup?"
"Nope. Thought I'd be stuck with nothing but a curved alcohol filled tube with a little ball in it attached to a weighted pendulum."
"The old stick and ball, dope and fabric, wind in the wires, scarf stretched out behind you, knight of the sky sort of thing?"
"Yep—simple and reliable—none of that electronic mumbo jumbo stuff that craps out when you really need it."
"You're one of the old school types, Freddy."
"Damn right I am, and just what you'll need around when that box of wires decides to go on the fritz."

Scotty smiled to himself, Fred may talk like he preferred the old days but he knew every system on this bird down to the last nut and bolt, and that thought was a comfort on any new plane.

Although they had the capacity to continue non-stop to Europe, the flight had been scheduled to land in the Azores for refueling and a quick check of all systems by downloading the data collected by special recording devices provided by the engine manufacturers. This would satisfy yet another FAA regulation about flight times and engine hot/cold cycles. Besides, it would be nice to stretch one's legs for a bit. In addition, Eastern Skies had flown a team of public relations people to take pictures and prepare brochures for an upcoming advertising blitz. Scotty brought up the mapping function on one of his screens. Selecting the Azores from a list of destinations within the remaining fuel on board, he punched a key and the autopilot calculated the plane's course towards the islands. The autopilot contacted Atlantic control and advised them of the course settings. In the operations room of the Trans Atlantic control room, the updated numbers appeared on a console. This was the same as an aircraft in flight requesting a course change via voice radio. In this instance, it was immediately available to the controller and there was no chance of misinterpretation. The controller pressed a key acknowledging receipt, and another a few seconds later, indicating the course settings were approved. Only then did the autopilot make the actual course changes required. Scotty looked over the screens and wondered if he just witnessed the birth of fully automated passenger flights, and with it, the death of his profession. The steady hum of the engines and the noise of air rushing past the outside skin continued its soothing lullaby.

CHAPTER FIVE

Matashuita Laboratories, Tokyo, Japan

 At 8:00 AM the security guards positioned by the huge glass doors of the main laboratory building stood by to throw a switch that would signal the locking mechanisms on those doors to release. Free from their mechanical and electronic restraints, the doors would pivot on ball bearings and soundlessly allow the employees to enter. This was, of course, merely a formality. Never in the history of the company, except for testing purposes, had any of the white gloved guards actually had to push the button. Computers controlled every aspect of the building's operation. In any event, the doors admitted few people, save visitors. The employees were already at work. Tradition in Japan meant workers routinely arrived early and stayed late, providing the company with many hours of unpaid work. This advantage allowed Japanese companies to flourish against their foreign competition.
Unlike the mainstream Japanese enterprises, Matashuita Laboratories was established, not to join the myriad of companies to market a new electronic device, nor was it to provide research and development for such products.

 Its sole purpose was to model the world.

 The Japanese islands sit smack on top of a massive battle between the earth's tectonic plates. Like the San Andreas fault that runs up the west side of North America, the fault lines that Japan rests on, produce devastating earthquakes. They are, in fact, one of the most active fault lines in the world. Riding this geological tiger spurred the Japanese to model the entire Earth's crust in a bank of super computers. This allowed the tracking of the many small disturbances in the Earth that seemed to shake one part or another of the islands every month or so. The goal was to be able to analyze the quakes, and hopefully predict the occurrence of the next "big one" in time to warn the overpopulated cities that might be hit. An added capability was the prediction of the path that any tsunami or tidal wave might take. On this day, the entire staff was present for a special celebration. The final piece of code had been completed, and was being implemented. It was also, and not by coincidence, the birthday of the company's president, Yoshi Matashuita. In recognition of the enormous achievement, and as a measure of the gravity with which the Japanese took the subject of earthquakes, the Emperor himself was to attend the ceremonies.

 Thus, for the first time in its company history, and likely the last, all employees were instructed not to arrive prior to 8:00 AM. Instead they would assemble in the parking lot and witness the arrival of the emperor and his staff. They were also encouraged to bring their children and spouses.

It was not every day a god visited their place of work.

Alan Freeman was not of the opinion that the emperor was a god, but he recognized that the native born Japanese would treat him as such. Along with Yoko, his Japanese wife, he waited in the parking lot with the rest of the employees. Alan was technically not an employee at all. He was a consultant. His work at Woods Hole Oceanographic Institute in the States had involved mapping underwater features such as fault lines, mountains, and valleys. He was here to oversee the transfer of that data into the software models the Japanese had built. The American Navy had essentially mapped all the world's oceans, at least as far as the current level of technology allowed. There were always holes in the data. The Japanese computer incorporated new algorithms that would fill in many of those blank spaces. The U.S. Navy had been chiefly concerned with the presence of other nation's submarines and such underwater features that may affect their operations, rather than pure science. It was also Alan's job to ensure no "sensitive" information ever reached the Japanese computer. Like other maritime nations, Japan operated a fleet of submarines. The fleet was small in number, much smaller than the fleet operated by India for instance. In addition, none of the Japanese subs were nuclear powered. This was due less to the much publicized aversion to all things nuclear that they espoused as the only nation to ever suffer a nuclear attack, than the realization that diesel electric boats were, by far, harder to detect. Adapting the revolutionary Scandinavian design of an engine that ran on thermal energy and powered by liquid air, they had increased the ability of the submarine in both power and duration. The result was a boat that could run in as close to complete silence as was possible for almost a month. In that month, the boat could run fast enough to operate off the Pacific coast of America for over two weeks. The Americans claimed they could still track such a boat; truth was they could but get the occasional glimpse of its passage. Since the information that flowed from Wood's Hole came from the same source of instruments as the U.S. Navy, that information was, in theory, scrubbed of any "military significant" data prior to entering the data stream.

Still, shit happens, and Alan was there to ensure that when it did, it did not hit the fan.

But these things were not foremost in his mind at the moment, as he waited with Yoko and the other workers. A platform had been erected by the front entrance; over it a canopy of silk decorated by cherry blossoms shielded the seats and their expected occupants from the sun. Yoshi Matashuita strode through the crowd, meeting with executives and workers alike. The feeling throughout the company was that of a large and happy family. In the two years Alan had worked there he had met with Yoshi many times and his presence in the company cafeteria was a common sight. During that time also, Alan had never heard of anyone leaving the company. This ran against the current trend in Japan where the downturn in the economy had led to the, unheard of at the time, practice of letting employees go.

Yoshi made his way in Alan's direction, bowing to this person and that, greeting everyone. When he came to Alan, he bowed to both him and Yoko, and then shook Alan's hand. "This is a great day, Alan, a great day."
"Yes it is, Yoshi, to be visited by the emperor himself, is an unheard of honour for you."
"For all of us, my friend, for all of us."

Their attention was diverted by the sound of approaching sirens. Soon a coterie of motorcycles manned by the national police appeared. In their midst a long black sedan was the only vehicle. Unlike the heads of other states, no extraordinary security precautions were necessary. To the Japanese, the thought of harming their emperor was simply nonexistent. The police were there only to ensure a quick and safe passage through the legendary Japanese traffic. The motorcade came to a stop in the parking lot, and the driver, wearing white gloves, quickly went to the rear door and opened it. As the emperor and his wife exited, the crowd bowed as one, including Alan. Not to do so would be a huge insult. The emperor acknowledged the crowd with a bow of his own and stepped to the podium.

Alan had studied Japanese before leaving the States, and his wife had tutored him since his arrival. Still, the emperor spoke in the traditional style and Alan had a difficult time following. He was grateful for Yoko's whispered translation.

"It is said our country lies at the top of a quivering mountain, and that one day, the mountain may cast the nation into the sea." The emperor continued, "But we have learned that the mountain is a vast and restless giant that, like our nation, is a living thing, and needs to grow. When it does we feel that growth in the shaking of the ground. The mountain does not mean to harm us, but does what it must do. We also have done what we must do. We have learned to listen to the mountain and to react to the warnings it sends us. This place is the center of all that we have learned, their instruments listen and tell us when and where the mountain must move, and when we in turn must respond."

The crowd listened in rapt silence. "For the first time in its history, the nation of Japan will know beforehand where and when the earthquakes will strike, and we will be ready."

The emperor turned, and with Yoshi at his side, headed into the building to begin the official tour. The employees scattered into small groups to take advantage of the food and entertainment laid on for them and their children. Inside, the computer screens displayed not only the islands of Japan and their surrounding topology, but the entire globe. Every fault line, plate, and volcano was modeled somewhere within the software. Now they could see how any geological disturbance, anywhere in the world, could affect the home islands. A few mouse clicks brought up the active volcanoes in Hawaii, Italy, and the continents of Africa and South America. They showed the level of activity in the lava dome of Mount St. Helens in the state of Washington. They showed Mount Etna and even the recorded eruptions of Krakatoa. Everything was rated in terms of its potential threat to Japan. The further away they were, the lower the threat. Even the threats were categorized; the most hazardous were from volcanic activity such as lava, or more likely ash. The ash from Mount St. Helens had circled the entire globe, and she was again showing signs of awakening.

The emperor stood, engrossed in the demonstration and occasionally asking a question. As a final display of the computer's power, Yoshi had the programmers put in a stunning 3D visual spinning globe, with all threats to all countries marked on it anywhere in the world. The emperor stared at the slowly spinning rendition, then turned to Yoshi and asked a question. In response, Yoshi keyed in a few parameters and the globe spun slowly 'til it revealed a dot in the waters in the Atlantic. A few more taps on the keyboard brought the dot into view and expanded the scale. Beneath it the legend for tsunami was at its maximum. The countries most at threat for damage were the Bahamas, Puerto Rico, Cuba, and...the United States.

CHAPTER SIX

Office of the Secretary General of the United Nations

"Is this true?"

"Apparently so, Mr. Secretary, it came straight from the ruling council itself."

"This is amazing!"

"So it is, sir, so it is, a tremendous achievement."

Sir Rodney Clarke, the British ambassador to the UN and the current head of the nuclear disarmament team, had just presented a single sheet of paper to Jorg Petersen, the current Secretary General. The information had been received only a few moments ago from the hands of the Iranian Atomic Energy Chief, Ali Urique. No one else in the office had seen it, but Sir Rodney had of course, sent a copy by tight beam communications directly to the government in Whitehall. He had no doubt whatsoever, that the Secretary of the United Nations would soon be receiving phone calls from most of the nations in Europe, and of course, the United States. Who, he wondered, would be the first to call?

The question was about to be answered as one of the buttons on the Secretary General's phone lit up, followed by another. "Good morning, Mr. President," he heard Jorg say into the handset. "Yes it seems to be true, wonderful news, is it not?, and may I say, Mr. President, it proves once again that careful and respectful negotiations can yield these kind of results without resorting to the violence of your predecessor, but we will save that argument for another time, agreed?"

Sir Rodney chuckled behind his smile. Let the UN have its moment. He rather thought the spread of democracy from Iraq to Lebanon, and thence to Syria had a lot more to do with the change in the Iranian position than all the talking in the world would ever do. Besides, Britain herself had been part of that same use of force to free Iraq from Saddam Hussein. With a nod to the Secretary General, he took his leave.

He had much to do before the end of the week.

CHAPTER SEVEN

Office of State Security - Tehran, Iran

Aram Mohammed Al Bazir was sitting on a bench in a long hallway. During the time of the Shah, the hallway had been decorated with art from around the world. Paintings, rich rugs, and gold statuary had lined its walls and decorated the finely crafted tables that stood there. The hallway had led to the offices of the various ministers and had been filled each day with foreign dignitaries and high ranking members of the citizenry. Now the building was the home of only one minister, and those who walked its halls were there, not by choice, but by summons. Aram sat between two "escorts," burly men who spoke very little. They appeared used to this duty, and sat staring at the opposite wall, waiting for the doors to the office to be opened for them. They had made this trip many times. Those who had been summonsed would wait until they saw the minister, then the same escorts would take them to one of the many state prisons for disposal. Upon their return, the guards would be given a new name to seek out, and the cycle would be repeated.

After a short wait, the doors were opened and a steward nodded to the party to enter. The guards rose in unison, and each placed a hand under Aram Mohammed Al Bazir's arms to "assist" him forward.

Together they walked through the open door.

The room they entered was as austere as the hallway. Furnishings were sparse, consisting only of a large desk, to the front of which were positioned two large chairs. The minister sat in his chair and hardly seemed to notice the arrival of the three. After a few minutes passed, he looked up in seeming surprise, as if the parties' presence was unexpected. The guards had experienced this many times of course. It was part of the physiological game played to unsettle those who had been summoned. Next the minister would consult a sheet and read out a number of crimes that were attributed to the attendee, and with a curt nod, indicate to the guards which prison would be the next stop. As if on cue, the minister took a sheet of paper from a folder in front of him and began to read.

"Aram Mohammed Al Bazir, you are hereby relieved of your position as head of El-Hahimin prison."

The guards moved closer, intending to catch the man should he faint, or try to run.

Aram himself took a deep breath and steeled himself for the inevitable to follow. Although he had faithfully followed his superiors' instructions, he had seen many people enter his own prison through no apparent fault of their own. He had accepted, as had many others, that things happened despite what you did. I wonder, he thought, if they are going to send me back to El-Hahimin in chains, or do they have somewhere else in mind? Perhaps it will be a short ride ending with a bullet in the head.

After a short pause the minister continued.

"You have now been appointed to the staff of the President of the ruling council; we welcome you to your new role."

The guards, paused, and then quickly took a step back from Aram, who had just now become one of their superiors. The minister nodded to them and they quickly turned about and left the room.

"I can see from your face Aram that this is a surprise to you," Minister Sahkirez said. Motioning for Aram to sit, he took a bell from his desk and rang it. Immediately a side door opened and a serving cart and steward appeared with tea. The ritual of serving tea to guests was still honoured in Iran. The steward left through the same side door and the minister came around in front of his desk and sat in the opposite chair.

"I have the honour to inform you, Aram, that you will now serve as chief advisor to the ruling council for matters concerning the handling of prisoners throughout the country. Of course from time to time there may be other duties assigned to you as you are no doubt aware."

"Why me? I am just an ordinary man."
"That is why you were chosen Aram, precisely because you are in many ways an ordinary man, and unlike many others in your position, you have not succumbed to the power that circumstances gave you."

Aram knew what the minister meant, other heads of prisons, had become cruel and bloodthirsty, some had simply gone mad. The minister leant forward, "We are not all fundamentalists Aram. I knew your father, and he was a good and honest man. I have watched you over the years and you have never wavered in your faith, but at the same time you have resisted the more extreme views that others have adopted."

Aram said nothing, this could all be a way of tricking him, the guards could yet be summonsed, and his day, and his life, ended in a instant. The minister put down his cup, and stood up signifying the end of the conference. "There will be a car brought to the front doors, it is yours to use now." Placing his arm on Aram's shoulders he escorted the still dazed man to the office's doors. As they approached, the doors opened, and two new uniformed guards stood waiting in the hallway. "These men will be your servants and your guards, the car contains a radio phone for you to use, and your new office, at the grand council complex has a well informed secretary. His name is Ahmed and he will assist you in getting used to your new duties. One of the first will be to recommend a replacement to take charge of your old position. We will talk later."

With that, the minister kissed Aram on each cheek and turned back to his desk. Aram left the room, still in a daze. Was this a new test of his loyalty? Was this a trick? He looked at his new body guards, and they, sensing his uncertainty, indicated the path to the front door.

"This way, sir, your car is waiting."

CHAPTER EIGHT

Office of the President of the United States

 The sign on the doors read "Office of The President," but in truth Shelly Burns thought, it should have been renamed to reflect the purpose of the building—"You Call, We Answer." When the American public calls their President, they don't want to talk to "no damn machine." While they rarely expect to actually talk to the President himself, they do expect a human voice at the end of the line. The office was in reality a large room, like many similar large rooms, with a staff whose job it was to filter an incoming call and direct it to the proper department. Most calls were about some program or another, Social Security, the Post Office, troubles with the Internal Revenue Service, or something similar. Where the concerns could be met by switching the call to the area responsible, it was done. So when a call actually got to the room where Shelly worked, it had already run a gamut of filtering and redirection. Most of the calls were folks who insisted on talking to, or leaving a message for, the President. Each call was taken in a polite manner, by someone who was, they assured the caller, a Presidential assistant or secretary. The call was of course, traced. The Secret Service, charged with the protection of the President, and other members of the government, had a duty to collect such information in case one of the threats routinely received turned out to be genuine.

 The number the public called to reach these offices was the general information number for the government of the United States. Anyone who had a routine need to access the President, or any other member of the government, used numbers not in general circulation. These would be other government agencies and foreign government departments. News organizations, such as CNN or FOX also had their own methods of communicating directly to the heads of various departments and their functionaries. Occasionally a journalist from another country, who was "out of the loop" so to speak, would resort to using the general number and attempt to have it routed to a department head. When these calls came through, as they did a few times per week, they wound their way to Shelly's desk.

 Her job was to take the message and based on her judgment, to forward the gist of it to the desired department, or in extreme cases, to attempt to send the call up the line to the department itself. Shelly had been at this job for the last seven years, starting with the previous administration. In that time she had fielded many calls, the vast majority of them simple inquiries that could have been answered much earlier in the cycle, but due to an unfamiliarity of the staff with the caller, had not. She had never met any of callers personally but had learned of their personalities.

There were the European reporters, big fish in their own countries, and insistent on their own importance. It had become a game for them to attempt to access some official or another by this "backdoor" method. If they could end up talking to some junior staff member or intern, they felt confident they would gain information not available through the regular channels, and thus "scoop" their counterparts.

The reporters from the newly liberated eastern bloc countries were still feeling their way around the world in an era of openness. Few had had the time to develop a "network" of other reporters and sources they could use to confirm a story, or to check facts with. Some had of course. In fact, they had been set up in record time by a western press eager for contacts in a country that had been previously "blacked out" to the democratic media. But that had not lasted. After a few years, the American and European press had grown tired of hearing about the failures of communism and moved on. While stories of missing nuclear weapons or biological labs would always raise a surge of interest, they were extremely hard to confirm. In the end, it was the lack of a credible confirmation of facts that killed most stories, just as the existence of a "freedom of information" procedure kept things alive in the west. The public demanded a new fact every few days, especially if they could be woven into a cloud of conspiracy.

Reporters from the Middle Eastern regions tended to be anti-western and came across as shills for Al-Jazerra. They certainly had their believers, but they had not yet mastered the subtlety of western style reporting. Instead of alluding to things that might be, and revealing those that were provable as simple fact, they tended to play to their home audiences. Almost all their contact with American news agencies came from high level contacts and interviews on the cable networks. No one phoned in out of a Middle Eastern capital and asked point blank to speak to the President of the United States about an issue of international importance.

Until today that is.

Technically, Joachim Spuntz was still an American. He had been born to middle class, hard working Farm folk in West County, Iowa. His uncles had served in Vietnam, both in the Navy Construction Corps, and both had returned alive and whole to take up engineering at the state college. The youngest of three boys, Joachim, long dreamed of leaving the farm life behind and heading for the lights of the big city. Which to him, was any community with a population greater than two thousand people. Unlike his brothers, Joachim had not been blessed with the genes that produced a powerful and muscled body. His eyes were weak, and from junior high onwards he had been one of the few kids in school with glasses. Instead of adding to the collection of athletic trophies that adorned the family fireplace and were inscribed with the names of his brothers, he found books more to his liking. His natural abilities lay with the written word, and while the yearbooks may have had his siblings' names on the pages of the sports teams, his was the one listed as editor. The sports scouts from the colleges and universities routinely made an appearance at the high school football games, and as good as they were, neither of his brothers was offered a scholarship for their sports achievements. Joachim however received three offers for literature. After much consideration, he chose to attend the University of California at Berkley. He did this for two reasons, it offered the best programs, and it was the furthest away he could get from West County, Iowa.

Berkley campus, despite its massive state funding, was not known for its conformist approach to education. It in fact, took pride on being "on the edge." While this is a good thing in such disciplines as science and medicine, it is somewhat less attractive in the field of journalism. It quickly became apparent that there were two schools of thought on campus when it came to the written word. One was that "shock" value was more important than truth, the other was opposite, that without truth, no one would take what you wrote seriously.

Joachim wanted to be taken seriously.

He quickly recognized two things; the first was that those who called the loudest for "tolerance" on campus were usually the least tolerant of all the groups. Secondly, there was a large amount of outside influence on the direction the written word was encouraged to pursue. First there were the communists, a group now waning in their influence since the fall of Russia; their dogma of the sixties, seventies, and eighties now shown to be a lie. Since their fall from grace, a new group stepped forward. These were the radical fundamentalists proclaiming their particular brand of Islam to be the one and only true path the world should travel. Well financed by those who saw democracy as a road block to attaining and keeping power, they attracted the young and disaffected. Like the groups before them, they had no respect for any views but their own. Any attempt at a free and open debate was greeted with hatred and violence. Using the proven tactics of bullies and dictators, they targeted specific groups like the Jews, Christians, and even those adherents to the Qur'an who believed that it was a book of peace. Like the regimes of old, they had the courts on their side. Well intentioned laws designed to protect minorities from hatred and discrimination were used to brand anyone with a view opposing theirs as bigots. Lawsuits designed to harass and bankrupt were targeted against small businesses and people who wished nothing more than to live their lives as they believed they should do. Joachim knew that to survive in this atmosphere of hate he would have to bide his time. Many of his fellow journalists had chosen to either jump on board and ride the current wave of expression, or in some cases to oppose it. The first group was destined for a comfortable career of conformance, the second for a brief flash of fame, and then to be swallowed Jonah like, in the belly of the whale they sought to harpoon.

Joachim had a different plan. He wanted nothing less than a Pulitzer. The best way to do this, he reasoned, was to infiltrate the enemy camp. So Joachim became Ali Al Hassam, he left the Baptist faith of his childhood behind him and became a follower of Islam. He had expected that the conversion would be painful and he was not sure at first if he could carry it off. It came as a relief then, that he found more likenesses than differences. Upon graduation he made his way to the Middle East, settling in Jordan. Here he found the people to be more tolerant than most Islamic countries. He learned to speak and write Arabic, and slowly built up a number of contacts in the news organizations of Israel, Palestine, and Lebanon. When Al-Jazerra began its rise in that part of the world as the local CNN, he cultivated a network of trustworthy people there also. The small newspaper he worked for was included in the automated newsfeed from the new network, and like all such organizations, it wanted to be first with the news.

Joachim was sitting in his office, composing his regular column of local news when the automated wire began its chatter. As a matter of routine he scanned the story. One of the Al-Jazerra writers was in Iran, doing what was called "local colour." In any country, local news was used to fill in gaps when there was nothing of great importance on the international scene. If the available space was large enough, pictures were used to give added emphasis. The column on this day was about a local building project in Bam. The ancient city was hard hit by an earthquake and reconstruction had been proceeding at a slow but steady pace. The column detailed the construction of a new religious school, and the picture showed trucks lined up with supplies waiting to unload. Smiling children surrounded the column of vehicles and several of the cities elders were shaking hands with government officials. It was all the usual stuff from any city anywhere in the world. Here are your tax dollars working for you. Joachim studied the picture; there was something odd about it, something he couldn't put his finger on exactly. The trucks were new, but that was not that unusual. Government agencies usually had the newest equipment. No, it was something else. He looked closely at the people standing around, apart from the townspeople, they all that unmistakably military look about them. Not just a militia or local unit, something more. More elitist, more guarded, more alert. Joachim looked closer.

Then he reached for keyboard. Quickly he pulled up the feeds for the past week, where was it now? He was sure he had seen something—yes that's it, Natanz, the up 'til 2002 secret nuclear facility that was designed to enrich uranium. The town was 250 kilometers south of Tehran, Bam was 700 kilometers southeast of Tehran. The building materials on the truck all had the name of "Natanz" stenciled on them. Why would so much material destined for a secret establishment suddenly show up in Bam? He searched some more, calling up all the news feeds for the last six months. He had heard rumours, but rumours were always rampant in any news organization. But now, now he had proof. Calling up another screen on the Internet, he copied down a phone number, and then made a long distance call.

On the other end a voice answered and he eventually found himself talking to Shelly Burns.

CHAPTER NINE

Office of the Press Secretary - The White House

Wade Stiller was a veteran newsman. He got to be a veteran newsman by knowing when to talk, and when to listen. Listening for him included scanning the foreign press and reading the body language and small talk from the dozens of officials he came into contact with every day. He had learned that when something as miniscule as an official arriving at the office outside of their normal working hours could mean something important was happening. When that official was the head of the U.S. Atomic Energy Commission, and he was followed by the Ambassador to the UN and the head of the Joint Chiefs, then that was something really important.

He made a cell phone call. In the offices of CNN, the phone rang at the desk of the senior correspondent for the United Nations, "Hey, Dick, how they hanging?"

"Same as usual, Wade, what's up?" Dick Norton held the phone to his ear with an expectation of one of two things, either he was going to get some information that no one else had, which was good, or he was going to be asked to supply some information, which was bad. In journalism, it was always better to receive than to give, unless the giving part involved a byline with your name accompanied with a front page spread or prime time slot, something which would help with the advancement of your career.

"Got something happening here—thought maybe you had a hint of something on the wires."

"It's Washington, Wade, there is always something happening and no one believes the wires anyway," Dick chuckled into the phone. "What in particular are you looking for?" Dick's body language betrayed the lighthearted banter in his voice. He knew Wade from years back when they studied journalism at Berkley. Wade was no wet-behind-the-ears cub reporter who got excited every time a suburban with dark windows pulled up. He also knew the town and the players. He had an instinct that led him to, and kept him on a story in a town with more secrets and actors than Hollywood. As he was talking Dick flipped on the plasma screens in front of him, each displayed a news feeds from the old standards Reuters and the BBC along with the newer European news agency, and the newest international feed from Al-Jazerra. Nothing here, nothing there, he thought reading the headlines in the multiple windows. "Nothing earthshaking, what are you seeing?"

"It could be nothing, but it appears like the UN and the Atomic Energy Commission are meeting with the Joint Chiefs."

"Unusual, but it could be any number of things."

"I agree, thing is, the meeting is taking place next to the office of the CIA."

"OK, well, as I said, nothing breaking here...except maybe something from the Brits, coming in now on the offer line."

Dick clicked the mouse on his desk and brought up the window marked "offers." It detailed breaking news that an agency was offering to share over and above the regular pre-negotiated content. It meant there was a story breaking that the offering agency thought was worth something extra. The rules of the game meant the story could be picked up—for a price, as long as the originating agency got its name on it. It also meant the offering agency has reason to believe it was the first to get the story and that it was time sensitive. The primary rule in reporting, be it print, radio, or TV, was get the story first, the second rule was never let someone else broadcast it first if it could be avoided.

Dick looked at the tickler, a synopsis of what the story contained. "Holy shit," he exclaimed, on the phone, with Wade still listening, "The Iranians are going to cave in on the nukes!"

The tickler marched across the screen in big letters, "The Iranian government has just announced to the United Nations that they would immediately halt all enrichment activities at their site in Natanz. Their ambassador went on to say that they are doing this in the name of world peace and not because of any pressure from the United States or any other country. A confirmation of this is expected to be announced at an extraordinary meeting of the United Nations today."

Dick pressed some keys on the keyboard signaling acceptance of the story at the demand price of 500,000 English pounds. The story would now be directed automatically to the "breaking news desk." In a few minutes, whatever programming was happening at the CNN desk in Atlanta, Georgia, a red bordered window would begin to overlay the regular news items on the computer screens of the anchors. Behind the scenes, the staff would be scrambling. First they would type the story verbatim onto the computers the anchors read from. Simultaneously, the ticker bar across the bottom of the broadcast would begin flashing the headline with the banner "Breaking News" bracketing it. Other staff members would begin calling their contacts at the BBC to confirm the story and get more details. Still others would start bombarding the press office in Washington for the government reaction. Background on the Iranian government, its officials, file tape of previous presentations at the UN, all this would begin to be collated and woven into a news clip. The length would depend on its importance in the scope of the news of the day. Today that meant a full 15 minutes.

At the other end of the line, Wade whistled slowly into the phone. "Well, that explains the reason for the meeting, but I'm not buying the 'world peace' bit, I wonder what the real reason is?"
"Could be a combination of things," responded Dick. "Maybe they hit a brick wall with the science, maybe they ran out of money, maybe it was a deal with the Israelis or us, or who knows?"
"And that, my friend, is the million dollar question. Who knows, indeed?"

CHAPTER TEN

Eastern Skies Flight 196

 One person who definitely did not know was Alfred Newton. Sitting in the upper lounge of the aircraft he was talking to Richard Smith. They were joined by Elijah Longeyes and a young gangly, baby-faced kid who, like Smith, was also from the N.Y.P.D. Newton had guessed his age at about 23 to 24 years old. His thinness accentuated his height, one of those folks with long arms and legs who will always look awkward and out of place, except perhaps on a basketball court. "Jason here is going to be doing the presentation," Smith nodded at the young man seated next to him. "I'm just going along for the ride. Why don't you get your kit and show Detective Newton here your marvelous invention?"
 "That would be Mr. Newton, not Detective, I'm retired now."
 "Pleased to meet you, sir," Jason mumbled in a muted voice. "I'd be very interested in your discoveries Jason, if you have the time to show them to me." Newton said gently, sensing the young man's unease. "Even though I'm retired, I'm always interested in learning something new."
 Jason nodded and headed down the stairs to retrieve his briefcase from the overhead locker above his seat.

 "Nice kid," said Smith, "but truth is he doesn't fit in well, more the techie type than a street cop. He only got into the academy because his uncle was a captain in the 29th. This trip is his last chance to make the grade, and I've been appointed his evaluator."
 "Not everyone can work the street," said Newton. "And now we depend more and more on those 'techie' types to support the investigators, so I'd say he was in a field that will be growing over the years."
 "Yeah, you're right about that, but his lieutenant is a real pain in the ass, has this notion every guy has to do his time on the pavement before getting an inside job."
 "So what does his 'invention' do?" asked Newton
 "Actually, the kid is onto something." Smith brightened and Newton suspected the detective would do everything in his power to see that Jason got a good evaluation. "He has come up with a way to cross match the DNA results from different countries and methods."

 Unlike the portrayal in the movies, DNA testing is not done by a single method. Each country's judicial system had specified which method of analysis it would accept as being the test to use. This worked fine within its own borders. However some countries advanced quicker than others, and in so doing developed testing procedures that were both faster and more reliable than those methods employed in other countries. As a result, it was possible for a lab in Europe to come up with a result that would not be accepted in South America. For years, police agencies and labs had been working towards a standard set of tests that all countries could agree on. Naturally, the N.I.H., or Not Invented Here, attitude took hold and there were endless debates about which method to use. Countries without the sophisticated labs really needed a cheaper and easier test than the well funded countries were offering. According to Smith, Jason had devised a way to do this. If this was true, thought Newton, putting such a talent out on the street to shake doors and wake up drunks was a colossal waste of his talents.

A chorus of "excuse mes" and the banging of a metal case against the railing of the aircraft's circular staircase announced Jason's return. Smith rolled his eyes and shook his head slightly back and forth. Headed towards them clutching a large metal equipment case, the "techie" seemed to be well on his way to annoying every passenger with an aisle seat between him and the lounge. The case was bigger than a briefcase, more like one you would see as professional photographer use. The letters N.Y.P.D. were clearly stamped on the outside. Holding it like a shield in front of him, the young technician was concentrating on not banging into any more passengers, tables, or chairs in the last few feet to where they were sitting. Elijah rose from his place at the table and deftly maneuvered the last obstacle, a piece of carryon luggage, out of his way.

Jason plopped the case down on the table with a thud.

A quick re-arranging of their seating gave him enough room to open the lid of the case to reveal an inset panel on the bottom, while the top of the case served as a storage area for small vials and envelopes. The panel held a receiver for a telephone handset, a number of electrical jacks, and a small LCD panel. At the bottom was a sub panel which Jason popped open to remove a small cable. It looked to Newton to be a telephone extension cord. Jason searched around the aircraft interior until he found what he was looking for. A small jack built into the bulkhead and repeated at regular intervals where passengers could plug in their laptops to get the latest high speed internet access. The same network of satellites that provided in-flight cell phone connections also served to relay the internet requests and responses. A flip of a switch on the panel brought the unit to life and the LCD screen flashed on with the N.Y.P.D. logo. Another search of the storage compartment brought forth a small keyboard and mouse. After a few moments a small rectangular light glowed red on the panel beneath the LCD screen. Jason held his thumb against it for a few seconds and the light turned to green.

"Finger print reader," he explained to the group, "restricts access to the chosen few." The N.Y.P.D. logo disappeared from the screen and was replaced by a series of numbers indicating that the unit was now running and communicating with a computer back in New York.

Newton was impressed, not only with the machinery, but the obvious change in the demeanor of Jason. The awkwardness was gone, replaced by a look of competency and even his voice took on an authoritative tenor as he described the workings of his "invention" to them. "All I need," he was saying, "is a drop of blood, or other bodily fluid, and I can set up a search for a matching DNA pattern from any country in INTERPOL."

"What if the country in the International Police Agency doesn't use the same tests as we do?" Newton asked.
"Ah," said Jason, "that's the beauty of this machine, it knows which testing parameters the various countries do use, and it assigns a weight—or degree of confidence, if you will, to those results, and then interpolates what they would be if a standard test was used."
"So it would come back with a weighted match then, something like, this match has a 90 percent degree of accuracy?"
"Right, tell you what, let's test it. Who wants to volunteer a sample?" Jason asked, taking a small black instrument from the case. "This is the same thing as a diabetic would use to get a small drop of blood from the end of his finger to test the blood sugar level. Only in our case, it does a quick DNA analysis."
"Amazing, something that small; how accurate is it?" Newton had never seen a DNA analysis that did not require a lab full of equipment and a 24 hour time span to complete.
"Most of grunt work is done back in New York, that's where the main database is stored. Think of this as the "front end" of the process. It reads the blood parameters and sends them back to the mainframe for analysis. Accuracy is sufficient to narrow it down to a probability of one in a billion or so, of course for court presentations you need the full meal deal. However, this little gadget can eliminate most suspects immediately so that you don't waste time headed in the wrong direction, and it offers a much larger search base, which in this day and age is becoming a requirement."

"I'm certainly not an expert at this," Elijah said, "but can't you get the same results using a quick blood typing test?"

"Sure," Jason responded. "But you can only get that with blood, this also gives the same results using any bodily fluid."

"Fantastic." Newton added, "I can think of a lot of cases where this machine would have been of great help."

"So then, who's up for a test?" said Jason smiling, holding up the small black tester. "Who wants to sacrifice a drop of blood for science?" After a moment's hesitation, Elijah offered his finger. "I don't really know what to expect from this, I've never had a DNA sample taken before so where would the match come from?"

"You never know, perhaps some long lost relative. Remember, it's not searching just for you, but for others who have a similar DNA marker set." Jason placed the tester on Elijah's offered finger and there was a small, almost inaudible snap as the spring loaded point drew a single drop of blood. A tiny motor whirred and a strip of paper emerged from tester. Jason took the paper with the blood spot on it, placed it in a transparent envelope and dropped it into a slot on the panel. Next he unscrewed the top of the tester and replaced the used needle with a new one from a supply in the top of the case. The LCD panel came alive with a series of numbers and a set of graphs.

After what seemed like a very short time it blinked out an "analysis completed" message which was replaced with "search?" when Jason clicked the mouse pointer on it. He clicked again and the machine reported it was in search mode. In a few moments a series of three names appeared, each with a number beside it. At the top of list was the name "Shaun O'Reilly," the number beside it was 29%.

"Hah!" said Newton, "always suspected you were a leprechaun in disguise!"

Elijah looked confused and turned to Jason for an explanation, "Ireland is a bit of a ways from the west coast of Canada."

Jason smiled and clicked on the name. In a few seconds the built in printer pumped out a single sheet of paper.

NAME: O'Reilly, Shaun
SEX: M
AGE: 49
CAUSE OF DEATH: Death by Asphyxiation
LOCATION: Ballycotton Harbour, County Cork Ireland
DATE: Jan03, 2001
CIRCUMSTANCES:
Deceased was found dead in a house fire on the morning of Jan 03, 2001. Remains identified by DNA analysis. Deceased was a sailor employed by EYRE SHIPPING. Cause of fire traced to careless disposal

of smoking material.

"OK, you have my attention Jason, how accurate is this?"

"Accurate enough, ever since Francis Crick and James Watson first modeled the DNA helix in 1953, an enormous amount of the scientific communities' resources have been devoted to the study of DNA and the genes of the human race."

"What about the cloning of sheep and other animals?"

"Ah, yes, that's the focus of the press for you, it comes with pictures, so they can understand it, and what's more important, they can put it in newspapers and on TV."

"So cloning is not an important activity?"

"Sure it is, but it is not the focus of the research, only one of the most displayable sidelines."

"What about O'Reilly, my supposed 'match'?" asked Elijah. "What about him?"

"Well, let's start from the beginning then, we all agree that DNA is like a fingerprint, it is unique to every individual on earth. That is the basis for much of our field work, correct?"

"Not entirely true," said Newton. "Identical twins, formed from the same egg, have identical DNA."

"Exactly!" said Jason. "Fraternal twins, formed from separate eggs, have the same genotype also, but their DNA phenotypes are expressed in different ways, which means of course that they would have different fingerprints also. So apart from identical twins from the same egg, science has not found any two people with the same DNA genotypes and the same DNA phenotypes. With me so far?"

They all nodded agreement, some more slowly than others.

"All right then, so the question from Elijah is how some lad in Ireland shows up with some of his DNA traits from half a world away. The answer to that is given in the five mothers' theory."

"The what?" asked Smith.

"The five mothers." Jason continued. "Not a rap band but a theory proposed by the bulk of the scientific community investigating the human genome. The theory is that all of the members of the human race can trace their maternal genes back through time to five mothers who once lived in ancient Africa. As the human race expanded, their descendants moved out to different parts of the world over thousands of years and populated the world."

"Puts a whole new light on the 'We are Family' song, doesn't it?" Newton said.

"Exactly," added Jason. "And that is why you can share DNA traits with someone halfway around the world and not be aware of it. So, you see, the results are accurate after all."

"Does everyone agree with this 'five mothers' theory?"
"No, not everyone, and for many reasons, the presence of DNA samples from even a few hundred years ago is very limited. Unlike movies portraying the cloning of dinosaurs from blood samples sealed in amber from millions of years ago would have us believe. DNA is relatively fragile, and obtaining a sample that is strong enough to do a complete set of tests on, is still not within the realm of our abilities."
"Well, that is a lot to think about—what about the rest of these guys—do they have any far flung relatives hiding in that box?" Elijah asked.
"Let's see," said Jason. "Who's next? How about you, Detective, er, Mr. Newton, would you like to see if your ancestors once sat under an apple tree?"
"Why not, we still have an hour before landing, but how would the real Sir Isaac's DNA wind up in your database?"
"One of the first things they did was track down samples of hair from famous figures to make up the database. I believe even Shakespeare has a slot in it. Tons of people were willing to spend money to have their DNA checked for a lineage to someone special, and having famous folk in it provided a means to finance the early work that was required to make the database a reality."

Newton offered his finger and a few moments later the machine began its work. He did not expect to be linked to his famous namesake, his ancestors had already traced the genealogy and found no connection. Yet, still it was an interesting exercise. As the machine went through its analysis, Newton asked, "How many responses to a single inquiry do you get? If as you say we are all related to the five mothers, there must be a large response set for each inquiry."
"We set the limit to five responses, or we can set a threshold, for example in Elijah's case I had it set to the single top response, for you let's set it at the best two."
In a few moments the screen blinked indicating the analysis was complete and Jason started the search.

A few moments after that, Newton's life changed forever.

CHAPTER ELEVEN

Tehran, Iran

The Japanese made Lexus was quite comfortable with leather seats and what westerners would call "all the goodies." The sound system was the factory CD/FM/AM with a large LCD screen on the dashboard. The screen was a GPS receiver that showed every road and town in Iran. Unlike the factory supplied one, this instrument also transmitted the vehicle's location back to a central office. That office was in the Ministry of State Security. The vehicle's movements were recorded, and then reviewed by an officer reporting directly to the minister in charge. Aram Mohammed Al Bazir found that the further up the ladder one went, the less the degree of trust. In any case, it would not matter. He had no interest in taking advantage of the "freedom" his new position afforded. The illicit gambling establishments, with satellite TV from the west and the presence of a large number of women available for a day's marriage, held no attraction for him. Instead he devoted his time to his new position as advisor. His responsibilities now included organizing the cadre of lower level security officials that would accompany any government official when they went out of the country. Part of that entailed ensuring the official's family was adequately provided for. This he quickly learned, meant sending a number of armed guards to "protect" the family members left behind. There were always family members left behind. The charade fooled no one. Any official who suddenly decided to seek refuge out of the country was in effect sentencing his family to death. So far there were few refugee claimants from Iran on foreign shores.

Aram had been directed to set up a plan for two low level delegations. The first was to the Interpol conference on policing. It was always good to study the ways of those considered to be the enemy. In that way one learned how defeat him. The second was a scientific delegation to the Canary Islands. The purpose of that gathering was to talk about and plan for the next earthquake disaster. Those going to the first meeting would consist of medium and low level security people. Some of them would be traveling outside the country for the first time. Aram's job was to go through their records and recommend 10 of the possible 89 candidates. To do this he would investigate their backgrounds, check with the local Mullahs from their hometowns, and in some cases interview them personally. With so many possibilities, it would be a relatively easy task to narrow the list down. The second group was more or less decided at the outset. There were only a few officials with the required expertise to have been invited in the first place. These people would be going without exception. Aram's job here was to come up with a list of five security personnel to accompany them. For this, he needed four experienced and trusted mid level officers, and one higher ranking official from state security. The list had been provided to him already and unless he came up with a reason to disqualify someone, the list would stand.

Aram knew why he had been given this task. The newest arrival in the organization had not yet had time to foster any relationships with the others on the team. Thus, he could, more than anyone else, be untainted by considerations of friendship or even bribes. Aram had himself used this simple system to vet the guards at his old job when reassigning of positions took place. Intent on his task, he took the first of several file folders that had been placed on his desk, and began to read.

Unknown to him, the subject of one of those folders, Dr. Mohammed Al-Maquir, was also studying a folder in his office located across the city in the Ministry of Science. Unlike Aram, however, he had not been left alone to study it at his leisure. It had come directly from the hands of a colonel wearing the black patches of the Iranian Military Intelligence Corps. Accompanying the colonel were two well armed guards, one of whom had a briefcase chained to his wrist. It was from this briefcase that the folder had been taken. The colonel held a stopwatch in his hands. Dr. Al-Maquir had been given exactly five minutes to read the contents of the folder, and the time was ticking down. At precisely five minutes, the stopwatch beeped, and the colonel reached out his hand for the folder. It was given to him and he immediately placed it in the briefcase. The case snapped shut. During this time it had remained chained to the guard's wrist, secured with an electronic lock for which no mechanical key existed. The briefcase itself could be opened once and once only, when locked again a security system came online. If someone attempted to open the case again, without the proper protocols, the documents, the guard, and everyone within three meters would be incinerated.

Dr. Al-Maquir had not needed the entire five minutes to read the contents of the folder. He was the author of the paper it contained. He had only needed to assure himself that the proper authorities had affixed their signatures signifying approval of the plan. He nodded to the colonel who wordlessly saluted and left the office accompanied by the guards. As he opened the door to leave, Dr. Al-Maquir's secretary entered, flushed with excitement.

"Have you heard the news, Doctor? The work at Natanz has been halted!"

"Yes Omar, I have heard."

"But why? We were so close, why did we give up our research, why did we allow ourselves to be bullied by the UN and the Great Satan?"

"Because Omar, we have accomplished all we need to do, Please send out these notices right away."

Dr. Al-Maquir handed his secretary a sheaf of pre-typed messages, and then rose from his desk.

"I shall be away from the office for the next few weeks Omar, please summon my car."

A few minutes later an old black Lincoln Continental, left over from the days of the Shah arrived at the front of the building. Two small flags were mounted on the front fenders signifying the vehicle was being used by a member of the ruling council. No police officer on the streets of Iran was authorized to stop or interfere with its travel, and its movement took priority over any other traffic, save a similarly equipped vehicle. Mohammed sank into the leather upholstery of the rear seat, "The docks, berth 1-A," he ordered the driver through the open glass panel separating the driver from the rear. With that done he pressed the button that raised the panel and ensured complete privacy. Dr. Al-Maquir thought it ironic that he was riding in such a well crafted vehicle, while he set about destroying the country that made it. Now, he thought to himself, to ensure the Chinese have done their part.

CHAPTER TWELVE

The White House - Washington D.C.

Alexander Wells loved the smell of the cherry blossoms, and paused for a minute before leaving the White House gardens. He had just left the meeting with the President, the Head of the Atomic Energy Committee, and as usual the National Security Advisor. The meeting had been called to discuss the response to the news from the United Nations that Iran had suddenly reversed course and agreed to abide by the Nuclear Non-Proliferation Treaty. In addition, it had invited representatives from the UN and all the major powers to witness the dismantling of the Natanz nuclear enrichment facility. In return, Iran had asked for inclusion in the European Common Market, and, a seat on the new Security Council. The first request had seemed to be achievable and the reasons for granting it of more benefit to Europe than to Iran. Wells expected them to grant it without much debate. The second would be a lot harder to push through. Even with the expansion of the Security Council planned by the UN, the problem would be that they had already announced a seat for Israel. In order to take their seat at the council, Iran would have to recognize the legitimacy of the State of Israel, just as Israel had been required to recognize the existence of the State of Palestine. Successive Iranian governments had repeatedly stated they would never do this. While the talkers and negotiators in the State Department were slapping themselves on the back at what they considered to be the obvious success of negotiation and reason, Wells was not so sure. The supporting signs were simply not there. All the old players were still in power. The widespread, but still impotent, movement of students had not achieved sufficient power to challenge the ruling religious council, and the requisite driving force for change was absent.

Added to the mix was China.

The rapid and relentless emergence of China into world trade had brought about enormous problems for the United States and other members of the western World. The trade deficit with the U.S. was now approaching two billion dollars a day. Cheap labour and a controlled work force ensured Chinese goods a preferred price point with American buyers. It was ironic that the "throw away" society brought about by American marketing agencies had laid the foundation for the public's willingness to put quality aside in favour of flash. Introduced to sell a new model of automobile, appliance, or TV set each year, and keep the factories in full production, it had led to the buying of cheaper offshore goods. The jobs that these represented were thus transferred to developing countries, and, inevitably, the factories in America closed. The original thought was that as the developing country prospered, its citizens would see their standard of living rise, and the prices of their goods would rise to fuel their workers' demands for increased wages. It would all even out in the end. There were even some benefits to the State Department. A country whose workers enjoyed a high standard of living would demand the freedom to enjoy the fruits of their labours. Democracy would reign, despots and dictators would fall, and everyone would be happy. No one thought about what would happen when the inrush of cheap goods inundated the marketplace. In order to compete and satisfy their shareholders, American companies had to move entire factories offshore. The brand "made in America" became harder to find, save on weapons systems and aircraft. With the rise of the European Common Market, even that position of prominence was now in jeopardy.

The continued advancement of the Chinese in world markets meant another, much more threatening set of realities. They were now major competitors for the supply of raw materials. Already America was dependent on others for her energy needs, and the demands of the Chinese economy coupled with its success, meant it could outbid the United States for those dwindling supplies. Increasingly, American firms were successful in obtaining the metals and timber they needed only after the Chinese had taken first pick. American firms tended to buy on the short term market, looking for a better spot price on some commodity or another. The Chinese now had the money to simply buy a controlling interest in the company supplying the required product. As the civilian marketplace grew, so did the military-industrial complex behind it. As the military modernized its equipment previously based on outdated Russian designs, it needed to take over control of previously civilian run factories. As long as these concerned the land based components of the military, the State Department remained an interested observer.

Now a disturbing set of rumours had reached their ears. One of the Chinese shipyards had been taken over by the military. The Chinese navy to this point had a limited blue water capability. The U.S. Seventh Fleet guarded the straits between the island nation of Taiwan and the Chinese mainland. As long as American sea power remained supreme in that body of water, the chances of a conflict arising from the constant war of words between the two factions remained remote. With the placing of an entire shipyard under military control, the indications seemed to be that the mainland government had decided to make a challenge to the status quo.

When Wells had learned from his contacts in the C.I.A. that they had been busy building a number of what appeared to be deep sea drilling rigs, he was puzzled. These types of ships were standard civilian products, available at a number of shipyards worldwide. Offshore oil exploration had been going on for years. Any number of the rigs could be seen in action in the shallower areas of some countries' continental shelf. Their construction had been more or less standardized for years. With the required changes to account for local ice conditions, the platforms pretty much all consisted of the same basic design. Submersible legs that were filled with ballast such as sea water and anchored to the sea floor provided the stability required to drill. Flexible drilling couplers and pipe allowed a degree of lateral and vertical movement to compensate for the wave motion. All of this worked—in shallow water. When the exploration area moved out to the deep ocean, other answers were necessary. Many solutions had been proposed. From remotely operated submarine platforms that were designed to be fixed to the sea floor up to one mile below, with the pipe fed from above, to a new carbon fiber type of pipe which could be used by a "conventional" offshore platform. All the indications were that the Chinese had developed something that allowed them to drill in much deeper waters than the state of American technology would allow. The C.I.A. was convinced they had perfected it already—why else would they build five ships instead of one to test the theory with? The construction of the vessels by the military added to the feeling that this was a done deal. If this was all true, Wells believed, then not only would the Chinese have assured themselves of a large supply of cheap oil, they also would have a stranglehold on the newly emerging technology. If not for the complete takeover of the shipyard, this would simply appear to be the latest step in the Chinese industrial march.

Further to that, it appeared the Iranians were also involved, possibly as the major financial backers. If true, then that would explain why they had abandoned their expensive nuclear plans. With their on shore oil reserves and now an apparent partnership with the Chinese in the plentiful but hitherto unreachable deep sea reserves, they would control the supply of oil for decades to come.

Why else would one of the ships, the "Shinning Way," be berthed at this moment at Bandar Immam Khomeyni, one of the largest Iranian ports in the Persian Gulf? Neither Wells, nor Major O'Conner were aware that at that precise moment Dr. Al-Maquir was boarding the

"Shining Way," and was about to meet her captain. Major O'Conner was finalizing the details of the flight to Tehran which was due to leave in less than four hours. There were many details to work out. One of the most vexing was not present, however, on this trip. The usual protocol for an American official to visit Iran was not to go there at all. Meetings were arranged through third parties in another country. Officials from the United States and Iran would rarely schedule face to face talks. The mood in the oil rich Islamic Republic was still officially anti-Western, and specifically anti-American. Anything that required discussion was done by "chance meetings." Both parties would attend some common diplomatic function, during which the two would, "by chance" find themselves in the same room. There, any required exchanges would take place. Nothing was ever "officially" done. Such was the world of the diplomats. For this trip, however, a direct invitation through the new Iraqi embassy had been extended. There was even talk of re-opening the embassy in Tehran.

Peace and democracy were apparently breaking out all over the world.

Major O'Conner was waiting for Wells when he opened the door to his office. She was dressed in a definitely unmilitary long dress. Even though it stretched from the floor to her throat, the dark blue material did nothing to hide her curves. The matching scarf would be used to cover her head once they landed in Tehran. As much of change as the news from Iran indicated, they still were not likely to accept a woman in the standard U.S. military garb. His housekeeping staff had already sent over the suitcases that he kept packed and ready for trips on short notice. Even now they were being loaded on the Grumman Gulfstream II business jet.
"So, Major, what do you think of this sudden reversal of the Iranians?"
"Welcome news, sir, but I'd consider the possibility that there may be some other reason other than good relations at the root of it."
"Really? Why?"
"Because there is no apparent reason for them to suddenly change their way of doing things. Everything in that part of the world is planned on a longer timeline than we use. We tend to look ahead four years at a time to the next election. They look ahead to the next century. "
"Some of those in the State Department believe this is all just the result of their hard work and dedication," said Wells, rocking back and forth in his chair. "They believe that the Iranians have come to the conclusion that it is too expensive to continue with their nuclear

program."

"Sir, with respect to them, and their hard work, they are wrong. Every time the price of oil goes up another dollar a barrel, the Iranians make another two and a half million a day. I don't think finances are a great concern. Their social programs are, unlike ours, a minor part of their budget. Their investments abroad earn billions, and they don't need to invest in the military end of things since Russia fell. And none of that has changed in the last two weeks."

"As it happens, I agree with you, Carol, but there are those agendas, or ideologies, that do not allow that kind of thinking. I'd like you to get together with the folks from the company who are accompanying us, and see if you can find out the real reason behind this."

A knock on the door preceded the entrance of Wells' secretary. She announced that their departure may be subject to a small delay.

"What's that all about?" Wells asked, "We have a time table to meet."

"It's really no problem, sir, you will be landing in the early morning in Tehran, and you are not scheduled to meet with the ruling council until later that day at the British Embassy." Throughout all the problems in Iran, the British had maintained their embassy. Their history in the region predated the American presence, and besides, their embassy had not been overrun.

"One more thing, sir, you'll be making a refueling stop in Azores instead of Diego Garcia."

"That's odd; the Gulfstream can make Diego easily, why stop on the other side of Africa?"

"It's at the request of the V.P. Sir"

"Ahh, I see," said Wells.

That request had come at the behest of one J.J. Ogden. J.J. was the current CEO. of Eastern Skies and it was under his personal direction that the airlines had pushed for the acquisition of the new aircraft that was currently headed towards a landing in those same Azores. The 10,000 foot runway at Santa Maria (SMA) was the main refueling stop for civilian air traffic. The military field at Lajes Air Base (TER) was slightly longer at 10,800 feet, but traffic there was restricted. J.J. was not a happy man. He had spent a large amount of company money to fete the aviation and tourist press on a trip to the island of Santa Maria and put them up at a five star hotel. Included was a tour and a flight aboard the new plane in the exotic locale. Now he learned that someone in the bloody maintenance department had not bothered to read the newest directives and shipped seven cartons of the wrong type engine oil to the company facility at the island airport. They had assumed the oil would be the same as normal and not the new lighter type demanded by the new engines design. J.J. had been forced to call in a few markers to correct the situation. The call had been to the new V.P. begging space on the Gulfstream he knew was taking some weenies from the state department to Iran. The V.P. had been happy to approve the request. It meant one less marker outstanding, and in this case J.J. and Eastern had been a very generous contributor to the V.P.'s election fund. All in all, the V.P. got off easy, all it took was a small diversion in the flight path of a jet already scheduled to head that way. The V.P. was in a much better mood than J.J. The delay caused by the wrong oil type meant the airline would now have to delay the departure of the flight on its way to Europe. That meant the passengers would be entitled to, and would receive, a complimentary stay in the same hotel as the press. That meant they would probably not all be happy. Unhappy passengers would go to the bar. The press would go to the bar as a matter of daily habit for most of them. The two groups would meet and some of the press would sympathize with the disgruntled few. That would taint their stories and all the careful planning J.J. had done to bring the new aircraft to the public in a good light stood to be undone. No, J.J. was not a happy man, and when he was not happy someone else was damn sure going to be unhappy.

A few phone calls later, J.J.'s unhappiness was made known to the maintenance shipping department. The poor slob who had not read the company directive about the new oil requirements was called on the carpet and told to personally supervise the delivery of seven cases of oil to the government Gulfstream preparing for a trip to Iran. The poor slob, a newer employee, decided that in order to make good his mistake he would also ship seven cases of the regular oil, so that there would be a plentiful supply of the stuff. Yes-siree, he would not make the same mistake twice. The 14 cases were delivered and quickly disappeared into the Grumman's cargo hold. The total delay to the flight turned out to be less than five minutes, less time in fact than it took to taxi the Gulfstream into position for takeoff. Spouting black smoke from its four rear mounted engines it roared skyward and quickly made up the time.

CHAPTER THIRTEEN

Eastern Skies Inaugural Flight 196

 Two hours west of the Azores, the in-flight communications screen in the cockpit came alive with a message from the company headquarters. The channel was normally used for private communications, and the messages concerned the minutiae of all aircrafts flights. On this occasion, the flight engineer was alerted to the mix-up with the oil types and the captain told to announce an extended stay-over to the passengers. The public relations and marketing department of Eastern Skies had been busy, and with the announcement came a list of room numbers assigned and pre-booked for each passenger. The company had a lot of pull with the island's tourist department and they had used that to ensure that though their passengers were delayed, they would at least be comfortable.

After the announcement, the predictable chorus of dismay emanated from the passengers aboard the plane. There was a flurry of cell phone calls and folks consulting their electronic planners. In the lounge, Jason used the situation as an opportunity to demonstrate another feature of his box of tricks. Flipping open another compartment, he popped out a web camera and attached its cable to another jack on the panel. In minutes he had contacted the conference organizers and confirmed that their hotel reservations would be held over. The conference itself would not require their attendance on the first day, so the delay would have no other effect. That done, he turned to the task he was doing prior to the interruption.

The machine had returned two matches to the DNA sample provided by Newton. Both were female.

NAME: Ellie Newton
SEX: F
AGE:19
LOCATION: Yonkers, New York
DATE: 11 July 2005
CIRCUMSTANCES:
Subject found unconscious on subway.
Taken to Memorial Hospital for treatment.
No identification.
Treated and released.
Malnutrition and dehydration.
No drug use. No trauma.
BASE RECORD: Victoria Police Service School Child Identification Program September 1994

NOK. Alfred and Winnifred Newton
NOTE: Parent is a serving member - Do not release address

"Hey," said Jason, "this is you!"
Smith and Elijah, who had been chatting by themselves looked over expectantly. Smith took note of the expression on Newton's face and turned immediately to Jason. "Turn it off."
"What?"
"I said turn the frigging thing off, do it now."
Sudden understanding came over Jason's face and he reached for the machine.
"Sorry 'bout that, man, I didn't know."
Newton grabbed Jason's arm, "It's Ok, leave it on."
"Is she your daughter?"
"Yeah," said Newton.
The table grew quiet, and Smith turned to Jason, "Better turn it off, Jason."
"Print it first please," Newton asked Jason. "Both sheets"
After the printer spat out the two sheets with a whisper, Jason disconnected the machine and packed it away. "Sorry 'bout that, man."
"No problem, she is my daughter, she left home right after my wife and I divorced, she was 16 and I haven't heard from her since. In a way, it's a relief to know she's OK, so I thank you for that."
"When we land I'll make a few calls, I know some of the guys in Yonkers and I'll see what they can find out for you." said Smith. "Funny they didn't contact you at the time."
"They wouldn't have known, and no doubt she asked them not to," said Newton. "And really, there was no reason for them if she was not in trouble, so in one way it's a good thing."
"Would she have contacted her mother?" asked Smith.
"No, she was killed in a car wreck shortly after we split up, I think that was part of the reason Ellie left."
"The curse of the job," Smith said. "It's one of the hardest professions on relationships. Marie and I split ten years ago next February."
A few moments of silence passed with all the men deep in their thoughts. "Hey, what about that second sheet, what does it say?" Newton asked.
"Jason scanned the sheet quickly, "Geez, that's odd," he said, "your name's on this one too."
"What?"
"This one also has markers that.. Sure. See this," Jason said pointing at the sheets. "There are the same sibling markers on both, but, umm, only on the mother's side,"

Newton took a look at the other sheet for the first time

NAME: Jane Doe
SEX: F
AGE:18
LOCATION: Victoria B.C.
DATE: March 2004
CIRCUMSTANCES:
Body of young girl found on beach. No identification. Cause of Death - Drowning
Case open. Investigating Officer Det Alfred Newton

"Now that is just weird," said Smith.

"Jason, explain this to me, how is it the markers are similar, and why didn't this come up when we first submitted the DNA back in 2004."

"The answer to your second question is easy, different methods of testing that were not correlated. The match is between a sample taken in 1994 and a newer method ten years later, and the sample I just got from you. That is what this machine does, takes all those different methods and generates a new screening as if they had been done with the same tests. The answer to the first question is that, according to the results, there is a good possibility that both samples had the same mother. But remember, this is just an approximation, it's meant to focus the investigation, not define it. The logical next avenue would be to see if your wife had an identical twin or something like that."

"No, she didn't."

"Was she married before?"

"Not that she told me about. But maybe, I never did meet her parents. She told me they were dead."

"When did you two meet?"

"Just a year before we got married, she was 23, I was 28."

"Well, it could be a number of things, I wouldn't read that much into it," said Jason.

The seatbelt sign began flashing, and the lounge began to clear out as the passengers returned to their seats in preparation for landing. As they made their way to their seats, Elijah took the opportunity to whisper a few words to Newton. "Life is full of surprises my friend, this is good news, is it not? Your child is alive and well."

"One is," said Newton, looking at his friend, "but apparently one is not."

Back in his seat, Newton slipped on his headphones. The background music was an easy listening channel, and the soft sounds soothed his spirit. Emotions, long held in check, rose to the surface. On one hand, he was relieved his daughter Ellie had been seen alive and well a few months ago. On the other, his brain cycled through the myriad of memories from her birth, to the day he came home to find her gone.

The snapshots in his mind flickered on and off, like an old movie projector. Black and white and color, all mixed together. A sleeping form in a crib wearing a pink sleeper, teddy bear clutched close. Her first steps, well not the very first, he had not been there for that. He had been on a case, solving someone else's problems, unaware of his own. She had tottered across the hardwood floor arms raised, outstretched to him as he waited kneeling down a few feet away.
"Here, honey!"
"You can do it"
"Good girl!"
She giggled, and laughed the laugh only babies and toddlers have. A deep throated chuckle ending with a high pitched "Whheeee." The next few days were full of padded thumps and giggles. Occasional crashes as an object came within her reach and small fingers grasped for support.
Birthdays arrived and passed. Some he was there for, some he was not. Pink sleepers became PJ's with bunnies; they in turn gave way to night gowns. The hugs and carrying her off to bed changed to stories read and then to a quick "'Night, Daddy." Prams became trikes and bikes, bikes eventually a car, not hers, not his, but a friend's. The refrigerator door sprouted colored pictures and drawings, then essays mixed with reminders, "Piano lessons at 6, skating at 8."

He didn't notice at all when frilly dresses turned to jeans, blouses into shirts, and the first applications of makeup appeared. Suddenly they were just there, and then they were gone with her. The house, which first rang with laughter, then shouts and tears, grew quiet again. The reminders on the fridge replaced with a single note.
"Bye, dad, I love you. Don't worry, I'll be OK—Ellie"
He still remembered that day. It had started out so well, a case solved, someone taken off the streets, again, this time for a longer period than the few months they had received the last time. He had made her a lunch for school and hoped she would take it this time. Many times she didn't, but today was the last day of school and there was to be a party of sorts. He had fixed her favorites, added in a large bag of chips for the class, and put ten dollars in an envelope so she could purchase pop or whatever for the group. Graduation had been two weeks ago and he had made it there. She was lovely in her cap and gown, long black dress, and Birkenstock sandals. He didn't know much about her friends, they rarely came over, or he was rarely there.

The class valedictorian had made a great speech about this being a crossroads in their lives. He spoke of challenges past and future, the roads ahead, and most especially the roads that they now had the opportunity to travel. Newton thought then that the young man had a career made in the travel industry if he should choose to take it.

After, the kids all gathered around her and then they split off into groups, some had plans, some had dreams of plans, and some were still just planning to dream. She had attended the prom with Roger Wilcox, her on again off again boyfriend. Out the door at seven, home by eleven.

Later, on the day she left, the weather had turned sour; the morning sunshine gave way to clouds, the clouds to rain. By the time he wrapped it up at the office and filed the last report it was windy and the rain lashed out at him when he parked the car and struggled in through the front door. He had taken but two steps when it hit him. The house was quiet. No radio, no TV, no sounds of people moving. The air was still, too still. The kitchen table held the note and nothing else.

He had searched for her of course, but by then she had left the island. Gone to Vancouver, Seattle, or some other place, and then gone from there to another. He had placed some calls to friends and colleagues in other police services, sent the pictures, surprised at how few he had, and waited. Occasionally a call would come and he would leave town, only to arrive too late.

Then she came, the Jane Doe. With her came the flood of emotions that he had buried over the months. With her came the clue from an informant named Rusty, the news that Ellie had been seen again. The search for the Jane Doe's identity had led Newton to the rugged Queen Charlotte Islands. There he had found some clues but more questions, and he had found love. A love he had thought lost to him, and that too had awakened more emotion. Now he found that that girl may be somehow related to his daughter? How could this be?

When he met Winnifred, she had been on the island for less than a year. Working in the court system, she had been trained as a legal secretary, and was starting her own business as a paralegal. At first their relationship was all business. He wanted to buy a house, and she provided the legal conveyance and property title search required for the transaction. The lender she was working for required that the lot be measured and its dimensions verified. Not unusual for a hilly region. She had made arrangements to meet him in the late afternoon and together they had found the white surveyor's stakes that marked the property boundaries. He had offered dinner, she accepted, and then everything flowed from that. They were married within a year, and a year later Ellie came along. The strains of his job, and the absences it demanded left her feeling alone more often. With Ellie becoming more independent, the days began to lengthen and she returned to her first job. In the beginning it was exciting and filled the empty hours, at the end it became more important than home and she left. Shortly after that, she was the victim of a drunk driver. Her loss, not only to him, but to Ellie, precipitated his daughter's leaving also. He had not asked her much about her life prior to their meeting. There was never a reason for him to be interested in it, until now.

Newton held the sheets in his hands, he had received a limited amount of training in the art of reading DNA profiles, but even to him, the similarities were obvious. The quality of the testing was always a wild card. Ellie's had been part of a "Child Identification" program, and the tests were not as rigorous as one which would be done today. Still, the markers could not be denied. Either Winnifred had another child previous to their relationship, or she had a twin sister who did.

Newton's thoughts were interrupted by a hand on his shoulder.

"The world is a small place my friend, is it not?"

"So it would seem, Elijah, so it would seem."

"Now you have more up-to-date information on where your daughter has been, that is a good thing," Elijah went on. "Perhaps Detective Smith will be able to help you find her."

"Yes, Elijah, perhaps he will, but will she welcome it? If she wanted to, she could call home at any time."

"Our children do the same as yours," said Elijah. "For some, the journey is part of a plan they have to expand their view of the world and find work. For others it is different, they leave in a state of confusion, and in order to do so, some of them convince themselves that this is something they must do because they do not feel there is a place for them at home. It is the same in the big cities, is it not? In a few cases it is true that the children cannot find peace at home, in others they create that view in their minds because they do not yet have the experience to appreciate the circumstances that a family may find itself in."

The seatbelt sign flashed on overhead and the intercom announced the aircraft's descent into the traffic approach pattern for the airport.

Elijah went on, "These children then feel they cannot call home, because if they do, they fear they will not be welcome because they had left for no solid reason. Even if they are welcome, then they would have been wrong, and that for some would be the worst thing of all."

Newton knew Elijah was right, he had seen the same thing many times in his career, but it was different when the home was your home, and the children your children. He had, when he was younger, wondered how parents could be so blind, so occupied with making a living that they forgot to make a life. Later he had come to realize that nothing was so cut and dried. Children went on their own path, regardless of social or economic situation. The best parents sometimes had the worst kids, and conversely, the best kids sometimes came from the worst situations. Like an arrow, they could only be aimed, once loosed, they found their own way in the winds of life. Newton had managed to solve most of the cases he had been involved in. Not always to a legal conviction, but certainly to level of certainty that was, more often or not, proved true by later confessions and convictions. His last case was an exception. His Jane Doe remained unidentified. The *why* of her death still unanswered. He had felt a connection to her from the beginning when she was discovered on the beach. He thought at first this was due to his own daughter's disappearance. Perhaps a natural consequence of similar situations, or rather possibilities. Seeing her there naturally brought up questions in his mind about where his daughter would be, and the fear that she would one day be found dead.

But now he knew she had been found, at least for a while, and he knew that after this conference was over, and he was back home, that he would actively take up the search again.

A thump below him signaled the landing gear being deployed. They had arrived at the Azores.

CHAPTER FOURTEEN

Bandar Immam Khomeyni

Dr. Al-Maquir was seated in the captain's cabin aboard the "Shining Way." He had been offered tea and a small plate of sandwiches, both of which he had politely refused. The master of the vessel was officially Chung Wey, and he was not pleased. He was not in reality the master of any vessel; in fact, he was not a sailor at all. The trip to this port from China had been spent in his cabin fighting seasickness. Chung Wey was a diplomat of sorts. He had been put in charge of this project by his government to oversee the search for oil promised by the Iranians. His regular job was as a political officer for the Party. His regular duties were to ensure the government officials under his control kept the State's interests ahead of their own. With the economy booming, the attractions of capitalism had led some of them to stray from those duties. In some cases it had required the expenditure of a pistol bullet to bring the rest back into line. The Chinese government had built these five deep sea drilling vessels at great cost. Even though that cost had been borne chiefly by the Iranian government, the space available for shipbuilding was limited. Constructing these five vessels had taken three years away from the building plans of the Chinese Navy. As a consequence, the plan for reuniting the province of Taiwan with the mother country had been delayed. During that time the Americans had made huge strides in the perfecting and deployment of their anti-ballistic missile systems. Although publicly parroted as a work in progress—and not much progress at that—the Chinese knew the system was a success and that the first operational batteries had been deployed to both Taiwan and Israel. The next installation was set for Japan as a hedge against the unpredictable plans of North Korea's dictator. Thus the Chinese government had to revise its plans for reunification yet again, as the delay in naval construction had eclipsed the window of opportunity to use the Navy to spearhead the invasion of the island state. The promise of increased oil reserves by the Iranians had not come to pass, and the Chinese government had begun to lose patience.

There were the usual pleasantries being exchanged, small gifts given and received in the rites of diplomatic niceties acted out everywhere. In due time, the secretaries were dismissed, the pictures taken, and the two men got down to business. Wey had been given strict instructions by his government. He was here to tell the Iranians that the Chinese had decided to end the partnership. The instructions had arrived in a sealed container, the key to which had been given to the

Ship's captain, and not opened until the vessel had set sail.

"Minister," began Wey, "I am charged by my government to express disappointment at the results of the drilling program that we have undertaken at your insistence. Our geologists have studied the core samples taken from the La Palma basin and confirmed, that as they expected all along, the chance of the finding any significant hydrocarbons is, to say the least, remote."

Al-Maquir sat there, his face stolid.

Wey continued, "As you know, we have invested significant resources into this project and we now feel it necessary to move on." He paused and studied the face of the Iranian, no clues as to how his words were being received appeared on the bearded face, or in his body language. Wey had been told that his Farsi was excellent, but he couldn't help but wonder if he was getting through. "I have a copy of the agreement here minister, and according to our agreement, we are exercising our rights to withdraw—and to keep four of the five ships as compensation."

Dr. AL-Maquir finally nodded, "I understand, and the ships you wish to keep are still on station at La Palma?"

"Yes, Minister, as required, they will be there two more weeks."

"Very well, Mr. Wey, please convey to your government that we also are disappointed in the results of the drilling. It is not our intention to penalize the People's Republic of China for our failure to assess the potential of the basin. Therefore The government of Iran asks that you accept fifty percent of the Ahwaz-Asmari oil fields' daily production of 700,000 barrels a day. This request comes directly from the new President and the Majlis. All we ask is that we be allowed to recover some recording equipment that is presently aboard those four ships."

Wey was speechless. He had expected a much different response. The mark of a good diplomat is that he never let their counterparts know they were surprised and in this Wey was indeed a good diplomat. He merely nodded his head. Recovering his voice, he said "I will communicate that to my government. Although I cannot give you an official answer, I cannot think of any objections they would have." Indeed, the whole scheme had been premised on a forecast production of 500,000 barrels a day of which the Chinese would get half from the La Palma basin. Now they were being given more than that with no further work on their part. Wey was reminded of an old Chinese saying "never look a gift dragon in the mouth." Minister Al-Maquir rose and handed over an envelope. "Here are the details, in anticipation of your government's acceptance, we have made arrangements to have some of our scientists visit the vessels this coming week and retrieve our equipment."

"How will this be done, Minister? The vessels are still at sea."

"There is a geology conference at La Palma in the next few days, the attending scientists will be able to find time to visit the ships."

"That conference is not related to the study of oil as I recall. We ourselves have two geologists attending, but they are volcanologists."

"As are our attendees, but dirt is dirt, Mr. Wey, and the equipment is applicable to both fields of study."

The two men made small talk for a further ten minutes, then Dr AL-Maquir left. Immediately thereafter, Wey headed for the communications center of the ship. Once there, he made use of the secure radio phone that had been installed. Less than half an hour later, he had an answer for the Iranian government.

The next stop for the minister was an army base located at the port. Ostensibly, the army was responsible for port security. The huge amount of piping, several hundreds of kilometers in total length, would be a prime target for terrorists. Despite its apparent wealth, Iran ran a budget deficit every year. The reason for this was the subsidy for gasoline and social programs. The price of 40 cents a gallon was far below the cost of production. This presented the Majlis or parliament, with a dilemma. In order to reduce its dependence upon oil, it was necessary to diversify the economic base of the country. The more that succeeded, the more internal fuel consumption rose, and the subsidies took a larger part of the countries budget. The expectations of the masses also rose with the changing economy. Increased computer use made the outside world much more accessible, and the masses were beginning the inevitable move towards a desire for greater freedom.

Arriving at the military post, the minister was met by a general. The general had been at the post only a few hours, announcing a surprise inspection when he arrived. The major in charge of the post had been summonsed from home and the general's staff had insisted the major and all his officers take them on a personal inspection of the facility. This left the general alone at the post when the minister arrived. The minister stayed only long enough to hand the general an envelope, and left. When his staff returned, the general had a brief conference with them, pronounced the post acceptable with a few minor changes in security procedures, and promoted the major to colonel on the spot. The new colonel, still in a daze from the whirlwind inspection, was left sitting at his desk wondering what the hell just happened. He had been around long enough not to ask questions and accepted that there must have been a greater purpose to the whole charade than he was supposed to know. That was the kind of thinking that had kept him alive during the transition from the Shah's rule.

The general, now in his staff car, opened the envelope he had received. It held but one sheet of paper and on that paper was one word. With but a moment's hesitation he opened the shield between his compartment and the front seat. He motioned to his aide to pass over the briefcase that accompanied him wherever he went. Receiving it, he put the shield back up and entered the day's key code into the electronic lock. The case snapped opened and he selected a black plastic container that had the same word imprinted on it as the sheet of paper he had received from the minister. Snapping the plastic in half, he removed the laminated sheet it contained and read the instructions printed on it. Next he picked up the phone and gave the driver new instructions.

"Tehran, Mujad, take the fast lanes."

"Yes, General," the driver responded and took the lane reserved for government traffic. He knew then that this was a "special" trip. The reserved lanes allowed the driver to complete the trip at high speed. They also marked the vehicle as a high importance target for any "insurgents" that may be in the vicinity. Despite the picture presented to the outside press, the activity of such groups was very much on the upswing. Lowering the shield, he passed the briefcase back to his aide. These steps completed he said a silent prayer and settled back into his seat.

The driver headed south to Tehran. The road took them past small villages and larger town centers alike. Traffic was light, and in places consisted of the centuries old donkey carts that still rattled around the country. It was not unusual to see a farm with modern tractors and machinery next to family plots served by donkeys and oxen. On the highways, modern cars and trucks, mostly from Asian countries, whizzed by with little regard to the posted speed laws. The general's car sported small flags from the front fenders. Any local police force or militia would ensure unimpeded passage through the many checkpoints that dotted the countryside.

They arrived within two hours and went straight to the army command center located in the massive telephone center at Immam Khomeini Square. The telephone center was the communications hub of the entire city of twelve million people. While a nightmare to maintain and an engineering headache to build, the centralized system allowed the authorities to easily monitor any telephone they wished. The main downside of such an arrangement, aside from the extra costs involved in building it, was that any group controlling the complex controlled all the landline communications in the city. This explained the presence of the army. It was their job to provide the required physical protection of the facility. The main listening duties were assumed by the religious council. If it was felt that a matter concerned national security, then the army could be invited in. The technical expertise required to provide the means to listen in to the millions of phone calls came from the signals section of the army's engineering corps. In the process, there were those in the remnants of the Shah's intelligence service who managed to ensure that the army was not kept completely at the mercy of the largely uneducated group of religious fanatics who ran the country. The same exchange that tapped into the communications of the masses also listened to the government. The main computer complex that controlled the forest of cell phone towers was also situated at the site. The signals corps had overseen the foreign contractors who built it. The illusion of being unable to tap into those signals had been deliberately fostered by the army. As a result, most of the government ministries relied on cell phones rather than landlines for their communications. The army, it turned out, had been less than forthright in its descriptions of its own technical expertise.

The general made two calls when he arrived in his office that night; one was to the special forces group located at the Doshan Tapeh Air Base. This call consisted of the same code word he had received from Minister Al-Maquir, and the code word printed on the card he had retrieved from his aide. Upon receipt, the commander would retrieve a similar card from an office safe located in his office. If that card had the same code word as the general's, the commander would execute the instructions printed on the reverse side. This procedure had been the subject of many exercises, and until today the instructions were simply to call a number and speak a code word. Today the instructions were to execute the orders contained in another sealed envelope. In accordance with those orders, four small packages were loaded onto a civilian aircraft. The aircraft was then positioned to load civilian passengers headed to La Palma Airport, Canary Islands.

The second call was to a number he had committed to memory many years ago. That call was made from a connection within the complex that simulated a phone call made from a public phone booth located in the metro subway system.

"Hello, is Amar there?"

"No, you have the wrong number, this is the museum."

"I'm sorry, I must have dialed wrong."

The computerized phone records would show a call received by the museum. What they would not show is a high speed burst of radio traffic to a weather satellite in geo synchronous orbit over Iraq. The signal was relayed to the national listening post in Washington D.C.

There the coded markers on the signal were matched to a preprogrammed list buried in a computer program which searched every incoming signal for those telltale bytes. When they appeared, the signal was relayed to another computer screen and marked in red. That computer was monitored by the signals section of the C.I.A. and a click of a mouse on the red lined box brought up the required protocol.

CHAPTER FIFTEEN

The Azores

"Ladies and gentlemen, this is your captain speaking. Eastern Skies Inaugural Flight 196 welcomes you to the Santa Maria Airport here in the Azores. Please remain in your seats until the aircraft has come to a complete stop. As this is our inaugural flight, we would like to present you with a complimentary one night stay at the Hotel De Santa Maria. As we pull up to the ramp you will see a large group of photographers assembled in the terminal. They have been granted access to the aircraft to take pictures, so we ask that you ensure all personal items leave the aircraft with you. Buses have been provided to take you to the hotel. On behalf of Eastern Skies I'd like to thank you for flying with us today and we look forward to continuing our flight tomorrow." Scotty hung up the intercom microphone as he said to no one in particular, "And so the dog and pony show begins."

Newton, Smith, Jason, and Elijah waited for the rest of the passengers to deplane. They sat at the rear until the crush of people had gone through the routine of getting up from their seats, jostling for room to remove their belongings from the overhead racks, and waiting until those in front moved towards the exits. Some still protested the unplanned delay in the completion of their flight, but most were resigned to the fact that there was nothing to be done. Besides, the airline was going to foot the bill for their hotel rooms and meals—including the bar tab. Even though the stopover was going to be limited to one night, the passengers were going to make sure the airline paid dearly for the inconvenience. Many of those same passengers may well be wishing they had exercised greater restraint when the flight did continue. Experiencing rough air while strapped into a seat that prevented one from lying down whilst under the effects of a hangover exacted its own measure of revenge. In anticipation of the possibilities, the flight crew had already scheduled the aircraft for a complete cabin cleanup when they reached Europe.

At last, the crowd ahead thinned enough for the group of four to proceed. Each carried whatever luggage they brought on board, and Jason had the additional burden of his DNA machine. Their checked luggage was already on the way to the hotel, or so they were told. But most of the travelers had enough experience with airlines to stock their carryon luggage with a change of clothing and other items to keep them comfortable for an overnight stay. As they exited the aircraft, each received an envelope from one of the stewardesses at the main cabin door.

"Thanks for flying with us, enjoy your stay!"

"Like we have a choice?" one passenger, grumbled as he left.

Newton gave them a welcome smile and thanked them for their service during the flight. The delay was not due to anything they had control over, and unlike some of the other passengers, he saw no need to vent whatever frustrations he may have. Detective Smith, at the end of the line, took the time to joke with the crew about the situation and struck up a conversation with an auburn haired crew member. In the short time it took for his turn to exit to arrive, he had gained a promise to look for each other in the hotel bar.

"Whew, we're not in Kansas any more, Toto," Elijah said, as they went down the portable flight stairs.

The hot sun and humidity were a shock after the closed air conditioned environment of the plane. Newton felt the sweat spread on his back. Even mitigated somewhat by an ocean breeze, the air was heavy and clinging. They had all dressed for the more temperate climate of the European continent rather than the tropics. The walk to the assembled buses was interrupted by a sudden tropical shower. Newton marveled that so much rain could come from such small clouds, even though his region of the world, the West Coast of Canada, was noted for a high annual rainfall. They boarded the last bus and took seats at the rear.

"Aren't we special," Elijah said. Looking around they found they were the only passengers on this particular bus, the rest of the seats were for the flight crew.

"Serves us right for being the last to exit I guess." With the exception of the captain, the flight engineer, and two of the cabin crew, the rest of the planes complement boarded shortly after them. To Smith's delight, one of the crew not detailed to show the press around the new plane was the auburn haired girl he had chatted up earlier. He was even happier when she took a seat across the aisle from him. The bus left the terminal and arrived at the hotel a half hour later. Even though they arrived later than the rest of the passengers, they found most of them milling about in the lobby. Taking a seat until the confusion sorted itself out, they examined the envelopes they had been given. Newton and Elijah found they had been given a room on the top floor.

"Well, here's a bit of luck, looks like we get the top floor," Elijah said with pleasure. Obviously one of the more expensive suites, it featured a balcony that, according to the travel brochure included in his envelope, "provided a great view of the ocean." Well, he thought, it shouldn't be all that hard to do on an island. The desk was understandably busy, but managed to get them their room key and directions to it. Not bothering to wait for the hotel staff, they found their luggage which had actually arrived at the hotel before they did, and took the elevator up. The room did indeed provide a spectacular view of the ocean, and while he waited for Elijah to make use of the shower, Newton sat on one of the provided lounges to relax. Not long after he had sat down, he saw the Eastern Skies aircraft in the air followed by two plane loads of photographers. They headed out to take pictures of the plane in flight with the setting sun and the island as a backdrop. Elijah padded out wearing a hotel supplied terry cloth robe and slippers. He carried a cup of coffee from the kitchenette and sat down in one of the other lounges.

"A little warmer here than home," said Newton.

"Yes, it's nice, but sometimes I miss having all four season in the same day."

"What time do they serve dinner here, I wonder."

"I would expect that to be most any time. Hotels that cater to the tourist crowd tend to expand their hours of service. What with folks coming in from all over the world and the differences in time zones, which is a good thing—given that my time zone says it's almost dinner time now."

"OK, I'll grab a shower and we'll head down."

Newton found the shower refreshing after sitting for all those hours on the plane. It was a new design, in keeping with the upscale appointments in the suite. Adjusting the temperature, he slipped into the full body coverage the multiple shower heads offered. This would be a great thing to put into his house he thought. After retiring, he had decided to move away from the city and find a quiet spot in the country. His apartment held too many memories for him now. Some days, he was sure he could smell her perfume.

Before leaving, he had packed everything into the standard two and four cubic foot boxes from the moving company. While he was on this trip, the contractor would be putting up the large workshop he had dreamed about having since he first joined the force. On his return, he would start living out of the shop whilst building the house. He could have had the whole thing contracted out if he wanted to. But retirement was a time to do all those things you dream about when you're working. One of Newton's dreams was to build his own house. Well, as much of it as he could. He would be acting as his own general contractor. The digging of the basement would be handled by the same crew that prepared the shop foundation and floor. He expected the hole to be dug and graded when he got back. He had already bought the house package, a panelized post and beam plan that offered a large glass faced living room, and open, airy spaces. After living in an apartment for most of his working life, Newton needed the unfettered feeling such a plan offered. He was a little claustrophobic, and over time, the apartment had felt more confining every year.

The rest of the bathroom was appointed in the same luxurious style as the shower. Twin sinks and an assortment of various sized towels, face cloths, and the ever present tiny bars of soap. A pair of complimentary terry cloth housecoats hung by the door, and two pairs of slippers were laid out underneath. Everything a first class suite should have. The living area even had a mini bar complete with a well stocked fridge.

Drying off, he selected a comfortable pair of slacks and a short sleeved golf shirt from his suitcase. Elijah was similarly dressed and talking on the phone when Newton entered the living room. Elijah hung up and turned to him and said, "Richard and Jason are heading down to the restaurant and wanted to know if they should get a table for five or three."
"Five?"
"Apparently our New York Lothario has persuaded the young lady from the airline to join him for dinner."
"And he wants us to tag along?"
"No, she does, a condition of his acceptance was that we all be there. Safety in numbers I think."
"Ah, beauty and brains—a nice combination. What did you say?"
"I said we would be glad to lend our good offices to act as chaperone."
Newton chuckled, "I gather it was Richard on the phone then?"
"Correct, Jason was fiddling with his magic box, trying to see if he could connect with the Internet."
"Any luck?"
"Not so far. I gather the appointments of their suite do not extend that far, something about incompatible telephone jacks."
"Well, he can give it a try up here if he wants. This place," Newton looked around the suite, "seems to have been upgraded from its original standards."
"Sure has, I'm guessing we have what they would call, the 'Presidential' suite."
"I'm glad we aren't footing the bill, but I would have thought that the air crew would have got first pick."
"Something we can ask Ms. Georgia Thompson at dinner then."
"That's her name?"
"So I'm told, a southern belle from Atlanta."
"Dinner," said Newton, "should be interesting."
With that, they both checked to ensure they had their pass cards, the modern day equivalent to a room key, and headed down to the restaurant.

The restaurant was located on the ground floor. It was composed of a large indoor area, which led out to a covered veranda and terrace. All the tables appeared to be occupied, and there was a small lineup forming at the entrance, the sudden infusion of an unexpected plane load of people meant the kitchen was operating at capacity. Waiting in line, Newton and Elijah were soon joined by Richard and Jason.

"How's the magic box doing?" Newton asked Jason.

"Not so good, the phone jack in our room seems to be of, how do I say this, 'original design'."

"Well, the one in our room is more modern, after dinner you can give it a go. What are you trying to hook up anyway?"

"This," said Jason holding up his electronic room pass. "The machine has a magnetic strip reader because some countries use them for recording the DNA profiles on."

"You want to find out your own room number?"

Jason laughed, "No, it's just an experiment of sorts. You see, the key locks are electronically reset for each guest every time someone new checks in. That way the old cards can't be used to enter the room after you check out. It's a security feature."

"OK, and you want to use it to do what with the card?"

"Oh, well, you see I didn't bring any spare cards with me, and I'm not sure anyone at the conference would have any, so I hope to program a sample profile onto my card and use it in the demo."

"It keeps him off the street at night," said Richard. "At least that's what I tell his mother."

"Hey, this is important stuff!"

"Listen, my boy, you are in need of serious help. Here you are a young man on a tropical island surrounded by God know how many young ladies, free liquor, free dinner, a room in a swanky hotel, and all you think of doing is playing with that box of wires. I think it's time we had a little talk." Smith put an arm around his young partner's shoulders. "It all starts with the flowers you see, think of yourself as a bee, whose job it is to spread pollen to all the pretty flowers."

Elijah and Newton both looked at each other and rolled their eyes. Just when Smith seemed ready to continue, they were interrupted by the arrival of two of the stewardesses from the flight. One was the aforementioned Georgia Thompson, and the other was a younger dark haired girl, who introduced herself as Julie Bent. Both were dressed in civilian clothes suitable for the tropics, short sleeved blouses and skirts with sandals. While their uniforms were flattering, they definitely shone in their off duty outfits.

"I thought it would be OK to bring Julie with me—the rest of the aircrew are all busy with the press and company people and the new plane. She has only been with us a short time, and this is her first transatlantic flight." Georgia introduced Julie to everyone. As she did, Newton caught a look at Jason. For the first time since he met the young man's acquaintance, Newton believed his attention was on something else other than his work. Apparently Julie had found a kindred spirit; they could hardly take their eyes off each other.

The waiter arrived and showed them their table; the two girls took chairs between Richard and Jason. The restaurant was understandably busy, and the staff was doing their best to keep up with the demand. The group used the time to get to better know each other with small talk.

"How long are you going to be at the conference?" Georgia was asking. Richard answered, "It runs for a full two weeks, but while we will be there for that time, I expect that we will be in the conference proper for only a couple of days. Most of the good stuff takes place one on one."

"What are you presenting?" asked Julie.

"Ah," said Richard, "That's the province of our boy wonder. Jason here can explain it much better than I, since he did all the work."

Julie turned to look at Jason, and he blushed in response.

"He built this amazing box for DNA comparison, first of its kind, I understand, truly a brilliant achievement"

"Really?" said Julie. "Do you use polymerase chain reaction or nucleotide sequencing?"

"Both! And also molecular cloning, and gel electrophoresis," Jason responded. "You know about this stuff?"

"Yes," said Julie, "I majored in bioengineering."

"And you wound up being a … a stewardess?" asked Richard. "How in the world did that happen?"

"Oh, you know," said Julie. "Be a stewardess, see the world. I wanted a break after my degree, some time to think about where to go with my life. So I thought it would be fun to do this for a while."

"Cool," said Jason. "Beauty and brains!"

"Well," said Newton, "I hope you two can put aside the urge to discuss the relative merits of nucleic acid probes and Southern Blotting and hybridization long enough to choose from the menu."

Jason looked up at him with a quizzical expression.

"I thought this was all new to you, Detective Newton?"

"I've picked up a little from time to time, and it's Mr. Newton, not detective anymore"

"Once a cop…"

"Yeah, I know, always a cop."

"I'll just bet you get called 'Isaac' a lot," chimed in Georgia

"It's inevitable," added Elijah.

The waiter arrived and took their orders.

"How long have you been a stew?" Elijah asked Georgia.

"Oh my, about seven years now."

"All international flights?"

"Yes, Eastern Skies is an international carrier, we don't have much in the way of domestic traffic. Our aircraft are all configured for long haul routes."

"You must like it then, what is your favorite destination?"

"That depends on the time of year. In the summer I like the northern European countries, like Norway, and in the winter any place warm!"

"Have you ever been to my part of the world?"

"Where is that?"

"The Queen Charlotte Islands, west coast of British Columbia, just south of Alaska."

"No, not yet, though I have been on a cruise to Prince William Sound, and it was spectacular."

"Very similar to the Charlottes then, but of course it would be missing one important thing."

"And what would that be?"

"Me, of course."

Georgia laughed with a deep throaty sound, genuine, and from the boots up. Richard Smith, on the other hand, was not liking the direction the conversation was taking, and that his '"date" was now appearing more interested in Elijah than she was in him.

Julie, Jason, and Newton were engaged in their own conversation. Having someone who shared his interests had stripped Jason of some of his shyness. Newton was able to learn an amazing amount about DNA analysis, far more than the peripheral knowledge he had picked up on the job. He had been aware of the many different ways that DNA was processed, but he had never been sure why there were different methods.

"Two things," Julie was saying, "determine the method you would use; first would be the technology available to you, second, the quality of the sample."

"Right," added Jason. "Even though it is theoretically possible to get a full DNA profile from a single cell, that is still science fiction at this point."

"The 'Jurassic Park' theory?" asked Newton.

"Exactly," Jason and Julie responded together laughing.

"Though, interestingly enough, in Montana they have been able to get soft tissue samples from fossils."

"Not the blood sample in the mosquito trapped in amber scenario?"

"No, even though there are many examples of insects trapped in amber, to date, every time the insect has been examined, they have been found to be dried up shells."

"So then, the soft tissue samples could be used? How did they do that anyway—get tissue from samples? I thought fossils were more or less mineral deposits laid down over time in place of bone tissue."

"You're correct," Julie said. "The operative phrase is 'more or less'. You see, they found a fossil bed with a broken bone in it. A leg bone I believe, and since it was already broken, one of the experts there decided to see what was inside, and after breaking through the fossil shell, found connective tissue."

"Like tendons?"

"That sort of stuff, pliable and stretchy is how they describe it, and once that was found, then other groups began to investigate the bones they had in storage, and found similar results."

"Why did it take so long for them to discover that, I wonder," said Newton.

Jason laughed, "Think about it, you go to a great deal of trouble and expense to recover as complete a skeleton that you can, with as many bones as intact as possible, the last thing you want to do is take a hammer and bust the bones up looking for what conventional wisdom tells you will not be there."

"Yes," said Newton. "I see what you mean, that sort of thing would not endear you to management."

"So right, I imagine you would have a great deal of trouble just getting permission to work on a broken piece."

"OK, so now instead of a drop of blood, they have a much larger sample to work with; do you see dinosaurs roaming about anytime soon?"

"No," said Julie. "They have been actually trying to recover enough DNA from one of those frozen Mastodons they dug up in Siberia with no success."

"One more very important point to consider also," said Newton.

"Which is?"

"The amount of oxygen in the air has fallen in the last 65 million years, it is calculated that it was almost three to five percent higher back then."

"Really?"

"How significant is that?" asked Julie.

"Think of it this way, when you are flying at eight thousand feet altitude, the measured amount of oxygen in the air falls to around eighteen percent. This is enough to affect all but the healthiest people. You would see this in your passengers after a long flight, Julie. In fact, you may have experienced it yourself, it's that hung-over feeling you may get."

"What is the regular amount of oxygen then?"

"Twenty-two to twenty-three percent."

"So our new dinosaurs would be feeling jet lag?"

Newton laughed. "No, not quite, I don't see them getting frequent flier miles! What it really means is that those huge bodies require the higher oxygen levels just to move and find food. The natural decline in oxygen levels means dinosaurs would have evolved into smaller and smaller creatures, even if the big rock hadn't wiped them out."

"Ah," said Julie, "that must one of 'Newton's Laws'!"

They all chuckled as the waiter brought their orders. The conversation over dinner was light, none of the group had been to the Azores before, and they were curious as to what sort of activities tourists could take part in. There were the beaches, of course, and the history of the islands was long with many historical sites. It all depended on the time available. In their case, it was not expected to be long. The girls had been told to contact the airline at 8:00 AM in order to learn when the flight would be resumed. There were some sunrise photo shots to be made, the aircraft would be serviced, and then off they would go. The press would have had their evening flight around the islands with lots of wine and there was a late evening reception laid on at the airlines office. Every airline knew the game. In order to be profitable, the airline had to fly a minimum number of seat miles every month. The revenue returned by ticket sales had to exceed the fixed costs of flying the route. This included not only the fuel burned and salaries of the crew, but also the costs of the office buildings, maintenance hangars, and technicians. In addition, the airports they landed at charged landing fees and there were also other service costs. In order to fill those seats, the primary sales agents had been travel agents, and they in turn relied on reports by the travel press. Contrary to popular belief, few travel agencies could afford to send their employees around the world to try out the services of the various airlines and hotels. To get that information, they turned to those members of the travel press who made a living doing just that. Great work if you can find it. These chosen few were well known to every airline and hotel chain. A good report in a well read travel magazine could persuade enough people on the merits of a particular airline to ensure those important seat miles would appear. In a surprising number of flights, the difference between profitability and failure could be as little as ten fliers. It was that close. With those sorts of figures, airlines viewed the press correctly as an investment.

As if on cue, the hotel shook slightly with the approach of the new airliner to the airport.

Georgia looked up and said, "That should be the last flight of the night,

I'd expect the rest of the crew to be here in about an hour."

"Well then," said Newton getting to his feet, "that's my cue to bid you all good night."

"And I also," said Elijah. "Ladies, it's been a pleasure, I expect we'll see you tomorrow."

With that, they left the restaurant.

"Have you known them long?" asked Georgia.

"Just met them on the plane actually, but I know a fair amount about Newton, not so much about Elijah though."

"Oh?"

"Alfred, also known as 'Sir Isaac,' as Julie picked up on, is, or rather was, a detective working in Victoria B.C. up in Canada. He has the reputation of being a very thorough investigator. As you would expect, he has given a few lectures, did a tour of the B.C. Police College as an instructor, and of course his techniques got tagged with the heading of 'Newton's Law'."

"Which would be?"

"Why?"

"Why what?"

"No, the thing that got tagged as 'Newton's Law,' primarily at least, was 'why.' Why did this happen, why did that not happen, why do you see this, why do you not see that. He always stressed that if you can figure out why a crime happened, then you had a very good chance of finding out who did it. When you look at it like that, it makes sense."

Jason looked up, "Now when I went through the academy, they stressed 'follow the evidence' and that will lead you to whoever did what."

"That is one method, for sure, and with DNA and modern forensic techniques you can sure narrow down your list of suspects, but these things take time, and we know that the first 48 hours are critical, especially in homicides and the best chance to actually catch someone comes in that time period. If you are in a small department without those kinds of resources, and let's face it, that is the majority of law enforcement even in the States, then your best chance is still to find out the 'why'" component."

Jason thought for a moment. "I can see that, heck, even in New York the sheer volume of stuff we have to work through pretty much guarantees you won't get an answer from forensics within that 48 hour period unless it is moved to the front burner."

"Did he just say 'heck' Julie?" asked Georgia. "I haven't heard that since the schoolyard."

"I never even heard it there," said Julie.

Jason blushed, "My apologies, ma'am," he went on in an affected southern accent, I was taught never to use bad language in the presence of such beauty as we have been fortunate to have here tonight."

"Why, sir," Georgia replied in her authentic southern accent, "we may appear to be fragile as magnolia blossoms, but I assure you we have heard worse. But I do thank you for your consideration." She fluttered her eyelids and looked away demurely, just like the all the old movies portrayed.

Julie laughed. "Please go on, Mr. Smith, what else can you tell us about Mr. Newton? There must be a woman in his life."

Smith paused for a moment.

"Sorry," said Julie, a look of confusion on her face. "Did I say something wrong?"

Jason looked at Richard and cleared his throat. "Actually, that is a sensitive area, you see, earlier today I ran a DNA check as a demo for the conference, and he found out his daughter, who incidentally he hasn't seen in years, may have a sister."

"What?!"

"Well, it's kind of complicated, but I suspect his ex-wife had a daughter before they met, and he just found out about it."

"Ex-wife?"

"Well, sort of, she was killed by a drunk driver after they split, then his daughter took off and he hasn't seen her since."

"How sad," both girls said at the same time.

"That's not the half of it, unfortunately," said Smith.

Georgia looked at Julie then back at the detective. "Maybe we shouldn't talk about this when he is not here; I didn't mean to pry into his life."

"To understand the man, or the woman," said Smith, nodding at the girls, "you need to understand his life, and once you understand the man, you understand his teachings and his methods, both essential in police work. I'm not telling any secrets here, it's all in the press and out in public. On the last case before he retired, Newton and a woman he was with were both shot, he survived, she didn't, a tough blow all around."

"Well, I, for one, think that's probably more than I need to know," said Georgia. "It appears to be turning into a lovely evening out there," she said, indicating the view of the beach from the restaurant windows. "I think I'll take a little walk before turning in, anyone want to come along?"

Richard rose from his chair and bowed, "Certainly, ma'am, I'd be honored if you would allow me to escort you."

"Why, sir, that would indeed be nice," Georgia said in her best "Gone With the Wind" impression. "Are you two going to accompany us?"

Julie spoke before Jason could reply "No, I'd like to pick Jason's brains on his machine, if you don't mind, I haven't had the opportunity to delve into this stuff since college and I'd like to see how far behind I've fallen."

"Well then, we are off," said Julie offering her hand to Richard. "We'll see you later."

CHAPTER SIXTEEN

Santa Maria Airport - The Azores

Hangar 7 was the largest structure on the airport. It was also the most modern, built of steel, concrete, and aluminum. Designed to shelter a Boeing 747, it contained the maintenance facilities for all the major airlines who serviced the tourist trade. Since it would be too expensive for each airline to own its own hangar of such a size, it was shared by all as needed. The airport authority maintained the building and rented it out as required. To store supplies specific to each organization, a number of compounds, secured by chain link fencing and topped with a corrugated iron roof, were assigned to each user. The mechanic's pool serviced any aircraft that required it, under the supervision of a representative of the specific airline's maintenance force. This co-operative arrangement worked well for the most part. Major repairs were not anticipated, and if they were required, a team of mechanics specially trained for the job would arrive on the next plane and the repairs would be accomplished quickly. The advantage to the airport was that they could boast a trained pool of mechanics that were experienced in servicing many different types of aircraft. Given the island's main industry was tourism, the airport became the center for technology. There was always a keen competition amongst the young people to get a job connected to airport. A year or two of experience there was a ticket to a faster paced life somewhere else.

Juan Dominguez was such a person. He was what is known to airport staff everywhere, a "ramp rat." As a child he had hung around the airport at every opportunity and was soon given odd jobs washing aircraft, fetching parts, and pumping gas. When an opportunity arose to join the mechanics' pool as a helper he jumped at it. Always the first to arrive each day and the last to leave, he had earned his reputation of being reliable and careful in following instructions. The older and more experienced mechanics, always happy to teach a willing student, had taken him under their wing and tutored him with an eye to his winning his Airframe and Power plant ticket. Juan studied hard, and today was graduation day. Under the supervision of the chief mechanic, Jorge Manuel, he had written his exams two weeks ago. His practical exam had come when, unknown to anyone else, the chief mechanic had arranged for an examiner to come to the island under the guise of an Eastern Skies mechanic. Assigned to assist him, Juan had stripped down and rebuilt a Garret Air research turbine. Normally this would have taken the manufacturer's facilities to accomplish. Juan had managed to complete it with the limited machine shop at the airport. He had correctly determined which parts needed replacement and which could be repaired. After submitting the results of the exam for review, the examiner had telephoned Jorge with the good news. Swearing the rest of the mechanics to secrecy, Jorge had prepared a surprise party scheduled for this morning to award the coveted certificate to Juan. All the mechanics save one were more than happy to welcome Juan to their ranks.

Peter Billinghurst was the lone holdout.

Billinghurst had arrived on the island as part of team of mechanics assigned to do an engine swap on a European-owned 737. He had never left. Originally he trained in the United States where he managed through his work habits and dedication to graduate at the bottom of his class—and pretty much went downhill from that point. At this airport he had been relegated to such things as driving the forklift and changing the oil. None of the other mechanics trusted his work and were not shy about letting him know. Peter had found solace by returning to the root cause of his problems—liquor. On this day of celebration, he had turned up after a night of drinking, which was becoming his usual state. Not wanting to spoil Juan's party, which he knew would piss Peter off, Jorge sent him with the airport truck to retrieve some oil that had arrived on a Gulfstream now parked on the opposite side of the airport.

The Gulfstream had arrived late last night and was itself awaiting a repair to the new electronics it carried. Leased to the U.S. government, it had been outfitted with a "black box" that identified the aircraft to airport controllers as a government diplomatic jet and allowed it clearances not available to normal air traffic. The electronics had failed in the flight over, and a replacement was on its way via a U.S. Navy F-14 Tomcat. Obviously, this aroused the curiosity of the airport staff, and they would be on the lookout for a firsthand view of the famous Navy fighter.

Peter arrived at the compound in the old truck and since both he and the truck were known to security staff they were waved through to the secure area. After checking in with staff, Peter backed the truck up to the loading dock and tossed in two cases of oil. One case he recognized as being the usual type for the large turbo fans the big airliners used. The second case was a new type he was not familiar with.

Whatever, he thought, he didn't care much anyway. Those pukes at the maintenance hangar had sent him on this chicken-shit run so they could give that kid his ticket. Big deal he thought, like he could care less. In his anger Peter demonstrated why he was in the position he was in. He failed to check the truck bed for obstructions prior to tossing in the oil cases. The first one landed with a thud in the box. The second landed on top of the first. If he bothered to check, and he never did, Peter would have seen that the bottom case was now oozing oil onto the truck bed. A number of old bolts that found their way from some other task had pierced the thin metal of the oil cans and their contents were leaking out. This in itself was a bad thing, but nothing compared to what was about to happen. Peter threw the truck into reverse and in his anger stomped on the gas. The truck motor roared and in the rear view mirror Peter saw the wing tip of the Gulfstream disappear out of his line of sight. He smashed down on the brakes and the truck rocked back and forth. Dropping it into first gear he mashed the accelerator and the truck rocketed towards the gate. Behind him Peter left a brief pattern of tire marks, and a dented wing tip on the Gulfstream.

Juan was feeling great, Jorge had personally given him his A&P licence mounted and framed. The rest of the guys had pitched in and bought him a set of tools and a large "Mac tools," tool chest on wheels. Each drawer had been lined with cotton sheets, and the new tools set lay shining and pristine on the white cloth. A basic set did not take up much room and Juan knew he could borrow any special tools that he was missing for a particular job. Over time, he would amass his own collection of additional tools. The rolling tool chest had his name on it, and there was his own space and bench in the shop. What more could he want? On the wall of the dispatch office hung a number of clipboards, one for each mechanic. Jorge looked for, and found, his name on the wall along with a brand new clipboard. Each time a job came in, the supervisor would assign it to a mechanic by adding it to his clipboard.

Usually the jobs were allotted in a simple rotation, provided the job was within the capabilities of the mechanic. The system worked well, spreading the work out in a more or less even pattern. The shop charged the job out on an hourly basis, and the mechanics received most of that in their pay. Apprentices were paid a standard rate no matter what job they worked on. To complete their apprenticeship they had to spend a certain number of hours in each phase of the work, from refueling to a complete engine overhaul, all under the supervision of a licenced mechanic who received a small bonus for the extra time the supervision took. As a licenced A&P, Juan would now be entitled, and indeed expected, to teach one of the new people.

Even the arrival of Peter did little to dampen the festive attitude of the shop. Sensing the disgruntled mechanic's mood and not wanting to have it poison the good feeling in the shop, Jorge sent Peter and two of the helpers to the Eastern Skies plane with the newly picked up oil. When Peter looked as if he was going to complain about this obvious simple task Jorge took him aside.

"Now, Peter, you realize that this is a big deal for Eastern because of the inaugural flight and all."

"Umm, well, sure I do," said Peter, who had not yet heard of it.

"Well, they specifically asked for one of my best men, so I'm sending you, you have to look like you're in charge, confident, and sure of yourself 'cause there are a lot of reporters there. Can you do that?"

"Sure I can, boss, you know me—always put the company first."

"Good, Peter, I know I can count on you, just let the young guys do the work, you're the supervisor, so stand back and let them do the grunt stuff."

Peter puffed up; at last he was getting some recognition, "You bet, boss, I'm on it."

What you're on, thought Jorge, is too much bloody booze, so I'm keeping you away from doing any actually work so you don't fuck it up.

"Off you go then—and thanks, Peter."

The truck left the compound a few minutes later with the two helpers riding in the front along with Peter. True to form, it headed down the wrong road, screeched to a stop, reversed and at last roared out towards the Eastern Skies plane. Jorge shook his head; at least the press would not be there for another hour he muttered to himself. Enough time for even Peter to get the job done without a problem. Trouble was, there was always a problem when Peter was involved.

Jorge sighed again, and picked up the list of jobs for the day. Scanning the list he found what he wanted, a top overhaul on a light plane engine, just the thing for his new mechanic. A couple more like Juan and this would be a shop capable of almost anything. He took the sheet from the pile and clipped it on to Juan's clipboard. As he turned around he saw Juan waiting nervously. As soon as he saw what the job was Juan smiled, set his shoulders and headed for his tool chest.

Yep, thought Jorge, this is going to be a great day.

The pickup rocked its way along the service road towards the Eastern Skies airliner. In the front cab Peter was feeling better than he had in a long time. This was more like it. He was being recognized for his true abilities—and what did Jorge say? Ah yes, the press was going to be there. He glanced down at his clothes, not too bad. He would have worn a cleaner set if he had been told about this beforehand. Shit, why didn't they tell him last night? They must have known. Damn it, he thought, his mood turning dark again, was this some kind of set up? Did Jorge send him out here to fall on his face? Sure! That was it. Jorge expected him to fuck up and then they would have a reason to can him. Growing angrier, Peter didn't notice he was pressing harder on the accelerator and the truck was bouncing crazily on the old potholed road. In the back the oil cases were beating themselves against the debris in the back of the truck. More and more cans were being punctured.

"Senor!" one of the helpers cried, pointing at a large hole in the road. "Look out!"

Peter wrenched the steering wheel to the left and the old truck bounced over the edge of the hole. The two helpers held on for dear life, and in the back the oil cases bounced high in the air, and came down on its side, causing a new row of oil cans to puncture. The Eastern Skies plane came into view, and Peter, scaring even himself, slowed the truck and drove carefully up to the side of the plane. Getting out of the truck, Peter noticed for the first time, a freshly cleaned set of coveralls wrapped in plastic and stuck behind the cab seat. Shit, Peter thought, guess I was wrong, Jorge must have meant for me to wear this. Maybe this isn't a set up after all. Like most alcoholics, Peter's moods swung wildly from one extreme to another. The sight of the coveralls had swung his mood back to euphoria. He quickly donned the overalls and began to look around for the press.

Sally Westerman was not a real member of the press. Even though she carried press credentials, she was actually a travel advisor. The small magazine she worked for only had one reporter/writer/photographer and he was away on vacation. Sally had volunteered to take some pictures and do a small column on this new airplane as a replacement. She had enjoyed the all expenses paid trip out here but found the regular press a closed club. They tolerated her presence, but made it plain she was not "one of them." In fact, the only attention she got at all was from one of the middle-aged photographers from the mainstream press. He had offered to take her down to a beach he knew, for a "private photo shoot." The only way she could get him to stop pestering her was to agree to "think about it." She had no intention of meeting up of course; in fact, she was out here an hour early to take a few pictures and then head back to the safety of the hotel. If he asked she would say she wasn't feeling well and relax on her balcony until time to head back to the States.

Sally saw the truck pull up and a man and two boys get out. This is a bit of luck, she thought, maybe I can get a few pictures of these guys working on the plane to go with the solo shots. I should be able to get this done in half an hour and take a taxi back to the hotel before the crush of press show up.

"Excuse me," she asked going up to the oldest man struggling into a set of coveralls, "are you in charge here?"

Peter turned around to look at the young lady. Pretty nice he thought to himself. "Yes, I'm in charge. What can I do for you?"

"Well, I'd like to get some pictures of you working on the plane, that's what your doing, isn't it?"

"You bet Miss, umm, what did you say your name was?"

"Sally, what exactly will you be doing?"

Peter puffed out his chest and looked at the dispatch sheet. "Well, miss, we are here to service the engines, it a very important job. What we will be doing is checking the fluid levels and adjusting things as required to keep the engines operating at peak efficiency."

"So you're a mechanic then?"

"Yes I am, I'm the chief mechanic and these are my crew."

Peter had the helpers take a ladder out of the truck and leaned it against the engine nacelles. Then he told them to take the oil out the cases. When they saw that some of them had been punctured, they started to talk quickly in Spanish to Peter. God damn it, Peter thought to himself, what the fuck is going on here. With the photographer looking over his shoulder he pulled out the cans from the now soaked cardboard cases. In doing so, he did not pay particular attention to which case they came from. Smiling at Sally, he checked the required amount of oil against the dispatch sheet. Even with the damaged cans removed, he had just enough to fill the wing oil tanks. He told the boys to wipe the cans off, and then took a couple up to the auxiliary tanks.

"Here," he told Sally, "come up on the wing and you can get some shots the others will never have."

This was an irresistible offer for any photographer. An original shot was a coup. Sally climbed up the ladder and leaned against the wing. Peter, clean coveralls and all, struck up a professional pose as he opened the hatches and removed the filler caps. Each was secured by a small wire twisted into a small channel on the cap.

"See this wire?" he asked Sally. "This is here to prevent the cap from coming loose in flight, because if it did the rush of air over the wing would suck the oil right out of the tank."

"Have you been doing this long Mr., umm, I'm sorry I didn't get your name."

"Peter Billinghurst, that's 'B I L L I N G H U R S T'," he replied as he poured the oil into the tanks. Wait 'til those pukes at the shop see this in the travel magazines, he thought. This will show them I'm not a washed up drunk. Peter made a great show of checking the level and opening a new can of oil. The helpers, eager to be in the picture, clambered up the ladder passing the one liter oil cans and smiling broadly whenever they saw Sally look their way. She smiled back and made a big production out of taking their pictures. When the oil had reached the correct level, Peter cleaned the area, carefully replaced the tank cap and hatch and moved over to the next engine where he repeated the procedure. Sally took a few more pictures of the plane from different angles, including one with the sun behind the cockpit. Not bad for an amateur she thought, at least it will fill up the column space. Those kids were cute and made a good "human interest" photo that would fit well into the travel magazine. She managed to get away from the airport before her ardent admirer from the day before arrived.

Peter and his two helpers made their way back to the shop at a much more leisurely and safer pace than the trip out. Peter was feeling much better now. So good in fact, he even stopped at the field vehicle wash station and had the two young men clean out the truck and wash it down. He put the old oil soaked cardboard in the garbage and cleaned the accumulated junk out of the cab. Hell, he thought, maybe this is the start of a new period in his life. When everything was clean, he and the crew drove back to the shop. Jorge immediately noticed Peter's new attitude, or rather his lack of bitching. He was grateful for the change, and was treated to the sight of Peter walking up to Juan and shaking his hand whilst offering congratulations. Now that, thought Jorge, was something I thought I'd never see. Maybe miracles do happen.

Later that day, he was to learn they did not.

CHAPTER SEVENTEEN

Eastern Skies Inaugural Flight - Continuation

Georgia and Julie, dressed in their newly pressed uniforms, took their usual places aboard the aircraft. They were both cheerful and chipper, talking lightly with the passengers—and for good reason.

Georgia had arrived back at the hotel with Richard after a long relaxing walk on the beach. As usual for this time of the year, the air was warm and the ocean was calm. Several brightly painted fishing boats, which as a sign of the times carried a larger load of tourists than they ever did fish, were drawn up on the sand. Richard carried a large beach towel rolled up under his arm. He had grabbed it from a lounge chair on their way out of the hotel patio. The beach wound its way past the cliff side that the hotel was built on, towards a fishing village. Between the village and the hotel property it followed the shoreline dotted with a number of small bays. Finding a secluded one, Richard unwrapped the towel and spread it on the sand in the shadow of a lone overturned boat. In the middle of the bundle was a bottle of wine and two glasses.

"My," said Georgia, "how on earth did you get those out of the hotel?"

"The staff are accustomed to their guests wandering about at all hours of the night apparently, and this sort of request is not unheard of. In fact, they even have it itemized for the hotel bill. The glasses, you will note, are shapely, but plastic, as is the bottle. They do request that all refuse be accounted for and deposited in the trash."

"They told you that?"

"Nope, it says it right here on the label," he said indicating the printing on the back of the bottle. "I told you this was not an uncommon thing, but they do guarantee that the contents, however packaged, are nothing but the best porch crawler they could squeeze into the bottle."

They both laughed and settled onto the towel. The lights of the nearby village made a dim showing over the edge of the cliffs. Out to the sea, the moon was full, and the stars twinkled like Christmas lights. Making small talk soon changed to long deep kisses, and Richard was again thankful for the fashion designers who chose to equip their ladies' blouses with large buttons. When he reached to undo her skirt, Georgia gently grabbed his hand.

"Let's go skinny dipping," she said.

"What!"

"Come on. What could be better—you're not embarrassed are you?"

"No, but..."

"But what—scared?"

"Of course not," Richard said, peeling off his shirt. "But what about our clothes?"

"Always the cop," said Georgia. "What, you're expecting a gang of desperate clothes thieves to suddenly rappel down the cliff side and steal our meager rags?"

Richard smiled, "Well, since you put it that way, last one in is a chicken!"

In the end, Richard was the chicken, but the view was worth it. High on the cliff behind him someone else was taking in the view. Unlike the couple on the beach he was wearing black, specifically so that he would blend in with the night sky. He put down his binoculars and prepared to wait until they made their way back to the roadway.

Julie and Jason had left the restaurant after the others. Jason had been eager to try out his idea to reprogram the key card with a representation of his DNA. There had been some problems in that the card was not cut the same as a regular DNA profile recorder, and the magnetic stripe was not in the right place. A strip of paper and a little tape fixed that and the machine was coaxed into working. While he was doing his magic with the machine, Julie busied herself with studying the written presentation Jason had prepared. While technically accurate, she noticed he had missed the mark in some of the terms, and with his encouragement made some changes. A few clicks on the laptop made the changes permanent, although he would have to find a printer somewhere to produce the amended copies. But there was sure to be one at the conference. While he was doing that, Julie had disappeared into the bathroom. Returning clad in one of the hotel robes, she snuggled up to Jason and whispered huskily, "I think we should take another DNA sample, just in case."

The morning dawned bright and sunny, as it often is in the tropics. Later in the day, the heat from the sun would draw water from the ocean and the afternoon rain showers would begin. But at the moment, Newton and Elijah were enjoying the warmth of the new day in the restaurant.

"So, is this what paradise feels like?" Newton asked his friend.

"Depends on your expectation of paradise I suppose."

"This would not be yours then."

"No, it's nice enough, but there are no salmon in the rivers, no pine trees scenting the wind, and the spirits of my ancestors don't call to me every day as they do at home."

"Ah yes, but on the bright side, there are also no rapid changes from snow to sleet to rain either."

"True, I miss that also."

Newton chuckled, the Charlottes were a special place indeed, and truth be known, the sudden changes of weather, unpredictable in their frequency and duration, were truly a part of the experience one must have when visiting there. His recollection of the last time he had visited brought back bittersweet memories.

"Ah, here is the bus I think, time for us to get to the airport."

In order to keep confusion to a minimum and ensure no one was missed, the airline used the same roster to load the buses that they had from the day before. Newton and Elijah found themselves back in the company of Richard, Jason, and the flight crew.

"How was your evening?" Newton asked Richard. "Did you get out to see any of the night life?"

"In a way," Richard responded. "In a way." Then he turned serious. "Funny thing though, I'm sure we were followed."

"Followed? You and Jason?"

"No, Georgia and I, we went down to this secluded beach and I'm sure there was someone following us."

"You saw someone?"

"Nope, just a feeling, you know how that goes."

"Yeah, I do," Newton said knowing exactly how after a few years of being a cop certain instincts are honed and heightened.

"What about Jason, did he see anything?"

"Never left his room, spent the time with Julie playing with that box of wires I think."

"Probably just one of the locals trying to sell you something," Elijah said. "There are street vendors all over this place, I even saw some in the hotel trying to sell stuff to the tourists."

" No, no, it was different than that, I thought I saw him getting ready to come up and talk to us, but the lights of a car coming down the road made it difficult to see, and when the car was gone, so was he."

"He got in?"

"No, the car never stopped, hardly even slowed down."

"Probably nothing to worry about, these islands attract folks of all kinds, maybe he was just watching the stars. Not much background light to worry about here."

"Yeah, maybe you're right." Richard said, but he didn't sound convinced.

After a ride that seemed shorter than the one from the day before, they arrived at the airport and went through the ritual of having their bags checked and loaded aboard the plane. Most of the passengers were eager to get aboard and get on with their journey. Some were still complaining at the delay and everyone was relieved to get aboard.

There had been a few changes in the passenger seating for the second half of the flight. Not only had Newton, Elijah, Jason, and Richard been upgraded to the mostly empty first class cabin, they now had two new passengers. Newton noticed the presence of Carol O'Conner by the way she carried herself. She arranged for a rear row seat for her companion quickly and efficiently. It was as obvious that he was a civilian, as it was apparent that she was not. He also judged correctly that theirs was a purely business relationship, from her side of the aisle anyway. He was not so sure about the guy. What he was sure about was that he was a government man. The volume of papers scattered about the seats soon grew past the confines of the row they occupied. He was also a ranking government man, judging from the fact that the pilot had come back to personally speak with him. Of the three flight attendants assigned to first class, Georgia and Julie were paying particular attention to the Richard and Jason. No surprise there. The third was seemingly assigned exclusively to what Newton had tagged as "The G-Man."

"What do you figure, Alfred, some kind of chief?" Asked Elijah.

"Yep, and one with a lot to do by the looks of the amount of paper he has."

"Too much paper in the way you guys run things."

"You got that right, my friend," said Newton remembering the hours he had spent filling in forms on his old job. "There are much better uses for trees."

The "G-man," Alexander Wells, was more than pissed off, he was truly angry. His fast trip to Iran for this very important conference had been first delayed so someone could toss aboard a couple of cases of oil. Then some idiot from the airline getting the oil, which was entirely due to their own incompetence in the first place, drove his truck into the wingtip of the government jet and dented it. Now, ironically, he was forced to continue his journey on the same plane that required the oil. Outwardly he was the same calm and deliberate persona as always. Such are the required skills of the diplomat. The combined delays had meant that he would have to complete all the paperwork on board, instead of at the consular office. At least he had been given a first class seat in which to complete the task. Already he had spread out the papers on the two seats assigned to him, and was working on the third. The papers were innocuous; a casual look from one of the other first class passengers would reveal nothing. They were chiefly position papers from various government departments that he had to absorb. In truth, any of them could be found by a determined search on the Internet as all were previously published and opened to the public.

Major Carol O'Conner had moved up a couple of rows to give her boss the room he required to work. He would be totally immersed in his tasks until the plane landed. She took the opportunity to relax and rest for the grueling schedule ahead. All arrangements were complete as far as she could manage them. The rest was the responsibility of others in the State Department. As her training and nature dictated, she had taken a quick survey of the other occupants of the first class cabin. There were only four others besides themselves. Three of the aircrew looked after getting them all the coffee they could drink, and anything else that was available. She noticed straight off that two of the crew seemed to have formed a special relationship with a couple of the passengers. This she shrugged off with nothing more than mild curiosity. Her own love life had been eclipsed by her work. This was something she welcomed after a messy divorce. Thank God her son was already on his own and making his own way through the world. At least that part of her marriage had turned out good. No, she mused, better than that, much better. Cody seemed to be everything his father was not, kind, sensitive, and confident. Mildly successful in college athletics, much more successful with the ladies and with a natural flair for business, he was doing well in Seattle working for some computer outfit or another. Carol sighed inwardly with the kind of contentment that comes only to a parent who sees their offspring achieving despite the obstacles life puts in everyone's way. Settling into the plush seats, she started to doze off. Flying was a regular part of her duties in the military, but the seats were never this nice.

One of the stewardesses, with the name "Georgia" on her name tag was talking to her.
"Would you like a pillow ma'am?"
"What? Oh, no, thank you, I'm OK." Carol woke from her cat nap and looked at her watch. Only five minutes had passed. Why do they always wake you up when you just start to doze? The attendant had moved to the row in front of her and was now chatting to the two men seated there. They were known to her, she judged, because of the familiarity of their speech. What was it she called him? Detective? That fit, he was either military or police. Short cut hair, eyes that took in the whole cabin, and a way of being relaxed, but still alert. The other fellow, what was the name—right—Elijah, he looked like an interesting guy. Carried himself like a military officer, but different somehow from his companion. Could also be police, but, no, something else.

"More coffee, Detective?" The attendant was asking in a sweet southern accent. "Georgia," hmm, well named, thought Carol. So she was right, the guy was a cop.

"No thanks, Georgia, and please, it's Mr. Newton, I'm retired, remember?"

Unable to return to her catnap, Carol headed up the aisle to the restroom. On the way she passed the other two passengers. One was fussing with some kind of briefcase sized machinery, and was the object of attention of the attendant with the name of "Julie" on her nametag. The other was dozing in his seat. The restrooms in first class were larger and better equipped than those on the rest of the plane. A small drawer held an assortment of soaps and even cosmetics. A razor hung from a hangar on the wall, and the towels were real cloth, not paper. Carol had never flown first class before, and was mildly surprised by the appointments. Sure is better than anything in the military inventory she thought to herself. A surprising thought crossed her mind, no wonder there are so many members of the "mile high" club in first class. At least there would be room to tango here.

Elijah moved over to the row opposite Jason and struck up a conversation about his apparently long lost Irish cousin. The possibility of an as yet undiscovered branch of his family tree intrigued him. Newton was himself wondering about the accuracy of Jason's machine. Turning up an Irish connection for a Haida elder was incredulous enough, but linking the Jane Doe who had been the subject of his last case to his own family was a stretch he was still suspicious of. In his career, he had come across many coincidences that seemed to defy logic until thoroughly investigated. When he got back to Victoria he would have to dig into that in a big way. He glanced around the cabin; the "G-man" was still fussing with his papers. No matter what the organization, he thought, paper is the blood that flows in its veins. Mildly curious, he wondered about what kind of mission would require such a load of paperwork. He never even saw the major until she landed, literally, in his lap.

Just as Carol O'Conner had passed the retired detective, the plane lurched in the sky. She instinctively grabbed for the seat next to her, missed as the plane lurched again, lost her balance and wound up square in the lap of the passenger who she heard addressed as "detective."

"Hello," said Newton to the attractive package sitting in his lap, "allow me to introduce myself, I'm Alfred Newton. Are you OK?"

Carol struggled to regain her feet and only succeeded in wrapping her arm around Newton's neck. Then grabbing the back of the seat to her side, she raised herself halfway up, then the plane lurched again and she fell once more into Newton's lap. Resigning herself to remaining there until the aircraft settled down, she looked up at Newton.

"Carol," she said offering her hand. "Carol O'Conner."

In the cockpit the flight crew were concentrating on the aircraft's instruments. Tapping a few keys on the keypad the co-pilot, Michael Alan, brought up the weather charts and overlaid them onto the planned course. The screen blinked and displayed the standard IACO charts with the routes marked in red. Another tap of the keys and the screen changed the display into a 3D presentation.

"Whew," said Scotty, the pilot, "looks like a solid front for miles." The screen showed a bank of clouds squarely across the flight path. Another tap of the keys and the computer showed a number of suggested route changes that lessened the impact of weather on the aircraft. Selecting the one promising the smoothest flight, the co-pilot sent the request to the International Trans-Atlantic Air Control center for approval. A few seconds later the request was approved and accepted. The changes required the flight to gain altitude and the autopilot commanded the attitude change and increased power to the engines to initiate a smooth climb to flight level 35, or 35 thousand feet. Outside, the air temperature began to drop.

Newton sensed the change in the aircraft's attitude and helped Carol to her feet.

"There, you should be OK now."

"Thank you. Sorry to have dropped in on you like that."

"No problem, Miss O'Conner, I'm always happy to provide a lap to fall in, so to speak."

They both laughed, and Carol looked to the rear where Wells had commandeered the remaining seats and covered them in paper and file folders. She dropped into the seat across the aisle from Newton. "It seems as if I'm temporarily displaced," nodding at the rear of the cabin. "My seat has been put to better use."

Newton nodded in agreement, "I'm sure you can stay where you are if you want."

"Of course you can," said Georgia, coming up the aisle towards them. "Can I get you anything, Major?"

"No thank you," said Carol, "I'm fine."

"Ah," said Newton, "are you a member of the Army or Marines?"

"Marines, of course."

"Good outfit," replied Newton.

"Were you in the service?"

"Air Force, a long time ago, but it was Canadian, not U.S."

"Also a good outfit," said Carol. "Your Snowbirds aerobatic team is considered one of the world's best."

"Yeah, they do wonders with those old planes."

"And now you are a detective, I mean a retired detective, yes?"

"Yes, more than twenty years."

"And now?"

"Now I'm a consultant of sorts, we did a lot of things with a small amount of resources, and apparently that sort of expertise is in demand. Along with those fellows up front we are heading for a conference on doing more with less. How about you, on vacation or headed for a new posting?"

"Neither actually, I have a civilian boss now and he also has a conference to attend."

"Well, I'm happy you're on this flight, Miss O'Conner, I hope the rest of your trip will be smooth."

She smiled, "I think we are headed up to a better flight level to get above the weather, and the air is calmer up here."

"Yes it is, but turbulence has its advantages," winked Newton.

"I suppose it does," she said rising and heading back to the rear of the cabin where the blizzard of paper had at last been corralled and replaced inside the briefcases of Mr. Wells. "It looks like it is safe for me to return."

"Very nice of you to drop by," said Newton. Perhaps we will meet again."

"One never knows," Carol replied.

In the cockpit the flight engineer was scanning his panel. Unlike his predecessors, he had very little adjusting to do. Everything was computer controlled on the new engines. His role was strictly to monitor and record. If he noticed anything going wrong with the engines or any of the other onboard systems, he had the option of talking directly to the maintenance facilities to remedy it. Right now he was watching the readouts march across the screen. The software was working as it should, and the computers were adjusting the fuel flow to allow for the increase in power required by the change in altitude. The engine RPM was spooled up to 98 percent. Unlike their piston powered counterparts, jet engines do not read out in revolutions per minute. Jet engine turbines rotated at over one hundred thousand revolutions per minute. Piston engines were normally in the range of zero to three thousand. Unlike automobile engines, aircraft piston engines were designed to operate efficiently at the same speed that their propellers were most efficient. That meant they provided their power at about 2300 to 2800 RPM. Jet engines provided their best power in the top five percent of their RPM. range. To be meaningful, the jets reported in percent of full throttle. At 98 percent, the engines were providing power to push the aircraft higher. The demand meant the fuel flow would increase, but this would be compensated for by a faster cruising speed brought about by encountering less drag on the airframe due to the thinner air. The increased power also meant an increase in the oil consumption of the massive engines. The small oil tanks mounted in the nacelles were soon exhausted. Sensing this, the computers signaled the pumps that transferred the reserve oil from the wing tanks to begin operation. The software also monitored the oil flow rate so that the pump speed could be adjusted for maximum efficiency. This prevented pressurization of the tank receiving the oil. If pressurized, the oil could escape the tank via the air breather holes and present a fire hazard.

The operation of the oil reserve pump assumed a higher importance when it was running than when it was not in use. As programmed by the computer, the monitoring screens displayed engine operations in a sequence determined by what was happening at any specific moment in time. Thus, when the signal is received by the pumps to begin operation, the monitor also switched to display how well the pumps are operating. At first, the color on the instrument background was green, indicating normal operation. Within a few minutes, that changed to yellow. Tapping the keypad in front of him, the engineer isolated the specific readings for each pump, one for each engine. The oil levels in the reserve tanks indicated full, but the rate the oil was being transferred was dropping. First one, then the other pump indicators changed from yellow to red. A tap of the keypad sent the data directly to the flight maintenance facility at Eastern Skies' head office. In response the intercom alert started to beep, indicating a voice call over the radio.

Joe Zacardi was chomping down hard on his unlit cigar as the engineer on the plane came onto the circuit. "Whatchya got there buddy?"

"Damnedest thing, Joe, the oil transfer from the wing tanks doesn't seem to be working." The head engineer studied the screen in front of him.

"Why you flying at flight level 35?"

"Weather below. We have a government passenger from State on board."

"OK, I see, well, tell the pilot to head back to level 32, weather there is reporting OAT at least 10 degrees warmer. Meanwhile, limit the pumps duty cycle to no more than ten seconds. Got that?"

"Got it."

"OK, we'll see what's what on this end, meanwhile watch the pumps; they get their lubrication from the oil, so if it ain't flowing they'll pack up on you."

"OK."

"Also, reduce power to 93 percent, if them engines ain't getting any oil they'll pack it in also, what reading do you get for nacelle oil levels?"

The computer already had passed that information to the data link, and Joe could see it on the larger monitor screens he had in front of him. The reason for asking was to keep the engineer's attention focused on it. Once the giant fans ran out of oil, the bearings would likely fail within minutes. Even more dangerous would be the loss of cooling the oil would no longer supply. The metal would expand in the fan hubs and the clearances were manufactured so close that the expansion would cause the parts within the engines to touch. At 125 thousand RPM the time to failure would be measured in fractions of a second. The engineer picked up on the warning and brought up the readings on his smaller screen.

"Hey, Joe."

"Yeah?"

"Looks like maybe fifteen, twenty minutes without the pumps."

"That's what I see too; maybe the higher outside air temps will help."

"Right."

They both knew it wouldn't.

CHAPTER EIGHTEEN

Maintenance Hangar - Santa Maria Airport.

Jorge had been heading out for lunch when then the pager he carried went off. The buzzing intruded on the good mood that had been building all day since the presentation to Juan. Well, he thought with a sigh, nothing lasts forever. The text screen reported a code that designated the importance of the message; "311" was an incoming query from a customer about having a job done, the sort of queries he answered when he got back to the office and had the schedule in front of him. "411" meant a mechanic had a question about a job he was engaged in. Usually that meant more repairs than were anticipated were required. These he answered whenever it was convenient for him to find a phone. Extra repairs meant more revenue for the shop, but sometimes an angry customer. If the customer was a good one with a long record, he would cut a deal on the parts. The markup in the aviation field was fairly large and there was always some room to move. If the customer was not a good one, well, that's the way things shake out some times. "911" meant trouble. On those calls Jorge pulled out the cell phone he always carried but left turned off. Only one reason was sufficient for the 911 code, it meant the shit had hit the fan—big time.

His pager read "911."

Jorge pulled over the old truck onto the shoulder of the road and with a sigh reached for his phone. Punching in a number from memory he waited for the connection. It was answered on the second ring.
"Eastern Skies has a problem with the oil transfer to the engines."
The announcement came with no fanfare, no "how are you, how's the kids." Jorge knew why. Without the constant flow of oil the engines would quit, and as cutting edge as the aircraft was, it was no glider and there was a lot of water between it and the shores of Europe.
"What do you need?" Jorge answered
"Check the empty cans for the grade and lot numbers; check the sheets for quantity and type, report back ASAP."
"How long?"
"Eastern says no more than 15 minutes."
"Shit!"
"Ain't that the truth."
"On my way." Jorge clicked the phone off. He turned the truck around and hit the amber rotating beacon switch that activated the light mounted on the roof. All airport vehicles were required to have amber

lights and to keep them on when traveling on airport property. It kept the big birds from running into you. Turning the phone back on and punching in his office number, Jorge aimed the speeding truck at the nearest airport gate. Luckily he had just been heading out, the airport was a good five minutes from town, and it would only take another minute or two to get to his office.

The phone was answered on the third ring.

"Maintenance," came the response.

"This is Jorge, find that fuck-up, Peters, and get him in my office, next tell his two helpers to dig out the empty cans and cases from the garbage and haul them over to the office also. Tell them they got two minutes, then pull the sheets on Eastern Skies and put them on my desk. I'm on my way in."

"We got trouble, boss?"

"Yeah, we got trouble."

The phone went dead and Jorge tossed it onto the seat as he rocketed through the access gate with a bang and onto the dirt access road. Fuck the lock, he said to himself, I'll buy them a new one. Behind him the gate swung around on its rusty hinges and collapsed onto the ground. The hood of the truck now had fresh scars on the metal work. Luckily it was old enough to have been made with heavier steel than the new crop of lightweight, but more fragile, vehicles. In his mind Jorge was running the request sheets from Eastern through his memory. It was a simple job, pick up the oil that Eastern supplied and put the right oil in the right tanks, a child could do it. The sheet called for eleven quarts of light oil for the wing tanks and fifteen of regular weight for the engine tanks. Each case was clearly marked and Eastern had supplied more than was needed. So how could Peters have fucked it up? The tires screeched on the paved portion of the taxiway as the truck shot from the gravel road onto the hard surface. The runway prep crews were already in their sweeping trucks and heading towards the spot. Up in the control tower, the ground controller watched as the service truck broke every rule in the book about traveling on airport property. Vehicles were required to travel at no more than 25 KPH so that they didn't kick up rocks and debris onto the taxi ways and runways that could later be sucked into jet engines. The ground controller was the one responsible for ensuring vehicles followed this rule to the letter and had the power to ban any outfit from airport property for infractions of the rules. The controller also had a sheet in his hand that detailed the problems Eastern was having, so on this occasion he was keeping other airport vehicles and aircraft out of the speeding truck's path instead of the other way around. As the truck made its way, he directed the sweeping crews to trace its path and sweep the paved surfaces clean.

Making record time, Jorge pulled up in front of his office in a cloud of red dust and flying stones. The mechanics in the shop, its doors open as usual, watched as the dust cloud made its way into the building and contaminated the clean parts spread out on the benches. All of them would have to be cleaned again. They had already heard the news. Such things travel on the airport gossip network at light speed. If they hadn't heard the official version, the sight of Peters being summoned to the office was enough to foretell that nothing good was happening. Shortly after the truck pulled up, the two kids were seen hauling in a bag of empty oil cans and oil soaked cardboard into the building. Most just shook their heads and returned to their tasks. Nothing else they could do.

On the desk in front of him, the empty oil cans were removed from the bag, and Jorge was looking at the markings on them and the cardboard. The first thing he noticed was the number of cans that had been punctured with the tell tale marks of the oil filling tool, and that a number of empty cans did not have those marks. He realized in seconds what had happened and picked up the phone on his desk.

"Get me Eastern," he growled into the phone.

The look on Peters' face was proof enough that he was responsible.

In the cockpit the call button on the panel glowed red. It signified a call direct from the head office for the flight crew.

"Eastern 196."

"Get me the engineer!"

A moment later Fred came on the line. He listened along with Scotty to the voice of Smoking Joe and then reached over and punched a series of buttons on the cockpit panel.

Two things happened immediately with the code the pilot punched in. First was the little box on the Mid Ocean controller's radar screen that represented Eastern 196 changed from a single bar to a flashing red box. At the same time the "fasten seatbelt" sign started blinking in the passenger cabins. The box was designed with two different colored lights for the border. Instead of blinking with the normal white light, it was now blinking red. The chief flight attendant noticed it straight off and walked rapidly to the cabin phone mounted on the bulkhead outside of the cockpit door.

"How long?" she asked picking up the phone.

"Ten minutes," came the response and the phone went dead.

The navigation panel now went into a new mode. The screen showed a new course, the readout included the direction to steer and the estimated time to airport. That read nine minutes. The pilot looked over at his partner and nodded, 60 seconds to spare, lots of time.

In the rear of the aircraft, passengers were being directed back to their seats. Newton immediately sensed the change in attitude of the aircraft and the flight crew. Georgia and Julie had been busy setting up the meal service when the seatbelt light started flashing. Without a word they smoothly rolled the carts back into the meal service bays and locked the hatches down. The flight crew's expressions took on a mask of confidence. Their smiles conveyed an air of normalness, but their eyes held the fear that those skills they had trained so diligently to perfect were now about to be put to the test. There was no need for them to know the specifics of whatever emergency required the rapid decent of the aircraft, nor its destination. If they had looked out the windows just behind the engines they would have seen a delicate stream of whitish smoke trailing behind. The oil pumps were not able to pump the cold congealed oil from the exposed wing tanks. Deprived of its super thin coating of oil, the main bearings had heated up beyond the level of tolerance designed by the aerospace engineers.

Normally the outer surface and inner surfaces of the bearings were separated by a distance of two, one thousandths of an inch. This provided enough space for the oil film to lubricate and cool the metal. The inner and outer bearings, constructed of the same material, would expand at a known rate per degree of engine temperature. The inner bearing, being smaller but denser, would expand slightly more because it received more heat. The outer bearing was thinner and was shielded from the heat by the ceramic blades of the fans and cooled by virtue of being close to the moving air. The oil was designed to cool the inner bearing sufficiently to keep its expansion rate within the design parameters. A pump fed the oil to the inner bearings within a narrow range of pressure. The spinning outer bearing had tiny holes drilled in them that allowed the now heated oil to exit via centrifugal force into the engine airstream where it was consumed along with the fuel. This carefully engineered system allowed cool fresh oil to constantly be pumped around the inner bearing. Proven by thousands of hours of use, the system was simple and reliable, as long as there was a steady supply of oil. The now congealed oil from the wing tanks had interrupted that critical supply. The inner bearing had expanded enough that its outer edge was beginning to contact the inner edge of the outer bearing. Wherever that happened, the metal scuffed and built up ridges, the ridges impeded the progress of whatever amount of oil made its way into the bearings, and slowly the process accelerated.

Dropping to a lower altitude meant the heavier oil was warming, and becoming thinner. So it had became a race. The oil transfer pumps began to refill the engine tanks. The increased oil supply meant the amount of lubrication available would also increase. But by this time the damage to the engine bearings was extensive enough that it was too late to save them. They would fail. The engines would stop, or worse, catch fire; in the process, the aircraft would be turned into a very inefficient glider. The computers took all that into consideration and offered their best guess of how much time there was left until complete engine failure. Initially this was given as ten minutes, with the time to the air port at La Palma being twelve minutes. But the pilots knew that as then engines failed, they would lose power and the time to the airport would inevitably get longer. The computer would respond to the drop in power and report the estimated time accordingly. The flight crew watched as the process began, the time to engine failure, and the time to the airport began to head towards each other. Now it read nine minutes to failure, and nine minutes fifty-five seconds to the airport. The pilot prayed that when they crossed the airport boundary there would still be enough power in the engines to run the hydraulics and operate the flaps and wheel lowering mechanism. The engineer, more steeped in the knowledge of the new engines operation, knew that the computers would not allow the engines to deteriorate to the point where they would catch fire. They would shut them off prior to reaching that point. If they still had not made the airport at that time, he would have to manually override the black boxes and try to coax the last bit of power from the dying turbofans. Problem with that was no one had ever done it before, not even at the factory. To do so was to risk destroying several million dollars of machinery and no one had authorized that kind of testing. He watched and waited as the numbers inexorably continued their march across the screen. Like an onrushing freight train, the moment of truth was coming closer with each passing second, and there was absolutely nothing he could do about it.

Strapped securely in his seat, Newton knew the aircraft was in trouble. A pilot for over thirty years he had developed a "feel" for flying. His senses told him that the nose of the aircraft was pointed down and the increased turbulence signaled passage through the storm layers. A normal descent was a slightly nose down attitude accompanied with a marked reduction in power. Gravity would, of course, pull the aircraft to earth with the volume of the wings passing through the air providing slightly less lift than the weight of the aircraft. This, according to the laws of physics, Newton's laws, meant the aircraft would descend. But now the aircraft was in a much more accentuated nose down attitude. The engines were putting out more power than required for a controlled descent. The aircraft was accelerating on its downward course, shedding altitude as rapidly as possible. Ergo, they were in trouble. What kind of trouble it was,

Newton didn't yet know. But even as they plunged down, his mind went through the reasons which would demand such a maneuver.

First on the list was a decompression event. The aircraft's cabin was kept at a minimum eight thousand feet altitude by law. This meant there would be a pressure differential between the outside environment and the inside of the cabin. A sudden loss of pressure would result in several things happening at once. The first indication would be a rather loud noise as the structural failure of some part or another announced itself. Next would come a rush of air as it left the high pressure area of the cabin for the lower pressure outside the aircraft. The cabin itself would fill with all manner of debris such as papers, dirt, coffee cups, clothing articles, and anything else not secured. The air inside the plane would turn whitish as the higher moisture content suddenly condensed into fog or ice. The movies like to portray these events with scenes of people being sucked out into the sky through impossibly small openings. This view had been pronounced by folks on the ground with their slide rules and such as being so much bunk.

In theory it is said there is no difference between theory and practice, in practice there is. This was another of Newton's laws. People on the ground tended to look only at the pressure differential between the air inside and outside of the cabin. They forget about Bernoulli's principle. Simply put, the principle dictated an additional pressure differential caused by the speed of the air outside rushing by the hole in the cabin. This is illustrated by the destructive power of a hurricane or tornado, whose winds speeds can attain a reading of over 200 miles per hour. Modern aircraft fly twice a fast as that. Scenes played in his mind of a local airliner in Hawaii that suffered a decompression event. Metal fatigue had caused a structural failure in the skin, some of the flight crew had been sucked out of the fuselage and Newton instinctively scanned the sides of the cabin walls for signs of cracks. If it was such an event, then he would see the automatic dropping of the yellow oxygen masks from their compartments above the seats. Since none of these things were apparent at the moment, Newton ruled out a decompression event.

Next on his list would be fire. This would usually be heralded by smoke. Modern aircraft ventilation was largely a self contained system with the introduction of less than ten percent of outside fresh air. This was done to lessen the energy costs of heating the cabin air to comfortable levels. Air at normal cruising altitude was well below zero in temperature and heating it took energy. All energy was supplied by the engines, and that took fuel, and fuel was an ever increasing expense. Reusing the already heated air was the method of choice. A secondary indicator was the loss of one of more electrically driven systems, such as the cabin lights. He could quickly see that none of these was occurring.

Third on the list would be engine trouble. Engine trouble was usually depicted as a sudden loss of power, accompanied by large unnerving noises, and bits of metal flying around. Structural damage was a potential byproduct and the subsequent attempt to reach an emergency airport quickly was a race between the strength of the aircraft and time it would take for a vital control surface or engine part to become unusable. This was a race rarely won by the aircraft. Engines could fail gradually, however, and as in this case, would be caused not by an engine fault but by the failure of an engine subsystem.

Newton correctly suspected door number three and attempted to tune his senses to the performance of the huge power plants. He looked over at Elijah; the native elder was sitting calmly in his seat, seemingly unaffected by the events that Newton knew he too was aware of. Elijah's attitude towards life spoke of his native heritage. Certain that all things were connected and therefore nothing happened without a reason, he was sure there was a reason for this too. Besides, there was absolutely nothing that he could do about it. What would happen would happen regardless of any action he could take.

What was happening was the emergency descent of Eastern Skies towards the field at La Palma. The airspeed had built up to the maximum safe descent speed. The captain knew the dangers of doing this. If the engines failed to run the hydraulic pumps they would not be able to use the speed brakes. If that happened, they would not be able to slow the aircraft to a safe speed to deploy the flaps and lower the landing gear.

"Eastern 196, La Palma." The radio crackled into life. Up until now the communications had been mainly done via the computer network. But La Palma was not connected to the link, and used the standard radio channels. 121500 Khz is the designated frequency for aviation distress calls, and it was on this frequency that the controller at La Palma was communicating.

"La Palma, Eastern 196."

"Good morning, sir, I have been apprised of your situation by your head office, conditions at La Palma are wind 010 at 5, barometer 1016 Kp, temperature 25 degrees. Radar has you at 45 nautical miles out, you are cleared number one for 01."

"Eastern 196."

With that, Scotty acknowledged receipt of the information from the tower.

"Sir, do you wish to have the emergency equipment?"
The pilot looked at his instruments and tried to make a judgment on the chances of the aircraft landing safely. Seconds counted if they were unable to deploy the landing gear or flaps. The runway was 2200 meters long, more suited to a 737 than the huge plane they were flying.
"Affirmative, La Palma."
"We'll let them know, and good luck."
"Eastern 196."

The La Palma airport was located on the west side of the Island. So in order to make the landing into the wind, it was necessary to head south from their present position and then turn 180 degrees to the left, coming in from the sea in a gentle turn to line up with the runway. The deteriorating condition of the engines meant that they would have likely only one chance. Adding to the problem was the weather. As is usual with tropical locations, clouds and showers were the order of the day. One of the large cloud cells was at this moment drifting between the route of the aircraft and the runway. In a normal approach the pilot would wait for the cloud to drift out of the path by slowing the aircraft and using a long approach. But this was not a normal approach. The flight engineer studied the readout on his screen. As the predicted time for engine failure and the estimated time of arrival at the airport grew closer to the same value, he called out the differential to the pilot.
"Forty seconds, skipper!"
"Roger that."
"Eastern 196, radar has you at 38 nautical miles."
The radar controller at the airport came onto the radio circuit and would give a constant update of the aircraft's position. Even though the plane had the best GPS systems that were available at the time, their operation would depend on the continuing supply of power from the auxiliary generators. These generators were designed to run independently of the main engines. However, they were fed from the same fuel system. If the pilot needed to shut off the master fuel valve because of the condition of the engines had deteriorated to the point where they may come apart, that power would stop. In those circumstances, the GPS would not function and the only guidance available would be from the radar readings. In addition to the auxiliary generator, the aircraft was fitted with a slipstream generator. This device resembled a small windmill. On command it would be deployed into the slipstream outside the aircraft where the rushing air would spin the turbine inside it and generate power. This should provide enough power to run the radios and some of the instruments. The cost

of generating the power would be increased drag. Not a lot, but any increase in drag would slow down the aircraft and lengthen the time it would take for it to reach the airport. Time they did not have.

The continued voice communication with the airport was a comforting link.

Scotty did not respond, the procedure common to emergency situations dictated that he was deemed too busy flying the aircraft, and no acknowledgement of ground transmissions would be required.

The onboard weather radar showed a large cloud cell drifting onto the airport property between Eastern 196 and the threshold. The colored screen flashed between red and orange indicating heavy rain and possible electrical activity within the cloud. The pilot had flown hundreds of hours through clouds and rain before, and normally the prospect of doing so presented nothing more than an interesting challenge, at least as long as the onboard navigational instruments continued to operate.

Michael Alan had the emergency checklist out and was reading down the list of things that were required to be accomplished, time permitting. Every airline had prepared such lists for every possible combination of events that they could think of. A single engine failure was not that uncommon, even in today's world. A dual failure was rare. Complete failure of all engines practically unheard of. In fact, the last time Michael had even heard of one was an Air Canada flight that suffered fuel exhaustion due to an instrument failure, and the switching over to the metric system from imperial where there was confusion about the quantity of fuel to be loaded. That aircraft had made a nearly impossible landing on an old military airfield in Gimli Manitoba. The incredible skill of the flight crew had made the difference that day. Michael hoped it would not require the same level on this occasion.

"Auxiliary power master switch on."

"Emergency door release armed."

"Emergency locator beacon armed."

"Master fuel transfer on."

"Emergency hydraulic system pressurized." And so the list went. Scotty continued flying the aircraft alone until the end of the list was reached.

"List complete, Scotty," Michael reported.

"Thanks, buddy, follow through on this with me."

Michael now put his hands on the controls, and followed Scotty's moves. If the captain were to become incapacitated, he would be able to continue flying the aircraft without interruption.

"Eastern 196, twenty miles out," reported the radar operator.

"Emergency equipment rolling," noted the tower.

The buffeting increased from the cloud layers they passed through, and the aircraft began its turn towards the runway threshold.

"Skipper, we are down to thirty seconds!"

"Roger that, Scotty."

Out on the wings the bearing on number one engine had reached their breaking point. Every bearing is manufactured to a range of strict tolerances. But even with the use of modern computer-controlled machinery, it is just not possible to produce an exact part. The inner bearing had been made less than one ten thousandths of an inch bigger than its counterparts. This was well within the specs for a normal running assembly. But this was also dependent upon an interrupted supply of oil. Since this was not the case, the inner race of the bearing had now expanded to the point where it touched the outer sleeve. In the blink of an eye the metal parts heated from friction, and failed. The inertia of rotating mass of the fans kept the engine from coming to a complete halt, and in the process guaranteed the destruction of the engine. Fred noted the accelerated drop in RPM.

"Number one is going, Scotty!"

Scotty had already felt the change in the aircraft's response. The loss of power on one side of the plane meant he had to apply greater pressure to the control surfaces to keep the airliner on course. The drop in engine speed also increased the drag on that side of the plane, which in turn required more power to compensate from the number two engine. This accelerated the rate of failure for that engine.

"How long on number two, Fred?!"

"Any time now, skipper!"

On the instrument panel, the estimated time to failure for number two engine was now in the minus figures.

"Eastern 196, 15 miles from the threshold, cleared number one," came the tower operator's voice over the radio. A shudder shook the plane as the number one engine bearings seized up.

Michael punched a key on his control wheel and one of the screens in front of him listed the emergency shutdown procedures. Rather than manually follow the checklist as he had done earlier, Michael pressed the key again and the computer took over the shutdown tasks. In the number one engine nacelle, things began to happen faster than any human could dictate. The fuel valves snapped shut, cutting off all fuel flow to the engine. The oil transfer pump ceased its futile operation, cutting off that source of combustible material. Within the engine itself, sensors registering the heat of the bearings now fed their information directly to the fire control system. Without the flow of air through the massive fan assemblies, the residual heat began to soak into the components. As it did, the fire suppression system detected the rise and fired the first in a series of carbon dioxide bottles. This had a dual effect, it cut off any oxygen to prevent a fire from starting, and the minus 125 degree temperature of the compressed CO_2 immediately cooled any overheated components.

On his panel, Fred monitored the computer's progress. "Bottle one fired, skipper," he called out on the intercom. "Bottle two firing!" There were five separate fire suppression circuits available for the computer to use. Each had a separate CO_2 bottle and each bottle could be routed to any circuit.

"Bottle three, Scotty!"

"Roger that," came the response.

The bearings in the number two engine were now beginning to overheat. The added stress of the extra power it had to supply taxed them to their limits, and beyond. By now the aircraft had passed through twelve thousand feet. The cabin pressure was almost equal to the outside air, and subsequently the pressurization system was no longer needed. This reduced the strain on the number two engine which drove it.

"Eastern 196, eight miles out, on glide slope," the tower reported.

Scotty was concentrating on the instrument panel. The local storm had swathed the aircraft in heavy cloud and rocked it from side to side. Visibility from the cockpit was reduced to nothing. Scotty's favorite description for this was "flying from the inside of a cow." On the screen before him the runway was clearly marked as a series of lights within a box. The outline of the aircraft was electronically shown along with the route to fly. On the edge of the box an electronic representation of the glide slope appeared. This told the pilot if the aircraft was too high or too low in his approach to the runway threshold. It was shown as a series of two lights.

If the lights were both red, the aircraft was too low for the required three degree rate of descent. "Red over red, you're dead," was the pilot's refrain that came into Scotty's mind. Both lights white meant you were too high, "white over white, you'll fly all night." The display on Scotty's screen was red over white, a perfect rate of descent.

"Eastern 196, 4 miles out, wind 15 at 010, altimeter 1001, cleared for landing."

The tower called out the normal information, fully aware that Scotty did not have the luxury of time to do other than check the setting of the instruments. Even though the aircraft had all electronic instruments, regulations required all aircraft be equipped with a basic set of manual ones for backup, and they were mounted to a sub panel. Instinctively Michael checked the settings on the altimeter and adjusted them to the local conditions.

"Eastern 196, two miles out."

Onboard, the number two engine began to shudder. The computer sensed the imminent failure of the bearings and started the shutdown notification. Fred's screen reported five seconds to engine shutdown.

"Five seconds, skipper!"

"Override Fred, I need it now!"

Fred, anticipating the request, had already started the key sequence that told the computer not to engage the automatic shutdown checklist. On the wing, number two engine started to die.

"Eastern 196, one mile out; good luck, sir," came the tower's final communication.

On the runway the red lights of the emergency vehicles showed through the envelope of cloud and rain. The various fire suppression trucks and rescue crews were lined up on the taxiways alongside runway 01. They were aligned to race down the runway parallel to Eastern 196's anticipated landing rollout. In theory, they would be in the right spot to race to the site of the final landing spot within 30 seconds.

Scotty felt the aircraft yaw to the left with the loss of power to the number two engine. "Flaps," he called out. Michael pushed a button on the control console at the same time as the "flaps deployed" notification appeared on his screen. Along the rear of the wings the large sheets of metal that made up those control surfaces began their descent into the slipstream. This caused two things to happen. The increased drag slowed the aircraft, and also provided increased lift to the wings. They also caused the aircraft to pitch down slightly.

In his seat, Newton sensed the pitch change and felt the rumble of the flaps coming down. This was immediately followed by a bump as the landing gear assembly was deployed. Damn, he thought, the pilot is really leaving this to the last minute.

With the gear down and the flaps deployed, the aircraft entered the landing phase of its flight envelope. The added drag and pitch changes provided more stability and the aircraft was dead center over the runway numbers as it passed the runway threshold. The added strain of the hydraulic pumps working the flaps and gear exceeded the capabilities of the engines. Numbers three and four failed simultaneously. Their onboard computers automatically shutting them down as the plane touched down on the tarmac. The aircraft, now accompanied by an escort of emergency vehicles, rumbled down runway 01. With all the engines dead, Scotty now faced the problem of stopping the plane prior to reaching the end of the pavement. Watching the speed bleed off on his instruments, he had to wait until it fell below 80 knots before he could fire the emergency braking system. Any sooner and the brake pads would burn off prior to stopping the plane. Any later and they would not stop before the runway ended.

"100!" called out Michael.

"95!"

"90!"

"85!" Scotty had his finger on the key.

"84!"

"83!"

"82!"

"81!"

"80!" Scotty pushed hard on the key. Under the aircraft, pressure was released from two compressed air bottles and the brake shoes on the main wheels snapped against their drums. The computers monitored the slippage of the wheels and interrupted the flow of gas as required to prevent full lock up. In the same fashion as the automatic braking system on a modern automobile, the ABS on the plane worked to allow the wheels to generate maximum braking power.

Newton felt the skipping action of the giant wheels and looked over at his companion. Elijah was still serene as ever, he returned Newton's gaze and grinned "We there yet?" he asked.

"Apparently," Newton replied with a smile.

Within a few seconds, Eastern 196 had slowed to a speed that allowed the emergency vehicles catch up with it. On board the fire trucks located on each side of the plane, the crews were aiming the nozzles of their equipment at the engine nacelles. The nozzles were mounted like tank guns on a swivel mount at the top of the truck. To the side of the nozzle was a small screen. Like the aiming equipment of a modern tank, it was connected to an infrared sensor. On it the outline of the aircraft filled the screen; the colors were shades of orange and red, with the brightest sections the areas of greatest heat. This allowed the fireman to direct the fire retardant foam at the hottest part of a fire, even if the target was engulfed in smoke. Essentially the truck was a rolling metal tank filled with foam generating chemicals under pressure. When released through the nozzle it generated huge amounts of foam. The foam would cut off the air supply to the fire and cool it. But it would also cut off the air to any survivors caught in the stream. The crew trained many hours to perfect their techniques. As they came up to an aircraft, they would scan it for hot spots and concentrate on them. The truck on the left side of the plane scanned the number one engine and found it fairly cool, due, no doubt, to the fact that it had been shut down while still in flight and had been cooled by the cloud and rain.

Number two engine showed several hot spots and the truck pulled into position to direct a stream of foam into the rear of it. The problem they faced was the proximity of the emergency exit doors to the engine mounting. The crew chief told the crew over the radio to be prepared to direct the foam at the rear of the engine only. The massive fan blades at the front of it would deflect any of the fire retardant delivered there. The aircraft was still rolling as the truck pulled in behind it, keeping a safe distance away.

On the left wing, the automatic braking system was beginning to fail. As the number two engine failed, it had shed small bits of debris into the fuselage that had been undetected to this point. The actual number of vital areas that could be hit by pieces of a disintegrating engine were small. Ever since an airliner's control systems had been severely disabled by the breakup of one of its rear mounted engines, engineers had actively designed redundant routings of essential control cables and hydraulic lines to prevent similar occurrences. In the case of Eastern 196, the wing-mounted engines lessened the probability of such damage in the first place. Preventing it entirely was impossible. The tip of a fan blade that had broken off of engine number two had struck the brake line of the left main landing gear assembly. The strike had not cut the line completely; rather, it had pierced it leaving a small hole. As the emergency braking system rapidly cycled the valves that alternately applied and released the brakes, the reserve air escaped through the hole until it became depleted. Sensing the loss of pressure, the computer applied the brakes in full as a last desperate act to slow the giant aircraft. When it did, the right side of the plane was still working as designed, that meant the straight ahead inertia of the rolling mass of the plane was now slewed to the side.

The landing gear was not designed to handle the resultant sideways force and the left leg snapped off dropping the wing to the ground in a shower of sparks. Riding on the left wing tip and engine nacelles, the plane was dragged around suddenly to the left, surprising the emergency crew and passengers alike.

One of the rescue trucks was too slow in reacting and piled into the rear of the plane, its roof catching the bottom of the fuselage. The right hand gear then collapsed under the extra force and the plane wound up skidding along on the underside of main fuselage.

Inside the plane, Newton and Elijah lurched against their seat belts as the plane bumped and ground its way along the runway. The emergency lights blinked on and off as the oxygen masks dropped from the upper compartments. Articles in the overhead racks flew around the cabin when the doors popped open under the bending stress.

The increased drag brought the plane to a quick stop in a cloud of dust and smoke. Gaps appeared in the aluminum skin and the rain poured in. Even before Newton and Elijah had released their belts and struggled to their feet, Julie and Georgia along with other members of the crew, had the emergency doors, at least those that would operate, open and the exit slides inflated with a bang. On the ground a blanket of foam covered the wings and filled the engines, all of which were now leaking fuel. Thankfully there was no sign of fire.

Newton got to his feet and with Elijah took a quick look around the cabin. Jason and Richard were also on their feet and already making their way to the exits. At the rear of the cabin, the "G-man" had received a large cut on his head from a piece of flying debris, and was being helped to his feet by Major O'Conner. Newton and Elijah made their way back and each grabbed an arm to support the injured man. He was muttering something about his papers and fighting all attempts to get him to leave.

"I have them, I have your papers!" yelled Major O'Conner. "You have to get out of here!"

Dragging the injured man and followed by O'Conner, Newton and Elijah made their way to the door. Julie was already at the bottom of the nylon slide, helping exiting passengers and Georgia was standing at the door urging them to jump. After literally tossing the injured man down the slide, Newton and Elijah pushed the protesting O'Conner onto it and then jumped on themselves, followed immediately by Georgia. In a few seconds they were bundled in blankets by the rescue crew, and taken to an ambulance at the side of the runway.

Eastern 196 now sat in the middle of the runway. A pile of aluminum wrapped in a foam blanket. Deep gouges traced the path of the landing gear legs along the runway surface. Pieces of the wings, engine nacelles, and bits of the fuselage lay scattered about the scene.

Her crew and passengers had been taken to the terminal, there had been a few injuries, some serious, but no fatalities. Newton sought out the pilot and rest of the aircrew, who were gathered in a group of their own.

"Hell of a good job you did there," Newton told Scotty reaching out to shake his hand.

"Thanks, but I don't think the company would agree."

"Sure they will, landing with all engines out, on a short runway in a rain storm, at an unfamiliar field, that's one hell of a great job of flying."

"How did you know the engines were out?"

"I felt it, been flying for thirty years, not anything like this though, just the small stuff, but you still sense things."

"Well, I thank you for your comments, but I think this was my last flight."

"Whatever happens, Captain, you have my support, and I intend to be very vocal about the good job you did."

"Me too." said Elijah.

"What they said!" added Richard.

"Also count me in," piped up Jason, still holding the case he had been clutching throughout the whole incident.

"I do have one question though," said Elijah.

"What's that?"

"What carousel do we pick up our luggage at?"

The whole group chuckled at the comment, garnering confused looks from the rescue airport personnel within hearing range. Across from their group they noticed a small man in a very agitated state. Wearing a business suit and speaking Spanish rapidly he was gesturing to the chief of the rescue crew.

"What's that all about?" asked Jason.

"He is pissed because the airport is closed and they do not have the equipment to move the aircraft," translated Scotty. "There are no maintenance facilities on La Palma; it's just a transient stop. With the damage to the runway and the remains of the plane where it is, it is going to keep the airport closed for some time to all but small planes and helicopters. Naturally, the tourist trade is going to suffer a bit. Eastern will foot the bill for us to stay a local hotel after we get checked out at the hospital. But no large aircraft will be able to land until they get the runway cleared. And that appears, from what he is saying, to be some days in the future."

"So this flight is going to be a disaster for Eastern, economically speaking," said Elijah.

"Actually, no," Scotty replied.

"How can that be?"

"Eastern contracted for 15 aircraft at a set price with the option to buy an unspecified number later. If they buy more then they get a reduction in the price of the first 15 planes also. Since they will get the full cost of the plane back from the insurance claim, they will now order a new plane to replace it, so their total order goes to 16, and that means the other 14 of the first order drop in price. When you add up the money they get back plus the drop in price, in the end they will come out about 2.5 million ahead. The loss of the plane and all associated costs will also affect their tax position resulting in that figure going up a little also."

"So what caused this all anyway," asked Newton

"A problem with the engine reserve oil tanks," Fred responded. "Someone screwed up in the Azores is the word I got."

"I'd hate to be in his shoes," said Jason. "The insurance companies will hound him for the rest of his life."

"I wonder who the poor bastard is."

At that time the poor bastard was sitting on the beach in front of the disheveled shack he called home. The empty bottle in his hand fell and joined its companions at his feet. The dismissal notice sat unopened in an envelope on the cluttered kitchen table. He didn't need to read it. He had really fucked up this time, a multimillion dollar aircraft wrecked, the last shreds of his integrity wiped away. Luckily no one on the aircraft was killed. There were a couple of serious injuries from flying debris, but the Federal Aircraft Administration's report on the incident would not list any fatalities. At least he had no deaths on his conscience. Except one, of course. He stripped off his shirt, carefully pulled out his wallet and keys and left them on top of the chair. His mechanic's certificate, which would be revoked now, was in a frame propped up in the sand. Strange, he thought, how most suicides don't take any identification with them. It was if they didn't want anyone to know who they really were. I guess, he thought with his last functioning brain cells, that in the end God knew who you were, and the rest really doesn't matter. He kicked off his shoes and stumbled into the sea.

CHAPTER NINETEEN

Tenerife Airport - Canary Islands

Aram Mohammed Al Bazir gripped the armrests of the small business jet so hard his knuckles turned white. He had never been in a plane before, and if he had any say in the matter he would not do so again. The Cessna Citation had made the trip from Tehran in a short time, flying East across the top of Africa and refueling in Spain before touching down at Tenerife. There had been some consternation amongst the pilots when the Cessna had been diverted from its intended destination of La Palma due to a problem on the runway there. Aram had been informed by one of the flight crew that an American airliner had crashed, rendering the runway unusable. He was still not used to being in a position where people reported to him in this fashion. It would take some time to get used to this new job. Already he had experienced the uncertainty in planning that came with it. His choice for an "escort" for the five scientists on board had been approved by the security office, only to be informed that he was unavailable at the last minute due to an appendicitis attack. With only half an hour before departure, he had been told that he would personally take the escort's place. Deep down, he suspected this could be a further test of his loyalty. The scientists were a low risk to defect. Their work was well funded, their families had access to "special areas" not open to the general public, and the government tended to leave them alone to do their work. The study of geology was not a hot button issue in any country as far as security went, especially in the area of volcanoes. The only odd thing that had piqued his interest was the youngest member of the five man group. Salim Pashar was not your typical volcanologist, if there was such a thing. His credentials had come straight from the minister himself, and were impeccable. What he was lacking was any record of published papers in the field. He was still young, only in his early thirties, and that might account for it, but others in this field had already been published, some as the lead, but at least as a contributor. Indeed, the main competition amongst the group was a drive to publish some paper of some sort in the field. Salim carried himself more as military man than a scientist. He was seldom dressed as his compatriots, forsaking the casual dress of the group and always impeccably groomed. One other thing seemed out of place, and that was that the older members deferred to him in a way that went against the usual practice. Aram had found that more than in any other field, experience garnered respect, and Salim was too young to have achieved such experience. Obviously, Salim was a plant, Aram thought, and the reason for it was plain; Salim was there to keep an eye on him.

The Cessna landed with the usual chirp and puff of smoke as the tires came in contact with the pavement. Aram started to breathe easier as soon as he felt the plane begin to slow. Man may be meant to fly, he mused, but not, praise Allah, this man. Reaching the taxiway, the plane turned towards the charter terminal on the opposite side of the airport from the main concourse. Through its small windows Aram glimpsed his first views of life outside the confines of Iran. The most obvious difference was the place of women. Dressed in the same garb as men, without their heads covered, women were operating machinery and doing the same work. Aram exited the aircraft along with the rest of his group who seemed nonplussed about the sights. The crew of the Cessna began to unlock the cargo hatches as a freight dolly was rolled into place to take their bags. Two large black limousines pulled onto the apron flying the Iranian flag from their fenders. The doors opened and a small man in a business suit alighted and came towards them.

"Praise be to Allah, I am Shaba Al Habrid, the consul general here. Your bags have been waived through customs and will be taken to your hotel, please come with me." The drivers of the cars, both dressed in Iranian military uniforms, stood by the open passenger doors of the vehicles. Talking lightly amongst themselves, the group of scientists split into two parties and entered the cars. Aram noticed Salim whisper something to the driver of his vehicle. He also noticed the man stood a little stiffer and almost tried to salute. Yes, thought Aram, I am correct, this man is not who his papers say he is. Am I expected to watch him, or is he to watch me?

"You are Aram, are you not?" asked Shaba.
"I am."
Shaba sat next to Aram, with two of the volcanologists sitting across from them, studying papers they had pulled from their briefcases.
Shaba looked up from a photograph stapled to a folder sitting on top of a leather case. The folder was sealed.
"You were not expected," Shaba stated. "Sign here."
Aram signed the routing slip signifying receipt of the folder.
"Do not open that until you get to your room, I have made arrangements for your party to stay at the Sol La Palma. The crash of the American airliner has thrown things off schedule somewhat. You will find an updated itinerary for your group in the folder, and the latest security reports from Tehran."
"How are we going to get there?" Aram asked.
"You and your party will be traveling to La Palma by helicopter; we

have arranged it so that you will leave within the hour,

"Thank you," replied Aram. "Have you been here long?"

Shaba looked closely at him, as if trying to decide something, then replied in a more relaxed tone. "Ah yes, this is your first trip abroad is it not?"

"Yes, I have never been in such a place as this."

"You will find many differences from our homeland, Aram, the most obvious being the dress of the women, it is shameful, is it not?"

Aram did not reply.

"This is nothing," Shaba said, "Wait 'til you see them at the hotel, they have no shame, and the television, such things should not be broadcast."

Aram nodded, wondering if the consul was saying these things as a warning or to state his position for the record. His words were one thing, his eyes said others.

"Praise Allah, I will be on guard against these temptations," said Aram.

"Yes," said the consul. "We must all be on guard against them."

In the other car Salim had also been given a folder, as he sat silently reading it on a seat alone, the other passengers remained absolutely silent. A few minutes later, the two vehicles pulled up in front of an unmarked hangar. The doors were open and attached to a large tractor; a Russian made Mi-8T Helicopter was being towed to the apron in front. Aram got out of the car and inwardly groaned. Flying in a fixed wing aircraft had seemed bad enough, but now he was to continue this journey in a helicopter? He had seen this type of machine many times. Prisoners of "special interest" to the state had been delivered to his prison occasionally by such means, landing in the main yard in a cloud of dust and noise. Sometimes they had left that way also. When they did, they were never seen again. The machine now being prepared for flight differed little from those which had visited his former workplace. The paint was white, with standard civilian markings. The helicopter still had the stubby wing pylons that marked it as a military model, even though nothing was currently mounted on them. The crew were dressed in civilian clothes, but their manner was still military. The huge rear doors were open and Aram could see the interior held boxes of equipment, and the canvas chairs that folded against the wall to make room for cargo when required.

Shaba motioned to the rear doors, "You will continue your trip from here, Allah's blessings be upon you."

Aram nodded and boarded the craft with the group. He noticed that some of the crates on board had Iranian Air Force markings. Folding out one of the canvas seats he buckled himself in and waited as the aircrew checked the stowage of their bags, then went to each person and checked the security of the seatbelts. With an increasing whine the two turbine engines started and quickly wound up to speed. The vibration level increased and with a clatter of its blades the helicopter headed north to La Palma.

The hospital at La Palma was well equipped and well staffed. The climate and locale had played a great part in luring many healthcare professionals to the island. Apart from the normal ills of the resident population, there were the usual tourist complaints to deal with. Changes in food and climate stirred some digestive systems into complaint. The long hours of sunshine brought on sunburns and there were, of course, the accidents. Parasailing, diving with the sharks, rock climbing, and just the general boisterous nature of being on vacation guaranteed a steady stream of work. Ever since the horrendous collision of two fully loaded 747s on Tenerife, the hospitals had upgraded the emergency response capabilities of their facilities. The crash of Eastern 196 had turned out to be well within the limits of the medical establishment. At the end of the day, there were only three admissions to the hospital. The rest of the passengers and crew had been sent to the hotel after being checked out. Most of that checking out had occurred at the airport terminal itself. A triage team had arrived at the terminal when notified by the tower and were already set up when the aircraft crossed the threshold.

Newton and Elijah had been seen by a triage nurse when they came into the terminal from the runway. A quick look put them into the "check later" group. Soon joined by Richard and Jason they waited patiently, watching the activities of the rescue crews. Satisfied that the more serious injuries had been seen to, Newton's group, which included the aircrew, were checked once more and then sent down to get onto the bus taking them to the hotel. For the second day in a row, Newton found himself checking into a strange place on an unplanned stay. This time he was unsure of the length of time he would be staying. Unlike his last stay, he and Elijah found themselves in a regular tourist room. There was still the obligatory balcony and view of the sea, but it was not a suite. Like most of the passengers, they took the opportunity to rest for the afternoon.

CHAPTER TWENTY

Sol La Palma

Newton was sitting in a lounger and staring at the sea lying beyond the beach. There were the expected sail boats carving the clear waters as they made their way from one spot to another. Most of them were small craft, rented by the various hotels and tourist establishments. Two larger boats, both with two masts and large sails, plied the waters of the outer reefs. Newton guessed they were dive boats, headed out with their complement of neophyte divers to try their hands at scuba. All the hotels offered quick courses in diving for those who wished to try it for the first time. The reefs provided a rich vista of underwater flora and fauna for photographing by the cheap digital cameras supplied for a small extra cost. Newton had never been a diver, suffering from mild claustrophobia; he couldn't picture himself in such an environment. The beaches held the usual suspects. Cabanas filled with food and drink catered to the crowd of sun seekers, hawkers walked slowly up and down the sand peddling sunscreen and umbrellas. The tourists, for their part, had separated into their respective groups. The younger crowd, couples and singles, flocked to the bars and volleyball nets. Some rented the jet powered "personal watercraft" and raced up and down outside the swimming areas. Some sought the spaces near the water's edge to set up their towels and umbrellas, out to see and be seen. Still others went no further than the hotel pools and spas. The families congregated near the swimming beaches. Large red buoys marked the safe areas and shallow waters suitable for children. On the beaches, tall towers marked the lifeguard stations. The sound of children laughing was audible even now. The older crowd spent their time mostly around the pool areas. Dressed in full bathing suits and broad hats, they claimed their stools and chairs. Seated at tables with a cool drink and a book close by, they settled for the warmth of the sun, and perhaps the memories of younger days.

Alfred had never before been to the tropics, let alone a beach such as this. In his mind he could see himself as a younger man in better times taking part in the various activities. walking on the beach hand in hand with Winnifred, watching Ellie playing on the beach.

"Mommy! I found a shell, you can hear the ocean if you try! Can I keep it? Can I?" Ellie ran down the beach clutching her treasured shell, 'til she found another. At last she returned, her arms filled with the various bits of flotsam of interest only to a child. Bits of string and wood that would be just junk to an adult spoke of heroic adventures and tales of pirates long gone. This bit of rope and wood must have come from such a pirate ship, or maybe the raft of some castaway, lost for years on a deserted island. That piece of worn glass, made smooth by the action of the sand and water, was obviously from the lights of some freighter, lost at sea during a terrible storm.

Winnifred would take her hand and smile. "That's right, honey! It must be so, we will ask Daddy when he gets home, I'm sure that will be soon."

They continued down the beach, their footprints tracing the path of the life they spent together. On the smooth sea washed sand they stood out, strong and deep. Well, not his, his were faint and in most spots gone altogether. In the distance the tracks faded, first his, then Winifred's, then at the end Ellie's, 'til finally his came back, faint and alone.

"Seems like we are stuck in paradise doesn't it?"

Newton snapped out of his reverie and looked up at Elijah. "Sorry, you were saying?"

Elijah smiled, "I was thinking that we seem to be having a problem getting away from the tropics, first in the Azores, and now here."

"Yes, yes it does, weird isn't it, at least the accommodations are suitable, and one good thing, so far it's been pretty much a free vacation."

"Speaking of which, what are you planning to do about dinner?"

"Head down to the restaurant I guess, why? Do you have another suggestion?"

"Not me, but Richard and Jason have called and asked if we care to join them out on the town."

"Why not, sounds like a good idea. What do they have in mind?"

"Apparently Georgia has been here before and knows of a small out of the way place where the food is the local variety, not the usual restaurant fare."

"I'm in, what time?"

Elijah looked at his watch, "You have about 3 hours and 45 minutes, and here is the good news, they managed to deliver our luggage from the plane."

"Covered in fire fighting foam?"

"Nope, but I recommend sending everything out for cleaning, which brings me to my next suggestion."

"Which is?"

"A little shopping, the hotel is next to a mall, and I for one, could use some clothing more suited to the climate, than what I left home with."

"A capital idea, let's do that."

A quick trip down the elevators brought the two men to the front lobby. As with most tourist hotels, several private businesses had made arrangements to advertise their services by the concierge's station. One of these was that of a local cleaner. Newton quickly learned that the way things were done required him to place those items that needed cleaning in a bag, seal it, and then drop it off at the desk. Within 12 hours the items would be returned.

"Well, what do you make our chances to be?" asked Elijah.
"As in...."
"As in, will we be here for 12 hours, or will they have to forward our laundry on to whatever island we land on next?"
"The official word is not yet out; however, I suspect that it will take more than 12 hours to clear the runway so that we can continue on. Which I strongly feel will likely not be to the conference, but rather homeward. The investigation will probably take several days. Removal of the plane to a suitable hangar is top priority I'm sure, but that will require more heavy equipment than is likely to be found locally. I'm sure the Spanish government will respond quickly, but it will still take time. Helicopters and smaller planes will be able to use the shortened runway in the meantime, but they will have to be arranged for out of Tenerife or some other airport. Also Eastern will want to send their folks to talk with everyone, for all the myriad of legal reasons that go along with a crashed plane, and they will want to do that prior to everyone scattering. Luckily there were few injuries, but I still expect a minimum of 24 hours before things begin to shake out."

"I had thought much the same, but why the Spanish government?"
"Because the Canary Islands are theirs—administratively anyway. Expect to see any number of Spanish aviation officials popping up soon. Bottom line is we are safe from being separated from our meager rags for the near future."

"A rather good summation, Mr. Newton," came a voice from behind them. They turned to find Scotty and the rest of the crew. They were now dressed in civilian clothes, with large bags under their arms. "I have been informed, officially, that it is safe for the flight crew to submit their laundry for processing."
Newton and Elijah both shook hands with the captain. "Did they tell you anything about when they expect to start sending the passengers home?" Newton asked.
"A minimum wait of 24 hours, everyone will then be asked to undergo another medical checkup to be sure that there are no lingering after effects from the crash. I understand that the hotel will be making a room here available tomorrow for that since we are all here. The three passengers who required hospitalization will be airlifted to Spain

tomorrow if the doctors give their OK."

"Well, once again, captain, our thanks for bringing us safely in, have you found out any more information on what caused the engine problems?"

"Still a maintenance snafu on our previous stopover is the most likely cause, other than that I'm not allowed to say." Newton noticed the look in Scotty's eyes; it told him the captain knew the exact cause and circumstances.

Leaving the captain to deposit his package, Newton and Elijah made their way to the mall on the street just outside the front entrance. The signs were in Spanish, English, and French and they found a number of small outlets that catered to the tourist trade. All carried the expected garish shirts expected of any tropical locale. Straw hats, sandals, and brightly colored pants filled shelves and racks, all meant to catch the eye of the passerby. Impulse spending made up the bulk of the trade in these stores and their stocks reflected that. The large stores also had a presence, although more subdued than their counterparts, and Newton and Elijah found one of those at the far end of the mall. Although more European in nature, the clothing tags were the same and they both soon found sizes and styles that suited them. Weighed down with their purchases, they headed back to the hotel.

"We had better try to get hold of the conference officials and advise them of everything that has happened," said Newton, heading over to the desk. "I expect they have heard of the crash by now."

"Good idea, I hope they will be able to find someone to fill the time slots."

"I expect they have plans for that, you can never be sure that all attendees will arrive at an international conference."

As they headed to the desk, they were hailed by Richard and Jason, who were just exiting the manager's office. Richard was holding a number of fax sheets in his hand.

"Ah, just in time," he said.

"For?"

"I just let the conference staff know that we are amongst the uninjured but unlikely to arrive in time for our presentations. I took the liberty of including your names with ours, so that they know you are OK also. I hope that was all right?"

"Perfect, in fact we were about to do that very thing. So you have saved us the trouble."

"No problem, Jason here is disappointed he won't be able to demonstrate his little box, but I've assured him there is always next year."

Newton smiled, so Richard was going to give him a passing grade when they returned to New York. Good, the young man may not fit the image the old school police school folks had, but he represented the way things were moving in the world. In time Jason would lead the "old boys" kicking and screaming into the new millennium.

"I also have the proposed timetables from Eastern for our departure, seems like we will likely be here a couple of days at least."

"Why so long? I thought they would expedite us out as soon as possible."

"I'm sure they would like to, but, with the airport closed, all the other tourists will have to be shuttled by small plane to Tenerife to make their flights in and out, and since Eastern caused the mess, they have been relegated to the bottom of the list, except for medical cases."

"So, here we stay then," Elijah added. "Well, I for one think we should take in some of the local color, what sort of things does one do here?"

"I would think the usual tourist stuff; obviously the beaches are a great draw, lots of coast line to explore."

"Cumbre Vieja," said Newton.

"Who-the-what a?" replied Jason.

"Cumbre Vieja, the volcano."

"There's a volcano here? Where? I don't see any smoke?"

"That would probably be because the last eruption was over fifty years ago, in 1950."

"Alfred, you amaze me, how on earth did you know that?" Jason asked.

"I read a lot."

"You read books on volcanoes?"

"No, I read what's around me."

"Sorry, I'm not following you."

"He reads the signs," said Elijah with a twinkle in his eye. "Like that one over there," indicating a large sign by the doorway to a conference room. The sign said in large letters in English, Spanish, and French; 'CUMBRE VIEJA VOLCANO CONFERENCE—last eruption 1950'.

"Ah, of course," said Jason sheepishly. "I should have caught that."

"You'll learn, rookie, in time, you just need to spend a little more time on the street to develop your sense of awareness, takes a little time, no one is born with it." Said Richard.

"So, here we are, on a tropical paradise, loads of beaches, two very attractive ladies to share it with, all being paid for by someone else, and, let me get this straight, you want to go to the top of a volcano?"

"Nope."

"Excuse me, but you just said...."

"Nothing about going to the top of a volcano," continued Newton. "As I recall, this is the only volcano in the world with a railway built into it."

"Oh, now you're really confusing me. It has a railway, how did that happen?"

"Well, this volcano has channels in it, like most others, that lava flowed up in, but unlike most other volcanoes they travel horizontally as well as vertically. Also they are fairly close to the surface, so after the last eruption cooled off, it became sort of a volcano laboratory. In order to study it in greater detail, rail tracks were put in to allow scientists to travel deep within it to study the rock, etc."

"You got all that from the sign?" asked Jason.

"Nope," replied Newton with a grin. "I got it from this," and he held up a small printed tourist brochure, "from over there," he said indicating a rack by the front desk with tourist brochures.

"In police work we call that..." Richard began.

"A clue," Newton and Elijah added in chorus.

"I think I'll go lie down now," said Jason. "I'm obviously outclassed here."

"You'll learn, rookie," said Richard.

Newton and Elijah joined a group of people waiting for the elevator. There was a young couple, talking excitedly in Spanish, with a map of the various beaches in their hands. Apparently on their first trip to the island, the route they had marked out took in all the major tourist spots. Elijah nodded at the pair and winked at Newton. Like a first time visitor to a buffet, the young people seemed determined to not miss a single thing. Newton hoped they would not rush through so fast they sacrificed quality for quantity. Vacations should be marked not with a sheaf of half remembered pictures, but strong feelings that came easily to the mind.

Newton did not have many of those. His memories were chiefly centered on this case or that. Vacations were few and far between. Still, there were a few, like a day spent with Ellie walking along the shore of Half-Moon Lake on the island. The day had been warm, with light winds, early in summer, and the trees were just finished leafing out. She had been the first to spot the bear. A mother with two cubs, her fur just now returning to prime after winter, sat across a small glen watching them warily. One cub was swinging in a tree, its weight causing the small poplar to bend first one way, then the other. The other cub was at the bottom of the tree, uncertain how to climb it. Ellie was entranced, and wanted to get closer, but Newton whispered to her to begin walking slowly backwards. As their scent reached her, the mother stood on her hind legs, trying to get a glimpse with her poor eyesight of the strange odor. Newton checked the trail behind them, it was clear of obstructions and they continued retreating until they reached a place where they could still see the bears, but he hoped, they would not appear to threaten them. The breeze changed direction and the mother lost the scent. With a snort to her cubs, she turned back to feeding on the new berries that dotted the edge of the bush. Newton and Ellie watched with amusement as the cub up in the tree now had to figure out how to get down from its perch. Spurred on by the sight of its sibling feasting on the berries, the youngster let its grip slip and fell to the ground with a flurry of leaves and branches. The mother looked up and gave another snort. Kids, she seemed to be saying, they just don't listen anymore. Recovering its breath, the little cub waddled over to the berry patch and joined in the feasting. Newton looked at Ellie, and the wonder and joy on her face warmed his heart. Together they slipped back down the trail, still whispering excitedly about what they had seen. Later on, at dinner, Ellie told of the sighting again and again to her mother, ending up with a declaration that she wanted to be a conservation officer when she grew up. Ellie was eight years old at the time.

The bell announced the arrival of the elevator and broke into Newton's thoughts. They waited for it to empty and stepped in, selecting their floor. Along with the young tourists, they had been joined by another person who took a place at the rear of the car. The elevator started its upward journey with the two tourists still talking excitedly about their proposed plans. They got out on the second floor and the sound of their conversation disappeared down the hallway with them until the doors closed.

"You are American?" Newton and Elijah turned and looked at their fellow passenger as the elevator started up again. He was dressed in a business suit, clean shaven, and appeared to be in his fifties. He spoke with an even voice and his eyes held no malice.

"No, Canadian," Newton replied.

"Ah, I have been there, Canada that is, a most lovely country."

"Oh, what part of Canada?" Elijah asked.

"Vancouver, in May of 1980, I was there for the Mt. St. Helens event."

"So, you must be a volcanologist then, here for the conference no doubt."

"Quite so, allow me to introduce myself, I am Dr. Mohammed Al Zagrib from the Iranian Institute of Science."

Newton took his hand, "I am Alfred Newton, and this is Elijah Longeyes."

"Very pleased to meet you, I'm sure."

The elevator came to a smooth stop, and the door opened. "This is our floor," said Newton. "Mine too," replied Dr. Zagrib, and the group stepped out into the hallway.

"Would you perhaps be passengers from the Eastern flight?"

"Yes, we are."

"An unfortunate event, but as I understand it, no serious injuries, praise be to Allah."

"Very true, and we are thankful of that."

The group made its way down the hallway with Newton and Elijah stopping by their room first.

"I see we are neighbours then," the Iranian scientist said, "perhaps you would care to come in for tea. I have but one roommate and he is seldom around."

"I would enjoy that," said Newton. "However we are booked for dinner shortly, can I persuade you to join us?"

"Thank you, but no, I will not be able to do that. However, I expect I will be in the cafeteria later this evening if you find yourselves free."

"Quite likely," replied Newton. "With luck we will meet again."

The men shook hands and Newton and Elijah entered their room.

"For an Iranian, he had quite the English accent," remarked Elijah as they set out their new clothes.

"The British have a long history in the Middle East, longer than the Americans in fact. Most of the initial oil fields were found by the Brits and they provided the expertise to bring them on line."

"Seems like a nice fellow."

"Yes, but I think there is more to this than his just being friendly."

"Is he looking to jump ship do you think?"

"Maybe, but we will find out more this evening, if he is there."

The phone rang and Elijah picked it up. A few minutes later he called out to Newton, "Richard and Jason will meet us in the lobby in half and hour."

"OK, I'll be ready," said Newton heading to the shower.

The lobby had become noticeably busier when Newton and Elijah arrived to meet their dinner companions. The flow of people returning from a day at the beach or some other attraction ran up against the early evening crowd getting ready to leave for the night time activities. Predictably, the two currents of people met and swirled like water from a river meeting the incoming tide. The stationary objects stood rocklike in the current, with the flow separating around them. The designers of the lobby had anticipated this, and designed the placement of columns and pillars to separate the incoming and outgoing flows. The common meeting grounds were the elevators and, of course, the front desk. The harried staff behind it were trying to divide their attention between those coming in and looking for their keys and messages, and those requiring their services. Inevitably, there were those who believed their problems eclipsed everyone else's and demanded all of the staff's attention. Such a situation was occurring now. Newton and Elijah were seated in the lounge area, waiting for Richard and Jason, when loud voices from the front desk distracted them from their wait. An argument between a group of guests and one of the hotel staff was well underway. Some of the guests were shouting in Farsi, and the hotel staff were trying to first of all calm the agitated guests down, and secondly, to understand what the complaint was. Newton observed Dr. Zagrib trying to act as an interpreter. Eventually whatever it was that had upset the group was remedied and the lobby returned to the normal busy hum of activity.

The elevator doors opened and Richard and Jason accompanied by Georgia and Julie got off and came towards them.

"All ready?" Richard asked.

"All set." Elijah Replied.

The group headed out of the hotel and down the street. They passed several small stores and a couple of bars with names like "Senor Garcia's" and "El Cachon." Crowds of people still in beach attire mingled with those seeking the night life or, like them, a place to eat. The gentle evening breeze engulfed them in a blanket of warm air as they entered a small restaurant located off the main street and facing onto a beach. Unlike the eateries on the main road, this one had subdued lighting and but a simple unlighted sign above the door. "Conchita's" was family run and a favorite of the locals. The tables were of the simple wood designs found in almost any kitchen in the world. Each had four chairs, and when required, they were dragged together to form a larger surface. The clientele was made up of native islanders, mostly fishermen by appearance, and their families. The atmosphere was warm and welcoming, made even more so by the greeting they received.

"Georgia!" came a cry from behind the bar.

"Hola, Conchita!" A thin woman of about 40 years old put down the glass she was drying and came out to greet them. She gave Georgia a bear hug and talked rapidly to a man who had just emerged from the store room. "Gonzales, this is Georgia, my angel!"

The three of them chatted in rapid fire Spanish, none of which Newton understood. The feelings however were plain as day. Georgia and Conchita had some sort of history and whatever that was, it was a good thing. Conchita ushered them to a table and started again in English this time.

"Welcome!" She beamed. "Please consider yourselves my guests!"

In a few moments several bottles of wine were placed on the table, along with menus and napkins. Conchita hovered at their table like a mother hen, alternately hugging Georgia and talking to anyone who would listen at the other tables. After hearing what she had to say, they would raise their glasses in a toast, to which Georgia would smile in reply. At last Gonzales rescued them from all the attention, giving them time to collect themselves.

"Apparently, you two have met" Newton said, indicating the beaming Conchita.

"Yes, we have," Georgia said. "This is a bit overwhelming."

"I'm sure there is a good story behind it all," Richard added, "do tell."

Georgia, flushed with embarrassment, looked at them and began. "It wasn't all that much, really. I was getting ready for a flight from New York to Madrid and I heard one of our counter people talking in Spanish to a passenger. It seems the airline had been overbooked in tourists and she was going to miss her flight. I knew the flight had a free space in first class and since I had lots of points, I managed to get her upgraded so she could make the flight."

"Points?" Jason asked. "What are they?"

"Every employee gets a certain number of points per year they can use to apply towards tickets for a flight. There are restrictions of course, you can't bump a regular passenger, and the airline can refuse to allow them to be used if it wants too, but generally they are pretty good about it."

"So you cashed in some of your points to upgrade her ticket then," said Newton. "That was nice of you."

"It wasn't all that much, I had more than I could use anyway, but I guess it meant a lot for her," Georgia said, indicating the still bubbling Conchita. "She needed to get back in time for a family celebration, and it was important for her. She wrote down the name of her restaurant and told me to drop in if I was ever here, so here we are."

Gonzales brought a platter of pastries over and placed them on the table, "Enjoy," he said. "I will come back in a few moments and take your orders. Anything you like—it's on the house tonight!"

The menus were mostly Spanish, with English and French notations. "Anyone know what all this is?" Jason asked.

"Mostly native dishes, I think," Georgia responded. "Let me help you."

"First we have 'papas arrugadas', which are potatoes boiled in salt water, the 'mojo' is a native hot sauce, very good but I recommend that you go easy on it at first. The 'sancocho canario' is a stew of salted fish and mojo, very spicy. Also you have rabbit in 'salmorejo', that's a sauce made from water, vinegar, olive oil, salt and pepper, and a sweet black pudding. Not everything is 'tropical island' spicy though. For dessert you have native bananas, papayas, and avocado, also the tomatoes are superb. As for the rest, you're on your own."

"Lots to choose from then," Elijah remarked. "I always like to sample the native dishes, so it's the 'sancocho canario' for me."

The rest of them made up their minds and Gonzales soon brought heaping dishes over, and kept the wine glasses full. As the last dishes were cleared away, the restaurant clientele were coming and going as in any establishment of his sort. Conchita and Gonzales welcomed each new arrival as if they were friends and relatives, as indeed many of them were. Every now and then, a new face would appear. Some arrived based on the recommendation of others, and some by happenstance. Newton and Richard routinely scanned the entrance each time someone entered. Jason had not been a police officer long enough to develop the routine surveillance habits the older men demonstrated. If someone had brought this to their attention, they both would have professed surprise, so automatic had the practice become. Elijah smiled inwardly, he had seen this sort of watchfulness in other professions; fishermen were always watching the sky and the sea, even when their feet were on solid ground. Pilots noted every cloud and wind indicator, and when flying, constantly assessed every piece of open ground as a potential emergency landing site. As for himself, Elijah watched the watchers. As an elder his responsibility was to provide guidance when asked. Like any good guide, he was always aware of where the trail began and ended and what the dangers there were on the journey.

The doors opened as another group of diners said goodbye and left the restaurant. On their way out they held the doors open for others coming in. Newton saw Mohammed Al Zagrib enter and take a seat at the far end of the room. He was not alone. Accompanying him were two other Middle Eastern men. Their mood was lighthearted and he waved at Newton as they sat down. After conferring for a few minutes with his companions, Dr. Zagrib came over and greeted Elijah and Newton.

"So, you too have discovered that the best restaurants are not always the largest."

"Yes," Newton said. "Thanks to Georgia here." Introductions quickly followed, with Zagrib motioning to his dinner partners. "There is a tour at Cumbre Vieja tomorrow before the conference begins and my two colleagues are unable to attend, I was wondering if you and your friends would like to come, there is room on the tour for all and if you are interested in volcanoes this is a rare opportunity."

"What will the tour be about?" Julie asked; the interest showing in her eyes.

Dr. Zagrib pulled up a chair, politely refused a proffered glass of wine, and began to explain.

"There are many different tours available," he said. "Usually the tourist plan includes a trip up the side of the volcano, and a short look inside, but the trip tomorrow is to highlight the fissure, which is the focus of this year's conference. Last year the railway was extended and several exciting new discoveries were made about the volcano's internal composition."

"I'm in," Jason said, "sounds like an interesting tour."

"Count us in also," Georgia added looking at Richard and getting a nod of agreement.

"Will we need any special clothes or equipment?" Richard asked.

"The tour guide will supply anything you require, shall we meet at say 8:00 tomorrow morning at the hotel lobby? I will arrange for transportation."

"Sounds like a plan," Newton added. "But I have to ask how good is this tunnel, I'm afraid I have a touch of claustrophobia, and small windy spaces don't bring out the best in me."

"As it is with me my friend!" Zagrib laughed clapping Newton on the back,. "But don't worry, the tunnels are large and well lit, after all we had to run a railway through there!"

"We?" Newton asked. "You built the tunnels?"

"Oh no!" Zagrib replied, "We did not build them, at least not initially, but we did the extensions and enlarged them somewhat. After all, we are the sponsors of the conference, and the tunnels are the focal point, so naturally we would want to make sure they could be viewed comfortably by the rest of the attendees."

"Why the railroad?" Newton wondered out loud.

"Most volcanologists are old men, like me!" said Zagrib, "And like you, wandering about in small dark passages may make for a good computer game, but is too hard on our old bones. Besides, the lower reaches of the tunnel are below sea level, and pumps are required to manage the seepage. Also, there is the drilling machinery and crews to transport."

"Drilling?" Richard asked. "There is active drilling going on?"

"Oh no, at least not while we will be there, just a small maintenance crew looking after the pumps and such."

"What are they drilling for?"

"Exploratory only, after all, this is the only volcano in the world that is quiescent enough, and accessible enough, to allow an investigation this extensive. So one never knows what secrets could are there to be found. After all, the ultimate challenge for us is to be able to accurately predict eruptions."

"So this volcano isn't going to blow its cork any time soon, like when we are traipsing about within its innards and burp the lot of us out in some fiery belch?" Elijah joked.

"Not likely, it's been pretty much dead for decades, but of course," the Iranian scientist said with a wink, "one can never be sure."

He got up from his chair. "Tomorrow then!" he said heading back to his table.

"Well then," Richard said, "it appears we have our day planned for tomorrow."

CHAPTER TWENTY ONE

Cumbre Vieja

Newton and his party made a long goodbye to Conchita and Gonzales as they left the restaurant. Knowing they would refuse payment for the meal, Newton had placed a large tip under his napkin. The food had been superb and they had all promised to return the next night. Stepping out into the warm blanket that was the evening breeze, they walked slowly towards the hotel. Dr. Zagrib and his party left before they did, with a wave and a smile.

"He seems like a friendly guy," Jason said.

"I think," said Elijah, "that perhaps there is more to him than meets the eye."

"The Iranians were great allies 'til the Shah fell," Richard added. "I expect that many of them would like to go back to the good old days."

"What about this tunnel thing in the volcano though, doesn't that sound a little scary to you?" Georgia asked.

"Come on!" Julie exclaimed. "When will ever get another chance to do that?"

"Yeah," Jason added, the excitement rising within him. "I've never seen that before, think about it, we'd be in the inside of the thing, how cool is that?"

"What do you think about all this, Mr. Newton?"

Newton was not answering; instead he was studying the passing windows. Richard followed his gaze. "Yeah," he said in a low voice. "I see him too." To the rest he added loudly, "Well, I think it will be a great adventure, something to write home about, tell your grandchildren, that sort of thing."

Elijah picked up on what was going on and added his voice, "Definitely not something you'd be able to do on my island, I can tell you that."

The group picked up the pace a bit and were soon at the hotel.

The lobby had taken on a deserted look. There were a few stragglers coming in from a day's sailing or some other activity that kept them out longer than the normal times. These were usually those without children to keep track of. The younger set would change and head off to the bar, the older ones to the restaurants for a quiet meal. Jason and Julie decided to head off for the usual night spots, Richard and Georgia opted for a quiet bar. Elijah and Newton checked with the desk for messages and found there were none. Leaving a request for an early wakeup call, they headed over to the bank of elevators. The soft chime announced its arrival before the doors opened and they stepped in, punched the floor number and waited for the doors to close. They quietly slid shut, cutting down the ambient noise as they did so, until a hand suddenly thrust itself between them and caused them to open again.

A younger man stepped in, dressed in a western cut suit, with sunglasses and close cropped hair. His skin was olive and he spoke not a word. Newton recognized him as the man whose reflection he had seen in the windows of the stores they had passed on the way back to the hotel. He had thought then that they were being followed; now he was sure of it. He was also sure that he and Elijah were the object of the man's attention. The only reason he could think of that would lead to such an occurrence was his previous meeting with the Iranian scientist. The mysterious passenger had not picked a floor, and the only one lighted was the one Elijah and Newton were on. Elijah had picked up on the situation when they were walking back from the restaurant, but Newton could not be sure that he had knew what was going on. Turning to his friend, his eyes questioned if Elijah knew, the answer was instantly yes.

When the elevator slid to a halt, Newton was already on the balls of his feet, ready to move. Unsure of what lay beyond the door, he had taken a position against the rear of the car, as had Elijah. The doors slid open revealing an empty hallway. Their unwelcome companion slipped out without a word, turned to the right and walked straight to the Iranian scientist's room. A swipe of the key card he carried opened the door and he disappeared inside. Newton looked questioningly at Elijah who shrugged his shoulders in reply. With a glance at the now closed door, they opened the door to their room.

"So what do you make of that?" Newton asked.
"He was definitely following us, I saw his reflection in the glass, but I wonder what for?"
"The only thing I can think of is that it must be related to Dr. Zagrib talking to us."
"Well, there is one thing else it could be."
"Really, and what would that be?"
"The G-man from the plane."
"Right, I suppose he could figure into this, but I'm not sure how at this point."
"Tomorrow may give us a better look at things, if it has to do with the Iranian scientists, you can be sure he will be around there somehow."
Newton nodded in agreement and sat down to consider the next day's trip. The tourist brochures he found in the lobby mentioned the railway system. The regular trip featured a quick trip underground where you could see the actual channels the lava flowed up. Also included was a

look at a fissure that had developed during the last eruption. A large chuck of the mountain had moved away from the main body, and sat poised to slide into the ocean. Intrigued, Newton told Elijah he was going down to the lobby to learn what he could about the volcano.

"What more information would they have?" Elijah asked.

"I'm hoping that some of the conference material will be lying around, there is always some information floating around at these things. People drop papers, leave them behind, or there are some extra for folks who didn't make it."

"Well, have fun, I'm going to spend the evening here and turn in early."

Newton headed off down to the lobby, still wondering who the man was who shadowed them from the restaurant. The elevator opened and he headed over to the front desk.

"Good evening, sir, how may I help you?" The clerk asked.

"Good evening," replied Newton. "I was wondering of you had any extra papers about that." Newton pointed to a poster showing the volcano.

"Well, we have these," said the young man handing over copies of the same brochures Newton had already seen.

"Actually, I was looking for something a little more technical in nature."

"Oh," said the clerk, reaching under the desk and producing a large envelope. "They told me you had canceled, I'm glad you made it after all. Here are the conference materials and schedules."

The envelope bore the name "Patrick N. Schweering Bsc, Wood's Hole, U.S.A." On the top left of the envelope was the same conference symbol that the poster sported.

"I'm not really with the conference." Newton started to say, but when he looked up the clerk had moved down to the other end of the large desk to attend to another guest.

Well, thought Newton, gift horses and all that. He took the package and headed off in the direction of the coffee shop. He found it just off the main restaurant, with a patio open to the beach. The sun had set with the suddenness that is a hallmark of the tropics. One moment it is there, the next it seems, it is gone. Newton knew the scientific reason for it of course, that since the horizon is most likely the sea itself, there is nothing to reflect the light around and give a time of twilight. Still, it didn't dampen the beauty of it all.

A waiter came up to the table and Newton ordered a pot of tea, which he much preferred to coffee at this time of night. After it arrived, he set it to the side and opened the package of conference materials. There was a badge, with Mr. Schweering's name on it, a schedule, and a wealth of background information. A small packet of passes and tickets fell out. Every conference had its compliment of prizes and giveaways. This one was no different. Restaurant discounts led the way, along with coupons for a free paragliding flight, some scuba lessons, and a visit to a local winery. Newton slipped all these into his pocket, mainly to clear room for him to lay out the rest of the papers.

The first day of the conference was given over to study the number of active, and likely to be active, volcanoes in the world. Newton was happy to see that Cumbre Vieja was not amongst them.

"Hello again, Detective, I see you are the one with the papers tonight." Turning around, Newton saw the pleasant figure of Major O'Conner. He rose in his seat and shook her hand. "How nice to see you again Miss O'Conner, please join me."

"Oh, I don't want to disturb you, you are obviously busy with something, I just wanted to say hello." She was dressed in civilian clothes suitable for the climate. A light colored blouse and skirt combo with sensible shoes. Around her neck she wore a sweater with the arms tied in front. She looked just like any of the dozens of tourists out at this time of night.

"Please, take a seat, I'd be grateful for the company, is your hard working companion with you?" Newton said, looking around the room.

"Actually no, he is off doing other things, trying to arrange a flight and all that. This has been a strange few days."

"It sure has been more excitement than I care to have," Newton said, holding out the chair while she sat down. "Have your plans been disrupted then?" She asked, "Will you be able to make your conference?"

"Still uncertain about that," he said taking a seat, "the only thing I'm sure of is that I will be here a couple of days yet. Still, if one was to be stranded, there are far worse places I can think of, and far worse company."

She laughed at the suggestion; it was a laugh not unlike one he had heard before, not too long ago, and the memory still hurt. A look of pain washed over his face and she couldn't help but notice it.

Now what, she thought, do I leave or stay? "Are those papers helpful?" she asked, not wanting to choose the former. Newton had been dividing the pile into smaller groups, picking up one and grateful for the change in subject, he passed it over to her. It was entitled "Cumbre Vieja – Danger past and present."

"What do you know about volcanoes?" he asked.

"They tend to go boom, and spit out nasty molten rocks and other things harmful to the local flora and fauna. Still, many civilizations depended upon them for their survival. In some cases, such as

Vesuvius, they actually fertilized the fields with their ash. This allowed agriculture to flourish."

"I hadn't thought of that aspect of it," mused Newton. "But, yes you're absolutely correct, a symbiotic relationship exists, uneasy as it may be."

Carol scanned the paper in front her. "It doesn't appear as if this volcano is getting ready to erupt though."

"I hope not, I will be exploring the inside of the beast tomorrow."

"Really?" she asked, looking up at him. "How on earth are you going to be doing that?"

"Easy," Newton replied, "I'm going to take the train."

Carol laughed again, and this time the look on Newton's face was one of enjoyment. I wonder what that's all about, she thought, must be some history there. Strange thing is, why am I even interested? The Marine Corps, as any large group, is full of folks with history of some sort or another. I've not been interested in getting into that aspect of a relationship for a very long time, why now? Why him?

"Somewhere in this pile is...ah, here." Newton brought forth a separate sheet of paper with a map on it. "Apparently," he began placing the sheet between them, "there is a railway of sorts built right into the volcano." Carol moved her chair next to his and leaned forward over the map. She became deeply aware of his scent. No "Old Spice" or other fancy odors here, just man. Newton appeared to be studying the map, but inside he was both drawn to her, and afraid of the memories that came flooding back. Emotions swirled inside like the breeze from the nearby gardens. A mix of desire and caution, flowers and perfume bubbled up through his consciousness. If he had been in a group he would have focused on someone, or something else.

"Do they sell tickets for this train?" Carol was asking.

"Sorry," said Newton. "I was somewhere else, what were you saying?"

"I was asking if it was possible to get a ticket on the train, it seems like it would be an interesting trip."

"As a matter of fact," said Newton, "it just may be, let me look." He pulled the package of coupons from his pocket and shuffled through them. "Here we go," he said holding up a blue plastic conference tag that read "Delegate." Passing it over to Carol, he said. "There, now you will look like you belong."

"Is that legal?" Carol asked.

"Trust me," Newton said, "I was a cop."

"Right, like I haven't heard something like that before," Carol laughed.

"Here's the thing, we have been invited to accompany the conference tour, which apparently, will be much more interesting than the regular tourist trip. I'm told the railway has been expanded from what the pictures in the brochures portray. Normally, I prefer not to go into confined spaces if possible, but in this case it looks like a real opportunity to do something different."

"Now how on earth did you get invited to do all that? We've only been here a day or so."

"I happened to meet one of the scientists from the delegation from Iran, a friendly fellow, and he extended the invitation on behalf of his group. Apparently it's the Iranians who are hosting the conference this year." Carol's interest piqued at the mention of the group's nationality.

"That means something to you, that it came from the Iranians." Newton said.

"I'm surprised they did it, the Iranians are not exactly cozy with the Western nations at the moment."

"Dr. Zagrib appears to be from the old school," Newton said, "Educated in Britain and on the face of it, still retains a network of contacts with his peers in the West."

"So he is the contact you spoke of?"

"Yes."

"Interesting, very interesting, but yes I'd be delighted to go, umm, just one thing, are there any other Americans in the group?"

"Actually there are four, two flight attendants and two New York cops."

"I'll bet I can guess who the flight crew are!" Carol said. "I'm surprised they haven't been shipped home yet."

"The plane has more or less rendered the runway unusable for the next few days, or so I understand. In fact the only things I've seen in air recently are those things."

Newton indicated a Soviet made helicopter now beating its way over the hotel at a low level; its collision lights blinking and the sound of its rotors drowning out conversation. Everyone in the café watched as it made its way to a set of ship's running lights located on the horizon.

Everyone but one, that is.

Unseen by Newton and Carol, Salim Pashar had slipped into a seat across the room. His attention was not on the helicopter, he already knew its destination, and its purpose. His attention was on the Canadian detective. Twice now this evening he had tried to get close to him, and twice failed. Now he was sitting with an American woman, and from what he had heard, they were going to be in the volcano tour group tomorrow. Somehow he had to act before that occurred, but time was running out. Salim realized the chances of success with his original plan were now very slim. Fortunately, he had listened to his masters when they stressed the importance of having a backup plan.

In Tehran, a clock was ticking loudly, very loudly indeed.

CHAPTER TWENTY TWO

North West of La Palma - Drill Ship "Great Wall"

The Mi-8T helicopter thundered overhead. Its broad blades beating the air, causing a downdraft of warm moist air over the rear of the ship as it descended onto the helipad. On the bridge, the captain of the vessel, Ho Mung Chow, paced silently by the large windows. The deck was awash with light. In the very center of the ship, was a large steel mast, its lattice work lit like a Christmas tree, this central feature was the reason this ship, and its sisters, were built. A week ago, the deck would have rung to the noise of the drilling crew, machinery, and the clanging of pipe as sections were added to the thousands of feet already in the hole. But this night, only the noise of the chopper, now dying away, disturbed the gentle hum of a ship at rest. Ho watched as a tall bearded figure, bent over to avoid the arc of the blades, made its way off the landing platform. The figure straightened and adjusted a package under one arm. As the man was directed to the bridge by the first mate, Ho studied his movements. Military, he thought to himself, recognizable anywhere, from any country. The papers locked in the safe in his cabin had not mentioned a military man, only a scientist. He wondered briefly if he should alert his superiors in Beijing. No need of that really, if there was any warning to be done his political officer WoSun Koo would handle it. Koo was the real master of the ship, at least in terms of everything but operating the vessel. The cabin occupied by the political officer was slightly larger than that of the captain, a subtle reminder to the crew of just where the real power lay.

Ho sipped his tea and waited. The visitor bent his head as he entered the drilling control center of the ship. He handed over the package to Koo, who was waiting there. Koo bowed, "Welcome to the 'Great Wall,' Dr. Al-Maquir."

"Thank you. May I assume you have been briefed by your government?"

"That is correct."

"Then let us proceed without delay, the sooner we can wrap up this project, the sooner the 'Great Wall' and it sister ships can begin to be of service to China."

"I will let the captain know," Koo said picking up the phone, "so that he can issue the proper orders."

"Of course."

The phone rang on the bridge, and was answered by one of the crew. Chow accepted the receiver and began to speak. Putting down his tea, he made his way to the drilling center, accompanied by the tool pusher, the man in charge of actually running the huge drilling platform. Reaching the center, the captain shook hands with the Iranian and accepted the package from him.

It was a small cylinder, only a meter long, and small enough to fit into the bore hole. Three other identical cylinders had already been delivered to the Great Wall's sister ships. The tool pusher, who had already been in contact with his compatriots on the other vessels, had worked out with them the procedure for inserting the package into the pipe. On the drill head, a large fixture controlled the flow of the drilling mud. This was a specially formulated mixture of mud, water and other chemicals that served as the cooling fluid for the drill head. Forced down the hole by massive pumps, it circulated around the drill mechanism and returned to the surface carrying the bits of rock that had been chewed through. Next it entered a filtering screen where it was cleaned and the bits of rock analyzed to determine if any hydrocarbons were present. The cleaned fluid was returned to a large vat and re-circulated as required. The pumping pressure was adjusted to keep any gas or oil under control should a pocket be struck by the drill bit.

Closing a valve on the well head, the cylinder was placed into a section of pipe, and then the valves were opened and the pumps turned on. A large clock on the wall was started, it had been calculated that it would take up to three hours to reach the bottom of the hole. While this was in progress, another package was being unloaded from the helicopter. This consisted of a large buoy, and a small electronics package sealed within it. Its purpose, Dr. Al-Maquir was saying, "was to communicate with the sensor package in the cylinder." Now that the operation was underway, the Iranian "scientist" retuned to the helicopter after leaving a couple of small gifts with the captain and political officer. Once airborne a coded signal was sent to the Iranian Consulate in La Palma. There, in the signals room, a newly installed computer depicted the position of the cylinder, and its brothers, on a graph.

In Tehran the relayed signal was received and noted. An acknowledgement was in turn sent back. The chief signals officer on duty personally hand carried the message to the office of the Chief of the Iranian Armed Forces. A few minutes later, a number of unmarked vehicles left the headquarters' compound and headed along preplanned routes. Quietly and without fuss, the commanders of the Air Force, Navy, and Ground Forces and their families started out on their annual vacations. The commander of the Iranian Special Forces did not. For one thing, he had no family. For another, he had never taken a vacation. Thirdly, he had things to attend to, and together with his second in command, he set out to do them. A small jet left one of the unmarked desert airfields with them aboard, and headed west. A few minutes later a larger transport followed. Their ultimate destination was the Canary Islands.

CHAPTER TWENTY THREE

Hotel La Palma

The breakfast menu was pure tourist. Pancakes, bacon and eggs, bowls of cereal, and other western choices jostled for space on the waiter's trays with yogurt, fruit, and dry toast. Newton and Elijah sat drinking coffee and watching the early morning crowd on the beaches. Already the first of the fishing charters had left the marina, heading out to the lure of marlin and sailfish. Dive boats would soon follow, making their way to the reefs and shallow waters teeming with brightly colored fish and plant life. The young folks with their jet boats and scooters would follow on. Later the older crowd would head for the newly opened bars and pools as the tourist day swung into full gear. Around the restaurant families and adults mingled with young couples and singles at the tables, each of them trying to get this portion of the day out of the way so they could continue on to new things. Jason and Richard, accompanied by Georgia and Julie, made their way past the harried waiters and waitresses to join Newton and Elijah. Jason was again carrying his electronic box. Newton thought for a moment that Jason regarded the device much the same as that comic book character who was inseparable from his blanket. As soon as they sat down, Richard noted the extra empty chair by Newton's side. Raising his eyebrows in a quizzical look at Newton, he nodded to it.

"We have another intrepid spelunker accompanying us today," Newton began. "And here she comes." Major Carol O'Conner, clad in jeans and shirt, was headed down the aisle towards them.

"Good Morning," Carol said. "Looks like a wonderful day"

"I'm not sure you remember everyone from the plane," Newton said, as he made the introductions.

"So," Richard said, "what led you to join us moles for the day? Are you a volcanologist too?"

"No, merely a humble public servant, but I have an interest in unusual things, and you must admit it is not every day that one gets a chance to crawl around the inside of a volcano."

"Carol is a Marine major," Newton said.

"On vacation then?" Jason asked.

"Work actually; I was on my way to Europe when I wound up here. Mr. Newton asked me along for today, I hope I'm not intruding."

"Not at all!" Richard said emphatically. "We welcome all manner of travelers to our group."

"Speaking of traveling," Elijah added, "we are to meet our hosts in an hour out front, so perhaps we best order."

Richard signaled the waiter that they were ready, and an hour later the group was standing in front of the hotel. The jovial figure of Dr.

Zagrib alighted from a van as it pulled up in front. "Welcome!" the scientist said to Carol when she was introduced. "I hope you will enjoy the tour." A few minutes later the van was on its way to the site of the volcano. Along the way, the group listened to the scientists talk about the mountains they studied.

Each had their favorite, for Dr. Zagrib it was Mt. St. Helens, the recent activity there promised new opportunities for research in his field. Never before had there been proof that a landslide could precede the eruption, but the remarkable film shot at the moment of eruption provided new insight. For others the continuing eruptions of Vesuvius or Mt. Etna was the lure. The group of Iranians chattered on in a mixture of Farsi and English. Newton found the easy talk to be an affirmation that underneath the mantle of one's upbringing, people were pretty much the same.

"How many are there in the tour group," he asked during a rare lull in the conversation. "Other than yourselves, there are a dozen or so volcanologists from other countries, some will not be there of course, depending on their schedules. Also there will be the maintenance folks to ensure the railway keeps running. We don't want to have to walk back!"

"Will we be going very deep?" Georgia asked.

"Actually no, the railway drops only a few hundred feet in depth, but the length is two kilometers, too long a distance for this old man to walk comfortably."

"And this must be it," Jason said, pointing out the window at the two kilometer high mountain looming before them. "I didn't realize it was so big."

"Will we be climbing to the top then?" Julie asked.

"No, the railway begins about a quarter of the way up, and more or less travels down and to the north from there." The road headed up the side of the volcano, ending at a chain link fence and freshly painted visitor centre. Two other vans had already arrived and joined a number of service trucks and earth moving equipment parked at the front. As he got out of the van, Newton noted the newly built helicopter pad, and what appeared to be a small mountain of rock and debris at the end of a set of tracks.

"Ah yes," Dr. Zagrib answered the unspoken question. "That is from the new extension. It may look like a pile of waste to most people, but the composition of the rock is quite interesting. In fact, we have learned a great deal about the makeup of the whole mountain from the gasses that were trapped within that material at the time of the last eruption."

"Really, what did that tell you?"

"Well for one thing," the scientist continued as he held open the door to the visitor centre for them to pass through, "it is unusually dense; we were expecting a much lighter form of rock."

"Such as pumice?"

"You know your rocks, Mr. Newton, yes quite right, along with the igneous rocks that one normally gets at a volcano site, we were expecting the rock that floats—pumice. Strangely enough, what we saw was most prevalent was a much denser form of lava. Such are the mysteries of volcanology"

Newton was certainly no engineer, but it seemed to him the mountain of waste rock represented a larger effort at expanding the railway than could be accounted for by a simple extension. He kept these thoughts to himself. The group entered a large room in the building where the volcanologists were gathered. Large tables had been set up and on them a myriad of measuring instruments were arrayed. Dr. Zagrib took his place at the head of the group.

"Good Morning," he began. "Welcome to our little tour. As you can see, we have set up some of the most advanced seismologic equipment available in the world for you to examine, and we are pleased to announce that we will have the opportunity to observe some of it being installed underground. Now, you will notice that our group includes both delegates to the conference and some honoured guests. On that wall over there are a number of coveralls. To keep the respective groups together, we ask that the delegates wear the blue coloured overalls and helmets, the workers have yellow coveralls and helmets, and our guests will be wearing red." The room erupted in quiet confusion as the separate groups milled around selecting their attire and finding the correct sizes. Voices of many countries mixed in a cacophony more suited to a United Nations discussion than a trip inside a volcano. In due course, and with an admirable level of politeness, everyone sorted things out to their satisfaction. The only anomaly Newton noticed was that Carol had been assigned a set of blue coveralls when she showed the blue colored delegate's card Newton had given her rather than the red ones that the rest of the group got.

"You look marvelous, absolutely marvelous," Newton grinned while imitating the voice of Billy Crystal.

Carol pirouetted and batted her eyes "Why, thank you, gallant sir, but I seem to have got a different colour, and I don't know about the fashion style of these boots."

"Ah, yes the ubiquitous rubber boots, all the better to keep your feet dry."

"And these hard hats don't have lights on them, what if we get separated?"

"No matter, just stick close and we'll try to prevent you from getting lost."

Dr. Zagrib had disappeared down the hall, busy setting up for the arrival of the compact railway cars that would take them underground. Behind him, the groups mingled freely with each other. Several of the delegates sat down at the tables and examined the instruments laid out before them. Newton joined Jason and Elijah at the front of the group and listened to an explanation of each instrument and its purpose. "Once a techie, always a techie," Newton said to Elijah, indicating Jason.

"I'm sure they are helpful in this field," Elijah said. "In our history we relied on the actions and warnings of the animal spirits around us to warn of trouble."

"Unfortunately, these days, we seemed to have lost that ability, or rather we didn't take the time to learn it, more's the pity," Newton added in agreement.

Jason, for his part, was totally absorbed in learning how laser distance measuring equipment had been mounted on other active volcanoes in order to measure the swelling in their lava domes that often preceded an eruption. Live readouts of that information were then beamed around the world via the Internet to various international centers. On the table at that moment, he could see the readouts from Mt. St Helens and Mt. Etna on a split screen. Another screen showed measurements from inside Cumbre Vieja.

"How are those signals collected?" Jason asked.

"Same as the others, via the Internet, the density of the rock precludes radio communication, so they installed telephone lines and remote data collection points all along the railway, except for the tunnel we are going to visit. There we have mounted a number of high powered wireless modem relays. One of the sessions at the conference will feature live readings from special equipment we are still getting into place. The amount of data could be carried on copper wire of course, but this way we can have a larger number of wireless sensors. They are, of course, much easier to install than hardwired devices. The amount of information requires ADSL level equipment, but on the upside of that, is it is already Internet ready when we see it," explained one of the delegates. "Of course, with the railway activity today, the seismographs have all been turned off; they are so sensitive that they would be swamped by the vibrations of the railcars moving around."

"What about those ones?" Jason asked, indicating a set of reading labeled "La Palma" and showing some ongoing activity.

"Ah, those are from the fissure."

"Fissure?"

"Oh, my yes," the delegate continued, "this volcano has some unusual properties." The eruption in the last century opened up a north-south crack, and the general feeling is that the next eruption will cause the mountain to literally split in half and pretty much wipe out the east coasts of the Americas."

"How so?" Jason asked. "We are thousands of miles away and the blast would be pretty much diminished by the time it got there."

"Not the blast, old boy, the tsunami."

"Tsunami?"

"Of course, look at it this way; you sit at one end of a bathtub, with your nose just above the water. Something very big falls into the other end, that displaces the water and creates a wave that travels to your end of the bathtub and runs up your nose."

"How big a wave?"

"At this end, 900 meters, at the other end 25 meters, but there won't be just one, there will be a series of them, probably a dozen or more."

"Wow," said Julie, joining in the conversation, "but 25 meters doesn't seem high enough to wipe out the east coast."

"Ah, but that is just the height as it travels, when the wave hits the continental shelf the sea bed rises, and the wave with it. Some scientists believe it will be several hundred feet high when it sweeps through New York and Boston, and only slightly less than that for South America."

"How much rock would have to fall to cause that?" Jason asked.

"Worse case, about 500 square kilometers are available if you will, after all, this volcano is two kilometers high, but the island itself sits another 4000 feet or so above the seabed, and the fissure runs for at least 15 kilometers north-south."

"Yikes, that is scary," Julie said in awe, and looked at the instruments with a new fear.

"Luckily for us, this event, while inevitable, is far into the future. The volcano shows absolutely no signs of even beginning an eruption, and even if it did, it would take a specific type of explosive release to cause such an occurrence."

"Has this happened before then?"

"Oh yes, many times, last time about 4000 years ago. Why, a study of your own Hawaiian islands reveals a similar event in times past, and these Canary Islands have a wealth of evidence of the same thing."

Newton, who had been listening on the edge of the conversation, asked, "Wasn't there something like that in Alaska, in the sixties?"

"Quite right, quite right. There was, and even more incredibly, there was a witness to the event. A fishing trawler was carried completely over the top of a peninsula by a wave of 200 plus feet. The origin of that wave was a landslide in a confined bay, resulting in a scouring to the bedrock of the sides of the bay for a distance up to 140 feet."

"Thank you for the information," Newton said. "Is this your field of study?"

"No, not really, just a sideline, and excuse me, I've been remiss, my name is Charles David Hawthorne, Royal Academy of Science, London."

"Alfred Newton."

"Pleased to meet you, I'm sure." The rest of the group introduced themselves and they continued to chat until Dr. Zagrib reappeared.

"Ladies and gentlemen, if I may have your attention, the cars have arrived, please make your way to the doorway to my left and take a seat."

The crowd slowly shuffled their way through the doorway and found themselves in a long hallway. The chatting and conversations seemed to increase in volume as they selected a seat on the open rail cars. Barely wide enough for two people, the cars were less than ten feet long with narrow gauge wheels.

"These look like something one would find in an old Hollywood western movie," Jason said, swinging onto a narrow seat with Julie beside him. Richard, on the seat in front of the car, turned to Georgia and with his best John Wayne impersonation said to her, "Well, little missy, looks like we a'headin' into this here dark hole, now don't you be a'scared of nothing, I'm here to take care of you."

Newton smiled and shook his head; men sometimes turn into boys around women. Speaking of which, he thought to himself, I wonder how Carol views me. For that matter, how do I view her? The wounds on his soul still fresh from the events of his last case, he wanted to keep his distance and at the same time get closer to the Marine major now seated on his right. Sometimes he envied Elijah, who seemed to get through life unencumbered with relationship issues. Not that the Haida elder didn't have his admirers, Newton had seen that in abundance when he was up in the Charlottes.

Elijah was just taking a seat in the last row of the car, still chatting with Charles Hawthorne, who was a for real English lord, as Elijah was just learning. The amiable Englishman slipped into the seat beside Elijah just ahead of one of the other scientists.

Within a few moments the little train jolted to a start and the conversation level abated. All eyes seemed to be focused on the tunnel walls, now slipping by at little more than a fast walking pace. The cars swayed side to side like a carnival ride. Newton was keenly aware that in front of him Richard and Georgia were talking in low voices to each other, as were Jason and Julie behind him. Carol had said little since the ride began, and hardly looked his way. Well, he could hardly blame her Newton thought; I haven't been much fun to be with. I'm sure she gets much more attention from anyone else she would be with. Curiously the thought of that brought out some twinges of jealousy.

Anymore of this introspection and I'll likely wind up a basket case, Newton mused, better if I just concentrate on today, and not worry so much about what might have been.

"I said I think the tunnel is getting bigger."

"Pardon? I'm sorry my mind was drifting away there," Newton replied.

"The tunnel," Carol continued, "is it just me or is it getting bigger?"

Newton studied the walls, yes there was no doubt that they were further from the walls than before, and also, what was it—the lighting—the lighting was more modern in nature and brighter.

"You're right, we appear to be in the newer section already, funny I thought the old tunnel would be longer."

"Also we have been going down gradually for a while now," Carol remarked. "Do you remember how deep this goes?"

"Well, from where we started, I'd guess maybe a few hundred meters, but it's been gradually getting steeper."

The walls showed fresh work marks, and in some places, water seeped down them into ditches carved into the edge of the rail bed. Every so often these ditches ended in a catch basin where the water would collect and be pumped into a network of pipes that led up to the surface. Snatches of conversation flowed back to them as the train slowed for corners. The volcanologists could be seen pointing at this rock feature or that outcropping.

"Most unusual."

"Look at that piece."

"What do make of that, Boris?"

So it went, as the train rocked its way slowly downward, the air grew colder, then warmer and more humid. Occasionally Newton caught a glimpse of an air shaft carved into the roof of the tunnel. The roof itself grew and diminished in height as they passed underneath it. Obviously some areas were easier to excavate than others. Rounding a bend the train began to slow and continued at a reduced pace until it rocked to a final stop in a large and well lit cavern.

"End of the line," announced Richard as he slid out of the car and offered his arm to Georgia. A number of tunnels, each with its own set of tracks, fanned out from the central room. Their height was more than enough for some to walk along without bending over, and wide enough for two people to proceed side by side. Each tunnel had a large sign board posted beside its entrance. The rate of dripping and seepage from water had increased markedly since leaving the surface.

"Gather around here, please." Dr. Zagrib was standing in front of a large painted board that had been set up on one wall. "Now, you will note the sign boards posted by the auxiliary tunnels, each one has a number, and on this board here," he said tapping the large board to his side, "is a map of the tunnels and the particular rock formations they reveal. Please pick one that is of particular interest to you and gather in front of it. The tunnels are not long, and you will find they are easy to walk in. They are quite safe, but don't touch any of the wiring you come across. Now we will meet back here say, one hour, which should be sufficient."

The groups quickly assembled and headed down the tunnels that interested them, leaving Newton and his group feeling quite alone and out of place.

"Now then, my friends, are you ready?" Dr. Zagrib, smiling and rubbing his hands together, approached them. "I have saved the best for you I think." He led them over to a tunnel that did not have a sign posted on it. A small electric train with two cars sat on the tracks there. Several more were on a section of track behind it but unattached. "We are going to see one of the original lava pipes from centuries ago. It leads into a fantastic cavern, which in time gone by served as a collection chamber for the molten rock before gas pressure forced it up into the dome. The depth of the pipe is calculated to be over three kilometers, one of the deepest ever uncovered. Other than a few scientists like myself, you will be amongst the first to ever see it."

"Oh, I say," came a voice from the rear, "I'd dearly like to see that."

"By all means, Lord Hawthorne, by all means, please come along. It would be my pleasure to have you accompany us."

"Thank you ever so much, old boy. That is an amazing find, how did you come across it?"

"Pure chance, something you in the west would call serendipity I believe. Please everyone, let's get aboard," Dr. Zagrib said. "It's some distance away and we only have one hour."

The group quickly found seats on the little train and prepared to leave. Dr. Zagrib took a position at the front car and paused for one last look before signaling the driver to proceed. What he saw did not please him. One more passenger had arrived, unbidden, and his presence caused the scientist's eyes to narrow.

"I will also be coming, Dr. Zagrib," Salim Pashar announced as he took a seat. "I'm sure you will find that satisfactory." Without responding, Dr. Zagrib nodded to the driver and with a jolt the little train started down the tracks.

At the sound of Pashar's voice, Newton and Elijah both looked around. There was no doubt that this was the man both had seen shadowing them the previous night. Salim sat in the last row of the second car, and stared straight ahead, giving no sign he had recognized either of them. The train passed down the tunnel, passing a couple of donkey engines on a siding, and another smaller room carved out of the rock. Newton caught a flash of faces as they turned towards the noise the train made as it passed. A group of workers seemed busy with a number of large wooden boxes.

Aram Mohammed Al Bazir hardly noticed the passage of the train. His attention was almost entirely on the orders he had received that morning. Aram did look up long enough to recognize the last man on the train. He studied the papers in his hands again. The orders seemed simple enough; collect a number of boxes from a hangar which housed the helicopter that had brought him here from Tenerife. He found a crew and truck waiting for him there, already loaded. The orders specified their destination, which he had given the driver, and a second more ominous requirement. Aram was feeling uneasy, these sort of orders were the type one gave to a trusted member of the ruling class, not a newly promoted warden. His intuition, which had kept him alive all these years, told him there was much more to this than what appeared on the surface. Like the volcano they were now within, the real secrets lay out of view. For the moment at least, he stood back from the workers and let his mind retrace the events that had brought him to this moment in time. The workers in front of him went through their tasks in a well ordered way. He realized that he was the only person in the room with a piece of paper in his hand. The orders he received specified that the boxes held specialized mining equipment required for the conference. He looked again at the workers; the precision and purpose of their movements reminded him of a well drilled squad.

Why was it that none of them needed to consult a manual or booklet? Surely this equipment would be unfamiliar to them. Conferences such as this were held on every four or five years and never in the same country consecutively. How was it then, these ordinary workers could set up what must be very complicated instruments so quickly and with no wasted motions? Aram, looked harder at the equipment as it was unpacked and set up on tables. All of it looked used, as he would have expected it to be. Clad in grey chipped paint, it looked just like equipment he had seen many times over, equipment found in the military communications room at the prison. All right, he thought, communications gear would be part of any package he supposed. But the rest of the boxes should stand out as being something new, or at least out of place. Civilian equipment for a project such as this would have little wear except on the operating controls. Such equipment or at least scientific instruments would tend to be mounted and left in place for long periods of time. The wear patterns on these boxes were different. The mounting brackets were bright and scratched, showing where they had been put up and taken down many times. The answer then, was that this was not civilian equipment at all. It followed that these were not civilian workers either. Aram forced himself to relax and outwardly he displayed the harried bureaucratic façade that had served him well over the years. Occasionally one or another of the "workers" studied Aram from across the room. They saw nothing there other than what Aram wanted them to see, just another civilian wrapped up in paperwork and wanting to be elsewhere. "Everything is here and complete." Aram looked around to find a tall man addressing him.

"Indeed?"

"Yes, I will sign for them now, perhaps you would find it more comfortable if you took the train back to the conference center. These tunnels are cold and still somewhat dangerous, and frankly we will be able to do our job faster if we do not have to watch out for your safety." Aram stared back, the man in front of him was obviously in command, and used to the role. "Very well, I will return to the center and check on the progress for the conference tonight." The tall man simply nodded and turned back to his squad. Aram took a seat on the work train and headed back to the surface.

Dr. Zagrib signaled the driver to slow and stop by the second of three platforms in the cavern. A few moments before, the train had rocked and jostled its way from the tunnels into an open area about the size of a football field. With ceilings over 100 feet high in places, and lit by large halogen lights, it was a welcome sight for Newton. Never very comfortable in small confined places, he unconsciously began to breathe easier as soon as they left the tunnels behind. Elijah noted the look of relief on his friend's face, but said nothing. Although small spaces did not bother the elder, he too had his demons. One of those was the feeling of being out of control of his environment, such as he felt when forced to ride in the too small cars of the train. Give him a canoe or boat any day. For his own reasons he was also happy to see the end of the train ride. The group unwound themselves from the cars and stepped onto the platform. Jason slung his electronic box of tricks over his shoulder by its strap and took Julie's hand. Together with Richard and Georgia they stared at the jagged surface that made up the ceiling of the cavern.

"I had expected to see those things that hang down and drip," Georgia said.

"You're talking about stalactites," Dr. Zagrib said.

"They are the ones that drip down?" Georgia asked.

"Yes, and stalagmites grow up from the ground, but not here. Both are the results of water dripping through the ground, dissolving minerals, and then as they drip, evaporating and leaving the minerals behind. Here of course, the cavern is sealed by the ancient lava flows, and no water penetrates from above through the mineral layers. So, none of those cone shaped objects get a chance to form."

"How do you remember which is which?"

"Simple, the 'c' in stalactites means they come from the ceiling, the 'g' in the stalagmites means they grown from the ground up," he beamed.

"Cute," Georgia responded, "that's an easy way to remember."

"I'm getting older," the scientist joked, "and I need all the help I can get."

"But if no water seeps from above, then why is the floor wet and why are there puddles everywhere?"

"Rain from the tunnel entrance eventually finds its way in, and since it cannot evaporate at a large rate, it eventually builds up into puddles. Also there are a number of small air vents, that is, openings to the surface, which let water in. But don't worry; I'm sure they have installed pumps."

The lights created areas of shadow that were impenetrable to anyone on the platform, and the effect was to make the cavern seem endless. After a few moments for everyone to stretch and get accustomed to the light level, Dr. Zagrib called them to the center of the platform. The train driver had taken a seat on the rear of the platform where a small desk and a few chairs were. On the desk was an ordinary telephone, the wires to which snaked up the wall and disappeared into a metal conduit that had been affixed to the tunnel wall. "If I can have your attention, please," Dr. Zagrib began, "I have a few words of warning. As far as I know the extent of this cavern has not yet been fully explored, and like all caverns of this nature, the floor is neither flat nor without holes. So we have marked the safe areas of travel with these yellow nylon ropes," indicating a number of posts and roped off areas. "Please ensure that you keep within them. Now a few facts you may be interested in, the cavern has a number of natural vents that keep it ventilated, and depending where you are, you may feel a slight breeze. The ceiling is fairly stable for a cavern of this size, but of course nothing is guaranteed and occasionally a piece succumbs to gravity and falls, so keep your hard hats on. In a few moments we will be heading out to view the large vent. To do so, we will be heading along the path marked by those ropes over there," indicating a separate path, and I ask that you all keep together. Now, does anyone have any questions?"

The group, still in awe over the immenseness of the cavern, said nothing. "Good, now Lord Hawthorne, if I may impose upon you to put yourself in the middle of the group, perhaps between us we can answer all the questions that will inevitably come up."

"Oh, my, well yes, I'd be delighted, as much as I am able," the genial Englishman said. "But I'm not sure what help I may be."

The group prepared to move off. Dr. Zagrib took the lead and motioned Georgia and Richard, along with Jason and Julie, to come with him. Newton was about to step off the platform to follow Elijah and Lord Hawthorne, already chatting about something, when he felt a slight tug on his shirt. He turned to find Salim standing behind him pointedly staring out at the cavern. Newton was puzzled for a second, had he felt the tug or not? He started to move off again, and again there was a tug. This time Salim glanced quickly down at the wooden floor of the platform then stepped off it and joined Elijah and Lord Hawthorne. Newton looked down, on the spot where Salim indicated, large deep gashes marred the platform. Newton joined the group and began to wonder both what had caused such deep scarring, and more importantly perhaps, what the meaning was of Salim's actions.

"...and the molten rock would be forced up at enormous pressure from the vent into this chamber," Lord Hawthorne was saying. He winked at Newton. "I'm sure Mr. Newton can say what happens next."

"Boom?" Elijah quipped.

"Not quite," Newton chuckled. "Although that of course was the end result, before that would have been a period of hydraulic action."

"Hydraulic? Like a pump?"

"More like a pop bottle filled with water, take a two liter pop bottle, fill it completely with water and slap your hand over the neck. If there is no air trapped inside, the whole bottom of the bottle will pop and spray water everywhere. Same thing here, only the pop bottle is upside down, the neck of the bottle is the vent, and this cavern is the body. The lava flows up and fills the cavern, the edges cool and seal any leaks, but the lava keeps coming. Because the molten rock cannot be compressed, it exerts huge pressure on the walls and roof forcing it outward."

"Ah, I see, that's why the instruments in the observation center we saw earlier show the dome expanding at Mt. St. Helens."

"Precisely, old boy!" Lord Hawthorne said. "Well done, Mr. Newton, you are a credit to your namesake."

"Will it happen again?"

"Inevitably, I'm sure," Lord Hawthorne continued. "It's both the main building mechanism of these islands, and a sort of safety valve for mother earth. It has been an ongoing process since the earth was formed, and as long as gravity exists, it will continue."

"A shame we can't tap into it for energy," Elijah said, "and reduce the amount of green house gasses, etc."

"Actually, we can," said Lord Hawthorne, "and in many places in the world they already are. Take Iceland, for example, soon they will be exporting energy generated by the geothermal vents in that region of the world."

"A rather long way to run power lines isn't it?"

"True, so they don't do that, in actual fact, they use the electricity they generate to split water into oxygen and hydrogen, and then export those gasses to where they are needed."

"Unfortunately, not all areas of the world that can use the energy are fortunate enough to be located over geothermal vents," Elijah said.

"True, but since everywhere is somewhere on the earth's surface, there is always the potential to drill down and make your own vent."

The group continued on its way, with one eye on the ground to avoid the rocks scattered about the path. Newton bent down and picked up a piece of rock that had a particular sheen which caught his eye.

"What do you make of this?" he asked Lord Hawthorne.

"I'm no expert, you understand," the English volcanologist replied, "but it appears to be common lava remnants, yes, look you can see the striations formed as it cooled."

"Ah, yes," Newton replied. "But what about these marks here?" he said turning the rock over and indicating bright scrapes.

"Machine marks I'd say, probably from some path clearing project or another."

"Except," said Newton, "there is no indication that this path was manmade." Newton turned his attention to the roof of the cavern; he could not see the roof because of the glare of the lights. Now what on earth, he thought, could have required removal of rock from up there? The only thing that came to mind was to remove some dangerous outcropping that might have been in danger of collapse. Newton put the rock in his pocket.

The edge of the vent came into view; ropes marked the edges and the extent to which they could get close. In one area, a platform had been built that jutted out a few feet over the edge. There was only enough room for two people at a time to occupy the platform, and Dr. Zagrib invited them to take turns. Jason and Julie were first up. The group was silent as they made their way out onto the wooden platform, both holding onto the railing as they went. "Helloooo," Jason called, and a few moments later the echo returned. They returned to the edge and Richard and Georgia took their turn. After a few minutes of staring down into the abyss they came back and Newton and Lord Hawthorne went forward. As they started to return to the edge, Newton paused, took the rock he had put in his pocket and tossed it in. It clacked and banged against the walls of the vent, the sound getting fainter as it fell, until it could not be heard anymore, even in the silence.

Lord Hawthorne and Dr. Zagrib spent the most time on the platform. They could be seen pointing at some outcropping of rock or a particular pattern literally set in stone as the ancient lava had cooled. Most of what they said, had the others in the group heard it, would have been of mild interest at best. What was of interest, especially to Newton, was another pattern in the rock. This one, unlike most, was definitely manmade.

"What do you think, Elijah?"

"I would guess some very heavy equipment has been used here, and recently at that."

Both men were squatting down, peering at the surface of a rocky outcropping. The flat dark and smooth surface that typified the lava covered walls had been scrapped away to reveal a shiny underlay.

Newton took a pen from his pocket. Habit dictated he carry one, as he had done for all of his working life, and he pushed the tip into the scratch. "There, it must be three quarters of an inch deep," he said, holding up the pen tip for Elijah to check.

"What is?"

Newton looked around to see Jason and Julie standing behind him.

"We were just wondering about this mark, it must have taken a large piece of equipment to expose the underlying rock."

"Perhaps not," Jason said. "Lava can be quite brittle, and in some cases soft, let me take a look."

Jason bent down and examined the gouge in the lights of the cavern. "Can't really see too good, perhaps we can move that light a little," pointing to a halogen light mounted on a metal stand across the passage from them. Elijah crossed over and gripping the light adjusted the head so it shone in their direction. "Thanks, I think I can see it now."

The change in lighting pattern was instantly noticeable in the cavern. Both Lord Hawthorne and Dr. Zagrib looked up from their conversation, then around at the group gathered around Jason. In a few moments they too had joined it. "I say, what have you discovered young man?" Lord Hawthorne asked.

"Nothing much," Jason said standing up. "Just that it appears that the underlying structure of the cavern seems to be of granite."

"Quite right, quite right," said the Englishman, sounding like a professor whose lecture point had finally been grasped by the class. "But of course it would have to be, wouldn't it?" he continued with a chuckle. "Can you guess why?"

Elijah spoke up, "Strength of course, granite is a very strong rock, and if I remember correctly, it has a certain amount of elasticity."

"Spot on, old man, spot on!" The scientist clapped Elijah on the back. "Well done, I wish you had been one of my students, I would have felt that I had accomplished something."

"I'm sure you did very well in your teaching duties," Dr. Zagrib said. "My colleagues often mention how much they enjoyed your classes."

"Well, I'm glad I could get the ideas across. Now then, Elijah, where did you take your studies?"

"Denver College of Mining," Elijah replied, "mostly by correspondence."

Newton looked at his friend with a smile, "I never knew that, but I think I know why you would take that type of course."

"Why," asked Richard. "Did you have a mining job of some sort?"

"Close," Elijah replied. "Our people carve in argillite, a soft stone that is found in very few places. We mine it, and to do that safely, we need to know how to set up a mine, how to work it, what rock formations are safe, and what are not."

"So then, what makes granite so significant here?" Hawthorne asked.

"Well, remember we were discussing how a dome was formed, and how the hydraulic pressure of the molten rock forced it outward? In order to do that the rock of the dome has to be both strong enough to contain the pressure and elastic enough to stretch."

"Excellent" Lord Hawthorne said, "And correct!"

The group had been joined by Salim, who up to this point had kept pretty much to himself. He had been spending his time in the shadows and in some cases deliberately slipping past the guard ropes and poking about in the half lit areas beyond them. Salim stood behind Newton and said nothing. His dark eyes missed little and although he barely glanced at the gouge in the rock, Newton was sure it occupied a large part of his mind. Thirty years of interrogating suspects had honed Newton's abilities to read body language. The look in Richard's eyes showed he too was aware of something out of the ordinary.

"What's with him?" Richard asked Newton in a low voice, indicating the figure of Salim who had moved off to another part of the cavern and was intently studying the roof.

"Bit of a mystery man, have you noticed him before today?"

"Something about him looks familiar, not his features, just the way he moves." The New York cop thought for a moment. "Yeah, I did, he was following us last night."

"I saw him too; let me know if he speaks to you."

"Will do."

"Well, this has been a most interesting tour, has it not?" Dr. Zagrib was saying. "Now I think we should be getting back to the main body." He consulted his watch. "Yes, I think if we leave now, there should be sufficient time." With that, he turned and headed down the passage back to the platform.

Once again, Newton felt a tug on his shirt as he went to follow, glancing at Salim, he saw him glance quickly down before the Iranian moved off to follow the group. Newton looked in the direction Salim had indicated; there he found a small pool of liquid revealed by the change in lighting. Bending down in a quick motion he dipped a finger into the pool, rubbed it between his fingers and bringing them to his nose confirmed his suspicions before tagging along at the end of the column.

Arriving at the platform, they found the train driver bent over the little engine, its side panels were off and the driver was muttering to himself.

"What is the problem?" Dr. Zagrib said abruptly. "We have to get going."

"Just a problem with the battery Doctor," the driver replied. "I will have it going in a few minutes."

"We can't fall behind schedule. If you can't get it going try one of those other donkey engines."

"Won't do any good," the engineer said. "Their batteries are depleted and their charging cycle won't be completed before tomorrow night. Besides, their batteries are different than these ones."

A look of anger crossed Dr. Zagrib's face, but he said lightheartedly "Well, I'm sure you're doing the best you can." Next he spoke to the gathering group. "Please take a seat in one of the cars; we will be getting underway shortly."

Newton and Richard sat down in one of the cars to wait. Both men started to scan the platform, and both saw the same thing at the same time. When they left the driver had taken a seat by the lone table.

That table held only a phone attached to wires that ran to a pipe clipped to the tunnel walls. The phone had been half in the shadows, now it sat on the front edge of the table. Richard looked at Newton and Newton nodded back, both felt the hair on the back of their neck quiver. It was the ages old sense of something being amiss, honed in prehistoric times, and largely disregarded in modern ones. This same sense had kept both men at the top of their profession and they had learned, as had many before them, to trust it. Newton nodded at Richard and glanced at the tunnel entrance. Richard nodded back and changed his seat to focus his attention mainly there. Newton got up and touched Elijah's sleeve, and together they took a position at the other end of the platform, where they could watch the cavern. Elijah did not know what had caused his friend to take a defensive stance, but he instantly recognized that the situation in the room had changed. He looked at Newton with a question in his eyes, and Newton flicked his gaze over to the table. Elijah studied it for a few moments, then turned and nodded back, he had recognized that the phone had been moved, and put it together with the driver's sudden problems with the train.

Jason and Lord Hawthorne were gathered around the engine with Dr. Zagrib, who was now arguing with the driver. Julie and Georgia and Carol were standing off to the side. Georgia looked around for Richard, and found him watching the tunnel, She caught his eye and he silently motioned her to come over. When she started, he looked over to Julie, for a second Georgia looked confused, then understanding what he meant, tugged on Julie's sleeve and led her over to Richard. Carol saw the interchange between them, and started off towards Newton. Reaching him, she automatically took up a position behind him and Elijah. She was not certain what she should be looking for, but she was certain she should be looking for something. The Marine major had also learned to trust to her intuition, and it was now telling her that things were about to go south, and in a hurry.

CHAPTER TWENTY FOUR

The Cavern

The lights in the cavern flickered and went out at the same time as Newton was looking for Salim. He had disappeared once again into the shadows as the halogen lights ceased. Their white hot elements dying away into shades of red and orange and black. The animated conversation between Dr. Zagrib and the driver faded away with the lights. Newton felt the presence of Elijah and Carol press closer to his back, and then Carol slipped away. Down the platform Georgia or Julie screamed once when the lights quit.

"What the fuck?" Richard's voice carried crystal clear through the cavern.

"Listen, I hear something," Jason whispered loudly.

Why do people always want to whisper in the dark, Newton wondered, maybe Elijah was right, maybe we do it because we don't want to wake the spirits. Or maybe we are just afraid of what we can't see.

From the tunnel came a low noise, the sound of metal wheels on steel rails, and something else. Newton felt it on his cheek, a cool breeze from the tunnel brushed against him. It carried with it the scent of oil, electricity, and human sweat. The breeze increased in strength, rustling his hair, then it stopped and silence returned.

"Everyone,– look down and close your eyes, hands over your ears!" Carol's voice shouted in the silent room. Newton guessed why and he hoped the others did too.

Some did, some didn't.

A huge white flash filled the room and seared through his closed eyelids, accompanied by a deafening bang that reverberated from the cavern roof and walls and crashed through his hands which he held tightly over his ears. Newton felt himself slightly disoriented. He recognized from his emergency response team training the explosion of a "flash bang" grenade; its sole purpose to distract and disorient. "Everyone down," Newton called, wondering if anyone could even hear him.

The cavern lights came on with an optical bang. Shouting in English and Farsi filled the room, Newton was down on his knees, with dust in his nostrils, eyes and ears, and he opened his eyes. Several black suited figures were running into the room. Wearing helmets and carrying AK-47 rifles they headed quickly to the platform and surrounded it.

"Down!" "DOWN!" They shouted. Newton flattened out and felt Elijah do the same. Down the platform, Richard and Jason were already flat out on the ground, Georgia and Julie hugging each other and on their knees. Dr. Zagrib was staring in amazement at the men who had appeared suddenly out of the smoke and noise and confusion. His mouth hung agape and he was making incomprehensible sounds. Lord Hawthorne was on his knees, a dazed blank look on his face, dust and dirt covered him and he was holding his head in his hands. Newton looked up at a figure that came up to him pointing the muzzle of a rifle in his face. Someone behind him roughly grabbed his arms and fastened his hands together with what felt like a nylon strap. Doing the same to Elijah in turn and moving on down the platform, they repeated the process with the others.

Once everyone had been tied up, they were pushed into a group in the middle of the platform. One figure began to count their numbers. He did it twice and consulted a paper he had unfolded from his pocket. Turning on his heel he approached someone standing over by the tunnel entrance. Showing him the paper and gesturing to group he talked rapidly and saluted. The man in charge, as Newton now recognized, nodded his head and returned the offered salute. Taking the paper he looked at the group then approached Dr. Zagrib.

"Two are missing," he said in English. "Where are they?" Why in English? Newton thought, when they are both obviously fluent in Arabic. Dr. Zagrib looked blankly back.

Turning around, the leader barked a series of orders and his men came forward, taking bottles of water from their back packs they offered some to Dr. Zagrib, and then to Newton and the rest.

Getting no intelligible response from the Iranian scientist, the leader began looking at the rest of the bound group. He said nothing, studying their eyes and occasionally consulting the paper he carried. After looking at each in turn, he came back to stand in front of Newton.

"You are the Canadian," he announced. Looking closely at Elijah he added, "You are the, how do you say this, highdya?"

"Haida," replied Elijah. "From the West Coast Nations." The leader nodded, paused, and turned again to Newton.

"I see you are in the police forces, Detective Newton."

"Really, and how would you know that?"

The man grunted and struck Newton a blow across the face with the back of his hand.

"Let us start again, I see you are in the police forces, Detective Newton." Newton felt a trickle of blood run down his lip. "Used to be, I'm retired now."

"No one ever retires from our profession, Detective Newton, you should know that."

"Perhaps, but I like to think it's possible."

The leader laughed, "I am Hajib Al Faquir," the leader said nodding to Newton. "In my day job I am an interrogator, I trust you know all about interrogation procedures, Detective Newton?"

"Yes."

"You also know then that in my part of the world the techniques are, how you say, somewhat different, a little harsher than in the Western World."

"So I see," Newton replied.

"Very well then, out of respect for a fellow colleague I will give you the opportunity to answer my questions without resorting further to our usual methods."

"Very kind of you, I'm sure, but I have no idea what I could add to your obviously well developed pool of information," Newton smiled back. There was no sense in refusing. These men, whoever they worked for, held all the cards and were not shy about playing them. He decided to cooperate and try to learn as much as possible about what the hell was going on. As a hostage negotiator, he was well aware of the "Stockholm Syndrome." The more time the captives and captors spent together, the more reluctant the captors became to harm them. Eventually a sort of friendship formed. Newton had no doubt that Hajib knew of this also, but it was the only card Newton had at the moment.

Hajib turned to the subordinate who stood at his side, the butt of his rifle held ready to administer the usual "persuasion." At the barked order, a look of disappointment crossed the guard's face and he moved to Newton's rear. A sharp tug and his hands were released from their bonds. The guard made his way to the others in the group and also freed them. Having now established who the boss was, Hajib addressed the group.

"I would like to point out the obvious, there is only one way out of this cavern and," he said nodding to the tunnel entrance and the armed men stationed there, "you can see that it is blocked. You will be allowed to move freely on this platform, and also the washroom located behind it. Our stay here will be brief, but we will tolerate absolutely no interference with it. When we have completed our brief mission, we will leave with the train, and you, I'm afraid ,will have to walk out down the tunnel. This will provide us the time we need to leave without incident, and we will not have to resort to more permanent measures of ensuring you do not try to impede us. Is this clear?"

No one answered.

"Very well then, I'll take that as a yes." He barked an order to his men and from their packs they produced additional water and some wrapped sandwiches. "I regret that this is all I can offer you, but please help yourselves."

No one moved.

"And now Detective Newton, according to my list, there is one other person, a woman I believe who should be present and is not, and the driver has informed us of another man who also is not amongst this group." Hajib waved his hand around the platform. "Perhaps you can tell me where they can be found?"

"I really don't know I'm afraid. When the lights went out, I lost track of everyone, perhaps they are wandering around out there somewhere disoriented by your fireworks display?"

"I see," Hajib said, his eyes narrowing, the guard again looked hopeful. "And who exactly are these two?"

Newton looked around at the group behind him and counted heads. "The lady is someone I met on the plane, and whom I thought might be interested in spending some time with me, the man I would guess is one of your compatriots."

"Why do you say that?"

"He was not one of us," Newton said indicating his group. "You might get more information from Dr. Zagrib; he was attached to his party."

"Dr. Zagrib appears to be still a little confused," Hajib said, indicating the scientist who still sat with a blank look on his face and his hands, even though they were free, were still behind him.

"I think he was closest to the blast" Newton added, "maybe you should have your medic look at him."

Hajib turned looking for one of his men and finding him he barked another order and the man came over right away. Hajib indicated the injured Dr. Zagrib and the man went over to see to him. Pulling a flashlight out his pocket he shone it in his eyes, looked in his ears and muttered. After a few moments he gave the scientist a pill and came back over to Hajib, who had been barking orders to the rest of his party. Newton could see two of the guards unsling their packs and remove long black tubes. They set these up on metal bases and then set up huge lights that lit up the ceiling of the cavern. The medic had a short conversation with his leader, which ended with him shaking his head.

"I'm afraid Dr. Zagrib has suffered a concussion, Detective Newton, I ask you again what you know of this other man."

"And again I regret I can add nothing else, I never spoke to him and he never spoke to me, if it's any help to you, my impression was that he may have been Dr. Zagrib's boss."

"Why is that?"

"Zagrib was the only one I saw him talk to, and he appeared to be giving him instructions." Hajib considered Newton's comments for a moment. "Indeed, well it doesn't matter much, he cannot get out, and he cannot stop us."

"If I may ask," Newton said, "stop you from doing what?"

"Nothing that concerns you, Detective, please return to your companions."

Newton headed back to the rear of the platform and sat down next to Elijah who was busy with Lord Hawthorne. The English scientist seemed to be regaining his composure. Covered in dust and dirt his eyes were again focused and he was talking in coherent sentences.

"My lord, what has just happened?" he was asking Elijah.

"We've been mugged," Elijah responded.

Despite their apparent predicament Newton could not repress a smile, Elijah was as quick witted as ever. A look of confusion momentarily appeared on Lord Hawthorne's face, and then he grinned back. "Quite so, oh yes, quite so." Elijah held a bottle of water up to Newton who drank from it. "What do you think is the purpose of all this?"

"Not sure at this point, but whatever it is, we had better be ready to act damn fast."

"You think they mean us harm?"

"Rule number one is never let the hostages see your face, unless it doesn't matter."

"Maybe they don't care if we can identify them."

"I'm sure they don't, but there can only be two reasons for that, either they have a point to make and want their faces splashed across the world press, or they don't and will make sure they remain a mystery, only one of those is good for us." Elijah thought for a moment, and they were joined by Richard.

"So Alfred, got a plan?"

"Depends on their objectives I'm thinking, and I haven't figured that part out yet."

A pair of loud bangs interrupted their conversation and filled the cavern with another cloud of smoke and dust. The mortar like devices that had been set up had fired. Two ropes now hung from the ceiling. Each was being held taught and tested by a team of men on the ends of them. Satisfied the ropes could bear their weight, one man in each party attached a pair of metal handles to each rope, hefted a pack on their back, and started up the rope. "How do they climb like that?" Lord Hawthorne asked.

"Dumar ascenders, or something similar," Newton responded. "They have a locking mechanism that allows them to be pushed up the rope, then the weight of the climber locks it in place, when that happens they can heave themselves up a foot or so, take their weight on their legs and repeat the process."

"It seems quite efficient."

"Yes, these guys are well trained, definitely military, and that could be good news for us."

"How so?"

It means this is a military operation, not a terrorist or amateur group, and that means it's sanctioned at some higher level, which in turn means that this lot is more or less insulated against the consequences."

"So," Richard added, "they will not likely see any need to eliminate us."

"Well that's encouraging at least," Lord Hawthorne said. "But why on earth are they climbing up to the roof of the cavern, what could be up there that would interest them?"

The two climbers had by now disappeared into the gloom beyond the lights. Newton looked around for Hajib, and found him consulting a diagram he had removed from a pocket in his tunic. With the map in hand, he was directing his subordinates in various activities around the cavern. Some of them were beyond Newton's range of vision, their presence known only by the light of flashlights and small floodlights that popped on and off at seemingly random intervals. An occasional order echoed from the walls as tasks were assigned and completed. A few moments later one of the group approached Hajib and saluted, behind him the two climbers rappelled to the floor of the cavern, landing in a cloud of dust. Next they joined their companions, already forming up in ranks. Hajib shouted something and the group dispersed and boarded the train. The driver started to back it up towards the tunnel.

"Apparently," Richard said, "whatever they intended to do, they have completed it." As if to punctuate the remark, Hajib strode onto the platform and stood with his hands behind his back in a position that the military called "parade rest."

"If I may have your attention, please," Newton and the rest looked at him expectantly.

"You will now come up one at a time and give my sergeant here," he said indicating the man behind him, "all your personal papers, you may of course keep any valuables – we are not thieves."

"What on earth for?" Lord Hawthorne said.

"It may be necessary to convince certain people that you are here, and for them to take that into consideration."

"So we are hostages then?"

"I would have thought that to be self evident Lord Hawthorne, you disappoint me. Now then, in return for your – cooperation – we will leave you the rest of our food and water." He barked an order and one by one his men pulled out water bottles and food from their packs and piled them on the platform. Hajib watched each man empty his pack; suddenly he turned to his sergeant and questioned him. A look of surprise came over the sergeant's face. Quickly turning to the rank of men he screamed out an order, the group disintegrated into individuals and all began to fan out into the cavern, calling out a name.

"Rajish!"

Newton whispered to Elijah, "It appears someone has got lost."

Hajib was getting impatient, twice the sergeant came up to him and pointed to his watch. A moment later one of the troops returned with a helmet in his hand. A quick conference was held and Hajib returned to the platform with his sergeant. Behind him the troops were smashing the lights, turning the cave into darkness.

"I suggest that when we leave you confine your movements to the platform. We will leave the lights here intact. As you know, and one of my men has found out, there are dangers in walking around in the dark. The main vent is very deep, and I am told there may be others further in the cavern. Now then, your papers if you please." Newton handed over his driver's licence and was quickly followed by the rest of the group, even Lord Hawthorne reluctantly handed over some papers. "Once again, I warn you not to stray from the platform, for your own safety."

With that Hajib board the train and it jolted its way back up the tunnel.

As the lights of the engine disappeared up the tunnel, the cavern and its darkness closed in on Newton and the group. Elijah recognized the strain this was putting on his friend. Claustrophobic to begin with, Newton must be feeling the weight of the darkness coming down like a ton of bricks. He knew the best thing for Newton and the rest of the group was to get busy doing something, anything to take their minds off the circumstances in which they now found themselves. He began to count the water bottles and food, portioning them out in smaller piles for each of the members of the group. Jason had already moved to the phone and picked up the receiver to listen for a dial tone or something similar. The receiver came away in his hand, the cord leading to the main unit cut.

"Can you fix that?" Elijah asked.

"Sure, I'll just splice the wires," came the reply.

"Before you get carried away, where do you think it will connect to?" Newton asked.

Jason paused for a moment, "I suppose it's too much to think it will be a switchboard at the hotel. I guess it probably connects to the main conference room where we started out on this little adventure."

"Right, and who is likely to be there?"

"The same or a similar bunch to our visitors, I expect"

"Most likely. So be careful, we don't want them re-appearing with the conviction that we now have to be eliminated."

"Wait, didn't Zagrib say something about there being a wireless hookup of some sort down here for the instruments to feed their data through?" Lord Hawthorne asked. "Perhaps we can try to find that."

"That may turn out to be worse," Richard said. "Those devices all have indicator lights that flash when data is being sent – and that may alert them quicker."

"I don't think they will be able to tell at a glance if it's us or one of the sensors though," Newton said, "But try the telephone wires first, we know they go back to the conference center and hopefully out into the real world, the data network probably goes no further than the conference center."

"I thought it went to the Internet."

"I'm sure it may, but more than likely the data sits in a file waiting for someone to call it up, so I'm not sure we can use the connection to get out to the Web and make a call or send an email to anyone." Jason thought about that for a moment, then traced the wires back from the phone to the four wire clip mounted on the wall. He opened the machine that he had carted around wherever he went. Taking the cables he examined the ends and found what he was looking for, a cable that ended in two alligator clips. Telephone systems throughout the world worked on the same two wire principal. Even though it was common for a junction box to end in four or more wires, only two were required to establish a circuit, the rest were for adding a second or third line to the circuit. Four lines gave eight possible combinations. On the third try the circuit indicator on the board lit up. Jason punched numbers into the keyboard, and the screen came alive with an Internet browser.

"OK," he said. "We're in, what now?"

"Send an email to NYPD," Richard said.

"Who to, and what do you want to say?"

"Send it to Kleinschmidt, and let him know what the hell is happening."

"Will he believe it?" asked Newton. "If I sent something like that back to my partner, I doubt they would take it seriously."

"Yeah, maybe you're right, unhook that thing Jason, until we get a plan together, no sense letting the bad guys know we can get something out on the wire."

"How about the airline? Shouldn't we let them know? Maybe they could do something," Georgia said. "I know they have an operational disaster center"

"First," a voice from behind them said, "we must decide just exactly what we are going to say." Newton turned around and saw Dr. Zagrib, still looking shaken, coming their way.

"Are you feeling better now?" Newton asked the dust covered scientist.

Dr. Zagrib indicated his ears, a small trail of blood seeped from one of them. "My apologies, I still can't hear all that well. Other than that, I appear to have suffered no permanent damage, thank you."

"You were saying?"

"Ah, yes, I was thinking we should come to a consensus about exactly what we want to say, after all, Detective Newton is correct, we can't just say 'Help, we are trapped by a bunch of men in dark clothes in a cavern underneath a volcano on a tropical island.' Even though it may be accurate, I don't think it would be accepted as believable."

"Quite right, old boy, sounds more like a James Bond thriller than an actual set of circumstances, and of course we must be selective who we send it to," Lord Hawthorne added.

"Actually not," said Jason. "We can send the same message to any number of recipients, provided we have their email addresses, all at the same time."

"Well then, let's agree on what to send and who to send it to, before hooking up that machine again."

"Step one," Newton announced, "is for us to agree exactly WHAT our situation is, for instance, what were those men putting up on the roof ?"

"Only one for sure way we are going to find that out."

"I was afraid you were going to say that, Elijah."

"Lost your spirit of adventure, have you? I thought you were forever looking for the *why* of things."

"I'm trying to avoid the 'curiosity and cat' result."

"Well, I'm with you on that."

Newton and Elijah stepped off the platform along with Lord Hawthorne and Richard. The rest stayed back. With only the single light left, they soon found themselves in darkness and unsure of their footing. "Keep one hand on the ropes," Elijah said, "until your eyes adjust to the dark." Slowly moving forward, the group soon found themselves at the bottom of one of the ropes used to climb to the ceiling. The mechanical ascenders were gone, taken by the men who had used them when they left. Peering up in the darkness, Elijah said "I think I see a green light up there."

"Yes," Newton added, "I see it too."

"What are they?" Richard asked.

"I don't know for sure," Newton said. "But I'm guessing they are not something we would like."

"I'm afraid you're right, Detective Newton," Lord Hawthorne added. "I'm afraid it is certainly not something we would like."

"Do you know what it is, Lord Hawthorne?"

"Yes, old boy, I'm afraid I do."

CHAPTER TWENTY-FIVE

Iranian Consulate – Tenerife

Dr. Al-Maquir had just replaced the phone. The message on it had been brief and to the point. The next phase of the operation was ready. He sat at the desk of the consular head, who had been brusquely dismissed. In front of him lay a small black case which looked surprisingly similar to the one Jason had. Opening the lid, he activated the machine. A single panel glowed on the face of the upturned lid, while the main part of the case held a keyboard, keypad, and a number of switches and lights. He entered a series of numbers onto the keypad and waited for a green light on the panel to turn to orange. When it did, he removed a plastic envelope from his pocket. Snapping it in half he removed a smaller card that bore a magnetic stripe. Whispering a prayer to Allah, he inserted it into a slot on the machine. On the panel, the orange light turned red. Picking up the phone he pressed a button on its face. When the party on the other end answered he spoke curtly into the handset, and was immediately connected to the office of the President. The President was also sitting in front of a desk, and on it an identical case sat open. With a similar prayer, the President personally inserted an identical card into the open slot on its face. On both machines the light changed from a steady red light to a blinking green. Al-Maquir hung up the phone and repeated his prayer, then pressed the single large button on his panel. At the volcano, the seismic instruments registered four simultaneous disturbances below the sea floor surrounding La Palma. The readings were not large, barely above three on the Richter scale. The needles tracing sharp peaks on the recording paper underneath them; then settling down to the common background noise that is always present on the earth's crust.

The scientists, now gathering on their return from their various tours, were excited to be able to observe some activity during their presence. Gathering around the machines they talked excitedly in many languages at once. Some remarked that it was ironic their host had not yet returned, and so was missing this display of nature in action.

"Helmut, look at this, a standard infarction, yes?"

"Possibly, Olaf, possibly, but see, later on the trace it seems to be repeated." The two scientists closest to the bank of seismographs were soon surrounded by their peers. As in most professional groups that worked on the basis of interpretation, the meanings of the ink lines found champions in various circles. The firsthand thoughts were refined as more data became available.

"Soledad, this is your field, what do you make of it?"

"It is curious, but I agree that it is most unusual to see four separate spikes like that, especially delineated with such precision."

"And the amplitude, it seems almost too uniform does it not?"

"It could be an equipment problem."

"No, no look at this, the background traces are normal, it must be event related."

"Of course, I see it now, but how can that be?"

"Manmade perhaps?"

"Oh no, quite impossible, look at the depth, that has to be, umm, yes, about 1200 meters below the sea bed."

The discussion went on; each new printout was passed around the group as it became available. Off in one corner, two men were studying the printout on the newer sheets. One of them took out a pen and circled the spikes, a short conversation with his companion ensued and then they stood up and made their way to the crowded table.

"Excuse me, Dr. Owens, but I think you should see this." Dr. Wentworth Owens, a professor of geology at the University of Calgary turned and looked at the offered sheet.

"Dr. Spangler," he said. "How are things in Houston?"

"Same as always, hot in summer, tolerable in winter."

"What do we have here?"

"I'd rather not say, 'til I have your opinion."

Dr. Owens laid the paper on the table and noted the circled marks.

"Obviously, these are shot holes, yes, look at the rise and fall, classic, but rather large charges for mapping I would say."

"Exactly what we were thinking, Dr. Owens, it looks the same as oil field mapping charges, but why now, why here, and most especially why so large?"

"Why indeed, that, my friend, is a tale that will perhaps be told in the follow up tracings. What are we getting now? It's been what, twenty minutes since the readings?"

They hastened over to the equipment table. Grabbing the readouts as they came off the machines, they studied them like heart surgeons peering over an ECG. One by one, others in the group sensed that an important discovery had been made. Dr. Owens and Dr. Spangler were both leaders in the field of oil exploration and picked up on the graph's meanings faster than the rest. One of the others made the next determination, the seismographs showed the background noise of the restless earth being overshadowed, slowly at first, then accelerating.

"Magma movement," said one. "No, too light in density, and moving much too fast, it can only be one thing."

"Which is?"

"Water."

CHAPTER TWENTY SIX

The cavern – La Palma

"Water?" Jason asked.

"Yes, feel that breeze from the vent?" Lord Hawthorne motioned in the direction of the vent.

"Yes."

"It's colder isn't it?"

"Now that you mention it, yes I think it is."

"Well, it will be getting colder."

"Are you sure of this, Lord Hawthorne?" Newton asked the Englishman. "It seems a bit, well, science fiction oriented."

"Quite sure, old boy, quite sure. In fact, it is the only thing that makes sense when you stop to think about it."

"What is?" Richard asked, joining in on the conversation.

"The purpose of the commando raid, the placing of those boxes up there, the whole grand scheme."

"OK, I'm confused now," said Jason. "I just don't see the purpose."

"Quite simple," Dr. Zagrib announced, looking remarkably recovered. "The destruction of the West."

"Excuse me?" Jason said. "We are thousands of miles away, assuming of course that the 'West' you are talking about is the United States."

"Perhaps, but you are not immune to the forces of nature, no one is. I'm sure Mr. Newton would agree with that, would you not, Mr. Newton?"

Newton looked at the Iranian scientist and nodded. "Yes, Doctor, that is most certainly so."

"You're talking about the tsunami then," Jason said. "Bit there is no indication that the volcano is getting ready to erupt, much less split in half and cause a tidal wave."

"I'm afraid that an eruption will not be necessary any more, old boy, they have arranged for a suitable substitute," Lord Hawthorne noted pointing up at the ceiling. "And those little boxes up there are the triggers."

"Impossible," Richard exclaimed. "To do that they would have to be...."

"Nuclear!" Newton finished.

"Quite so," Lord Hawthorne added. "Quite so."

Jason looked up at the ceiling, "Is it just me," he asked, "or have those lights changed?" Everyone looked up at the little green lights which had now started to blink.

"Folks, I think," Richard said, "that it is time we got out of Dodge."

The group went back to the platform, going as fast as they could in the darkness. There Georgia and Julie were sitting amongst the divided piles of water and food. Georgia stood as the men approached, recognizing that something had changed. Where before the group were acting like explorers, unsure of what they would find or do, they now had been galvanized with a purpose.

"What did you find?" the girls asked.

"We need to get everyone together," Newton said. "I'll explain everything then." Julie took a quick look around. "I think we are all here now."

"OK, gather up as much of this stuff as we can carry easily." Georgia and Julie looked at each other and without saying a further word began to pull the supplies together. As they prepared to leave, Newton stood at the edge of the platform, anxiously scanning the darkness around him. "Carol?" he called. "Are you there? You can come out now, they've gone."

Elijah joined his friend on the platform, "I think she would have seen them leave, Alfred, and have rejoined us by now if she was able."

"My thoughts exactly," Newton said. "This cavern is a big place in the dark."

"Dangerous also," Elijah noted. "So when we go looking we will need this." Elijah produced a length of rope about 25 feet long. He had tied one end around his waist and offered the other to Newton. "I think we should start at the far end of the platform, that is where we last saw her, and perhaps more importantly, that is where we last saw Salim."

Newton turned to his friend, "I can do this by myself Elijah, and there is no need for you to..."

"Don't say it," Elijah interrupted. "Besides, who else is going to watch out for you when you're out there stumbling around like a tenderfoot in the wilderness?"

"It's pretty dark out there, my friend, and I don't want to lose you to some undiscovered hole in the floor."

"Don't worry about it, all that talk about natives not being able to operate at night is just some Hollywood screenwriter's fantasy, I'm usually at my best when the sun goes down," Elijah grinned.

Newton grinned back, "I'll just bet you are."

"Count us in," a voice from the rear announced. Newton and Elijah turned to see the rest of the group roped together like mountain climbers. "You didn't really think we would leave all the spelunking to you two now did you?" Lord Hawthorne said with a grin. "Simply not on, old chap." Newton thanked them with his eyes, and joined the free end of their rope to his waist. Setting out in as straight a line as they could manage in the dark, they stepped forward on command from Newton. "Step," he pronounced loudly and as a group they took a step into the darkness. "Step," he said again and in that fashion they moved forward, feeling as much with their feet as their hands, calling out Carol's name as they went. Around them the air grew colder. Newton was sure he could feel the air stir and move in new currents. The cavern made their direction change constantly and he never got a bearing on them that he could be certain of. In the darkness the sense of vision is replaced with the others, hearing and even smell became acuter. As a group they paused every ten steps, waited and listened. Jason and Julie were the youngest and their ears picked up the sound first, a faint tapping of rock on rock.

"Listen!" Julie whispered harshly, "I think I hear something!"

"Me too!" Jason added after a moment.

"Which direction?"

"To the right," Julie responded.

"Slowly now, folks," Elijah reminded them. "Let's not get tangled up, we have to move carefully." With agonizing slowness the group changed direction to the right, keeping the ropes taut between them and aligning themselves with the platform.

"Step," called Newton. "Step." He wanted them to go faster, but he knew that if they did they would likely get someone else injured. The tapping grew slowly louder, very slowly. Would it be Carol or Salim he wondered.

"Wait," Richard called suddenly. "I found something."

"What?"

"It's a pack of some sort."

The rope between them grew taut as Richard bent to the floor of the cavern and retrieved a canvas bag. The shoulder straps and pockets confirmed it to be a military style pack, and it was not empty.

"Got it," he cried slipping it over his shoulders.

"Step," Newton said and the group moved on towards the tapping noise. Then after the tenth step, "Listen!" The tapping grew more infrequent, "Carol!" Newton shouted and her name echoed off the walls and roof and flung itself back into his face. "Can you hear us?" Again the echo bounced back, a taunting reflection. "Step," Newton said. "Step!" and the grouped moved forward again.

It was Lord Hawthorne who found her. Older than the rest, his steps were more tentative and he moved his foot in a semi circle in front of him, like a dancer feeling his way on the stage.

"Newton!" he cried. "I've got her!"

The group started to collapse into the middle of the line, "Wait!" said Newton, wanting to get to her, more than he thought he would, and more than he dared to admit. "Keep your bearings, we can't allow ourselves to get lost in here."

"It's OK, Alfred," Elijah said, "I can still see the reflection of the platform lights."

Newton detached himself from the rope and made his way along to Lord Hawthorne who along with Dr. Zagrib was bent down and holding a limp form.

"She is breathing, but unconscious," Lord Hawthorne announced.

Newton felt Carol's head; it was sticky with blood, now clotting in her hair. Gently he picked her up and put her in a fireman's lift over his shoulder. Making his way back to his place on the line, he tied himself in with the help of Richard.

"Step," he said, taking up the chant again. This time though there was no stopping to listen. The group still had to carefully feel its way along the uneven floor, and to Newton, the journey was agonizingly slow. He could feel Carol's breathing and that was comforting, much more so than the warm blood dripping on his back. Eventually they made their way back to the welcoming circle of light around the platform. There they gathered around the still form lying in front of them. A check of her wounds revealed a gash to the back of her head. Elijah took the pack that Richard found and rummaged through it. He quickly found a wound dressing and wrapped the wound as tightly as he dared. He was rewarded by the blood ceasing to escape from the wound.

"I don't think she lost a lot of blood, Alfred, and I don't see any damage to the skull." Newton cradled Carol's head in the crook of his arm and raised the injured girl's eyelids. Both eyes reacted equally to the limited light and he breathed a sigh of relief. "No sign that she has a concussion."

"Thank god for that."

He ran his fingers lightly over her arms and legs, "No broken bones that I can detect either." Carol moaned slightly.

"Is she coming around?" Georgia asked.

"Maybe, can't tell at this point." Newton turned Carol's care over to Julie and Georgia, who took some water and patted it on the injured woman's face. Richard caught Newton's eye and motioned him and Elijah over to where he was standing with Lord Hawthorne.

"Tell him what you told me," Richard said nodding to Lord Hawthorne.

"Tell me what?" Newton asked.

"Well, it's most curious," the Englishman said, "Carol was quite unconscious when I found her."

"And?" Elijah said.

"Well, if she was unconscious, then who was doing the tapping of the rocks?"

"And," said Newton, "how did she get injured?"

Jason joined them carrying his black box. "How is she doing?"

"Fine, for now," Newton replied, "but we need to get out of here, and fast, it's getting much colder now."

"Do you think it's safe to go through the tunnel?"

"Not much choice, I don't see any other doors."

"What about the other guy, Salim, are we going to leave him here?"

"Yes," Dr. Zagrib, who had joined the group, said. "We can't waste time to find him."

"I have my doubts," Newton said, "that the tunnel is going to be an available route. We came—how far do you figure from the conference room?" Elijah thought for a moment, "I make it two kilometers anyway, given the time we spent on the train, and the speed it went, so it will take us about an hour with Carol in the condition she is, to climb out that way."

"That is, if the soldiers didn't mine it in some way."

"No need for them to do that, old boy, even if we did make it out, we would be on the wrong side of the volcano." Lord Hawthorne had joined the discussion. "I'm afraid we must find a different way."

Jason looked at the Englishman, "Can you explain that a little more? I know you started to say that there was going to be a landslide or something like that, but," he said looking up at the devices on the ceiling, "these things look too small to cause it. Even if they are nuclear, wouldn't the blast just take off the top of the volcano? I mean how powerful could they be, a few tons worth?"

"Ten kilotons each is their rated output" a voice from the dark intruded on their conversation. Newton and the rest looked outward, struggling to see. A figure entered the circle of light, disheveled, dirty, and with a torn shirt Salim stepped forward. He was carrying a rifle. "They are a Russian design of what the U.S. Department of Defence calls a 'suitcase' bomb. However, I don't think the Iranians were able to refine the plutonium sufficiently to gain the full rated yield. I would place them in the eight to nine kiloton range."

"You seem to have had a mishap," Newton said. "I would guess it came when you took out the missing commando."

Salim grinned, "Almost correct, Detective Newton, I see you have not lost your skills. But I didn't 'take him out' as you say; in fact, he lost his night vision and fell into the vent. I almost had him out but he decided to fight and is now, I suspect, floating at the bottom."

"Floating," Richard asked, "I thought Dr. Zagrib said the vent was dry."

"It was," Salim said, "until the explosions opened it to the sea."

"But why, what purpose would that serve?" Jason asked.

"Hydraulics, old chum," Lord Hawthorne added." As I was about to explain before this gentleman arrived out of the dark, the whole purpose of the exercise is to cause the mountain to split and drown the east coast of the Americas with a huge tidal wave."

"Hydraulics? What do you mean?"

"Think about it" Newton said. "The vent is a three kilometer hole in the mountain, with no doubt thousands of cracks of all sizes running off the core of the fissure. In order to split that part of the mountain, you need to apply enormous pressure to enough of those cracks to cause the fissure to expand enough so gravity would cause it to split away. Remember that the part that is poised to fall is already in a state of delicate balance, it almost tumbled off during the last eruption. So, in order to take it the rest of the way you have to both generate and transfer this force. The only way it can be done is the physics of hydraulics. In the last eruption the lava in its liquid state acted like hydraulic oil, transferring the enormous pressure building up from under the crust to the fracture points, and thus almost tipping the split part of the volcano into the sea. Since there isn't an eruption currently, substitute water for lava, and the nuclear explosions for the pressure wave and there you have it. The vent becomes a huge hydraulic ram, and the water, since it is uncompressible, will transfer the force to every nook and cranny causing the fissure to widen and the mountain to split."

"Capital! Detective Newton, you are a credit to your namesake," Lord Hawthorne exclaimed. "You figured it out perfectly. Now can you tell me how that can be avoided?"

"The only thing I can think of, Professor, is to prevent the generation of the pressure wave, but how to accomplish that I don't know."

"Spot on! Since we already know from the dropping temperature and increased air movement that the vent is being flooded, the only other course of action is to remove the bombs."

"How in the hell are we going to do that?" Jason asked.

"Only one way," Salim said, putting down the rifle and shrugging off the pack he had on his back. "Someone will have to climb up there and retrieve them."

"You're going to do that?" Richard asked warily. "How do we know we can trust you?"

"You don't," Salim replied, "but I am open to other ideas."

"Use that rifle," Richard said, "and disable them."

"It may come to that, but not at this point, the original design incorporates many anti-tampering devices. Although in this case they may have not thought it necessary to use them. I'm sure they were not expecting a group of 'tourists' to be wandering about the cavern. While a bullet may disable it, it would be more likely that it would set it off."

"You seem to know an awful lot about these things," Richard said suspiciously. "How is that possible?"

"I have been well trained," came the reply, "by some of the best in the business." Salim took hold of the rope and pulled sharply down, and then he grabbed hold and hoisted himself up a foot or so, testing the strength of the anchor. Dropping down to the ground, he tied a knot in the bottom of the rope.

"Will you hold this taut for me?" He asked Newton and Elijah. "I will try for this one first; however, I am not sure how well it is secured."

"Are you sure you can climb up there and hang on long enough to work on it with one hand?" Newton asked.

"I'm sure I can't," Salim replied. "That's why I'm going to use this as a tie off." Taking the pack, he used a knife to cut the straps off. "I should be able to make a foot rest with one of them. Of course, once I put it on, I doubt I'll be able to take it off again, so only one per rope."

"What about climbing aids?"

"I'll take whatever you have to offer," Salim grinned, "but if you can just hold the rope taut, I should be able to shinny up it using muscle power."

"No, I can't let you do that!"

Newton look behind him to see Dr. Zagrib holding the rifle leveled at Salim. "We should be spending the time getting away from here, not fooling with those things."

Salim looked coolly down the barrel of the rifle.

"You can leave anytime, Doctor.," he said, "but how will you do that? I doubt very much you can just walk up the tunnel. Even if you had the strength to get back to the conference center before these go off, what will you have gained? The conference center is on the wrong side of the fissure and will slide into the sea along with the rest of the mountain. No, the only course of action is to disable the devices and then find a way out by going up. There must be an air vent or alternate route we can take."

Elijah had stepped back when the Iranian scientist first pointed the rifle at them. Moving in the darkness he had positioned himself slightly behind the gunman. As soon as the muzzle of the rifle moved away from its target, he launched into action. Yelling at the top of his lungs he grabbed for the rifle.

And missed.

But the distraction was sufficient for Newton to grasp the barrel and give it a hard twist. With the barrel secured, he wrestled the weapon from Dr. Zagrib.

"What are you doing, Detective Newton? Surely you can't trust this man!"

Newton looked from one to the other. "So far, he has the only plan that makes sense, we can't outrun the blast, and with the injured, we will never be able to make our way back to the conference center in time."

"There is one other thing," Jason added coming up to the group.

"I'm all ears," Newton responded.

"It seems to me the key to this whole thing going off as planned, if you'll excuse the pun, is the correction functioning of those two things," he said indicating the blinking lights. "So if I were them, I'd make sure I had some way of monitoring their state of health, which of course would have to be from a safe distance."

"Of course!" Lord Hawthorne added, "It has to be so, but what? Radio waves wouldn't penetrate this rock for any distance."

"They wouldn't have to," Jason said, looking towards the entrance. "See those tracks, the signal would only have to go to a receiver connected to them, and the tracks would carry the signal like a wire back up to the surface."

"What about those wireless things they put up along the tunnel for the sensor readings?"

"That would be the obvious choice, perhaps too obvious, but then again, I'm sure they were not expecting anyone to be here."

"But here we are, and anyone planning such an operation as this would take the possibility of that into the planning process."

"So you think maybe they have a backup?"

"I sure as hell would."

"The only other thing would be the telephone wires, or the tracks."

"Aren't they grounded?" asked Elijah. "It seems to me they are all staked solid with big spikes." The group hurried over to the entrance and examined the tracks. "Just as I thought, look at those spikes."

"Yes but, aha, yes, they are spiked all right, but only into the wood ties and wood is an insulator," Jason pronounced. "Even with the moisture in this cavern, there should be no problem with a low level signal making it through. Now all we have to do is find the receiver."

"Elijah and I will take this side of the tracks, Jason, you and the rest take the other, it can't be far away."

"Almost certainly it would have to be in a place that has a direct line of sight to the bombs, in order to get a steady signal." Jason said. "Look for something attached to the walls."

"Jason, stand at the tunnel entrance and take a sighting in line with the spot where it would line up with the cavern roof. It won't necessarily be a direct line, but it should be pretty close." Jason stood at the entrance and played the flashlight beam down the walls like a searchlight. The rest watched the light and tried to pick out something, anything that looked like it didn't belong, a reflection off metal, or a shadow that shouldn't be there.

It was Elijah who spotted it first, a small thin wire crossing over a tie, and leading to a small black box wedged into a crevice in the wall.

"Here it is, what do you want to do with it now?"

"First," said Newton, "we need a plan, when we disconnect this thing. I suspect they will send someone, probably all of them, to investigate. That means they will have to come down this cavern by train at least part of the way, and probably by foot for the last few feet. So we have to be prepared to meet them, and deal with them when they get here."

"Deal with them! How?" Dr. Zagrib spat. "With what? Rocks?"

"Precisely!" Newton said, a slow grin appearing on his face. "With rocks."

Clearing a space on the floor of the cavern, Newton sketched out his plan in the dust. It wasn't the most elaborate one he had ever had, but it was the only one available to them.

CHAPTER TWENTY SEVEN

The conference room

While Dr. Owens and Spangler were discussing the chart and its readings, the rest of the group gathered around and offered their opinions. To have such a challenge in real time at the conference was an opportunity for all to express their particular views, and they were not shy about doing it. Soon the level of conversation reached a point where it was difficult for anyone to be heard at all. Taking the opportunity to leave the crowded room, the two scientists exited the center to continue their discussion and for Dr. Owen to light up his pipe.

"Seems every place in the world is now a 'non-smoking area'," he quipped to his comrade. "Yes, it's the natural swing of the pendulum, first the vice ,then the redemption." They both chuckled in the warm sunshine.

"Isn't that a rather large amount of transport to be here now," Dr. Spangler said gesturing at the four rental trucks parked in the lot. "These weren't here when we arrived, I'm sure."

"You're right, they weren't, I wonder who they belong to?"

"Did you notice any maintenance going on during the trip?"

"No, I saw a couple of the work engines but they all seemed to be down for scheduled maintenance."

"Hmm, there is nothing inside," Dr. Spangler said. "I wonder if we have some other tour group in progress?"

"I don't think so. The only working trains were being used by our groups, perhaps they belong to the maintenance staff."

"They belong to me." The scientists looked up to see Hajib and his men exiting the centre from a side door and headed their way. "You must be with the volcanologist conference?"

"Yes, I am Dr. Spangler and this Dr. Owens, and you are?"

"Unimportant," Hajib answered. "As your colleague has mentioned, we are only here to carry out some maintenance. I do hope we have not interfered with your conference, we try to be as inconspicuous as possible."

"No, not at all, we were completely unaware of your presence."

"Well, we will be off then, have a good time at your meetings." With a nod to the two scientists, they began to board the vehicles. Each was carrying a long canvas carryall, the type that hockey players used to carry all their equipment. Without a further word they entered the vehicles. Hajib waited until everyone had boarded then with a nod in their direction, led the vehicles down the road.

Dr. Owen puffed silently on his pipe, Wreaths of smoke soon curled around his head and he glanced at his fellow scientist.

"What was that all about?" He asked.

"I haven't a clue, but we should get back to the group." Dr. Owens tapped the ashes out of his pipe and they went inside. Down the road, the brake lights came on at the rear of the lead vehicle, followed immediately by the rest in line. In the cab of the lead vehicle Hajib was on his cell phone.

"The signal has ceased," the voice on the phone was saying, "nothing coming through at all." Hajib turned behind him and tapped at the window of the cab. In the truck bed a figure opened a case and put on a pair of earphones attached to a panel on the case. The panel also held a small dial, which the man was carefully turning first one way then the other. In a moment he turned to face the cab and shook his head. Muttering a few words into his cell phone, Hajib snapped the lid down and signaled for the trucks to turn around. A few moments later the little convoy had reversed on the narrow road and was speeding back to the centre.

The ashes from Dr. Owens's pipe were still warm when they drove over them into the parking lot.

The general murmur of conversation had risen during the sojourn into the parking lot. The banks of instruments had recorded an increase in activity along the sea bed to a distance of 14 kilometers from the island. The discussion of the moment was over the depth of the activity below the seabed, some of it apparently some two to three thousand meters below.

"And I'm telling you that cannot be true!" one scientist from Norway proclaimed. "We have extensive experience with undersea formations and the presence of a geothermal vent is marked by a much different signature."

"Aye, normally I would agree with you, Dr. Horjalds," replied a small thick man with flaming red hair. "But you will recall the problems we had scouting off of Iceland, after all we called you in to consult on that one."

"So you did, Hamish, so you did, but that was caused by drilling was it not?"

"Indeed it was, Artimus, so if it happened there, why not here, and that would make these tracings," the Scotsman pointed to the earlier readings, "evidence of something similar would it not?" Like conversations were continuing all over the centre, and with each passing moment, new readings filled the screens and were recorded on the seismographs. As each meter of paper spun off the recording reels, it was posted on a section of wall for all to see and accompanied by a rise in the volume of conversation.

Into this cauldron of discussion and opinion stepped Hajib.

Equipped with a small bull horn he shouted for the crowd's attention. After a few moments the din died away and he addressed the crowd.
"Gentlemen, gentlemen, I am Hajib Al Faquir, forgive me for interrupting your discussion, but I must ask for your assistance. Word has just reached me that the head of your conference is at this moment trapped by a rock fall within the caverns. Dr Zagrib is believed to be in good shape, but obviously we must begin immediately to extricate him. I only have a few men with me and therefore I must impose upon you for assistance. Fortunately, the electric train system is still running and with your assistance I am sure we will be able to shift whatever rock has fallen and affect a rescue. Now then, will you all assist?
"Excuse me, Mr. Hajib is it? As you can see, some of us are little advanced in years, I fear we will be more of a hindrance than a help."
"Everyone can contribute, I assure you. Those who cannot do much lifting can hold the work lights and pass out water and other such things. Please, I implore you, time is short and I would not like to see us fail because one or more of you failed to contribute."
The scientists looked at one another, for many it had been some years since they had engaged in hard physical labour and the idea simply didn't make sense. Some of the relatively younger ones shrugged and began to move towards the tunnel entrance. For the rest, after a short discussion, it was agreed that all should go and they filed out to the train. Hajib had pulled out a sheaf of paper from his tunic and handed sheets to his men. After consulting them, they had begun opening doors around the conference center and bringing out shovels, lanterns, water and blankets. Each of the scientists was handed something from the pile as they took a seat on the train. Crowded with its load of passengers and equipment the little engine strained to get up to speed. As it did the lights in the cavern dimmed with the extra demand on the electrical system.
Dr. Owens sat next to Dr. Spangler, and reluctantly put his pipe into a pocket. With his hands full trying to keep himself and a load of blankets from falling off, he would have no opportunity to smoke on the way. Probably a good thing he thought, it was time to quit the habit anyhow. He nodded to his companion who was deep in thought. Nudging him he asked, "Still trying to formulate a theory on those readings?"
"No, I was wondering how this Hajib fellow had a diagram showing where all that equipment was stored. It was like he had the plans of

the place or something. Another thing, we were at the only phone, so how did he find out about the cave in?"

"Well, he did say he was part of the maintenance crew, so I'm sure they would all be briefed where things were located."

"That's the point; they should know where all that stuff was without having to look at a floor plan."

"May be there are some new people, I'm sure they get new employees all the time."

"Well, they strike me as more of a military unit than a bunch of disconnected civilians."

"I'm sure all your questions will be answered in good time, Doctor, all in good time."

Dr. Spangler was not sure he would like the answer when he got it.

Beneath him the train bucked and swayed on its journey, the steel wheels clacking loudly against the joints in the tracks.

CHAPTER TWENTY EIGHT

Ground Zero

Newton and Elijah were sweating with exertion; it had taken them half an hour to split the railway ties using only rocks for tools. The end result was the loosening of five consecutive spikes on each side of the tracks.

"Think that's enough to do the job?" Elijah asked.

"It'll have to do; there just isn't enough time to do more." The two men walked back the short section of tunnel to the cavern entrance. Already the flashlights they carried were noticeably dimmer.

"Ready?" Newton asked Jason.

"As much as I will ever be."

"OK then, let's do it."

"Everyone take their places please." Newton said.

"You will kill us all!" Dr. Zagrib cried out. "You don't know that doing this will not set off the bombs!"

"We've already been over this Doctor," Newton said, "and we have no choice. While it's true that disconnection of the relay may initiate a countdown sequence on the devices, it's a chance we have to take. There is no other way to get out of here. The water is rising at a rapid rate. We can all feel how much colder it has got in here." Newton nodded to Jason, who took a deep breath and pulled the wire out of the black wrapped receiver. All eyes turned to the cavern roof, where the blinking green lights paused once, then returned to their sequence.

"Well, then, that wasn't so bad was it?" Lord Hawthorne remarked. "I mean we're still here and all."

"So far," Newton said. "Right then, next stage, Jason, start hooking up your box and sending messages in five minutes."

"Will do."

"Salim, are you clear on your part?"

"Perfectly, Detective, and I will be ready."

"What do you think you will do with just a handful of bullets for that thing?" Dr. Zagrib argued. "There will be too many of them."

"If I didn't know better, Dr. Zagrib, I could easily get the impression you didn't want to get out of here. Then I would have to ask myself why that would be?" Richard said. "Is there something you haven't told us about?"

"Why are you asking me?" Dr. Zagrib shot back. "HE is the one with the gun. HE is the one who was stalking you. HE is the shadowy figure in all this, maybe you should ask HIM!" shaking with rage, he pointed his finger at Salim, who just stood there.

"Really, and how did you know he was 'stalking' us?"

Zagrib paused, "I heard it being discussed by the women."

"I think you both bear watching," said Newton heading back to the platform. "We will find out soon enough what the reasons are behind both your actions." Reaching the platform, he brought the group together under the flickering light. "We have maybe a half hour or so before they come to find out why they lost the signal to the bombs. When they get here, they will have all the other scientists with them, so remember the plan. Get on the train at all costs and be ready to move. When the shooting starts, that will be your signal to go. Any last concerns?"

His question was met with silence and the group moved slowly to the front of the tunnel entrance. "OK, Jason, they should have had enough time to get aboard the train and start out by now, go ahead and start sending out messages. Jason bent over the telephone wires and twisted them together, on the front panel the LCD screen lit up and displayed a blinking 'connecting' message. Behind him Richard and the women were gathered in a group. All eyes were on the young police officer and his box. In a few seconds the screen message changed, it now read "connection failed." Jason grunted and examined the wires again, shrugging he twisted them tighter and started the procedure again. After a few seconds the screen cleared and "connection found" appeared. Jason breathed out audibly, "We're in!" He told Newton, "Who do I send this to?"

In the now empty conference room, a red light glowed on the phone face, but there was no one around to notice.

"Anything?" Richard asked.

"Nothing yet, but there's the time difference to take into account and even more worrisome is the automated spam detector. It's probably flushing everything down the toilet as we speak."

"Try this," said Carol as she pushed a piece of paper into his hands. "There is no spam detector on that system, and I can guarantee you that someone will check the messages, but I can't say when."

"Hmm, no name for the server, just an I.P. address, I'm betting this is some government machine in a dark room some place where you have to stare into a retina checker before the doors open."

"Something like that, you should be a policeman, Jason."

Jason smiled back and typed in the new address header. He clicked on the "send" button and hoped Carol was right.

"Any more suggestions?" he asked, looking back at the crowd behind him.

"No need," said Elijah, "I think we have just been cut off," and he pointed at the screen on the panel where "connection lost" was now being displayed.

"Damn," said Jason turning to the back of the box and inspecting the wires once again. "Nothing wrong here." After a few moments when the screen display did not change, Newton said "Save your efforts, Jason, it's not on our side. I think we have indeed been cut off."

"Ok then, let's go to plan 'B'."

"Plan 'B,' we have a plan 'B'?" Richard asked.

"Of course, isn't that one of the things you taught me, always have a plan 'B'?"

"Well sure, but..."

"Remember all those relays for the data sensors? Plan 'B' is to try and send a message out through them."

"Don't you need to know what IP address or something they are on?"

"I'm betting the guys who installed them left them on the ones they were shipped from the factory with."

"And you know which one that is?"

"Yep, at least close enough, the wireless components in this machine automatically search for a signal, and since there can only be one in this place, it has to be the one we want. When it finds it, it will start sending out the same messages we sent down the telephone. With a little luck we can get out that way."

"Do you need to watch it and set up something else, or can it run by itself?"

"Entirely automatic at this point," Jason said. "So we'll let it run."

"OK, folks, I think it's time we took our places, remember what I told you. Salim, Elijah, and Richard will go with me to do our thing while you folks set the stage here." With that he and the three other men took the best remaining flashlight and carefully picked their way to the bottom of the ropes. Salim tested his previously made loop and started up one of them.

"Hold it steady please," he called out, and with the strength of his arms inched his way slowly. It seemed to take forever, but he was soon out of the pale circle of light cast by the flashlight. Newton switched it off to save the batteries and because it would make no difference to Salim anyway.

"Elijah," he said in a whisper, "can we trust him?"

"Not much choice, besides, he is the best one to climb the rope, you may not have noticed this, but I'm getting a little long in the tooth for that."

"You and I both, old friend, you and I both."

"I have it," Salim announced from his position at the top of the rope. "It's secured by two straps fastened to the roof, but I think I can pry it away from them." His voice echoed down from the cavern. A few minutes later he called down again.

"Turn on the light please, I'm sending it down by itself." Newton sent the now weak beam of the flashlight upwards and saw that Salim had made a rope collar for the device, and wrapped it around the climbing rope. The friction of the collar allowed the device to slowly descend of its own weight. Newton and Elijah prepared to catch it when it reached their level. The beam of the flashlight traced its path until it reached their hands. Both men grabbed it at the same time, it was not as heavy as Newton thought it would be, and felt strangely warm in the coldness of the cavern.

"I judge it about 30 pounds," he said to Elijah. "What do you think?"

"About the same," he paused for a moment then added, "I thought it would be bigger."

"Hold the rope please," came Salim's voice from above them, "I'm coming down now." Richard stepped forward and put his weight on the bottom of the rope, holding it from twisting as Salim descended. In a much faster time than it took him to go up, he returned to the floor of the cavern. "Give me a moment to catch my breath, and I'll go for the other one." He said quietly.

"I think not!"

Newton turned the flashlight beam to a voice behind them. Dr. Zagrib stood there with a small caliber pistol pointed in their direction. "I'm afraid, gentlemen, that I cannot allow things to deteriorate any further. Please step away from that." He said indicating the still blinking box.

"What's this?" Richard asked.

"I'm not going to tell you again, step away from the box."

"I don't understand," Lord Hawthorne said. "How you can be involved in something like this? You who have traveled the world and had the benefit of the finest educations, how can you throw in your lot with terrorists?"

"As they say, Lord Hawthorne, one man's terrorist is another's freedom fighter. I may seem to be a poor choice as a terrorist to you, but I assure you, I am committed to my cause."

"But why? Surely you recognize the bulk of the advancements in society have come from those very people you wish to destroy."

"Advancements? What advancements? Yes, Western society has contributed in the material sense, but you have had us pay a very large price for it. We have lost out national soul!" Zagrib's eyes darkened with the force of his convictions. "And now you will pay the price of subversion, you will all be dealt a blow from which you will never recover. When the cavern is filled with water, and these devices go off, the age of Western influence will be over."

"You're mad, quite mad!" Lord Hawthorne exclaimed.

Newton caught the look in the Englishman's eyes, and as the argument raged, moved slightly away from them, increasing the space between Zagrib and the rest of the group. He felt Salim's eyes and looked across the short space at him. Salim glanced down at his hands, he had extended three fingers. Newton saw the question in Salim's eyes and signaled his understanding with his own. Now there were two fingers showing, then one, then...

Newton snapped off the light and felt a body hurl itself forward towards the Iranian. In doing so, the figure knocked the flashlight from his hands. In the dark he couldn't see who it was, not even with the light generated by the pistol shots. There were the sounds of a short scuffle in the dark, punctuated by first one shot from the pistol, then another. The sounds of the fight died away with a groan, and then silence. The flashlight, now in Elijah's hands, came back on and showed both Salim and Dr. Zagrib in a heap on the floor. The pistol lay to one side and Newton scooped it up. Next he examined both men, one was breathing and one was not, both had been shot.

Elijah and Newton bent over the two men. "I'm afraid he's gone," Elijah said indicating one. "This one is still alive, let's get him to the train platform." Rapidly they returned to small platform, where the rest of the group waited anxiously. Already nervous from the day's events, the shots they heard had only increased their unease further. As Newton and Elijah struggled with the combatants with Richard's help, Lord Hawthorne followed, holding the blinking bomb gingerly.

"What happened?" Carol cried out as she saw the group struggle into the weak light.

"He's dead," Newton said indicating one of the bodies, "and he's still alive, but bleeding."

Jason interrupted, "We have visitors on their way," he said indicating the tracks, "I can feel the vibrations in the track."

Newton strode to the rail bed and put his ear to the track, "Not long now, patch him up as best you can and get ready."

CHAPTER TWENTY NINE

In the tunnel

The overloaded train made its way while the volcanologists held on in the swaying cars. Hajib's men rode on their edges and took the bumping and swaying with the resiliency of youth and fitness. Dr. Owens for his part was concentrating on just staying on the rocking carriage.

"Look, Wentworth, doesn't this seem a little strange to you?"

"Yes, I've been thinking the same thing, if this is a rescue mission, where are all the timbers and tools we'll need? Those shovels won't do much. We need jacks and beams to properly attack a cave-in, and why didn't they take the time to call for help from the town?"

"Right, and those men, they must be military. Look at the way they ride in this contraption."

"Not to mention that they seem positioned more as guards than rescuers."

"Better keep our wits about us, Wentworth; something is very wrong about this."

The train slowed and came to a halt within the tunnel. At the front Hajib and some of his men got out and started walking forward, motioning the train to follow. They seemed to be studying the walls and roof looking for, what? Signs of a cave-in? Some of the other scientists were beginning to look uneasily at each other; they too sensed that this was not what it should be. As the noise of conversation reached them, Dr. Owens nudged his companion. "What are they talking about?"

"Mainly the lack of dust."

"How so?"

"In any cave-in there should be a huge amount of dust and possibly gas in the air, but here there is none and no breathing apparatus either."

"I'm beginning to smell a rat, and I think the head one is coming our way." Hajib and his men had returned to the train and were motioning everyone out of the cars. As he got out, Dr. Owens noticed that the way back up the tunnel was now blocked by a group of Hajib's men. Gathering everyone to the front of the train, Hajib began to speak.

"We are close to the end of the tracks," he explained, "I don't want to take the train in any further, loaded down with us all, in case its vibrations cause a further cave-in. Just down the tracks a way there is a cavern. There we will find jacks, timbers, and breathing equipment. My men tell me that the collapse begins a short distance past that and that is where Dr. Zagrib is likely to be. Please stick close together and tie yourselves to the rope being handed down. The cavern floor is very uneven and covered with holes, some quite deep. If you were to fall into one it would be very difficult to retrieve you." He nodded to his men who began to pass a rope back from the front of the line, and quickly secured each man to it with about five feet between them. "Please keep your distance, and follow the directions of my men, it's not far to the cavern's entrance."

With that, he turned and headed out at the front of the group, the rest followed, there not being anything else they could do. Hajib's explanation had calmed their fears for the moment. At first progress was steady, Dr. Owens found the track bed easy to walk on as long as he kept his head down and eyes on the rail ties. The train, now relieved of its burden, followed them. Occasionally he glanced over at his companion and found that he too was intently studying the ground ahead of him. In this fashion they made good time, stopping every now and then to rest for a few moments. Every time they did, Dr. Owens noticed, the air grew cooler and he swore he could smell seawater.

Sensing that the line ahead had come to a halt, the group paused while those in front sorted it out. When nothing happened after a few minutes, Wentworth and his companion unfastened the rope and followed the figures of the strangers as they made their way forward to see what was causing the holdup. They found a large pile of stones on the tracks with Hajib and his men gathered around Consulting a map.

"That," said Dr. Spangler, "is not the result of a rock fall." Tugging gently at his friend's coat, he motioned him to return to the train. "Obviously this is some kind of trick. Dr. Zagrib cannot be trapped by such a thing, something else is going on here."

"I agree, the question now is, what do we do about it?"

"I suggest we take the train and get the hell out of here back to the conference hall and warn the authorities."

"Can you drive that thing?"

"What's to drive, it only goes forward and backward, and not too fast at that." As the men at the front began to attack the pile of rocks with shovels, the two made their way back up the tunnel to the train as silently and quickly as possible.

The driver had taken the opportunity to adjust one of the cars linkages. Like all machinery underground, it had its share of rust and corrosion. He kept an oil can and a number of rags stored in the locomotive's storage locker and was in a constant battle against the forces of nature. A small can of kerosene supplied the required cleaning agents, and a small dab of grease on the coupler kept it working. Finished with his chore, he had left the items on the seat and was inspecting the other couplers when he felt the train suddenly reverse. With barely enough time to jump clear, the frightened man pressed himself against the wall of the cavern as the train scraped by driven by two of the scientists, one with a pipe clenched firmly between his teeth. A series of shouts came from the front of the group. A few seconds later one of the dark clad members of the leader's team ran past, shucking off his pack as he went, and producing a machine pistol from inside it. The sound of shooting followed by a flash of fire and smoke soon followed. The engineer peered cautiously around the bend in the tunnel and was greeted by a cloud of dust and a low rumbling sound.

CHAPTER THIRTY

The cavern

"What the hell was that?" The sound of the gunfire, followed by a rumbling permeated the tunnel. Newton paused and looked at Lord Hawthorne expectantly. The Englishman listened for a moment and nodded in return. All eyes were on the entrance which was filling with a fine layer of dust. "That's the real thing, I'm afraid," Lord Hawthorne said. "A real cave-in this time."

"Now the question is which side of it is Hajib on, ours or the outside?"

"We'll find out soon enough, I expect."

"It may not matter in the long run," Richard added, "if those bombs go off with us still here. Did you get any response to your messages, Jason?"

"Not yet, and I've not been able to reconnect to the 'Net either, the phone line must have been cut and the relay boxes disabled."

"So any change in plans?"

"Plans? I'd hardly call it a plan, more like reaction to the events of the moment," Newton said. "But no, no change, we'll still assume that Hajib will make every attempt to determine why he has lost contact with his bombs, and will have to physically get here to do that. I think events so far have proven that to be correct."

"But the cave-in, won't that mean we can't escape using the train?" Julie asked.

"Perhaps, but if we can't, then they can't, so they will have to disable the bombs or find a way out."

"Or die trying."

"Listen! I hear something," Georgia announced pointing towards the tunnel entrance. A few minutes later a number of frightened and dusty faces rounded the corner into view.

"Lord Hawthorne," one of them announced. "I didn't realize you were here, we have come to rescue Dr. Zagrib, do you know where he is?"

"Yes, I do, right here, but I'm afraid he is dead."

The group of scientists filed in, dirty and disheveled, most were exhausted, and slumped onto the floor of the platform, too tired to care about anything. Behind them came Hajib and his group, their attempts at disguise gone now, each of them brandishing a compact machine gun. One of them separated himself from the group and immediately went to examine the roof of the cavern where the bombs had been placed.

Hajib himself strode into the middle of the platform and looked around. He kicked at the body of Dr. Zagrib and satisfied himself that he was indeed dead. Then he did the same to Salim, who groaned in return. He turned to one of his men and nodded. That man in turn bent and examined the wounded man, then retrieved some medical supplies from his pack and began to dress his wounds. One of Hajib's men, the one who had gone to check on the devices returned with his face ashen. Quickly he spoke with Hajib, whose face turned grim. Looking over the group assembled on the platform, he made a decision and faced Newton.

"Where is it?"

"Where is what?" Newton asked.

Hajib drew his pistol and pointed it directly at Carol, "I will only ask once more, Detective, where is it?" Knowing that it really made no difference at this point, since they were all trapped anyway, Newton gestured to the far corner of the platform.

"There, under those rocks."

Hajib holstered his pistol and motioned towards the rocks. The bomb was retrieved and brought back. Two of what Newton now regarded as "terrorists" bent over the package and attached a variety of instruments. While they were doing that, another of their group arrived with a message. Hajib pointed to Newton and the men grabbed him roughly. Without any further word he was led down the cavern to the remaining bomb. Hajib pointed upwards at it and asked, "My men tell me it has been damaged, how did this happen?" Newton stared up at the casing, to him the only thing that was not as expected was the little green light. It was blinking much more rapidly now. "I'm afraid I can't help you on that score, other than to say it may have been struck by a stray bullet, things have been quite busy since you left."

"Where is the pistol?"

"Here," Newton responded, knowing there was no sense in hiding it.

"Give it to me."

Newton reached under his coat and removed the pistol, handing it over butt first. The same men who had climbed the ropes to secure the bombs in the first place now made a return trip. Once up there, they connected some type of meter to it and took some readings. In a moment the men had slid down, noticeably faster than the first time. Their faces were white and clearly showed fear. They jabbered excitedly to Hajib who listened in silence, then barked a command. At his orders, the group quickly gathered their equipment and headed once more for the tunnel entrance.

"You will return to your people," Hajib said curtly. "Tell them not to do anything foolish, neither I nor my men will hesitate to shoot." With that the terrorist leader turned and barked orders to his men. Two of them immediately left and headed down the tunnel where the train had been.

Lord Hawthorne had been getting reacquainted with some of the volcanologists he knew. After talking with them he returned with one of them in tow to speak to Newton.

"This is Dr. David Cummings," indicating a small bespectacled man who Newton thought looked like a poster boy for all the "mad scientist" caricatures ever dreamed up by science fiction writers. "He and I studied together, but he has one great advantage over me as he is fluent in Arabic."

"Pleased to meet you," Dr. Cummings said in a pleasant voice. "Though I would have preferred it be under different circumstances."

"Tell these chaps what you told me."

"Well, to be brief, we're in the soup so to speak. It seems the device on the roof," he said pointing towards the cavern, "is not working correctly."

"Yes, I agree, the look on the guy who checked it told me it wasn't good news," Newton said. "But could you tell how bad it was damaged?"

"Well, that's the thing you see, apparently not, and neither can they. If what I heard was correct, the damn thing is starting and stopping its countdown randomly. That chap," he said pointing to the man who had climbed the rope, "is convinced that it may go pop at any time."

"Do they have a plan to deal with it?"

"The leader does, but the rest of the group are not in agreement at this point."

"And that plan is?"

"Oh, well, quite simply, Mr. Hajib or whatever his name is, wants to go out with a rather large bang."

"You mean?"

"Precisely, he wants to set it off himself."

At that moment Hajib was listening to the two men who had just returned from scouting out the tunnel. The news was not good and the men were arguing loudly. Newton gathered everyone together and began to move closer to the walls. Richard and Elijah immediately understood what was about to happen. The tone of the conversation indicated that the men under Hajib's command were losing their discipline. For such a highly trained group to do that meant the situation was both intense and immediate. Hajib was standing facing his men with only his sergeant at his side. Newton noticed that the sergeant had flicked the safety off his machine gun and the barrel was moving ever so slowly towards the rest of the military force, who had gathered on the side closest to the tunnel. Some of them were glancing nervously, first in the direction of the train, and then at the bomb lying on the platform floor. Obviously they wanted to get going, and just as obviously Hajib did not want them to go. Dr. Cummings was whispering a translation as best he could.

"Hajib and the sergeant want to stay here, the rest want to leave immediately but apparently the tunnel is blocked. They're talking about the bomb now." Dr. Cummings strained to make out the words.

"The one on the platform is operational, but the damaged one will, no might, might go off without the trigger. Hajib is saying it is better to die as a martyr rather than trying to run away. The big guy with the testing instruments is trying to argue that he can rig a timer that will give them enough time to leave."

"Leave how?" Hajib is saying. "The tunnel is blocked."

"Not that bad, one of them says, it can be shifted in half an hour."

"They may not have half an hour, says Hajib and—oh oh!"

"Oh, oh?" Newton asked. "Oh, oh what?

"Watch the sergeant, he's losing it, he's beginning to pray, I think something..."

The burst of gunfire came as much as a surprise to the group of terrorists at the tunnel entrance as it did to Newton and his group. It caught most of them in mid argument and they went down in a heap. But their training had been excellent and two of the group had time to take cover and return fire. Both fired, striking the sergeant full in the chest with burst from their pistols. Hajib, standing next to the sergeant had heard him start to pray also, and he dropped and drew his pistol as soon as he felt the sergeant's gun begin to move. The first shot took one of the two survivors in the head; the next struck the second man in the throat dealing him a mortal wound. It did not disable him immediately however, and the return volley caught Hajib in the belly, just below his armoured vest.

The cavern filled with smoke and the stench of cordite and blood. Newton sprang forward as the soon as he saw Hajib start to fall, his leap carried him over the body of the dead sergeant and he kicked the pistol out of the terrorist leader's hand. Groaning in pain, the terrorist fumbled in his jacket pocket. Newton had made a grab for the fallen pistol, but the momentum of the kick was enough to propel it over the lip of the platform and out of reach.

"You are too late, Detective, too late."

Turning back to the terrorist Newton saw that him holding a small black box in his hand. It had a single blinking light and a small antenna. Hajib was grinning, with a small rivulet of blood running out of his mouth. He held his thumb over a large red button set into the device's front panel. "With this I will destroy the great satan, and end its influence on our world." Newton watched helplessly as the terrorist's thumb descended in slow motion towards the button, knowing there was absolutely nothing he could do to prevent it. Time compressed and his vision sharpened to the point where he was convinced he could see the veins in the man's thumb. And then that thumb disappeared in a spray of blood and a short, sharp report crashed into Newton's ears. Another blast of sound and the black box itself was torn away from Hajib and skittered across the platform trailing smoke and broken wires. Newton looked up to see Carol holding one of the fallen terrorist's weapons. Turning his attention back to Hajib he saw the look of surprise on his face turn to anger, then a realization that he was dying with his mission unaccomplished. The final expression was one of puzzlement, as if he was seeing something unexpected.

"I say, old girl, bloody good shot!" Lord Hawthorne broke the silence with a rush. "Damn fine show and a near thing at that." The rest of the group slowly regained movement after the sudden display of violence. Many had a look of surprise about them; some still did not fully comprehend what had occurred, and what was still liable to happen. Jason retrieved the pieces of the box Hajib had held, and examined it.

"Well, then, he said, that's that."

"What's what?" Richard asked.

"There goes our chance to disarm that thing."

"Wait a minute, wait a minute, wasn't he about to blow us all up with that thing?"

"Yes, yes he was, but this little box was the controller for the bomb, and I'm betting that it also has, or rather had, a disarm code in it as well as a detonation code. Am I correct, major?"

"You are," answered Salim in a weary voice. "The device has, or as you put it, had, both codes sealed in a computer chip inside it."

"How do you know this," Richard asked, "unless you are one of them."

"He knows because he is one of us," Carol answered slinging the machine gun across her back. "Or rather, one of you," she said pointing at Newton.

"As in?" Newton responded.

"As in Canadian, meet Charles Francis Lockerbie, born in Lebanon and who immigrated with his parents to Canada at the age of four."

"A pleasure, I'm sure," Newton said.

"Likewise," added Elijah.

"A plant then," Richard said, "but not one of ours?"

"We aren't the only country in the world who have used agents," Carol said, "and in this case, no one connected to the United States would have stood a chance at getting accepted by the Iranians."

"This is all very interesting, I'm sure," Jason interjected, "but putting international intrigue, man of mystery, and James Bond aside for the moment, let's not forget we are literally sitting on a couple of rather large nuclear devices, which may at any moment go boom."

"Right," Newton said. "We need a new plan."

CHAPTER THIRTY ONE

Washington D.C.

"And I'm telling you it's a valid message, Commander!"

"Right, someone we have never heard of sends an email over the most unsecured communication network in the history of mankind. Detailing a plot to blow up a mountain halfway around the world on some island and cause an earthquake and tidal wave so large it would drown the eastern coasts of both Americas. Not to mention a chunk of Asia and Britain and I'm supposed to take this fairy tale to the head of Homeland Security and present it as a plausible threat?"

"Yes."

"Based on what? Give me something that I can tell the director so she'll take it to the President and not tell me to take a flying leap off the Washington Monument."

"It's in the signature, right there at the end."

Mortimer J. Packinghouse, Com Spec. adjusted the thick lenses of his glasses and pointed yet again to a series of numbers following the name of Carol O'Conner, Major USMC on the bottom of the torn off sheet of paper.

Commander Edward "Jet" Jackson sighed inwardly and asked himself for umpteenth time why it had to be him, who on the first day of a new assignment, was the one who got the crazies? Late of the 14th fighter wing based at 21 Palms, he had ejected from a crippled Tomcat that lost an engine on its final approach and had suffered injuries that were sufficient to remove him from active flight status. His majors in mathematics and physics had qualified him for a narrow range of intelligence posts and his years of service were being "rewarded" with a desk job as military liaison with the Office of Homeland Security. It was only supposed to be a temporary assignment until his retirement in 9 months, 12 days, 21 hours.

"Mortimer, convince me this thing is real, that it could, first of all, actually happen, second, it will happen, and lastly this Major O'Conner whoever she may be, is in a position to observe all this, AND that this message came from her."

"Last thing first, each member of state is assigned a personal message ID number, like the PIN number on your bank card. They change it themselves after the initial assignment on a schedule that corresponds to their duties. In her case she is required to change it prior to leaving the country on any assignment. That's every time she leaves, and she did it prior to this trip. I checked and double checked and there is doubt that the number on the message is hers."

"OK, let's say that for sake of argument, the message IS valid, what about the content, it sounds too farfetched for me to believe." Jackson argued.

"Believe it, it can and has happened before, several times in fact, and not only at this particular spot. I checked, and both the University of California and the Department of Geological Sciences in the U.K. have confirmed it."

Jackson sighed inwardly and came around to the idea that this MAY be a valid communication. "What would we expect to happen?"

"Picture a chunk of rock, 500 kilometers square that is 25 kilometers long, 15 kilometers wide, and 1400 meters thick suddenly dropping into the ocean and displacing the water for 60 kilometers. All that occurs in the space of, oh, say two minutes. Like a pebble in a still pond, it generates ripples, each ripple is a huge wave. In nine hours they hit Florida with a wave height of up to 25 meters. It makes Hurricane Katrina look like a splash in the pool. The waves, the whole series of them, would strike everything on the east coast of the Americas. Once they strike, we estimate them running inland for up to 60 kilometers in some places. It would also hit Great Britain, Africa, and Europe; even Japan would see some effect."

Jackson stared straight ahead, focusing on the wall. "What can we do about it?"

"Absolutely nothing once it starts, so our best bet, our only bet, is to not let it start."

"How much time?" the commander snapped the question out, reaching for the phone.

"According to this message, the clock is already running, and we don't know what the alarm is set for."

At a small office in "D" ring in the Pentagon sits a bank of computers monitored 24/7 by a small group of technicians drawn from all branches of the services. Like any position so staffed, an ongoing competition existed between the representatives of each branch. This was by design; nothing honed the speed of response like good old fashioned competition. As luck would have it, the phone was answered by a Marine sergeant. Further to that piece of luck, the sergeant was a female, one of only two in the group. Equality on paper was one thing, equality in practice was another and Sergeant Paula Haskins had learned, as had many before her, that to be equal she had to be better. To be better required having "an edge" against the competition. Hers was the result of years of late night studies and constant practice. She had developed several sub programs for her computer station that tracked the constant stream of emails and messages that crossed her path. It was inevitable that in some form or another there would be times when "the shit hit the fan." The object of all this was to keep constant track of those people whom it would be her responsibility to contact when it did. Thus when the commander called she was able to relay his requests in well under the required 60 seconds that was specified in the standard operating procedures of the unit.

Assistant Secretary Alexander Wells was on his way to the British Consulate in Tehran when his cell phone activated. There was no sound, just a pattern of buzzing that told him it was urgent. Sitting in the rear passenger compartment accompanied by the assistant consular official for Iran from Great Britain he was chatting about nothing in the way diplomats have been known to do for centuries. Wells checked his watch; they were still some minutes away from the consulate. Removing the phone from his pocket and pressing a series of numbers on the keypad he read the single word on the panel.

Without missing a beat in the conversation, Wells noted the message and replaced the phone. His companion was an experienced aide and knew that the message was urgent; otherwise, it would have been ignored. He carried a similar phone and the cues were universal.

"Excuse me a minute, Mr. Wells," was all he said to indicate that he understood that things had changed.

"Of course."

The driver picked up the buzzing phone and listened for a moment and in response the car accelerated smoothly into the fast lane and headed directly for the consulate. Despite the weight of the armour plate all consulate cars were fitted with, the powerful engine responded to his touch with no hesitation. The traffic was unusually light and they reached the gates a few minutes later.

"The secure communications room is in the basement, you will find the stairway on your left as you enter. Your luggage will be brought to your room, second floor, and third door on your right," the assistant said to Wells as the car pulled into the courtyard.

"Thank you," Wells said. "Please convey my respects to the consul."

"I'll let him know you have arrived, his office is on the main floor at the rear when you are ready. He is expecting you."

Wells now knew that THEY knew he had a very urgent call to make, which meant that they probably knew what it was about. THAT meant that it was something international in nature, not restricted to the U.S. alone. THAT meant they expected to be involved. Further, the phrase, "when you are ready" meant that he was number one on the list. Whatever the consul was doing, it was not as important as the meeting he was to have with Wells. Armed with that knowledge, Wells did not vary his stride as he made his way down the staircase, the communications room was guarded by a Royal Marine in dress uniform, a holstered pistol at his side. Wells held out his credentials which were ignored by the blue suited communications director waiting by the now open door.

"This way, Mr. Wells," he said with a nod to the marine.

Hmm, worse than I thought, Wells mused. He was shown to a small cubicle fitted with an AN-237 secure communications console. It looked for all the world like a regular home computer. Removing a small micro CD from his wallet, he inserted it into a slot on the panel. The machine buzzed and the screen blinked. Bending close to a small scanner, Wells had his retina read. A few seconds later the screen flashed a series of questions to which only he knew the answer. He was required to know the answers to 50 questions, of which 10 were randomly chosen to be answered. If he failed to answer correctly, the communications link would not succeed and a warning notice sent to his bosses. Finally he was allowed to enter the code word that had been sent to him. Upon completion of that, the machine printed out a series of number groups. At this stage he was normally expected to retire to a secure location and use another piece of machinery that matched the number groups with those on the disk he carried. The result would be a message he could read. In certain situations, where speed was essential, he had been told that he would see a "decode immediate" line on the panel. If this ever happened, he had been told, it would only be in circumstances akin to the outbreak of war or similar in importance, so that secrecy became a secondary consideration. He would then enter his PIN number and the message would be decoded immediately. His instructors had assured him that it was very unlikely that he would ever see such a message during his service. They hadn't and they had been on the job much longer than he. He paused only slightly when the "decode immediate" instruction appeared. As the paper sheets appeared from the printer, he began to read. Grabbing the still warm sheets of paper, Wells retrieved his disk, shut off the machine, and opened the door to find the director waiting for him. He knew instantly that they had seen a similar communiqué from their own people.

"The consul will see you now, Mr. Wells."

Together they headed up the stairs towards the main floor to the consul's office where Sir Sidney George Rawlings, Consular General for Great Britain, was waiting. Without knocking, the director opened the door and in they walked.

"Mr. Wells, how nice to see you," Sir Sidney said coming around the desk and taking his hand in both of his and giving it a hearty shake. One would think they were old school chums, reunited after a year's absence. In truth they had never met before.

"Thank you, sir," Wells returned the handshake.

"Tea?"

"Thank you."

"Earl Grey to your liking then?"

"Excellent, thank you."

Wells was sure that even if the world were about to be invaded by aliens from some far off galaxy, or nuclear tipped missiles were falling from space upon London, the Brits were determined to put the world on "hold" and have tea first. The consul poured a cup for both of them and nodded to the director who left with a smile, closing the door behind him.

"Have you had enough time to look at your message?" Sir Sidney asked.

" Time enough," Wells replied. "But I must admit it sounds very, umm, strange."

"I understand that the originator is a person on your staff, a Ms. O'Conner, is that correct?"

"Yes, a very competent major in the Marines."

"And you can confirm that this message is from her?"

"Actually, no, I can't, the PIN number that authenticates the message is known only to her and the message center, but if they say it is from her, then I would put my trust in that."

"Thank you, Mr. Wells; it would appear we have a lot of work to do and not a lot of time."

"So you agree with the gist of the message then?"

"Yes."

"May I ask why?"

"We also have our sources, Mr. Wells," the consul said with a slight smile, "and they have confirmed that everything in the message as it pertains to the effect of such an event is not only possible, but very likely. For some time now, and this information has also been shared between our MI5 and your CIA; we have been tracking the resistance forces within Iran. As you are no doubt aware, the oilfields of Iran were primarily developed by the British for the Iranian authorities. We have had a long history with the country that goes back well into the original formation of the state. Many of the ranking families have had their children educated at our best schools. Your own country also has a history with the previous regime of the Shah. After the revolution, many of these people went 'underground' in terms of their political views. We have been able to keep in touch with them, both through this office and others from Europe and Canada. In the last few years we have learned that that the new President has a terminal illness, and wishes, as it were, to 'go out with a bang'."

The look on Wells' face didn't change at all. He had heard rumblings of this even in the short time he had been in Washington.

"I see this does not come as a surprise, Mr. Wells."

"There were rumors that the earthquake that destroyed the city of Bam had 'unusual' seismic signatures. The story offered there was that the new President had received less than enthusiastic support from that region."

"The stories, for once, were correct. The earthquake would no doubt have happened in due time, but we are convinced that it was helped along by a small nuclear package placed at the bottom of a drilled shaft. The purpose however, was not to punish the people of that city, but to test an idea. Well, perhaps it was both, but that was not the primary intent. The primary intent was to prove that the very limited nuclear assets of Iran could have an effect far beyond simply moving dirt around and destroying a small city."

Wells sipped his tea slowly and nodded in understanding.

"Our oil industry has remained the primary supplier of materials to the Iranian drillers. This is because their equipment is still, in large part, of our design. When it came to our attention that some of their best planners were pulled off jobs underway at the various sites on shore and transferred to Chinese built deep sea rigs, we became very curious. The oil patch is a tight network and nothing happens that is not known to everyone over the course of time. Even though the drilling rig was of Chinese origin, the drill bits were supplied of necessity from us. Accordingly, we have tracked the movements of the drill ships since they left the yards."

The consul unfolded a map and placed it before Wells.

"You can see the activity around the island of La Palma. Also, here are the latest sea bed seismic readings from Woods Hole, and your own undersea listening posts."

Wells knew the U.S. Navy had a series of listening posts and seismic sensors planted throughout all the world's oceans. The original purpose was submarine surveillance. Since the ending of the cold war it had been discovered that it also provided good data for the prediction of earthquakes. Something the people in California and Alaska were grateful for.

"You are giving me quite a lot of information, Sir Sidney; I'm not quite sure what I am to do with it."

"Apparently, you are the ranking state official in this part of the world, Mr. Wells, and therefore empowered to direct the operations of certain military forces with the approval of your Pentagon."

"You feel such forces may be required then, Sir Sidney?"

"I am sure of it. The seismic readings, which I confess are so much blotted ink and jagged lines to me, have been confirmed by our scientists and yours. The signatures are unmistakably those of four small nuclear explosions at a depth ranging from three to four thousand feet below sea level. Also, I'm told, there is incontrovertible evidence on those same graphs that the movement of water is underway in those areas."

The consul checked his watch, "I do believe it is about time for the last piece in this puzzle to fall into place. "We will have the head of Matashuita Laboratories, Yoshi Matashuita, on the video conference phone."

"I'm not familiar with him; what can he add?"

"His firm has modeled the entire world, and all its fault lines and zones. With his expertise, he can give you an exact picture of what will happen. He is scheduled to present this information in exactly seven minutes with your President and our Prime Minister."

"Will we be included in that conference?"

"Yes, Mr. Wells, we will be able to watch it, but not ask questions."

The consul flipped a switch and a large screen descended from the ceiling. The picture was fuzzy at first, and showed various technicians setting up microphones and computer screens. At last everyone appeared ready and a grey haired Japanese male appeared on the screen.

"Good day, Mr. President, Prime Minister," Yoshi said in perfect English. "What I am about to show you is the best prediction our computers could come with. Please bear in mind that the base data is supplemented by that from your own agencies and we believe it to be accurate."

The screen image switched to a satellite map image of the Canary Islands. "Now here we see the islands of La Palma, where the fissure and volcano are located, and also the adjoining islands of El Hierro to the south, with La Gomera, Tenerife, Gran Canaria, Fuerteventura, and Lanzarote to the east. Now, please note these areas here, where underwater surveys have already been carried out and confirmed the presence of previous landslides."

The screen showed new areas extending out from the islands mainly to the north, but also south and west where landslides had occurred in the past. "Now these have occurred here, and of course in other places like Alaska and Norway with their inlets and fjords over time, some as recent as in the last few decades. Now we know that during the last eruption on La Palma in 1949 a north-south fissure of some 15 kilometers was opened with an average separation of about four meters wide. It is calculated, based on the best geological data available, that the mass of material that would make up the landslide would amount to approximately 500 cubic kilometers."

Wells tried hard, but couldn't visualize a piece of land that big.

Yoshi went on, "The freed land mass would descend the steep western slope of the island until it reaches the sea floor."

"Excuse me, Mr. Matashuita, but how deep is the ocean there?" The President interrupted.

Yoshi looked at the data in front of him, adjusted his glasses and read the numbers. "Mr. President, the floor of the ocean on the western side of La Palma is 4000 feet below sea level."

"So this chunk of mountain is going to fall as it were, almost a mile?"

"Yes, Mr. President. That's the way physics say it will play out."

"How far into the ocean will it travel?"

"We calculate, umm, 60 kilometers." He pointed a small laser device at the screen and a jagged ring appeared around the image of the Island.

"Thank you, please continue."

"I think, sir, at this point we all understand the initial landslide will be composed of a block of land 25 kilometers long, 15 kilometers wide, and 1400 meters thick. I don't know about you folks, but I just can't visualize that properly, so here is how the computer sees it." The screen image centered on La Palma and a timeline appeared on the bottom. "Now this first image depicts the state of the slide at about two minutes after the initial collapse." The screen image froze. "We see that the slide area is calculated at 3456 square kilometers, the volume is 500 cubic kilometers, speed is 100 meters per second, the initial wave height is 70 meters, that's 210 feet."

The image ran forward, like a VCR on fast forward to five minutes then stopped again. "The wave height at this point is as high as 300 meters above sea level. Additionally, the water behind the wave has been depressed to a depth of up to 1300 meters below sea level, so from the backside you would see a wave height of 1600 meters. That, gentlemen, is about one mile high. Notice also that the wave is almost completely surrounding the island, so even though the landslide is towards the west, the resultant tsunami is radiated in all directions."

The image fast forwarded to a time of ten minutes. "Note that we are now seeing a well defined series of waves, kind of like splashing in the bathtub, the island mass is causing a series of reflected waves from a height of 700 meters to a depression of 500 meters. The first of these is scouring the nearby islands to a height of several hundred meters. The initial wave is already 100 kilometers from La Palma."

The image flickered and went forward to 15 minutes. "Notice here the follow up waves are starting to drop in height, down to 400 meters with a depression of also 400 meters, but the duration is lengthening. In other words, the tops of the waves are flattening out, staying at peak height for much longer, as are the depression valleys. The initial wave is now approaching 150 kilometers from the island."

Yoshi pressed a button on the remote unit in his hand and the image went to 30 minutes. "You can see now that almost all the islands have been scoured clean. The wave in the eastern direction is 30 meters high with depressions up to 50 meters. The western waves are still 100 meters high to a low of 130 meters and 250 kilometers from the island."

"Now at one hour past the event," Yoshi went on, "we have the first waves striking Africa at a height of 60 meters to a low of 120 meters. The Canaries are, of course, almost totally devastated at this point in time. Three hours brings the wave to mid Atlantic, still traveling at about 700 kilometers per hour, the height has diminished to 30 meters. Three more hours and the waves are striking Newfoundland and Canada and the coasts of Brazil with a height of 20 to 25 meters."

No one said a word in the consul's office.

"We believe Britain and Europe will already have been hit by this time. For the United States, the shallow waters along the Florida Coast will result in the waves reaching a height of 25 to 30 meters, and there will at this point be more than a dozen succeeding waves. The elapsed time will now be about nine hours." The waves will strike all along the coastal regions and travel inland for a distance of, umm, several hundred kilometers.

"Excuse me, Mr. Matashuita, but how can that happen, the wave is only 25 meters, that's 75 feet tall."

"Yes, Mr. President, that is so. However, it is not just a spike of water, like a ripple in a pond, it is a WALL of water several kilometers thick, as are the succeeding waves. As it strikes the shore, the leading edge of the wave will continue rising due to the push of the water behind it. When it recedes, it will encounter the next wave coming in and add its volume to that one. This cycle will repeat a dozen times. Where there are low lying sections of land, as in Louisiana, Florida, and Texas, the water will flood everything to an elevation of the original wave, which was 1300 meters tall, sir, lowest point to highest point. Where there are rivers with wide mouths, like the Mississippi, Potomac, Amazon, and St. Laurence, the water will be funneled even higher. Cities built along those rivers and coast lines, such as Rio de Janeiro, New York, Houston, Charlton, Boston, Washington D.C., Montreal, and Ottawa will simply disappear. On the European side the same fate will descend upon London, Brussels, even Paris. Low lying countries such as the Netherlands will be completely inundated. Even the Mediterranean coasts will suffer somewhat, although they will be protected by Gibraltar to some extent." Yoshi paused and looked into the camera. "To put this into perspective, Mr. President, the waves that devastated South East Asia in 2005 were a mere three meters in height, and there were only two of them."

"Does your computer model estimate the damage that will be wrought?"

"The experience with the waves in your state of Alaska, Mr. President, along with our study of ancient tsunamis from the past leads to only one conclusion on that point, sir, the earth will be scoured down to bedrock. Nothing else will remain."

"Thank you, Mr. Matashuita; that has been most informative."

Sir Sidney George Rawlings poured another cup of tea for his guest.

"You can perhaps understand how the Cumbre Vieja volcano has come to be called the 'ultimate weapon,' with only the two, and relatively small nuclear weapons they have placed at the top of that fissure, the terrorists can literally wipe the bulk of Western society off the face of the earth."

"Unbelievable," Wells replied.

"Oh, very much believable, old chap, that's the problem. You see, it's so bloody simple and quite, quite possible. Elements of the S.A.S., the British Special Air Service, are being mobilized as we speak, but that will take time. Now then, what assets do you have in place to assist?" he asked.

CHAPTER THIRTY TWO

U.S.S. Tarawa – Off the coast of Gibraltar

"And I say no way, gunny, eight out of ten maybe, but ten straight, it ain't gonna happen and I got 100 bucks to back that up." Master Gunnery Sergeant Lionel H Peabody of Lawrenceburg, Anderson County, Commonwealth of Kentucky smiled and plucked the bills from the hand of Seaman Melvin "The Mole" Potts. He knew a good thing when he saw it and this was definitely a good thing. "Anymore of you swabbies want some of this action?"

Off the fantail of the Marine Landing Ship Tarawa, a group of twenty or more sailors had gathered, ready to toss three empty oil drums over the side. The drums had 100 pounds of concrete in the bottom and to the top a standard International Shooting Federation target was affixed to a metal target holder. The target was of Olympic regulation size for the recording of scores fired from a distance of 25 feet with an approved .22 calibre handgun. Also gathered on the fantail were three teams of snipers. Each was composed of an observer, a recorder, and a shooter. Each team had the exact same firearm, a Browning .50 calibre sniper rifle fitted with a heavy barrel that had been bored to .338 inches. The chamber was machined for a standard U.S. .50 inch calibre casing. Normally the .50 calibre round fired a .50 calibre bullet, but it had been found through much trial and error that the .338 Winchester Boat Tailed full metal jacket had slightly superior ballistic characteristics. Especially when driven at velocities approaching 5000 feet per second from the powder charge of the larger .50 calibre casing. Although each weapon had left the factory built to the same specifications, they had not remained so. Each sniper team had customized their particular rifle to fit the characteristics and preferences of the one man in the team who would fire it. The relative merits of each set up were the subject of ongoing and endless debate.

"Aye, laddie, it's a sweet setup and that's no lie, but you canna say it's the best all around one." The talker, Sgt. Angus Stewart, was the observer for the British team, and his partner Master Sgt. Liam Walker nodded in agreement. "True enough, Angus, but we're not shooting pigeons on some windswept and rainy rock in the Hebrides now are we?" one of the Marine group chided.

"And a good thing too that we're not, by the time you pissed about with all the doohickeys and gadgets on that rifle the bloody bird would have passed away from old age from the wait."

Marine Sgt. Fred Sly smiled at the banter. "You forget, Angus, that you don't need to play with it all time, just use the things you need when you need them, and leave them alone when you don't."

The object of discussion was the battered looking rifle scope sitting on top of the Marine team's weapon. Typical of the American love of gadgets, it had a wide range of features built in for the shooter to use. A series of fine reticules on one side helped in estimating the range of the target, and the targeting reticule could be varied from a simple crosshair to a post and crosshair or a small lighted circle at the flick of a lever on one side of the scope. There was even an infrared filter that could be snapped over the front and a built in laser sight. Like all of the other rifles present, it had the ability to be used at night.

"What do you say, Bevan, would you like that on your rifle?"

"It's very impressive to be sure," Master Sgt. Bevan Anders of the Canadian Joint Task Force replied sighting down the scope and trying all the possible combinations. "But I think I'll stick with mine."

"If you folks are ready, we can proceed with the enrichment of my pension plan." Gunnery Sgt. Peabody said amiably. "I think I've got all from these fish that I'm going to get."

"Ready as we'll ever be," Bevan replied taking a position behind his own rifle. "Let's get to it."

As soon as the shooter from each team settled into their positions on mats laid out on the deck, the drums were tossed over. While the weight on the bottom held them more or less upright, the wake of the ship and the towing action caused them to skip wildly at the end of their ropes, never holding the same position for more than a second or two. On the bridge, the boom of gunfire told the captain, Henry Fernel, that the impromptu competition had commenced. Although all forms of gambling were officially prohibited on all American warships, the Navy was the Navy, and Captain Fernel had ten bucks riding on the Marine sharpshooters.

Every pair of binoculars aboard ship was in use, including the deck mounted high power sets normally used to identify distant objects. Behind one of these was the Officer of the Day Lt. Commander Norman Buchanan. His glasses were trained on the Marine target and he saw with satisfaction the center of the target was a ragged hole becoming slightly bigger with each passing shot. He also had ten bucks riding on the competition. An accomplished marksman himself, he focused on the target trying to judge when the likely moment for a shot would be. As the target bounced and skittered in the water, he squeezed his trigger finger at the time he would have judged it opportune to fire. So far he had been in sync with the Marine sniper for seven of nine shots. One more to go. As the target bounced in their wake, it balanced for a split second and the target spun to face the fantail, the drum stabilized and the ship's whistle pierced the air.

Startled, Lt. Commander Buchanan hoped the black mark in the target's nine ring was just water. The whistle blew again and the targets were immediately hauled in. The sailors felt the surge of the vessel's engines and noted that she was turning into the wind. On deck three of the giant Sea Stallion helicopters were spooling up, their blades beginning to pick up speed.

The shooting competition ended immediately upon the first blast of the whistle. Even if the change in the ship's direction hadn't alerted the teams, and they had somehow missed the blast of the whistle, the actions of the sailors would have been enough of a clue. Instead of concentrating on the targets, they had begun to haul them in from their tie off points below the lip of the deck. "Blimey," Liam said, "has the balloon gone up?"

His question was answered by the ship's loudspeakers.

"Attention on deck! Attention on deck! All team personnel report to your ready copter. All team personnel report to your ready copter. This is not a drill. This is not a drill."

Months of practice took over and the shooting competition had now turned into a race between each team to collect their gear and sprint for the Sea Stallion that had been assigned to them. The doors to the superstructure were open and teams of U.S. Marines were racing to take their positions in the machines also.

The U.S.S. Tarawa was a Marine landing force vessel. On its flat steel deck rows of helicopters stood ready to transport Marine assault teams to positions onshore to secure a beachhead. For protective cover, 16 Harrier vertical takeoff and landing fighters were available. Beneath her decks 16 amphibious landing craft could transport the remainder of the 1500 man force and its heavy equipment for the main assault.

The helicopter forces were designated as the first to arrive in the standard operational doctrine. Slower by a large margin than the Harriers, they would take off first. Once the deck had been cleared the jets would thunder down the short runway and up an inclined ramp, literally leaping into the air riding on a jet of hot exhaust gasses from the engine. They would then join up with the helicopters and provide air cover and suppression of any hostile fire.

One of the more radical maneuvers the ship and its crew were capable of was a "hot dust off" or HDO in the acronyms that the military loved to use. This involved launching whatever helicopters or landing craft were required, and sending them the detailed operations plan via a secure encrypted data link whilst they were enroute to the area of operations. This technique allowed them to strike faster and with more flexibility than any other group of comparable size. The success of such a tactic depended upon the degree of training and skill of the ship's crew and her fighting forces. Their ability to pull it off had been demonstrated a year earlier during the annual North Atlantic Treaty Organization's exercises off the coast of Britain. The original assault plan had called for the Tarawa to land her forces on a specific beach in advance of a main NATO striking force. Once underway, the planners suddenly announced a change in plans, and called for a rescue mission in force to be launched at a spot over 200 miles away. The expectation was that there would be a massive foul up resulting in the defending forces winning the day. To everyone's surprise, the entire Marine landing force changed direction in mid air as soon as they received the new directives. They landed intact, save for one craft which managed to tangle with a derelict fishing net, and completed the simulated rescue to the amusement of the local townspeople. Many of whom still believe they were impromptu extras in some blockbuster movie production.

As soon as the last Marine climbed aboard, the doors closed and the choppers lifted off. On board the designated command Sea Stallion the operations officer bent over the communications console, watching the map of La Palma print out. The noise level in the back of the machine was high and Bevan kept his shooter's ear muffs on. All around him the Marine force was buckled into their seats and doing the last minute check of their equipment, much of it prepositioned in lockers on the chopper's lower deck.

"Damn," Sgt. Bevan thought to himself, "these guys are good."
He was going to find out just how good, good was.

CHAPTER THIRTY THREE

La Palma

Aram Mohammed Al Bazir was getting worried. According to the instructions he had received, he was to escort the scientific team from the conference center and take them to the lecture hall in time to prepare for the presentations slated for that afternoon and evening. The instructions were explicit, and the timelines allowed little room for tardiness. After leaving the group to go on their tour he had traveled to La Palma to check with the consul on the progress of the conference. The blockage of the runway at the airport had caused delays in the arrival of some of the attendees and cancellations from others who could not fit the delay into their schedules. Every deviation from the prescribed plan had been recorded and he had turned his notes over to the consul for forwarding to Tehran. In addition, a second set of notes had been forwarded by him personally to his new boss. He had expected the consul to give him confirmation that both had been received. This had not happened and he was getting that feeling of apprehension that had served him so well in his life. Something was not right. Sitting in the hotel lobby he had been summonsed to use the desk phone by a clerk.

"Aram?"

"It is I, praise be to Allah."

"This is Shaba, I have transmitted your report as requested, and I am asked to direct you to proceed with the conference timetable as set out. Those who are not yet here will not be coming."

"I understand."

"I also have a message from Minister Sahkirez for you."

"Yes?"

"You are to ensure that all our attendees are back at the hotel in good time for the conference. Do you understand?"

"Yes."

"That is all I have." The line went dead.

Aram had expected such a message; one of the group was thought to be on the verge of seeking asylum perhaps? It would be an easy thing to approach one of the attendees from another country and declare their intentions. No doubt the foreign scientists had been briefed how to assist in such an event. No, that would not be it, all the scientists save Salim had been abroad many times, and had better opportunities to defect. It must be something else, something he couldn't put his finger on at the moment. But he had his orders and he must carry them out. Accordingly he had returned to the conference center earlier than expected and waited in the parking lot. At first, the presence of the military trucks had not meant much to him, but as time went on he paid them more attention. In Iran of course, they were everywhere, but why here? Did this have something to do with the message he had received? Finally, he entered the center and looked around. That it was empty was explainable by the tendency of those in the scientific world to lose track of time and immerse themselves in discussions about this and that. The instruments in the room continued to record the seismic conditions around the volcano and regularly spit out sheets of paper. Aram took a seat and continued his waiting. After a few minutes he began to study the instruments and their data, more from curiosity than anything else. Aram was not a trained scientist, but he was not an unintelligent man either. After looking at the new sheets of recorded data, he noted one value that seemed to be rising with each passing moment. Intrigued he rummaged through the piles of paper on the table until he came to the sheets that had first caught the attention of the volcanologists. There, marked by circles of ink, and commented by those who had studied them earlier, he noted the Iranian words for "water level." Cross checking that value with the newer ones coming off the machines he discovered that the level of water had increased substantially over the last hour. He looked at his watch; the group was now overdue by half an hour. Flipping open his cell phone he attempted to make a call but the phone would not lock onto a signal. Searching around the room, he knew there had to be a phone somewhere in the center he could use. The logical place would be close to the doorway, on the table which was now covered in the papers he had been studying.

Studying the walls he found a set of wires, painted over and leading down from the wall. They led to a pile of papers on the corner of the large table. Following the wires he discovered the phone and lifted the handset. No dial tone sounded in the ear piece. He examined the phone; no obvious problems with it appeared. Holding the wires in his hand he traced them back up the wall where they disappeared into a small black plastic box. The box was damaged, and he quickly recognized the presence of a bullet hole. The presence of the military vehicles, the bullet hole, the rising water, and the missing scientists added up to trouble and Aram knew he had to report this immediately to his new boss. The problem was, how to make sure it only reached his ears alone? Shaba was no doubt a loyal servant of the government, else he would not have been given the position he was in. His cell phone did not have the range, and he could not leave the center lest the scientists return in his absence. Perhaps, he thought, one of those vehicles in the parking lot might have a stronger cell phone that he could use.

Minister Sahkirez was at that moment attempting to contact Aram.

The secure line that had been assigned for his use and linked to his cell phone had gone unanswered. On his desk sat a full report from his "private" observers of the activity now going on in the British Consul's office. It merely confirmed what he had already known. The events presently unfolding on a small volcanic island off the coast of Spain had been one plan amongst many. When it had come up for consideration, he had abstained from voting on it. His reasons were so clear back then, many years ago in the heady days after the takeover of the American Embassy. He had been a small fish in the pond, the technical requirements were beyond the capability of the small nation, and Saddam Hussein had been a much larger and more immediate threat. He had not thought much of the plan since then, and now he was to pay a price for it.

The door to his office opened and a man in the uniform of the Presidential guard entered. Behind him a pair of much larger men in black uniforms with rifles stood guard.

"Minister Sahkirez, you will come with me." It was not a request.

The black suited men behind him held their weapons at the ready.

"Very well, general," the minister responded and got up from his desk. "My family?"

"They are already under our protection"

As they exited through the door Sahkirez noted that there were five or six more black suited men waiting. All were armed. In the corner lay two of the personal guards that had been assigned to him and both were dead, their heads lying at an unnatural angle. With no further conversation the group formed a circle around the minister and led him down the stairs to a waiting armoured truck, its engine idling.

Behind them in his office the phone began a ceaseless ringing.

Aram hung up after the low battery indicator started to flash on his phone. He had not found a phone in the trucks, but changing his position to a higher elevation above the center had brought the phone within range of one of the few towers on the island. Most tourists had wanted to escape the infernal devices to which they so willing enslaved themselves at home. Cell phone coverage was therefore limited to the urban centers of the island. Apparently the minister was no longer in a position to receive calls. Making a quick decision he left the building and went back to his car. Plugging in the phone to the car's power outlet, he waited for the unit to recharge. While he gave that some time to happen, he went over to the military vehicles to see what else he could find. The first truck contained some shovels and other digging equipment. A few personal packs littered the rear compartment and in the driver's cab he found a map of the island with the route to the mountain conference center marked in grease pencil. He also found two AK-47 rifles with folding stocks, each with a full clip of ammunition. Moving on to the other vehicle, he found a backpack with a small leather covered binder. Opening it he found some diagrams and a map of some of the passages. One of them which led to a large cavern with a spot circled in red. Some water bottles and packaged food and clothing made up the rest of the contents of the pack. The glove box held official looking papers which he recognized as Visas. All were from countries of the Middle East, Lebanon, Syria, and Jordan. None were from Iran. Returning to his car Aram retrieved his recharged phone and looked at his watch, calculating the change in time zones he phoned a number that he knew would be answered.

The ringing phone interrupted a conversation between the new head of El-Hahimin prison, Hatem Al-Quabar and the head of the guards on the third floor. The prison had been notified to expect a prisoner of "special importance" and this meant an arrival by helicopter or armoured vehicle. The discussion was centered on where to put the new arrival. Normally "special importance" prisoners were housed in one wing of the third floor, but this wing was suddenly full at the moment, and a decision had to be made where to either put him in a different wing, or where to move one of the already housed.
"Sir, the prisoners are required to be in isolation from each other and we have no more empty cells," the guard was saying.
"What about the second floor?"
"Already full, and anyway, the last time we did that the interrogators complained about the lack of 'private' facilities."
"I understand that, but they will have to realize that there is only so much room here." The guard said nothing further, but he knew that such mundane things as the prisoner population would not matter to the interrogators. They always considered their priorities to be of greater importance. Hatem finally acknowledged the ringing of the phone and nodded at the guard to leave. "We'll discuss this later."
"Hatem, is that you?" The voice on the phone said without waiting for an official greeting.
"Aram?"
"It is I, Hatem, listen carefully, I cannot get through to minister Sahkirez, and I need you to try from your end."
"You are in luck then, Aram, I have just received notification that he is on his way here."
"He is holding an inspection then? That is why I cannot get him at his office?"
"No, Aram, he is coming here as a 'special interest' prisoner; Minister Sahkirez has been arrested."

Aram closed the lid of the phone in stunned silence and as a matter of habit hooked it up to the charger again. Who could he contact now? His thoughts were disturbed by the distant sound of helicopters. In Iran, Hatem stepped to the window of his office and scanned the skies looking for the dark spot that signal the arrival of perhaps the most important prisoner he would see in his lifetime.

CHAPTER THIRTY FOUR

Aboard call sign "Tiger One"

The two pilots concentrated on the navigational readout on the screen in front of them. The Sea Stallion was equipped with a "glass cockpit." All but the most basic flight instruments were represented digitally on plasma flat screen readouts mounted in their panel. One of these was dedicated to navigational duties. Since lifting off the Tarawa they had received a flight plan sent from the ship via secure data link before reaching cruising altitude. In response to that data the three Sea Stallions had headed via the shortest possible route to the island of La Palma. Moments after getting airborne they had been notified that a twin engine tanker had departed the British military field in Gibraltar and been directed to a station halfway to the island.

"What do you think, Bobby?" Commander Zach Pederson said into the intercom.

"They don't pay me to think, just to fly," Bobby Anderson replied with a grin that was hidden in his mask.

"Good thing, they barely get their money's worth from that," Zach responded.

"Humph, well if they did pay me to think, I'd say we were going to either pull someone's ass out of a fire, or start one."

"Got that right. Look at the flight profile," he said tapping on the screen just below the required speed indicator. It read "maximum" instead of the usual knots per hour numbers.

"Hope that tanker is on time, we pulled off light."

Standard operating procedure was for the Sea Stallions to lift off with less than full tanks, so that the maximum load could be carried. Usually a tanker was already circling the ship and would immediately fuel the helicopter for its mission profile. Since a mission could come up at any time the choppers were left in a "light" fuel state, in their case less than one-third full.

"Tiger One, this is Big Bird, over," came the distinctly British voice on the radio.

"Big Bird, Tiger One, go ahead."

"We'll be on station in three. Co-ordinates are downloading now."

The navigation screen showed another blinking dot at a position forty miles ahead on their flight path.

"Got it."

"High test or regular?"

"We'll take the good stuff."

"Right then, regular fueling sequence I presume?"

"One two three, nice and simple so you can count it on your fingers," Bobby chuckled into the radio.

"Just the way we like it," the British voice responded. "Deploying boom, watch for the bouncing lights." Behind the tanker a long pipe with a small set of wings was reeled out, on the end was a carbon fiber meshed bucket about 24 inches in diameter. The Sea Stallion was equipped with a long probe on the front of the helicopter which extended a few feet past the arc of the rotor blades. The pilot's job was to set the helicopter in position so that the boom flyer on the tanker could, with the assistance of a television camera mounted on the end of the boom, "fly" the basket onto the probe.

"Tiger One is ready."

"Roger that," came the voice of the boom operator, "Stand by for hookup." The boom maneuvered a little from side to side, then the helicopter rocked slightly as it seated fully on the probe. A light blinked on the panel of the chopper and another on the panel of the boom operator. Zach punched a button and a valve opened and the fuel transfer began. The pilots of both machines began a synchronized ballet; the helicopter was getting heavier as the fuel was pumped aboard. The tanker was getting lighter and both pilots compensated to keep the positions within the required profile.

"Big Bird, Tiger One is reading full."

"Roger, disengaging now."

The valves closed and Tiger One fell back slightly, the boom disengaged with a small spray of fuel and Tiger Two curved into position for its turn. With the benefit of many hours of practice, the three Sea Stallions finished the maneuver and returned to formation.

"Tiger One, Big Bird, fuelling completed, returning to base"

"Roger, Big Bird, thanks. But next time do the windows will you?"

"Ahh, no chance of that, old boy, management gets upset if we leave our seats during the show."

"Right you are, sir, see you in Gibraltar next time, and the beer is on me."

"So long as it's warm. You Yanks have no taste for the good stuff," laughed the British pilot as he headed back in a sweeping turn.

"Tiger flight close up," Bobby radioed and the three choppers bored west at full throttle towards the fast growing dot in their arc of vision.

Below the Marine colonel in charge of the mission keyed a switch on the tactical radio that linked the teams on all three machines. Lt. Col. Granby Heliwell was a no-nonsense 35 year old on the fast track. This was his ninth mission since joining the Tarawa over ten months ago. He had been a major when he arrived and he intended on making the next selection panel. For all his ambition he was fiercely defensive of his men. Although he had taken casualties in his previous missions, only four had been fatalities. He insisted on the best equipment he could get his hands one. Much of it was not allotted to a Marine Corps Unit, but had been set aside for more "specialized" units like the Seals or Rangers. His first task had been to lobby that if the mission was considered "specialized" then so should the equipment. Someone further along the line had agreed and soon the men of his unit began to receive and train with things most servicemen would never even see. One of the lessons that 9/11 and subsequent operations had shown, was that inter-service rivalries were simply too expensive a luxury for the times.

On Tiger Two and Three the radios were already on and tuned to the mission frequency contained in the operational plan downloaded soon after liftoff. Printers mounted in racks silently spat out a series of written instructions and maps. The commanders of each team consulted the directives for their men then brought their respective groups together and handed out the assignments.

Bevan and his spotter Walter Sanchez were replacing the cleaning gear for their weapon when they received their mission orders. Every sniper knew that a rifle with a clean barrel shot differently than one with an accumulation of spent powder and other debris in the barrel. The rule was to always start a mission with a clean bore, that way they knew the exact spot the first round would hit. In many cases the first round to be fired would be the only one. Together they went over the detailed plans and orders. The presence of a volcano on the island was news to both of them.
"This thing about to blow then, Bevan?"
"Apparently, but not from as they say 'natural causes'."
"So, once again the fate of the world rests on our shoulders, eh?"
"And whose shoulders would be better able to carry such a burden?"
"Why, us of course. What rounds do you want?"
"Standard 50 round pack, 250 grain, oh and better take a ten pack of those new titanium tipped armour piercing jobs."
"Christ, we expecting to take out a tank?"
"One never knows what opportunities the day may bring, Walter, best to be prepared"
"What do you think of this then, sounds apocalyptic to me." The two men studied the op order detailing the possible consequences of the impending collapse of the west side of the Island. The maps and narrative sent a cold chill up both their backs. Bevan's home was in the Province of New Brunswick, a fishing town built close to the shore. He had seen the damage that could be done by a strong storm and in

his mind saw that a 15 meter tidal wave would completely inundate his home. Looking across at Walter he shook his head in wonder.

"What do you think, Walter?"

"It ain't Afghanistan, Bevan, and it ain't Kosovo either."

"You're right about that. Looks like we'll be traveling light, no packs, no food, no extra water, just a quick in and out."

"I sure hope they are correct about how they think this little gem is made."

"Time will tell, Walter, time will tell."

CHAPTER THIRTY FIVE
Volcano Conference Center

Aram watched with resignation as the three dots on the horizon grew closer. His mission here had been confusing from the start. Minister Sahkirez had sent him to observe the scientists and report back any incidents that might require action to be taken at a higher level. That had been made more difficult by the last minute inclusion of Salim into the number of personnel that were attending. Now not only had he lost contact with the main group of scientists because he was off looking for Salim. He had lost contact with Salim as well. With his direct superior being arrested, he wondered how long it would be before he too shared that fate. What of the trucks he wondered, what was the military interest here? The papers he found were obviously Iranian, despite the names and places of origin. What was the significance of the codes and orders he had taken from the truck and put into his pocket? Aram sighed inwardly, and adopted the same philosophy that had kept him alive all these years. What is written is written—and not for him to change.

He returned his focus to the approaching helicopters. They grew in his vision more quickly now, black shapes and shadows racing over the dark rock strewn sides of the volcano. Approaching the parking lot, they paused in the air and descended in a whirring cloud of dust. Aram shielded his eyes and opened them only when the noise of the spinning turbines died away. Shouted orders and the hurried movement of men greeted him when the dust clouds abated. Each machine disgorged its cargo of men and equipment. One of the men stood apart from the rest and directed the actions of the men unloading the choppers. Soon one of his men pointed at Aram and said something to the leader who barked something in return and came over to where Aram was standing. As he did, he consulted the clipboard he carried, flipping through the sheets before settling on one.

"You are Aram Mohammed Al Bazir," he said in a voice which brooked no argument.

"I am." Aram replied. For a moment, the man said nothing, studying the figure in front of him. "I have been sent from Minister Sahkirez."

Aram said nothing in return; did this man know the Minister had been arrested?

"I am Colonel Benadar; do you know what has been going on here?"

"I brought out a group of volcanologists to the conference event here, they entered the tunnels and they have not yet returned. I am to bring them back to the hotel in La Palma when they do."

Colonel Benadar looked at the vehicles assembled in the parking lot.

"Are these yours?" he asked.

"No, they were here when I arrived back from the town; they were not here earlier when I first dropped the group off."

"Do you know who they belong to?" The Colonel Asked, looking directly at Aram.

"Not entirely, but these vehicles and the weapons I have found in them indicate that there are Iranian military personnel here already. This leads me to wonder what you are doing here Colonel?"

"Those men are under the control of Mullah Shariz, and they are here under the orders of the President of the ruling council to put into effect a plan to kill millions of people from the west."

"And you Colonel, what are you here for?" Aram asked again.

The Colonel looked into Aram's eyes, and said nothing for a moment, "Isn't it obvious Deputy Minister Al Bazir? I am here to stop them."

One of the Colonel's men ran up to him with a radio transceiver in hand. "Colonel Benadar, the Americans are coming."

To the east, the beat of helicopter blades grew louder, around the edge of the volcano, just above ground level, three Sea Stallion helicopters appeared in formation. Sweeping in just above a growing cloud of dust they hovered as if waiting for further orders. A large cloud of dust obscured them except for the tips of their blades, a few seconds later they resumed their inward journey. Aram was sure the pilots had not expected to see three Soviet made Iranian helicopters parked at the center entrance. Evidently they had radioed for instructions and received the OK to proceed with the landing. As they approached, they changed altitude, lifting higher and dropping down in an intricate pattern designed to break up the heated rivers of air from their turbines to make tracking them with anti-aircraft missiles harder. Continuing on overhead they now swept in from the west, raising more dust as they did. Landing simultaneously, with their passengers exiting even before the landing gear had full taken the weight of the craft. As soon as the men had left, the helicopters were off and gone within seconds. Aram was duly impressed. He wondered if the Colonel was too.

If he was, he didn't show it. Joined now by a Captain, he handed over the clipboard he had been carrying, barked an order, returned the officer's salute, and waited for the approach of the American commander. Colonel Granby Heliwell came up in an unhurried walk; the Marines had already fanned out in a semi-circle and were approaching from a variety of angles and directions. At any given time half were hidden behind the man in front, all appeared nonchalant and unconcerned, but their approach was designed to allow at least half the group to survive an ambush and return immediate fire. Colonel Benadar gave no outward indication of any emotion. Inwardly he admired the easy movements of the Marine force; the way they advanced indicated both a high degree of training and discipline. Waiting until it was clear that the Marines were in position to control events, he barked an order and his men fell in behind him in three rows. The officers assumed their positions in front of the men and executed a "present arms" maneuver in as crisp a manner as any Marine Corps honour guard. Colonel Heliwell drew himself up to parade attention and returned the offered salute. He barked an order and the Marines fell in behind him and returned the honors. That done, the two commanders shook hands and the tension eased. The two groups fell out and did what military men the world over did when meeting soldiers from another country. They eyed each other's equipment and within a few minutes were exchanging greetings. Given another half hour, Colonel Heliwell thought, and they would be organizing competitions and swapping cigarettes.

The two commanders took a walk where they compared sheets of paper, plans, and diagrams and in the end came to a mutual decision on a plan of action. This took less than five minutes as both men understood the need for quick action.

"Captain GreyOwl," barked Colonel Heliwell. "Get the men ready, we move out in two minutes, here are your orders." The Captain saluted, looked at the order, and started rounding up the Marines. Within minutes they had left the parking lot and headed into the center. Colonel Benadar did the same with his men, who broke into small groups, taking positions within the centre and leaving a couple outside by the trucks. Aram waited patiently for the two groups to complete their preparations. While he was surprised at the cooperation of the Iranian and Marine forces, he had long ago learned to expect the unexpected. When the two groups had settled into their tasks, both of the commanders came up to talk with him.

"This is Deputy Minister Al Bazir, he is the personal representative of Minister Sahkirez, he will go with you and act as an interpreter if required. Politically he outranks me and will carry more weight with those inside." Aram nodded in agreement; it didn't look like he had much say in the matter.

"Good to meet you, sir," the Marine commander said, offering his hand.

Aram shook it and said nothing.

"Colonel Benadar has given me these," and he showed Aram a list of the Iranian delegates along with their pictures. "Can you tell me if there are others?"

"The tour was open to all the volcanologists from the conference,"

Aram said. "I believe many of them took advantage, I do not know exactly how many. That information in the possession of Dr. Zagrib, the head of our delegation. As I have explained to Colonel Benadar, Dr. Zagrib is still within the tunnel."

"Thank you, sir," Col. Heliwell said. "Captain, move them out." Captain GreyOwl, a radio strapped to his waist and an earphone embedded in his helmet, signaled the men were ready and the Marines moved out and headed at a trot down the tunnel. They had gone only a short distance when the point man held up his hand. As one they tried to melt into the walls, with not much success. The point man turned and pointed to the tracks and clenched his fist. Something was coming along the tracks, some kind of a train or perhaps a man powered cart. The tunnel ahead was lit with a series of low wattage bulbs; they provided light enough for the point man to observe the bend in the tunnel. His hand felt the vibrations grow in strength on the metal tracks. He held his rifle at the ready and selected the grenade launcher tube on the fire selector lever. He had loaded it with a high explosive contact fused projectile. He had his doubts how effective it would be against a steel train, but he could always take out a portion of the roof over top of the train if he had to. That would not be his first choice, however, since the likely result would be a cave-in of some proportion that may block the tunnel. The vibrations were stronger now, and in the distance he could hear the rumble and screech of metal wheels on metal tracks.

The earpiece he wore squawked into life. "Oscar one, Tango, over"

"Go ahead." Tango was the call sign for the Colonel. "We want them alive, Sherm, and there are civilians in the party"

"Roger that." He turned the fire selector lever to single shot for the rifle. Beneath him the vibrations grew stronger and the headlight of the train played dimly on the tunnel wall by the bend.

They were coming.

"Hold it just so," Jason said quietly, all his concentration on a small piece of telephone wire scavenged from the lines on the wall. Carol, Newton, and Georgia were all holding small pieces of the single strand copper onto the pins of a chip soldered into a circuit board. The board was part of the now disassembled controller and the wires connected the chip with Jason's DNA analyzer. Jason turned on the power and punched a series of numbers into the keypad. The machine had a built in diagnostic routine that allowed it to read the code embedded on a chip. It could also alter that code if required, and the chip was compatible, so that new instructions to update the machine could be added. It was this feature that now occupied Jason's attention.

"That's it, I'm getting something." A series of characters marched across the screen and Jason pushed the print button. A sheet of paper spat out with rows of numbers and letters in two character groups.

"What the hell is that?" Richard asked.

"That is the code sequence from the chip."

"We can disarm it then?" Georgia asked happily.

"Not so fast, if it's the complete code, part of it will be instructions for the computer chip inside, and part of it will be the data that it is to send."

"Which means?" Elijah asked.

"It means he has to separate the two parts out before he can decipher which is which, and that will take some time." Newton said.

"Do we have that time?"

"Doesn't matter if we do or we don't; it will not affect the amount of time that it takes to do it." Elijah said.

"You aren't going to accidentally set that thing off are you?" Richard asked.

"No," Jason answered. "I've disabled the transmitter portion of the controller, and I've only supplied power to the one chip."

"How difficult is this going to be?" Newton asked.

"Well, luckily, the analyzer is essentially a little computer powered by Linux, and the operating system includes a number of programs which can take a piece of code like this and make a pretty good guess what the original program looks like. But the trick will be to determine the type of computer that it runs, because they all have different code sets."

"Can you determine that from the controller?"

"I can to a limited extent, but there are no markings on it, so it will be by counting the pins and deducing the type from there. I suspect it is something like a PIC or similar chip. After all, the job it has to do is very simple, just read the correct code sequence and send the proper signal to the transmitter."

"We'll leave you to it then," Newton said, "while we go and investigate the blast we heard from the tunnel."

"May I make a suggestion?" Lord Hawthorne put forth.

"Sure."

"Take the weapons off the bodies of these men, and hide the remains, it seems to me that the chaps who went to all the trouble to set this up would surely have a backup plan and this is not the sole extent of their efforts."

"Good idea." Elijah and Lord Hawthorne gathered the weapons from the fallen men, while Newton and Richard dragged the bodies behind the rock outcroppings. That done, they gathered by the tunnel entrance. Elijah handed each of them a radio taken from the terrorists,

"In case we get separated, and, if any more bad guys are coming we may be able to pick up some radio chatter."

"OK, but that works both ways so everyone keep their fingers off the transmit key. We don't want them to know where we are either, let's go."

Newton and the rest headed up the tunnel as far as they could go. A broken light bulb swung in its hanging socket over a pile of rock and rubble. Newton stood back and observed the mess. "Well, it can't be too bad," he said, "the power is still on, so the cable isn't cut."

"What now?" Richard asked.

"Now we start digging. We still have to get out of here remember. The water is rising and the bombs are still active. I suspect that they will go off when the water hits them. But that may not be the only trigger. My guess is there is a timer or other backup function also."

"Well then, there's nothing for it but to get to work." Lord Hawthorne added, "So pass me that folding shovel and let's start at the top, we only have to clear a space large enough to wiggle through."

"What do you see out there, Sherm?" The radio clicked on in the scout's ear.

"Stand by, one," he replied, "I got a couple of guys on the train, but they don't seem to be military."

Wentworth Owens was having problems seeing. The debris from the explosion made when the kerosene and solvent bottle unexpectedly blew up still stung his eyes. His nose was thoroughly clogged with dust and smoke. A ringing pain had started in his head soon after the explosion, and his hand came away covered in sticky blood when he ran his fingers through his hair. Dr. Spangler was in worse shape, the man chasing them had managed to fire a burst from his rifle prior to disappearing in the blast and Spangler had cried out and collapsed, he had said nothing since then, but his breathing continued, although it was getting harsher. Owens had stopped when he felt safe, and packed the wound in Spangler's back with the rags he found on the train. Certainly not very clean, but the only thing he had available. The train had slowed appreciably in the last mile. Owens guessed the batteries were reaching depletion as the grade had not gone up much. Now the train was only going at the speed of a fast walk. The whole series of events had combined to sap his strength and leave him dizzy. For the last few minutes he had caught himself dozing off despite the swaying and lurching of the engine. He was even beginning to hallucinate, not the white rabbits that Alice had chased, but a stocky man in a uniform was trying to talk to him. Again, unlike the rabbit, this figure had a name tag, but he couldn't focus long enough to read it. God, he was tired.

"See, it goes down from here, no telling how far." Newton nodded to Elijah and examined the broken timber. It sat squarely in the middle of the heap, blocking the escape route they had labouriously dug to that point.

"Well, we can't go around it, or under it, or over it, so we'll have to go through it." Newton announced. "I don't suppose any of those guys had a chain saw in their packs did they?"

"No such luck," Lord Hawthorne said. "But, yes I think they had something that might help." With that he headed off in the direction of the platform. Newton sank down on the pile of rock and rubble they had shifted so far. Elijah passed over a water bottle.

"How much of that have we got left?"

"Lots, at least enough, the bad guys brought some with them when they came the second time. Also they left a lot the first time around."
Newton swallowed the cool liquid and put the bottle aside. "I wonder what Hawthorne has in mind?"

"Drink slowly," Master Sergeant Fredrick James Potter the Third said to Owens. The scientist shook his head to clear the cobwebs and took a welcomed sip of the delicious cool water. His vision cleared and he could clearly make out the Red Cross patch on the tunic of the man holding the water bottle.

"What, where ?"

"Slowly now," the medic said. "You're going to be OK, you have a nasty bump on the head, but the bleeding has stopped."

"What about Dr. Spangler?" Owens started and looked around. "Is he going to be OK?"

"He's fine for now, took a bullet in the back, and he's lost a lot of blood, but I have him stabilized." Dr. Owens closed his eyes and took another sip from the bottle, when he opened them to thank the medic, he found himself staring into the cool blue eyes of Colonel Heliwell.

"How are you feeling? Up to answering a few questions?"

"Of course, thank you I'm much better now, just a little tired."

"To be expected, now tell me everything that happened since you got to the center."

"I have to admit, it's a solution I would not have thought of." Newton remarked. The subject of the conversation was a thin piece of super strong piano wire wrapped around the offending timber. The ends of the cable terminated in two small wooden handles. "Just what the well equipped assassin needs these days," Richard said. "Will it really cut through that beam?"

"Oh surely," Lord Hawthorne said, "but be careful it doesn't cut through the handles as well."

"You take one Richard, I'll take the other," Newton said grabbing one handle, "We'll do the bottom end first; the top looks like it will slip out with a little pressure."

"Yeah, as long as the roof doesn't come down with it." The wire cut through the wood at a steady pace, and Elijah and Lord Hawthorne took a turn and slowly they worked through it. A solid kick from Richard broke the last remaining strands and it fell free.

"Great," he said, "only a few tons left to go."

Elijah grabbed a shovel and started hacking at the pile.

"What's the condition of that train, Sergeant?"

"Not so good, sir, the batteries are pretty low and it's beat up some."

"Can we charge it up?"

"Yes, sir, the charger is located back at the center. But it will take some time to accomplish, probably three to four hours to charge it completely."

"Get on it, Sergeant, those civilians say it's about a 45 minute ride to the cavern, get it charged enough to make it there and back, we'll go ahead on foot, make sure you bring the extra cars from the siding when you come, looks like a lot of people to evacuate."

"Yes, sir. Move out people."

"OK, Captain, the scientists are certain they blocked the tunnel when they made their escape, so move your people out in skirmish order, we'll head on foot as fast as possible to the cave-in, technical packs only. And everyone bring their shovels."

"Yes, sir!"

The Marines dropped their spare ammunition, food, and extra water packs. Taking only technical equipment such as radio and electronics gear, personal shovels, and lightweight C4 explosive packs they moved out down the tunnel. This amounted to a reduction of about 40 to 50 pounds of gear per man and their rate of movement increased accordingly. Behind them the battered train was switched onto the maintenance siding.

"What ya got there, Sparky?" Sergeant K.D. "Sparky" Bonds was the unit's electrical specialist, and as usual, assigned any task that involved wires, batteries, or other electrical equipment. He wiped his greasy forearm on his brow and looked up from the inside of the engine compartment. "Regular 24 volt industrial deep cycle silver type batteries, just like a diesel sub has," he spat out a chunk of tobacco. "Should take about four and a half hours to charge up fully according to 'sissy'." Sissy was the specific gravity meter he held in his hand. It measured the state of charge in a battery by checking the state of the electrolyte.

"No way to speed that up, Sparky?"

"Sure, If you got an extra charger in your back pocket, we could double up the current, but it wouldn't do the batteries any good."

"How much current do you need?"

"Anything above 80 amps would do, but..."

"Those batteries come out of there, Sparky?"

"Well, sure, but, Captain, they weigh about 250 pounds apiece."

"Grab that trolley, Sparky, get a couple of guys to give you a hand, haul two batteries out and let this charger work on the other two."

"What is your plan, Captain?" Colonel Benadar said, as he observed the work in progress.

"Those trucks outside are equipped with 100 amp alternators, sir, and if we can get those batteries hooked up to a couple of the trucks we can use them to charge them, that will cut the time in half, to say about two hours, but we only need to get there and back, say two hours running time. I expect that we will only need a half charge to accomplish that."

"I think we can give you a hand with that." Colonel Benadar turned and addressed his Sergeant who left at a run and returned a few minutes later with the two largest members of his command. With a nod from the Colonel, they immediately fell in alongside the Marines and began to loosen and wrestle one of the batteries free from its restraints. The Marines working on the other battery at the far end looked at each other and the Iranians and grinned. As quick as that the exercise had turned into a competition between the two groups.

"Move it, Johnson," one Marine told the other as he freed the last bolt on his side.

"Got it, Mike," the other replied placing the freed nut from his side on the side plate. "You ready to lift this mother?"

"Anytime you want, candy-ass."

"Where's that trolley?"

"Harvey," Mike yelled, "bring that over here," he said pointing at the trolley

"Fuck that noise, look at those guys," Johnson said indicating the Iranians who had freed their battery and not waiting for a trolley were hand carrying the heavy battery by means of straps built into the casing. They were immediately joined by two others of their force and they sprinted for the outside.

"Shit!" said Harvey. "Henry get your ass over here. Gerry. grab the door!"

The Iranians reached the door first and were through it before the Marines got four sets of hands on their battery. The Iranians stopped at the first truck and put the battery down beside it. They had the

hood up just as the Marines skidded to a stop beside the other vehicle. Mike freed the hood and jumped in the cab to start the engine. Another Marine exited the center door with a set of jumper cables, followed by one of the Iranians. Both truck engines were roaring and the last jumper connected at virtually the same time. Both groups looked up at the other when the last connection clicked into place. Since it was a tie, both claimed victory. Mike grinned broadly at one of the Iranians and gave him the thumbs up, the Iranian returned the universal gesture and the tired sweating men collapsed beside the trucks breathing heavily. Johnson reached in his pocket and took out a pack of cigarettes and tossed it over to the largest of the Iranians who caught it and nodded his thanks. Johnson pointed to his name tag "John-son" he said slowly, offering his hand. The Iranian grinned as he shook the Marine's hand and pointed to himself, "Kareem, and this is Hanjabar, Marqueet, and Sanjhat," indicating the others in his group.
"You speak English?"
"Yes, some," Kareem replied. "My father was soldier when British were in Iran, he teach me, he say Brits come back one day." Mike joined the conversation, tossing over a couple of bars of chocolate. "You guys are pretty good."
"Lots of, how you say in your army, 'fatigues, physical work as punishment for small things, yes?"
Mike smiled back, "Same in every army, man, same in every army."
Colonel Benadar and Colonel Heliwell stood and observed the interchange, and had the same thought, they now had a cohesive group.

They would need it.

"Hey," Richard yelled, "I think I see a light!"
"Yeah?" Jason, who had joined the diggers asked.
"Yeah!"
"Thank God," Elijah said.
"Amen to that," Newton added.
"About bloody time!" Lord Hawthorne concluded. With renewed energy they widened the space until there was enough room to squeeze by.
"Do you see anything on the other side?"
"Just the other side," was the response.
"Geez, look at that!" Jason said pointing to a swirl of dust rushing by and exiting the cavern up the tunnel.
"Water's rising faster now; we better get everyone together and get going."
"What about the bomb?"

"We take it with us."

"And the one on the roof, what about that one?"

"We leave it, no choice, it will either go off or not. Either way," Newton said, "there is nothing much we can do about it."

"What about that code you were working on, Jason," Richard asked, "will that work?"

"Fifty percent chance," Jason said. "I got the code deciphered, but I can't be sure which is the part that turns it off and which is the part that says 'go boom'."

Newton turned to Lord Hawthorne, "Any idea how much time is left 'til this place fills with water?"

"Can't be sure, old boy, but it is getting much colder now and that means the water is getting higher, and closer, when it reaches the ceiling then, well, it's all over then isn't it."

"This is the worst tropical vacation I've ever had," Elijah quipped. "I'm going to complain to my travel agent."

"Look on the bright side, my boy," Lord Hawthorne said smiling, "It can hardly get much worse."

"I'm afraid it can," Newton said from the top of the pile of rocks. "I see lights coming down the tunnel."

"Hey, Sparky, these things cooked enough yet?" Mike yelled over the roar of the truck engines and looked at the boiling liquid inside the batteries. Sparky tested both batteries and did some quick calculations in his head. "Yep, I figure they will run for about two hours so that gives us half an hour extra time." "Let's get'em moved then," Mike said motioning to the group. This time the groups consisted of both Iranians and Marines working together to wrestle the heavy batteries back into the engine. A few minutes later the engine backed into the spare cars, hooking them to the few already attached.

"Sparky, did you figure on the extra cars when you made your calculations?" Mike asked.

"Shit, no." Sparky did a few recalcs in his head, "OK, should still be all right, maybe ten minutes less running."

"If you are ready, Captain," Colonel Benadar was saying," I suggest you move out immediately, we are about to have company." Outside to the east three helicopters were sweeping in hugging the ground. To the west on the road a convoy of five trucks was speeding up the hill, clouds of dust behind them.

"Wilson," Colonel Heliwell shouted, "get the Tarawa on the horn, and let them know we have possible hostiles inbound."

"Roger that."

"Sparky, get that train moving NOW."

"Already done, sir."

"Wilson, after the Tarawa, let the snipers know what's happening."

"Roger that. Usual targets, sir?"

"Yep."

"Captain, deploy your men."

"Roger that, sir," Captain Fleishman turned to his men and pointed. In a flash they had gathered their weapons and packs and disappeared into the surrounding landscape. When he turned around again the Iranians had done the same. In the space of a few minutes the two commanders were the only ones left standing in the parking lot. With a nod to each other, they retired into the center. Overhead, the helicopters descended in dust and wind disgorging men from their doors. One of choppers lifted up and made a fast swooping turn over the center as the truck convoy screeched to a halt in the parking lot. For a moment, Colonel Heliwell wondered what their intentions were; he was fairly sure but decided to let the actions of the new arrivals dictate his response. Any doubts he had disappeared when a rocket launched from the lead helicopter took out the center's door.

"You there, in the tunnel, put your hands in the air and come forward."

"I say, old boy, would you be kind enough to identify yourself," Lord Hawthorne shouted back.

"This is Captain GreyOwl of the United States Marines Corps."

"Easy for you to say," Richard replied in his New York accent. "How do we know that for sure?" He passed Lord Hawthorne one of the captured rifles, "Who won the 2004 World Series?"

"The Red Sox," came the reply. "But everyone knows that, can't you come up with something harder?"

"Let me ask," Elijah said.

"OK by me."

Elijah scrambled up the pile of rocks and asked a question in the plains Cree dialect.

A few minutes later he got a hesitant reply

A couple of more questions and Elijah grinned at the others. "He's the real McCoy," he announced and put his rifle down and wiggled through the hole.

Newton watched as Elijah walked down the tunnel and shook hands with a figure in a Marine uniform covered in dust. Turning to his friends he waved them forward and one by one they came forward as more and more shapes materialized out of the tunnel.

"How many of you are there?"

"Not sure, some of the scientific types kind of melted into the cavern, some may be lost in there, most of them you will find on the platform, some may be wounded. We had a firefight of sorts with the bad guys," Newton said. "But we have bigger problems than that."

"I'm aware of that, sir." the Captain turned to his men, "Arty, get your ass up here." A small man with glasses ran forward carrying a small case, his helmet constantly slipping over his face. "Arty here is our tech specialist; can you show him where the devices are located?"

"Sure, we got one down and…"

"Wait a minute, you got your hands on one?"

"Yeah, we climbed a rope and…"

"You MOVED it?"

"Well, sure we did and…"

"Arty, get it in gear."

"Yes, SIR!"

"Jason, you go with him."

"Cool, hey, Arty, is it? Anyway, listen, I got the detonator code downloaded from the chip but I can't ID the CPU." The two men scrambled over the debris and disappeared into the cavern, no longer a Marine and a police officer, just two computer geeks focused on the same problem.

"Let me get this straight, you guys removed the bombs, dissected the detonator, downloaded the codes and dug your way out of a cave-in?"

"Not to mention the gunfights and the spy, but we only got one of the bombs," added Richard.

"Right. Well, I'd love to chat about your accomplishments but we gotta go. I understand that these things will detonate when the water level rises high enough. And by the feel of it, that may not be too far away." Captain GreyOwl barked out some more orders and the Marines began to clear away more of the rocks and wood that blocked the tunnel. That done they headed inside to collect the scientists and get them on their way up the tunnel.

The debris from the door had not hit the ground before the first mortar rounds impacted in the parking lot. The two military trucks, still with their hoods up, disappeared in a cloud of flame and smoke. The attacking force was well trained and laid on a carpet of smoke along with the high explosive shells. Anyone still on the parking lot when the shells landed would have been shredded. But they weren't on the parking lot; they were hidden in the depressions and behind the rocks surrounding the center. The Marines and their Iranian allies began to return concentrated and deadly fire. The attackers had not expected much resistance, especially of this caliber and their first wave crumbled and fell back under the accurate fire. The two Colonels were busy on their radio nets, directing their forces and receiving intelligence. Colonel Heliwell was most worried about the helicopters, they had the capability to take out his Marines and their allies one by one, and soon the casualty reports testified that the Iranian attackers realized that too. The sound of the attack choppers swooping overhead made talking on the radio difficult. It also kept the Marines' heads down whilst the hostile commander maneuvered his forces to outflank them.

"Wilson," Colonel Heliwell yelled, "what's the word?"

"Tarawa reports three Harriers inbound, sir, Tact 21, Call Sign Dagger, E.T.A. 30 seconds!"

"Roger that. Contact them!"

"Already done, sir!"

Heliwell punched a key on his handset that connected him immediately to Tactical Channel 23, the frequency the Harrier flight was on. "Dagger Flight, Tiger Actual over."

"Dagger Lead," the radio responded. "Approaching from the east, clusters and napalm on board."

"Dagger lead, call blue smoke," the Col. Punched the key again connecting him back to his troops. "Mark 'em with blue," he called. The Marines in the field loaded and fired blue smoke grenades out of their portable mortar tubes to mark the position of the enemy positions. "Dagger lead, smoke deployed, take out the choppers first."

"Roger that. Dagger flight, mark 'em and spark 'em." The Marine Harriers came in fast; each picked up one of Soviet helicopters and locked their air to air sidewinders on target.

"Fox One!"

"Fox Two!"

"Fox Three!"

Each call signified the launching of a missile. At the press of the firing button, the rocket motors lit off. In a fraction of a second the thrust built up enough to overcome the speed of the aircraft and the missile left the guide rails. The electronics package had already been locked on the target helicopter. Infrared heat sensors picked out the exhaust of the helicopters turbines from the background of the warm volcanic rock, and the radar seeker head noted the speed and position of the moving chopper. The missile accelerated with a maximum achievable speed of Mach 7, but none of them would be in the air that long. As soon as they became active, the radar heads on the missiles activated the threat receivers in the choppers. The pilots of two of them pointed the noses of their machines down and accelerated looking for rock outcroppings to shield them; they were not successful. The Hind Hi-8 helicopters found the ground as flaming balls of steel, aluminum, and jet fuel. The third took a different route and hauled his machine towards the sun. He prayed the missile would lock onto that glowing ball of heat and as soon as he had the sun behind him, shut down the engines and went into an autorotation. The trick confused the heat seeking mechanism of the missile, and the jamming equipment on board blanked out the missiles radar. Neither technique fooled the pilot of Dagger Three who had by now selected his forward firing Gatling gun and centered the helicopter in his sights. A momentary press of the firing button sent hundreds of steel jacketed rounds into the target, which joined its brother machines in a crumpled burning ball.

The Marines and Iranian defenders were now free to raise their heads and watch the Harriers as they began a bomb run. So were the attackers. They had arrived on scene armed with shoulder fired anti-aircraft missiles similar to the American "stinger" that had defeated the Russian helicopter borne forces in Afghanistan. The Marine Harriers were wonderful fighting machines, able to dance and weave like a boxer going for the heavyweight title. Their one drawback was their speed; it was not as great as a pure fighter like the Tomcat and left them vulnerable to ground fire. The attackers had three teams designated to an anti-aircraft role and when the Harriers concentrated on the Hinds, they took up their positions. In order to fire the missiles, they had to be at least in a sitting position. The moment they did so, the sniper teams, deployed from the Sea Stallions on their initial approach, found the targets they had been waiting for. Three shots from different directions snapped out and found the missiles, disabling two immediately. The third leapt upwards trailing smoke and flame and locked on its target. The recommended evasive action for a conventional jet fighter would be to jink around the sky and launch flares to confuse the missile. But the Harrier was not a conventional plane. As soon as the threat warning went off, all three aircraft immediately stopped in mid air, hovering on columns of jet exhaust. They swiveled towards the incoming missile and fired their Gatling guns, aiming for a point just ahead of the missile's flight. The hail of bullets, fired at a rate of six thousand rounds per minute, shredded the incoming rocket, turning it into a burst of flame and shards of aluminum. With one of the attack jets providing cover they resumed their ground attack role. Slim cylinders tumbled from beneath their wings and impacted the marked positions with searing flames that spread out and engulfed the rock outcroppings and depressions that were seconds ago affording protection to the attackers.

At the end of the bomb run, the Harriers reversed course, climbed for altitude, and release more cylinders. A small parachute deployed from the end of each, slowing its descent. When each of the devices reached an altitude a few hundred feet above ground level, they burst open scattering hundreds of bomblets, designed to explode on contact with the ground. At ground level, those of the attacking troops who had escaped the inferno of the previous napalm drop, now found themselves sought by thousands of spinning, tearing metal slivers. When they found a human body they ripped through it, tumbling and tearing. Hardly had this ceased when the attackers found themselves surrounded by the Marines and allied Iranians, who rose from their positions as one and charged, weapons firing. It was all over in a few minutes, any of the attackers still living and able to move surrendered with their ears still ringing from the noise of the multiple attacks. Here and there a wounded man was helped, but there were few who survived.

"Tiger Actual, Dagger Lead, over," the radio ear piece in Colonel Heliwell's ear came alive with sound.

"Go ahead, Dagger Lead."

"Ordnance expended, returning to base."

"Roger that. Thanks for the help, Dagger Lead."

"No problem. Call us again if needed."

The three Marine Corps Harriers accelerated to cruise speed and headed back east to the Tarawa. The next few minutes were spent collecting the wounded and treating them. The attack from the aircraft was so fierce that there were few attackers left to treat and the medics concentrated on the Marines and the Iranian allies.

"What's the count, Wally?" Colonel Heliwell said to his medic.

"Three dead, fourteen wounded, sir, two Iranians killed, one of ours, Master Corporal Harris, sir."

"The choppers are on their way from Tarawa to collect them, Wally, make them comfortable 'til they get here, how about the attacking force?"

"Those Harriers really chewed them up, sir, only 23 wounded left, the rest are dead, I estimate 80 killed, plus whoever were in the Hinds."

"Who is the senior member of their force left?"

"We're checking now, sir."

"Let me know when you find him."

"Roger that."

"This is the code block?"

"That's it."

Arty looked over the printout and hummed softly to himself, pausing only to push the ill fitting helmet back on his head. "Yeah," he said after a few minutes tracing the code, "I see what you mean, there's the switch, but it doesn't really tell us which state it is in to start, normally it would be off, but there is nothing to say."

"Arty, you got that thing figured out yet?" The earpiece in his ear crackled.

"Working on it, sir."

"Well, for now put that aside and check out the remaining device hung on the ceiling, follow the lights."

"Roger that. Gotta go. Why don't you take this back to the train, they've already moved the other bomb back there."

"OK, but be careful, that other one got nicked by a bullet earlier, so I don't know how stable it is."

"Oh, oh, we gotta problem."

"What's that? Oh, shit!"

Both men stared at the water lapping at the edge of the platform.

"Captain, better get in here, we got a problem," Arty said into his radio microphone. "Better get in here NOW, sir."

Newton and Elijah were standing by Captain GreyOwl when the call came in from Arty, without hesitation they headed into the cavern and reached the platform. As soon as they saw the two looking down they knew what the problem was.

"This isn't good," Captain GreyOwl murmured. "Either of you know how much time we have left?"

"Depends" Newton answered, "on how many other holes need to be filled."

"How so?"

"When the water rises to this level and floods the cavern floor, it will find other holes that it will drain into for a while, and then the level here will start to rise again, but there is no way of telling how long that will take."

"OK, everyone out!"

"We have to get that device off the cavern roof!"

"Yes we do, but meanwhile we can send the rest of you up the tunnel."

"You'll need someone to show you where it is."

"We can find it."

"I'm sure you can, sir, but can you find it in time?"

"I can't risk your life, Mr. Newton, you're a civilian."

"You're not risking it, I am. Besides, if we don't retrieve that thing and the water hits it and it goes off, it won't matter where in the tunnel, or on the island I am, no one is going to survive."

The Captain thought for a minute, "All right, I don't have time to argue, but I AM going to start that train up the tunnel."

"OK by me."

"Move 'em out" he called into his radio and the train began its journey back up the tunnel with its load of human cargo.

"OK, how to we get to this bomb with all this water around?"

"Arty?"

"On it, sir. We should have a couple of PLRs around somewhere close."

"PLRs?"

"That's marine corps designation for a personal life raft, a small inflatable boat carried on all over water flights, one per man, part of our basic gear." A moment later Arty returned with two brown packages with rip cords attached to their sides. Pulling hard on the cord he was rewarded with a hiss of gas as the little orange boat spilled from its wrapper. Inflating the next one he laid them both in the water. "It's kind of like using a paddle board, sir, not a lot of room, mostly to keep you out of reach of sharks and the like."

"Take Corporal Eric with you," the Captain said motioning to a young Marine standing on the platform. "He can shinny up that rope better than either of you two, right, son?"

The young marine grinned back and deployed another little boat, "Yes, sir!"

Carrying flashlights, the three made their way to the spot where the rope leading to the bomb hung with its free end in the water.

"Be careful," Newton called out. "There is a strong current here." The water rushing into holes it found on the cavern floor was creating whirlpools and currents as it spilled into the empty spaces. Everyone could hear the sound of water splashing and gurgling over the lips of the holes and around the rocks. Newton and Arty held the young Marine's boat steady as he carefully rose to a sitting position and took hold of the rope. Using the strength in his arms he pulled himself up high enough until he could use his legs and quickly reached the top where he wrapped the rope on top of his boots to hold himself. Newton and Arty shone the lights up from below.

"How's it looking?"

"Not bad," came the reply. "The bullet took out most of one strap and I can pry the other one loose."

"Not to rush you but the water level's rising again."

Arty looked around at the blackness. "Listen," he whispered, "I can't hear the water anymore!"

"Must have filled all the holes," Newton said.

"Got it!" came the voice from above. "Coming down now."

"Slowly!" warned Arty.

Inching his way down the rope with the device in one hand and using his feet as brakes, the Marine reached the bobbing boat beneath him. Handing it over to Arty he asked. "What the hell is this thing anyway?"

"Tell you later," Arty replied. "Let's get out of here!"

Newton led the way, guiding them back, with Arty in the middle and the young man taking up the rear. They had to go slowly, Arty held the bomb well clear of the water while paddling with one hand.

Rounding the corner of a rock outcropping they could see the platform engulfed in water. It still wasn't too high, the Captain and Elijah stood calf deep in it. A sudden roar reached their ears. The water had found another hole to fill and its force loosened the rock wall around it, making a channel it could flow through. Like a bathtub that has its plug pulled, it surged towards the hole creating a whirlpool. The edges of the current tugged at the little boats pulling them back away from the platform. Even with everyone paddling furiously it was all they could do to make any headway and the current was getting stronger. Both Elijah and the Captain leapt toward them at the same time, one grabbing Newton's boat, the other Arty's. The current grew stronger and the boat holding Eric disappeared into the darkness, his cries lost in the roar of the water.

The Sea Stallions made a deafening noise as they curved east along the volcano's flank. Three were marked with the Red Cross designating them as medevac choppers, the others brandished machine guns from their open doors. As they set down, the Marines ducked from the flying dust and waited for the rotors to quit turning. When they did the passengers exited, many of them bearing patch of the First Marine Expeditionary Force, others wore the patch of the Spanish army. In their midst a tall hatless man wearing a bullet proof vest over a suit emerged and bowing his head made his way to the center. Accompanying him was another man, also wearing a vest, and also dressed in civilian clothes.

"Colonel Heliwell, this is Senor Escardo D'Angelino, the Spanish Consulate, I have explained to him what the urgency and nature of this operation is about and he has graciously offered the assistance of his office."

"Thank you, sir," Colonel Heliwell replied, "and may I present Colonel Benadar who is in charge of the Iranian forces who so ably assisted us. This other gentleman is Deputy Minister Aram of the Iranian government."

"It would seem that you and your men had quite a fight here, Colonel" the Spanish Consul said, "May I ask if the devices of which Mr. Wells told me have been recovered?"

"That is being done as we speak, sir."

"I understood from Mr. Wells that time is extremely short, is that not so?"

"That is so."

"Well then, of what assistance can I be?"

"We will need transport for the scientists and others that were trapped below, and possibly some heavy equipment, if that is possible."

"Of course, Colonel perhaps you could direct me to a radio or something to contact my government with?"

"There is a phone in here, sir, which we have just repaired; it would give you greater privacy."

"Thank you, Colonel"

"When do you estimate recovering the devices, Colonel?"

"Sir, I have men down the tunnel now, and we will send another unit down as soon as we can."

"I'll go, sir." Colonel Heliwell turned and saw Sergeant Johnson, with one arm bandaged standing to attention. "Me too," said a voice from behind, and a large Iranian with his head swathed in bandages and the name of "Kareem" in Arabic on his tunic stood in beside him. One by one the other Marines and Iranian allies fell in beside the men with whom they had shared so much danger and death. Both commanders shook their heads and smiled to themselves. "I think we'll let the fresh guys do that, Sergeant, you have all done enough for one day."

"Sergeant, did you not hear my order to move this train out?" yelled Captain GreyOwl.

"Yessir, I did, sir, but it's them civilians, sir, they wouldn't go."

"What do you mean they wouldn't go?"

"Just that, sir, we no sooner got the train started than they all started jumping off, weren't nothing we could say to get 'em on again. They weren't going to leave anyone behind, sir, is what they said."

The Captain looked around and shook his head, "Well tell 'em to get aboard now, everyone is here, the water's rising and we can't stay a minute more." With that the combined group climbed on board and the little train started its painful journey up the tunnel.

"Glad to see you made it, old boy," Lord Hawthorne grinned. "It was all her idea you know," indicating Major O'Connell who was seated firmly beside Newton. "Bloody well wouldn't leave without you."

"I suspect it was probably the bomb she was worried about, not me."

"I wouldn't bet on it."

Newton Smiled and then his expression grew more serious. "We aren't out of the woods yet," he said, looking back down the tunnel towards the cavern.

"How do you mean?"

"I mean the water is still rising and once it fills the cavern it's going to come straight up this tunnel, and at a very rapid rate. I hope this little train has enough juice to get us up to the surface."

"How far do we have to go?"

"As far a sea level, which is about 275 feet from the tunnel entrance."

"Well we better hurry," Richard said. "I think the water is catching up with us."

Behind them, the flashlight, which he was holding was now reflecting off a watery surface and not the tunnel walls it had earlier. Newton wrapped his coat tighter against the increasing chill.

"How much further, Sparky?"

"Not too far, sir."

"You've been saying that for the last ten minutes."

"Yes, sir, so I have."

"Can you push this thing any faster?"

"Flat out now, sir, and we're not taking any cooling time."

"Cooling time?"

"It's the way they laid out the tunnel, sir; the uphill parts are broken up by flat stretches so the engineer could reduce speed and cool the electric motor off a bit before tackling the next section. We ain't doing that, sir and sooner or later it's going to cost us."

The Captain turned to the Marine behind him, "Pass the word, have the devices passed up to the engine." Sparky looked at the Captain with a question on his face.

"Might as well have them as far from the water as we can, Sparky."

"Yes, sir," Sparky replied, thinking that the most they would gain from doing that would be like a minute of time at the most.

"Everyone ready to move out?"

"Yes, sir."

"OK then, Lieutenant, make it as quick as you can."

The group of Marines left the center heading down the tunnel, organized in four man teams, each time carrying a heavy bundle. No personal weapons were carried and the Colonel hoped none would be needed.

The smell of burning insulation permeated the engine and Sparky looked anxiously once again at the gauge in front of him. The needle was red lined and not about to move down anytime soon.

"We gotta stop Captain, or this thing is going to die on us."

"OK, Sparky, shut it down for five, or until the water gets here."

The train had managed to slowly pull ahead of the water level. The branches in the tunneling siphoned off some of the inrushing flow, and the pressure it had behind it decreased with each foot of elevation the engine managed to claw back. The air in the tunnel was very cold now, something that would help the engine cool quicker, but also signaled the approach of the cold seawater behind them. Those who wanted to took a break from the bouncing ride of the train to stretch their legs.

"This is a lot longer than it took to get down to the cavern in the first place," Richard remarked.

"The key word there being 'down'," Newton responded. "Now we are going up, it's harder on the engine and with the extra load it can't go as fast."

"Why have we stopped," Julie asked, "is it broken?"

"Just cooling the motor I expect," Jason said. "We should be on our way in a moment."

"Better be quick," Lord Hawthorne said. "Water's just behind us!" He yelled towards the front of the train and in response it started up again. The red needle headed almost immediately upwards and as they topped the next rise the smell of burning increased. The lamp at the front of the engine grew notably dimmer.

"Shit!"

"What's up, Sparky?"

"Batteries are about dead, Captain. It's the heat, makes the motor draw more current than normal"

"Can we make that next rise?"

"I sure hope so," Sparky said pointing at the thing rush of water flooding the tracks beside them. "I sure hope so!"

The engine crawled up the rise, leaving the water once again behind them where it found a side tunnel and began to fill it.

"That's all she wrote, sir," Sparky announced as the light at the front of the train died away. "Them batteries is toast."

"Right, let's get these bombs away then." Two Marines, selected for their ability to run, had been fitted with packs with the bombs in them. As soon as they had been strapped tight they headed off up the tunnel.

"OK, everyone, get in line, we have to make our way on foot from here."

"Maybe not, Captain," Sparky said. "Look at that."

Ahead of them came a number of flashlights, and four man teams carrying batteries from the trucks.

CHAPTER THIRTY SIX

On the surface

They looked like astronauts exploring an alien planet. Four figures, each in a full decontamination suit hovered around the table in the conference room. Two were from the Spanish Nuclear Agency, and the other two from the Tarawa. On the table in front of them were the two boxes so recently recovered from the cavern. A discussion was underway as to the best method of disabling them. The tension in the air was palpable, both bombs could detonate at any moment and no one had anything but a guess as to how to disarm them. In the government rooms of the Spanish parliament a debate was raging over whether or not to attempt to fly them off the island or not. Oblivious to that process the four bomb techs had already decided the only course of action was to disarm then there.

"I'm ready when you are, Philippe, let's take the undamaged one first, it will give us more clues about the damaged one."

"Very well, Joseph, let us begin."

One Spanish and One American technician began the delicate task of dismantling the trigger mechanism. The one thing in their favour was that no one had expected the device would be found quickly enough to allow for such a procedure, and no anti-tampering devices should be in place.

The Marine search teams had brought in all the attackers for questioning; amongst them one man was sitting slightly wounded with his back against the wall. Aram had been studying the man. He knew him from somewhere, but so many faces had passed by his eyes that it was difficult to place him. A Marine guard motioned the men to stand up, and in single file he led them out to await a helicopter to take them away. As he stood up, the man glanced at Aram and a flicker of recognition crossed his eyes. He immediately looked down and shuffled to the door.

Aram watched him move. Yes! He had it now. He quickly turned to find Colonel Benadar, but he was not in the room. Following the prisoners out side he saw the Colonel talking on a radio and strode quickly to approach him. A few short words later and Colonel Benadar looked over to the line of prisoners.

"That man!" he yelled. "Bring him here!" At the sound of the shouting the man wheeled and grabbed something from his boot, holding it high above his head he began yelling rapidly in Arabic.

"Get back! Get Back!" Colonel Benadar yelled at the Marines. "He has the detonator!"

"Detonator to what?" Colonel Heliwell cried.

"The bombs, the bombs!"

Colonel Heliwell whispered a few words into the microphone of his radio, and the man crumpled like someone sucked the bones out of the top of his head. The sound of a single rifle shot echoed across the valley. Aram sprinted to the man and picked up the detonator. "I recognized him as the chief of Mullah Shariz's security force; it was the way he walked. So arrogant when he brought in the special prisoners."

"Call in the sniper teams," Colonel Heliwell said into his radio. "We got our man."

Bevan stretched the aching muscles in his back and stood up. "Now that," he said, "was a damn fine shot."

CHAPTER THIRTY SEVEN

New York City

Richard stuck out his hand, "Anytime you want to work as a consultant, let me know."

"Thanks" Newton said. "But I'm retired now."

"Yeah, right! I heard that some place. Don't believe it though, guys like us never retire for real," grinned Richard. Jason leaned forward and shook hands with Newton and Elijah.

"It's been an adventure to say the least; how long will you be staying in New York?"

"That depends on what progress I can make locating my daughter."

"Anything the NYPD can do, anything at all, just say the word; and of course now you have two people helping you to look for her."

"Thanks, just having all the extra eyes looking will be a big help."

"I'll make sure the circular doesn't get lost over time."

"I appreciate that."

Every day in every squad room and muster call, circulars are handed out to thousands of police officers to be on the lookout for missing persons, suspicious vehicles, and unnatural occurrences. Since 9/11 the quantity had grown to almost overwhelming proportions. Richard knew, as did every cop on the street, that there were classes of circulars, this one would not end up in the trash can on the way out of the squad room.

"So, when is your meeting with the President?" Newton asked him.

Depends on the schedules, his, the Mayor's, the Chief's. I'm sure I'll be informed at the appropriate moment." Newton nodded with a grin, the more things change, the more they stay the same.

"And the tunnels? What will become of them?"

Lord Hawthorne smiled, "Ahh, of course, I forgot to tell you, seems like I am in charge of a new United Nations mission to study the island. With the cooperation of the Spanish government the whole area has been declared an internationally protected area. I suspect a rather large budget to be at our disposal to try and stabilize the fissure and prevent what will inevitably happen anyway. Such is the arrogance of man, is it not?"

"Given the alternatives, I suppose there is nothing else we can do but at least try."

"Oh my yes, old chum, we certainly shall, and who knows, perhaps in the future we will succeed. But of course we have perhaps less time now than before, or perhaps more, depending on which theory you subscribe to."

"How so?" Richard asked.

"Well, one camp says the weight of the water introduced into the tunnels will cause the fissure to open at an accelerated rate. Indeed, they believe that was really all the terrorists had to do, and therefore they have accomplished their aims. The whole lot will tumble into the ocean within five years."

"Not a pleasant thought. And the other theory?"

"More adventurous, I must say. They want to punch a series of holes into the magma chamber and release just enough molten rock to, how did they put it, ah yes, 'weld' the fissure together."

"Surely they don't actually believe that?" Newton said.

"I'm afraid they do."

"How will they control the generation of steam when the lava hits the seawater?"

"Some large geothermal vents are planned to release it, that is my understanding, but then, I'm not an expert in that area."

"I think I will stay on the west coast for the foreseeable future," Elijah added to the conversation. "I don't see a lot of success for that plan."

"Time will tell, old boy, it always does."

"Any official visits planned in our fair part of the world?"

"Maybe, the next international conference will be here, and it's nice that New York will be here to have it."

"Would it have really done all the damage they say it would?" Georgia asked.

"No doubt about it, probably more, and no one can truly imagine destruction on that scale to that large an area." Lord Hawthorne added. "And who can truly say it won't happen yet?"

"I hope we will never know in our lifetime," Georgia said.

"But someone else will, in theirs. And now I must go and board my flight, the interest in volcanology has taken somewhat of an upswing of late."

Another round of good-byes and the English scientist left with a spring in his step, there were a wealth of new theories to exam and argue.

Newton waited with Elijah until it was time to board his plane after promising to go to Washington to make a detailed report and answer questions about the whole affair. He had also promised a certain Marine Corps Major, now Lieutenant Colonel, that he would be available to tour the town, and he was looking forward to it.

Newton turned to Elijah and asked, "Remember when you challenged that Marine Captain, you asked him something in Cree, and he laughed, what did you ask him?"

"Do you remember the first question, about the Red Socks winning the World Series?"

"Yes."

"Well, I asked him if thought the Cleveland Indians would do it this year!"

EPILOGUE

The helicopter turned and paused like a hummingbird before descending in a cloud of dust into the courtyard. Across the prison yard the guards had heard of the coming of another "special prisoner." This time though, the arrival had been announced beforehand to the entire country. For the first time in its recent history, Iran had held an open trial, attended by media from around the globe. Also for the first time, a ranking Mullah had been publicly accused and convicted of using the Qur'an to mask his own crimes.

The prisoner had been taken immediately upon sentence to the helicopter so as to avoid the angry mobs in the street. He still had many followers and they were vengeful. But the greater numbers in Iran had been ashamed of their government's use of religion as a weapon of hate. When the plot had been fully exposed over the Internet and other media, and acknowledged as true by those who had tried to stop it, the revolt was swift. Not only for the plan to wreak death on so many innocent people, but also at the revelation that the test case was the destruction of the ancient city of Bam and the thousands of dead and injured left there.

For this day only Aram had resumed his previous duties by decree of President Sahkirez. He led the prisoner to a particular cell, which contained a bed, a soccer ball, and a young boy's belt. Then he closed the door.

The End

The volcano on La Palma is real. The fissure described in this novel is real. The evidence of previous landslides from the island chain is real. The existence of tsunamis caused by such catastrophic slides is also real, and the danger and effects of such a mega tidal wave are not only real, they are inevitable.